RHYTHMS
of GRACE

RHYTHMS
of GRACE

Marilynn
Griffith

Revell

a division of Baker Publishing Group
Grand Rapids, Michigan

Published by Revell
a division of Baker Publishing Group
P.O. Box 6287, Grand Rapids, MI 49516-6287
www.revellbooks.com

Printed in the United States of America

Library of Congress Cataloging-in-Publication Data
Griffith, Marilynn.
    Rhythms of grace / Marilynn Griffith.
        p.   cm.
    ISBN 978-0-8007-3278-3 (pbk.)
    1. Single women—Fiction. 2. Parent and adult child—Fiction. 3. Domestic fiction. I. Title.
PS3607.R54885R48 2008
813'.6—dc22   2008020291

Published in association with the Books & Such Literary Agency, Janet Kobobel Grant, 52 Mission Circle, Suite 122, PMB170, Santa Rosa, CA 95409-7953.

This book is a work of fiction. Names, characters, places, and incidents are the product of the author's imagination or are used fictitiously. Any resemblance to actual events, locales, or persons, living or dead, is coincidental.

For Dr. Joseph Smith of the Central State University Upward Bound program and Oral History department. Thank you for putting the drumbeat into my spirit. I hear it always.

"Are you tired? Worn out? Burned out on religion? Come to me . . . Walk with me and work with me—watch how I do it. Learn the unforced rhythms of grace."

Matthew 11:28–30 Message

PART 1

CHORUS

1984

1

Diana

No one would miss me. They never did. And that was okay because I'd made up my mind. I was never coming to ballet class again.

Ever.

And I was also going to tell my mother what size tights I really wore. These things were killing me. Mom believes in squeezing in wherever you can, but not Daddy. He says that life is too short to be uncomfortable. I wonder then why he married my mother. Who knows? People are strange that way, making sense and not making sense all at the same time. Like Mom, thinking that wearing this pink leotard will rid me of that other dancing, the kind I do by myself to the beat always in my head. She saw me once. We didn't say anything about it but the next week I was here at Fairweather Dance Academy where girls are kept on their toes.

Right

I didn't tell Mom then, but there are two kinds of dancing: the kind people teach you and the kind you're born knowing, like some kind of dream. That's how I dance when nobody's looking: pushing it back, throwing it over, paying it forward, dropping it down. None of that pointy floor-pecking that my ballet teacher screams about. I can do that too, the pointy thing, but it's too polite sometimes, like the way Daddy's lips brush Mom's cheek when he pretends to kiss her. No, when I do my dance my feet smack against the floor, kissing it full in the mouth, flat-footed with no apologies. There's a long smooch when I forget myself and slide across the floor. It drives my ballet teacher crazy. Like now.

"Toes, Diana! Toes, dear." My teacher sounds calm, but don't be fooled. She's crazy.

I smile and assume the correct position, knowing better than to make a scene. There'll be enough to fight over when Mom finds out I'm not coming back. The teacher could make me assume the correct position on the outside, but in my mind, I was bent low, head down, shimmying across the floor, knocking all the bony ballerinas out of the way, including Miss Fairweather, who, despite her name, was no friend at all.

She started in on me again. "Lift the knee, Diana. The knee!"

Yeah, yeah. I lifted my knee and flapped my arms. It was a silly piece that ended with us flapping our arms. Swan's wings, the teacher said. I caught a glimpse of my body in the mirror and stumbled, almost laughing. So much for Swan Lake. More like the piggy in the puddle.

"And . . . stop. Very nice." The teacher's expression glowed as she looked down the line. Once her eyes rested on me, the flowing stream of "niiice" curdled on the woman's lips.

I froze, knowing that look meant a speech was coming, one I didn't want to hear.

Miss Fairweather forced her eyes from me and turned to the other girls, who weren't really girls any longer, but she kept calling us that anyway. "Thanks, everyone. Don't forget to stop in the foyer and get fitted for your recital costumes."

Forget? How could anybody forget the joy of being measured at the end of a line of twiggy white girls and hearing their even skinnier mothers scream, "Turn around, hon. That can't be right. Your hips are bigger than mine!"? Thank God I didn't have to do it anymore.

Trying not to think about how I never measured up, I started for the door. There was no rush to get into the hall because if I moved too fast, they'd try to whisk me off to be measured no matter what I said. I always went last anyway, giving myself time to recite "Phenomenal Woman."

"Hold on, Diana. I need to speak with you," Miss Fairweather said.

No good could come of this. "Yes?"

The teacher approached, then stopped in the middle of the floor. I didn't approach. After a few seconds of stalemate, she spoke. "There's more to ballet than dance, Diana. A ballerina has to be suited for dance. And if she . . . isn't suited, she must make herself suitable; do you understand what I mean?"

I understood all too well. She'd been talking to my mother, for one thing. I dropped my bag to the floor. Even Maya Angelou wouldn't get me through this one. This was going to require some Jesus.

The Lord is my shepherd. I shall not want . . .

"I mean your behind, dear. The way it pokes out like that. It's a distraction. We must be uniform, so as not to take attention away from the others . . . Speaking of that, your hair. Your mother is going to straighten it for the recital, right? It must be in a bun like the other girls. Totally flat."

So much for that memory verse. I did *want.* I wanted her to shut up. The big rock that I get in my throat when Mom talks to me like this started choking me. I fought to swallow it down.

He leadeth me by still waters.

The teacher gave a tight smile, taking my silence for agreement. "I've discussed this with your mother before, but perhaps I didn't make it clear."

What was the next line of Psalm 23? Something about a table and some enemies? My friend Zeely and I had won a gold bookmark for memorizing the whole chapter last year when we graduated eighth grade, but now it wouldn't come to mind. I closed my eyes. It helped sometimes, for remembering poems.

"Look at me, Diana. This is important. Are you listening? I need you to lose twenty pounds by recital. Thirty would be optimal, but twenty is a good start."

He puts my enemies on the table, roasted with salt and pepper—

And on she goes. "One thousand calories a day should do it. It's a bit much still, but I realize this is all new to you. A sensible diet—"

A door slammed at the back of the dance room. "Lady, your brain is on a diet." A man's voice.

My head snapped up. My shoulders relaxed. He'd come to save me. Daddy.

My father crossed the room in long, slow strides. When he reached us, he leaned down and took my bag with his left hand and took my hand with his right. "There's nothing wrong with this girl. There's something wrong with you."

Miss Fairweather's face scrunched up the way Aunt Ina's cat looked when it was hungry. "This is my school, Mr. Dixon. I like your wife, so I've tried to be patient, but you will not talk to me in that tone."

"I won't talk to you in any tone, miss," Daddy said before nodding toward the door. "We won't be back."

At first I tried not to smile. I almost made it out the door with a straight face. Almost.

When I was done laughing, I reached my sweaty arms around Daddy and hugged him hard—between coughs from the talcum powder he put on under his shirts. He'd done it, just like in my dreams, the ones only God knew about. Only better.

The pink pig was free.

I saw it first. A billboard at the corner of Kentucky Street and Main. It might have been up there awhile, but it was new to me because Mom never drove this way, not even to church. She preferred the highway to driving through "South Side," as my mother called the place where she and Daddy grew up. Testimony really wasn't big enough to have sides, but people need that type of thing to feel good about themselves. Mom especially. (I'd like to call her Mama like everyone else on my block, but she insists on Mom.)

Sunday was the only time Mom came to this side of town since all her efforts to get Daddy to go to one of the fine churches in our mixed neighborhood had failed. No matter where we tried to go, within fifteen minutes Daddy was snoring like some kind of mule. He was a peaceful man most times, but he knew how to win a fight when he wanted to.

Like today. Today brought us to the South Side, where Daddy came all the time. He ate here, worked here, shopped here, laughed here. He was a come-up man, people said, but he never forgot where he came from. Not like that wife of his—who knew she'd go off to college and come back stuck up like that? At least he still brought his girl around sometimes, but wasn't she a little strange too? All those books. It couldn't be normal. They said these things right in front of me, the South Side people did, but I didn't mind. I wasn't Daddy or Mom, just stuck somewhere in between both of them, with a book in one hand and a drum beating in my head.

And now, here I was with Daddy, who never skipped the rough parts in books or told you to cover your eyes when people acted crazy in the movies. He'd shake his head and tell you plain how things were and what God said about it. Sometimes, if you asked, he'd tell you what he had to say about it too. But most times not.

Instead, he'd hide behind the newspaper making that laugh-coughing sound (probably from his talcum powder) or disappear under the hood of his truck and let Mom do the explaining. I couldn't blame him either. There was no stopping Mom when she got started. She could talk faster than most people could think. Even me.

But Mom wasn't here now. Daddy was here, driving past Mount

Olive Missionary Baptist Church, around Heavenly Pastures Cemetery, and right up to the rec center where a tall, brown girl with big hips and wide, oval eyes danced in the sky on the billboard above it. She was leaping, but not like in ballet class. It was a backyard-basement-secret-dance sort of leap. And that girl was no pink pig. She was a tree, uprooted and set to music. Music like the beat in my head. It had to be. Nothing else could explain her dancing like that up in the sky for everyone to see, even with her "behind poking out that way." Was her teacher ashamed of her too? It didn't look like it.

I turned around backwards in the front seat of Daddy's truck so I could read it better. *Ngozi Dance troupe. African dancing for girls 12 through 18, 4:30 PM. 374-5343.* I said the numbers over and over, three seven four, five three, four three. Three seven four . . . Those numbers were tumbling in my head so hard that I didn't notice Daddy had turned his truck around and come to a stop right in front of the Charles Chesnutt Recreational Center. Right in front of that dancing girl.

Being at the Charles C—I'd only been there once, before we moved across town—would have been enough to knock me off my feet, but now there was that girl in the air on top of the building. Zeely, our preacher's daughter, was always telling me about the Charles C and how I needed to pray that my mother would let me go some time. "Prayer changes things," she'd said, sounding like the old ladies in the choir that she spent so much time with. I didn't doubt her words or God's power, just my mother's stubbornness. Besides, until now it really hadn't been worth fighting over.

"Parks and Recreation facilities are for common people," my mother said every time I asked, while Daddy whispered into his coffee that we *were* common people. At that point, I usually thought to myself that my mother was uncommonly stupid, but since hearing that sermon about the ravens plucking out the eyes of disobedient children, I'd blocked out thoughts like that. Without my eyes, I couldn't read and that'd be worse than not being able to dance.

Almost.

I followed Daddy toward the infamous Charles C, named by the town founders for Charles Chesnutt, the wonderful writer of "Dave's Neckliss," my favorite short story. Well, not exactly. James Joyce's "Araby" was my all-time favorite, not only for the writing but for the sheer curiousness of the words. I wrung my hands, realizing how nervous I was. I was rambling, even in my head. I paused to touch the dedication plaque on the wall as we passed, remembering the story behind it that my father recounted every Sunday when we drove by.

The town founder, so moved by one of Chesnutt's "funny Negro stories," had named the original recreation center after him, only to be horrified later to learn that he had shaken the hand of a very light-skinned Negro, not a white man, and even named a building for him. The first rec burned down soon after, but the name stuck and in the end they named the new one the same thing. Charles C it began, Charles C it would always be. And I, Diana Dixon, was going in.

I squeezed Daddy's palm as he opened the door. Nobody truly understood me, but at least Daddy tried. He worried I'd go blind reading so much, but he never made me turn off the lights. I'd hear his slippers on the carpet in front of my door and I'd click the light off, waiting for his calloused fingers on my face, his prayer so faint I held my breath to hear it. In the morning, when my mother rushed into the room and found the light out and my glasses in the case on the stand, she would smack her lips and say, "I know you were up reading. I just know it. I'll catch you one day." But she wouldn't. Not as long as Daddy was around. And he'd always be around. Well, maybe not always, since Mom swore pork chops would be the death of him, but he was here today. Here at the Charles C.

Either I let go of Daddy's hand or he let go of mine, but next

I marched up the steps, wondering if the dance class was held today. No days had been mentioned on the sign. Was Zeely here somewhere? I hoped so. If I tried to tell Zeely I'd been to rec, she never would believe it. I hardly believed it myself.

"Hold up, girl." Daddy ran behind me and I saw how far ahead of him I'd gotten. I also realized that I'd run up into the rec in a pink leotard and tights so tight that my thighs were rubbed raw in the middle. So much for looking cool. Not that I could anyway. The glasses and the braces sort of killed any chances of that. Daddy holding my hand was total overkill. I didn't care though. This was it. Whatever I was going to do, I had to do it. And fast. Daddy was going to pay big-time as it was.

I stood in the main hall, taking in the big brown front desk, the flyer-pasted bulletin board shouting DANCING, COOKING, and MEETING, PRINCE HALL LODGE #409. Basketballs bounced in time with the squeaks of shoes beyond the gymnasium door. There was another sound too, a thump down the hall. I moved closer, trying not to run when the thump became a beat and the beat became music. My music, the kind that pumped in my fingertips and strummed through my veins. Butt-naked music with no fluff on top. Music that made me move toward it, like so many times before.

Daddy, who was still doing some kind of cowboy gallop to keep up, ran into my back when I pulled up short in the doorway of the classroom. The dance classroom. We'd found it. I stood there with both dread and happiness sloshing in my belly, feeling like I did when we ate real mashed potatoes at Thanksgiving, knowing that the goodness would soon be over. The dancers weren't bothered by our stares, they went right on, leaving me with nothing to do but watch them. Feel them.

There were twelve girls in all. Zeely was there, right in the front, but she didn't smile at me. She didn't even act like she saw me. She was too busy being the blackest, prettiest tree in the foot-forest.

They were all different, some with thick trunks and others willowy and long-limbed, but they moved the same, growing roots inside the song. My song.

If there'd been time, I would have changed out of the leotard, ripped off my tights, or asked Daddy if he had some talcum powder in the truck to soothe the rash between my thighs. There wasn't time for that. There was only now. And now was time for dancing.

"Princess, wait. Let me—" Daddy's fingers slid down my arm like ice on a hot pole. I'd apologize later.

A lady, who had to be the teacher, parted the dancers. She wasn't what I expected. At first, she reminded me of Miss Fairweather, my ballet teacher. Then I looked into her eyes, heard her voice. On the inside, she was deep-down brown. On the outside, she was delicate, but strong—a sonnet, covered in white chocolate. Sweet like a good poem on a bad day.

She stood tallest of all of them, this teacher, letting go of her body, calling the others to follow her movement and add something of their own. She did the dance first, then they followed in four lines of three. The motions came to me quickly, like the verses in my notebook. Like wings. I wanted to soar over their singing feet, preaching arms, fingers reaching for the right movement, the right body-word. On the sideline, I mimicked every movement, flinging my arms and almost knocking Daddy down. He didn't say a word.

A boy in the corner beat the drum that made the wild, strong music. The beat shook through my chest, went through my heart. I turned back to the dancers, to the teacher whose eyes were on me, as she moved past me. The dancers looked straight ahead, trying to follow each new part of the dance, trying to find what they lacked. When the last dance came, none of them could find the punctuation to end it, the amen to finish their prayer. I alone held that, but not for long.

"Come." With a slight lift in her wrist and that one word, the teacher called me forward as they lined up to put the whole dance together.

She didn't have to tell me twice. My ballet shoes hit the wall behind me as I flung them off and ran to squeeze in next to Zeely, who looked straight ahead, but giggled under her breath at the sight of me. The teacher shook her head at my place in the lineup, motioning to the empty space beside her. When I hesitated, looking at the other dancers instead, the teacher turned and stared at me, talking with her eyes. *This is your place. I have the water, but you have the seed. The wild seed. Come and fertilize us.*

The skin on my arms itched as I heeded her eyes and her movements, sowing myself among them, planting the white-hot something that always got me in trouble. In the cradle of their arms, on the boughs of the beat, a new me was born, harvested for the first time in a dance.

The dance.

I went for it like it was my last dance too, knowing that it probably was. This moment might have to last me for the rest of my life. Everything that I'd been biting back in ballet class, choking down behind my bedroom door, I let it go all at once, let it birth, bloody and wonderful in a room full of strangers. It came out strong, this secret self, previously bared only in basements and backyards, scribbled in journals and scraps of paper. Strong and beautiful.

My feet slapped first, then slid and kissed the floor before I leapt, flying like the girl on the billboard, only higher. Wider. I left the spot I'd been given, weaving between the other dancers' pumping arms, open hands, and swaying hips. I twirled on, until I came face-to-face with the drummer, a boy with the crazy brown afro. I was close enough to see him now, to know who he was. Maybe even too close. His eyes were closed, but I knew what they looked like when they were open—gold-green.

Like Daddy's.

I dropped to the floor from mid-air, leaves shriveling, withering

18

away. When I hit the ground, it was over. I was nothing. Nowhere. Just a pink pig in Charles C with a big butt and buck teeth. A fool who'd just danced in front of that boy from Mount Olive who could skate backwards. He could even break-dance. What had I been thinking?

Thank God he wasn't looking.

The other dancers struggled to keep what we'd had alive, trying to coax me with their halfhearted lunges. I looked up to find the teacher standing over me. I tipped my head down, wondering if I'd misread those eyes, wondering if there would be more angry words today for a girl such as me, one "unsuited" for the dance.

There wasn't. "Welcome to Ngozi, I'm Joyce Rogers, your new dance teacher," the woman said in a voice as clear as the sky. "I've been waiting for you."

We locked eyes again and I knew it must be true. The woman in my dreams. My Glinda on the road to Oz. This was her. She got it. She got me. Finally, somebody understood.

Our eyes met and I knew it must be true. "I'm Diana. Diana Dixon. I've been waiting for you too."

2

Daddy wasn't home. I tried not to panic. Today was dress rehearsal for our first performance with Ngozi. My parents had the worst fight I can remember over it, but Daddy put his foot—both his feet actually—down on the subject.

"You weren't there. You didn't see it. She has to go. Joyce will take good care of her," he'd said.

Mom still stood there with her mouth poked out every time Daddy took me to practice. I was never late or missed even though Daddy had to leave the plant early sometimes to do it. Mom vowed never to take me. And now Daddy wasn't home.

I pressed my face to the stained-glass room divider behind my father's recliner. Everything looked yellow now and I could almost imagine him sitting there, half-asleep with his keys on his lap. Or worse, awake but playing sleep so he wouldn't have to argue with my mother, who was perched on the edge of the couch, glasses sliding down her nose.

"Don't come in here looking all sorry like that. He's gone to Cleveland, don't you remember?" She looked sad and happy at the same time.

Cleveland. For his job. Yes, I remembered now. Oh well. I kicked the couch. Miss Joyce had given me the lead this time. A solo. If I didn't show, Zeely would tear it up as my understudy, but I wanted to do it. This was all I had left. Mom had already made me quit the Buds of Promise choir. She said I had to choose. Now it seemed I was getting nothing for nothing. I took a deep breath and said the unthinkable.

"I need a ride."

"Pardon me?" My mother's glasses slid off her nose, but didn't fall. Too stubborn. Just like their owner.

Well, today was my turn to be stubborn. This was ridiculous. "I need an R-I-D-E. Please, Mom. It's dress rehearsal." I looked up at the clock and thought about telling her that we needed to go right now, or going to her room and bringing her her shoes and purse, but I thought better of it. Best not to look too desperate. "Please."

The glasses hit the floor then. No longer Mom, Emily Dixon, the hardest math teacher in the county, stood and crossed her arms. "If you think I'm driving over there tonight for you to hop around with those little jungle bunnies, you're mistaken. Sadly so." She picked up her glasses. "Besides, I'm heading out anyway I have a meeting."

My throat tightened. "But your school is—"

"I said I'm not going that far, Diana!" Her eyebrows stood at attention for emphasis.

I tried to raise my eyebrows too but it just made my head hurt. This whole thing was making my head hurt. Why did everything have to be a fight? All the other girls' parents would be there cheering them on. Then I saw something in her eyes. Guilt.

"Daddy asked you, didn't he? He asked you to take me and you said you would. And now you're going to go against your word?"

My mother didn't answer. She got up, walked to the closet and slipped on her shoes, one at a time, then she smoothed her skirt and headed for the door. On her way out, she opened her purse and flipped three coins onto the table by the door. Two quarters and a dime.

Bus fare.

"Make sure you have your key and come straight home," she said before slamming the door.

Where else would I go after walking home in the dark? The moon? "I-I will."

But I didn't come straight home. I died first, scratching and

21

screaming and trying to fly. I died loud and bloody, but nobody heard me, not even God.

So I came home and went to bed.

I had taken the bus.

Or at least I had tried.

There was a boy there, his face covered in a ski mask, though it wasn't quite cold enough. He had sad eyes and an unlit cigarette. I wished I'd worn my tennis shoes instead of trying to show off my new cowboy boots, two-toned black and gray. I don't know why I said hello—maybe because we were there alone, waiting for the bus, and since it was still in my safe neighborhood, I didn't have the sense to be scared yet. That was saved for the other end of the line.

The boy-man just nodded, mumbling to himself. I checked my watch. How often did these buses come again? There was nobody to ask, but I'd figured one would come eventually. Then he threw down that cigarette, the one that had never been lit, and smiled at me. It was a cold smile, the scary kind. I could see that, even through the mouth slit in his ski mask. When he grabbed me, I knew that no bus was coming tonight. That he'd only been waiting for me.

Mom says I should have run then, that I should have known how to get away. I tried to run, but my new boots were cute and pointy. I never was too good with heels and pointy toes. I ran a little while, but I fell behind the oak tree.

And he covered me.

The leaves danced like even they couldn't see, daring to be beautiful while I was dying. Maybe they were giving me something to look at, something to numb the pain. It didn't help.

Nothing did.

No matter how much I bit and kicked and scratched and yelled, no matter how hard I tried to rise up and fly, he just kept on. Fighting just made it hurt worse and I figured I'd die soon anyway, so I tried to think of heaven and stuff like that.

Mom said that was stupid too. She said that I'm a woman now, and I should have known what was happening. Evidently, *women* know these things. Information like that would have been valuable beforehand, but being just a girl who died at the bus stop, I really wouldn't know.

It doesn't matter what Mom thinks anyway. Not now. She didn't see his eyes. Only Daddy could have stopped him and he was in Cleveland. There's nothing left but this pain between my legs, between my ears. There's a buzzing sound that won't stop. They said at the hospital that's from him slamming my head on the ground. That was the only time I saw Mom cry. She never apologized for not taking me. She never will. She thinks it's my own fault.

Maybe she's right. I wanted to dance, to fly, so bad. It felt so good. Maybe God didn't want me to have that. I don't know. It doesn't matter now. I'll never dance again.

Miss Joyce doesn't believe that. She said that I should write it all down. The police said so too. They said to try and remember all of it. I'm trying to forget it. Daddy is still in Cleveland. This morning I walked to the bus, holding my stomach, feeling for the line where he broke me in half. Nobody spoke to me. They'd already heard my story, recounted by the mothers over breakfast. I watched as the gate went up for our school bus. It lowered quickly, letting down the little flag I'd read so many times before.

Safety is our business.

I would have laughed but it hurt too much. Someone should tell the people who write dumb things like that or show people in bed on TV and make it look like something wonderful. Some other girl, one without bloody boots and a black eye, one who still had stickers on her Rubik's cube, should tell them. They were grown-ups. They should know these things.

3

Ron

It always starts fast and horrible like a bug flying up my nose. And usually when I'm sleeping. Brian warns me if he can, but sometimes she comes back walking. Once, after she'd been gone three nights straight, she came back crawling. It's been six days.

Sometimes she can't find me in the dark. Maybe, if I lie real still . . .

"Run! She's in the back!" Brian's voice hissed up through the broken window before the rain drowned him out. I jumped off the bed and was almost under it when a cold hand choked my neck. I vowed not to cry.

"I missed you, hon. Did you miss me?" my mother said, her warm breath a steam of cheap beer and stale cigarettes. I nodded, swallowed, wondering if she really meant it, if she ever had meant it. Sometimes, at the beginning, it was hard to tell. By the end though, there was never any doubt. She lit up a Marlboro from the smell of it and took a deep drag. I bit my lip, trying to pray to Brian's God, begging silently for her to put it out. And not on me. After a sweaty kiss on my cheek and an assurance of her love, my mother answered my prayer, tossing her cigarette somewhere on the floor and stomping it out. I grabbed for her hands. Just in time. She was coming at me.

"Ow! Cut it out, will you, Ma?"

Her answer was another blow. Despite the dark, she could see my every move. Even if she hadn't seen, she'd know anyway. I'd learned every bit of my bob-and-weave act from watching her. It'd never worked very well for either of us, but it made the time go faster somehow. As punches rained down on my back, I turned and grabbed her fists. Her hands didn't hurt so much. Not anymore. It was the other things . . .

"Stop it, okay? Just stop it!"

She laughed, sounding eerily like my father used to when he was dealing out the punches to her. Didn't she remember how it felt to be on the other end?

"You want to make this hard, do you?" she said, grabbing a fistful of my hair.

I gritted my teeth and yanked my head away. It felt like I left some hair in her hand. My head ached, but I didn't care. I was sixteen. Long past begging. It didn't do any good anyway.

"You think you're a man, boy? I'll make a man outta you. Don't worry."

Teetering on a broken heel, she lit into me again—this time scratching, digging at any flesh she could find. I ran back to the bedroom, hoping Brian was still outside the window in case I needed to jump out of it. He'd catch me, I was sure of that. The problem was, my mother caught me first, just as I was trying to get a running start.

She tripped me from behind and we flopped onto the bed. The broken springs that I avoided at night jabbed into me now. My mother kept screaming at me, but I tuned it out, listening to the rain pounding against the window and the rattle of Brian's bike chain instead.

He'd gone home.

Sure he'd come back when it was over and sneak me into his room, but it wasn't the same without him outside, waiting. It meant something to know he was out there, that as soon as she left, he'd come right in and take me home, smothering all my secrets under his mother's quilts.

Mama got tired of fighting me and started singing a song I'd never heard. I couldn't make out the words, but it sounded like the songs from Brian's church that floated down the hill. I wished there'd been a service tonight.

Cold, hard rain coming in through the cracks and my mother drunk and crazy on my chest was all the hymn I had. For a little while, it was enough. I put my arms around her and smoothed her hair.

The street light clicked on, bright and blurry against the window. We both turned away from it, not wanting to see. I think that's why she always came at night, so that she wouldn't have to look at me. At herself. Tomorrow, she'd leave money on the table for me.

I'd take the money and wait a couple hours before Brian came and helped me limp back to his house, where I'd stay until Mama came for me in a few days, sober and pretty in a worn-out sort of way, standing on the sidewalk, thanking Brian's mother through her teeth. We'd pretend it didn't happen except for her saying sorry over and over. We'd get pizza and watch stupid movies, cut coupons and do homework. And then some man would call, come by . . . And then she wouldn't come home. And when she did, it'd be like this. Only tonight, it was raining, so no one would hear me scream.

So far tonight I wasn't too bad off, though. Scratches and bruises was all. We'd broken the bed frame and my last clean T-shirt was ruined, but I couldn't think about that now. The picture frame I'd hidden under my mattress rested on the floor: face up, broken and smiling. I hoped she didn't see it. I hoped she was drunk enough that she'd be passing out soon.

One hand on her back, my fingers eased toward the metal frame, one of the last things we still had from before. There were two photos inside—the top one of my parents as newlyweds, the one that I looked at to remind me of who Mama really was, and the one under that, a snapshot of me and Brian smiling on a hot day when everything seemed right. I memorized days like that to save for nights like this. It all evens out somehow.

26

She snatched the frame from me as quickly as I reached for it and sat up on the mattress. Like so many times before, I thought about giving her a good shove, running to tell everybody what they already knew. But I couldn't. I wouldn't. I was a man, not a punk. Men didn't hit women and they never ran away. I looked like my father, but I wanted the resemblance to stop there. He was dead now, but still haunted Mama's soul. Mine too. I'd never be like him.

She pricked her finger on the broken glass but managed to get into the frame. I sat up carefully, trying to gauge her reaction. Mama faltered for a minute as she looked at the wedding picture, squinting in the dim light to recognize her own happiness. She steeled her resolve when she saw the second photo. She crumpled them both in her fist.

"Been hiding this?" She dug up another cigarette and lit it first, then the pictures. Her hand was really bleeding now, but she didn't seem to feel it. She was too busy trying to be him, even though she'd hated him.

But she loved him too. So did you. Just like you love her.

She slapped me out of my reverie. "Best live for today, Ronnie. Now for the last time, are you going to leave them niggers alone?" She reached for the radio and yanked the cord out of it.

I let out the scream I'd been holding back and rolled off the mattress, trying to avoid the broken glass. I knew what came next. This part hurt worst. How could I have been so stupid as to leave the radio out. It was Brian's—set to wake me up. I'd been tired. So tired. The first lash sliced the air and landed across my shoulder blades, just under my arms. The cord came down again, this time around my neck. The plug whipped around and hit my temple. At least it wasn't my eye. I hauled myself up and ran out of the room.

She chased slower this time, but my heart beat faster, sort of like Brian's drum. I slumped in the corner, quiet, while she looked for me with the cord raised above her head. One time, she'd fallen asleep on the couch like that, with an iron cord over her head. I'd climbed out the window onto Brian's bike.

Blood trailed down the side of my face. I must have moved or something because the cord came down again. I ducked to miss the plug, but banged my head hard into the wall in the process.

That made me laugh. I don't know why, but suddenly everything was funny. Ridiculous. Everybody said I should just go to the shelter, go to foster care and be some old person's boyfriend like the other kids I knew who'd gone. They said Brian's mother was too old to adopt me and that there were other kids, black kids that she should take. My mother was in treatment, they said. A hopeful case.

I laughed harder at the thought of it, feeling hot and dizzy. So tired I wanted to sleep and never wake up. Maybe tonight I would be with Brian's Jesus, the man of the cross and the shame. If God would have me, I'd be glad to come. I wasn't so sure on the heaven thing, but anything had to be better than this.

Anything.

Maybe I'd go back to the shelter. Maybe nobody would touch me this time. I slid down the wall, but not before she got me one last time, with all her strength. I tried to catch the cord, but it cut my hand. I screamed, then cursed myself for screaming.

Punk.

The room flashed black. When I saw clear again, Mama was bending over me again, trying to stand up. When she bobbled back and swung down again, I didn't even try to block her. I closed my eyes, but not before I heard the screen door bang open and then the front door. I didn't see them, but I knew. I took a deep breath to be sure. Vanilla extract and Afro Sheen. Yeah. It was them.

I squinted to see Miss Eva's wrinkled hands around Mama's wrists.

"Marie, put it down," she said from somewhere so far away it seemed like a dream.

"I ain't putting nothing down. This is my boy."

28

She did put it down, though. Mama put it down and stepped away, backed up against the wall.

Miss Eva tried to talk to her while Brian helped me up.

"Thanks," I said, not really looking at him. I'd told him never to bring anybody, but this time I guess I was glad. Still, my mother was shouting with Brian's mother in the corner, and I didn't know how it might turn out. Miss Eva talked calm, but I'd seen her snatch Brian off a basketball court while he was in midair. She was nobody to play with.

"Yeah," he said back with a quick nod.

Miss Eva smiled at Mama and took a deep breath. "Marie, I know you and I knew your mama too. I know that man done you bad and I'm sorry, but this has gone on too long. Now stop before you beat this child to death." She walked over to me and touched the side of my face.

Child? I was no child. I was a man. And my grandmother? Miss Eva had never mentioned knowing her. I tried to recall what she looked like. A kind voice. A soft touch. And nice eyes. Brown eyes. No face would come.

I tried to sit up, knowing without looking that Mama was gone. Her shows were private. Though Mama would never admit it, she was embarrassed by Eva's kindnesses and hated them for knowing our secrets probably more than she was prejudiced against them.

That was Miss Eva's theory anyway. She restated it again as she crushed me to her bosom. "Don't you mind your mama. She's just shamed at me seeing her like this."

"I told him not to bring you. She's got a gun." I whispered the words into the flowers on her dress.

"Marie is bad off, I know, but Brian Michael was so upset. I was just going to come up here to talk before I called the police. Then I heard you scream when we was still a ways down the road. Lord, that scream . . ."

That stupid screaming. If I'd only held out a little longer, she probably would have fallen asleep and everything could go back like before. "I didn't mean to scream," I said without looking at Brian. "She caught me by surprise. I'm sorry. She could've got the gun and shot y'all or something . . ."

Miss Eva's chest moved up and down. It made my head hurt, but I stayed put.

"The Lord looks after babies and fools, right? It looks like we both qualify today. And don't worry about screaming, baby. Don't ever stop." She pulled away and held me in front of her. "Someday you might even have to scream for somebody else."

Brian draped my arm over his shoulder.

I grabbed on to the wall. "My notebook. In the room. Third drawer. Can you get it?"

A grin inched across Miss Eva's face. "The word of your testimony. Have you been writing every day like Joyce told y'all? That's almost half your grade, you know." She held me up while Brian darted into the next room.

It hurt to breathe. "I'm trying."

I thought about what the room might look like to Brian, even in the light of the street. I shrugged. He'd seen worse. He'd seen things that nobody else had. To prove it, he came back seconds later with the notebook shoved under his arm. "Let's go," he said, having had enough experience with Mama to see the wisdom in a quick getaway.

We went out the door and down the steps together, all the family each other had. There weren't any words to be said, so none of us looked for any. As the rain baptized us, curtains inched back at the windows we passed by. Even in the storm and shame, Miss Eva smiled and waved her hand as the drapes fell back into place.

Brian didn't slow down until we stopped at his place, a yellow frame house with pink roses. I tried to walk inside by myself, but Brian wouldn't let go.

I shook my head. "Don't, man. I've got this." I didn't have it, not my strength or anything else. If it weren't for the rain, I'd have passed out on the way. Brian knew it, but he let me walk to the door anyway, following me every step.

Once we were inside, he picked me up like a bag of bones and carried me to the bathroom. Miss Eva sat on the edge of the tub, touching my forehead, while Brian started the water for the rags, first hot, then just enough cold. I'd had to tell him how to do it the first time I showed up silent and bleeding, but he never forgot after that.

Miss Eva told me to hold up my arms and started to tug at my shirt. I struggled to sit up, staring at Brian in a panic.

His hand came out of the sink so fast that some of the water sloshed over the side. "It's not so bad, Mama. We can do it."

Brian's mother, much older than the other mothers on the block, but much smarter too, got the clue quickly and stood up and started for the kitchen. I hated to deprive her of being good to me, but sometimes pity hurt as much as the rest of it.

She seemed to understand. "You hungry, Red?"

My red-brown hair didn't look like much to me, but Miss Eva liked it a lot. I liked it when she called me that. "Yes ma'am." I pried off my soggy Chuck Taylors with my toes.

"Well, all right then. I'll go warm up some dinner." She paused at the door while Brian pulled my shirt up just enough to clean my back. The water went red on his first pass.

I sat up a little, feeling better already. "What you cook? Pork chops?" I toppled backwards when Brian put the hot rag on the cut across my back.

Brian broke my fall and pushed me gently before Miss Eva could get across the room. She took a step back. "No pork chops, baby. Chitlins, macaroni and cheese, greens and cornbread. All your favorites."

I stared into Miss Eva's eyes. Brown eyes. I laughed out loud. "You cleaned chitlins?" I twisted around to Brian behind me. "And you let her? You all must have thought she was going to kill me for sure." I jumped and winced as he put on the hydrogen peroxide.

Brian winced too, only at the thought of the pig intestines he hated so much. He shook his head in agreement. "Yeah, I let her clean them for your stupid butt. Now, I'm the only one who's gonna die. Pig guts. Who in the world would want to eat that?"

"Hush, boy," Miss Eva said from the kitchen. "You don't have to eat it."

"Shore don't." I gave Brian a playful elbow as he wound a bandage around my chest. "Get out the hot sauce, will you, Miss Eva?"

Brian shuddered with disgust, lifting my shirt up the rest of the way and pulling it over my head. "Sometimes I could swear you're black under there."

I stared at the blood staining Brian's fingers. So much blood. I swallowed hard. When it came down to it, there was only one color that mattered. "All blood runs red."

4

Rolls look boring at the store. They sit still in the package and keep real quiet. Those were the only kind of rolls I knew, silent ones. I didn't know about talking bread with crunchy outsides and soft bellies, begging for butter. I didn't know a ball of yeast could talk a bruised boy out of bed, but I was learning and not just about bread.

First off, there was the new sleeping rule. I didn't hear about this one until I'd healed up enough to get around. Miss Joyce brought my work over after school and Brian shared his notes. Just when I felt better and thought we'd be able to have some fun after Miss Eva went to bed, she laid down the new law: after the evening news, everything with legs, including critters and boys, had to go upstairs. No coming down until morning, not even to pee. That seemed a little silly, especially with those big rooms downstairs, but like Brian says, sometimes it's best to just go along. I think Miss Eva was more worried about my mama than she let on.

Women are that way, I think, knowing things that men don't quite get. Their rules don't always make sense, but the one time you don't listen, you're doomed. That much, I knew already. Brian had to elbow me the first few nights when the news went off to remind me that instead of whispering all night downstairs like we'd always done, we had to go upstairs. That part, the going up, took forever. Though Miss Eva moved fast in the daytime, at night, she turned old in the same way my mother turned crazy.

I decided right then, on the stairs, to spend some time with my wife after dark before marrying her. Can't be too careful about stuff like that. Slow stair-climbing I could deal with, but crazy was something else altogether. It took me awhile to get used to going so slow on those stairs. It was like being almost to the top of Mount Everest but only taking one teeny step at a time. Brian seemed disgusted to be sleeping upstairs at all, but for me it was something else new: dust bunnies, Miss Eva's snoring, and even Brian's elbow in my eye.

I loved it all, though it bothered me that I was starting to look forward to *Masterpiece Theater* on the radio. I'd be a total nerd if I kept that up. Still, every day, there was something to be eager for: the hum of hymns rising in the oven downstairs, soon to be covered with honey butter and gooseberry jam. And today, I had something else to be excited about, scared about.

Today, I was going to meet Jesus.

After the rolls, of course. Even God wouldn't expect me to pass that up, I thought, plodding down the creaky steps two at time in the direction of the smell. Brian had left me sleeping, probably hoping to get an extra roll or two, but it was "few-tile," as Miss Eva said so often. Those rolls were singing and I meant to taste them all— chorus, refrain, and all the delicious notes in between. Even after so many mornings of fresh, hot bread, I kept waking up expecting the wonder to end. As usual, I was happy to be wrong.

Brian sat at the checker-clothed table nibbling calmly, undaunted by the spread. He put down the paper and looked at me like he was my father instead of my friend. "Morning."

I took another step toward the table, but paused at the stove, where Miss Eva cracked the first of several eggs over a mound of frying potatoes. I breathed deep, trying to suck all this goodness into my mind, into my memory, so then when the bad times came, when the breakfasts ended, when Mama came for me . . . I'd remember how good it all was. All of it. The little things too, like the way Miss Eva's dress hugged the roll of fat on her back. Clinging for dear life.

"It's rude to stare, Rodney," she said, addressing me by her pet name, the name of her first son, drowned at sixteen. Our age. Brian quietly suspected it was the first sign of sin-ill-ity, as he so mercilessly mocked his mother's pronunciation, but for me, it was a badge of honor being called the name of her son. I couldn't remember the last time my mother had called me by anything other than "boy" or "laddie" or other things, things I'd like to forget. But this hot, sweet Sunday, I wanted to remember forever. Hence, the staring.

"I'm sorry, Miss Eva." I bowed my head, trying to remember the prayer Brian had taught me days before. Once I got the sleeping down, there was the training of prayer and sifting through all the church words that Miss Eva used while talking on the phone. He'd put me through a crash course in Church 101 the last few nights, but I still felt ill-prepared. Brian assured me that no matter how stupid I acted, the music would be too loud for anyone to notice. Since I'd heard most of those songs and sermons all the way down to my house, I knew that part was true. It wasn't the people who worried me anyway; it was meeting the Big Guy that had me a little worried. It's not every day that a kid meets God.

I must have been staring again because Brian stomped my foot under the table. My eyes pressed shut again and I drowned out the sweet-talking bread and sizzling bacon. I ran a finger over the scar at my temple, now scabbed and itchy.

Jesus, thanks for all this good stuff. I'm looking forward to meeting you today.

There, that should do it. The key is not to overthink it, Brian says. Not that I ever do that. I'm usually trying not to think about something, except this bread. I grabbed a roll and stuffed it into my mouth. Just as good as yesterday. Not better. Not worse. Just perfect, exactly the same. And nobody here seemed to think that was strange. I stared at Miss Eva again, wiping her wrinkled hands on her apron. I tried not to stare, but her hands always kept my attention. They were three shades: nutmeg to her knuckles, then a stretch of pecan ran into dark chocolate cuticles. Her palms were always pink and soft, probably from working all that bread. She narrowed her eyes at me. I was staring again.

"There's just so much to look at, I can't help myself."

Miss Eva laughed at the stove. "I guess there is a lot to see around here, baby. Just don't start with that excuse. It's a dangerous one. Pray and ask God to help you with it, hear?" She slid a mess of eggs and potatoes onto a plate and placed it in front of us.

I nodded in agreement. It had taken me awhile to realize what she meant when she said it like that, but now I found myself saying it too. It drove Brian crazy. "I think I'll pray about it at church this morning."

Miss Eva looked very pleased with this response. Before I could ask, she placed a bottle of ketchup beside my plate. "Brian Michael, get those preserves from the red-topped cupboard before this boy eats all the rolls."

"Yes, ma'am." Brian closed his paper and reached behind him into the cupboard in the corner.

Gooseberry. Please let there be more. I promise not to eat it all this time.

I stuffed another roll into my mouth while Brian knocked around in the cupboard, probably just to torment me. I turned away from the table and leaned toward the gas stove. Mesmerized by the little grease-people left behind on the skillet, I leaned even closer, watching them dance across the pan. A burst of oil popped up and missed my cheek by an inch.

"Lord have mercy!" Miss Eva spun from the sink where she'd begun washing dishes. "See there! Get back now." She jerked the pan off the eye of the stove.

My chest felt tight. The popping sound had scared the air out of me. I'd even stopped chewing. "I'm sorry, Miss Eva. I—"

She shook her head. "I know. You just can't help it. That's a sorry song you're singing, Mister. And a whole lot of sorry men sang it before you. If you're going to live here, you better learn to help it, you hear?"

Surprised a little by her firm tone, I nodded and slid back onto my chair, raising a tin cup of milk to my lips. Miss Eva had never raised her voice at me before. When she did, she sounded a little too much like . . . Mama. Suddenly the roll in my mouth didn't taste so good. I spat a ball of dough, covered with gooseberries, onto the plate.

"Man, that's nasty." Brian peeked over the edge of the international page with a frown.

"Bri, you look like an old Englishman sitting with his tea and crumpets. All you need is a pipe."

Brian tugged the paper down again, dragging his eyes from an interview with Nelson Mandela. "An Englishman with an afro? Man, please. Eat your food. We've got to get dressed."

Brian's voice was a little louder than I would have liked. It wasn't that Brian and Miss Eva were being mean, but they weren't being, well . . . perfect. And when things weren't perfect for me, they were bad. Real bad. There didn't seem to be anything in the middle. I didn't want bad things again. Not here. I slumped in the chair.

Miss Eva's doughy fingers touched my neck. "No need to go pouting now. I still love you. You just mind me and we'll all make out fine. Isn't that right, Brian Michael?"

Coating the last roll with the peach preserves he'd dug out from the back of the cabinet, Brian nodded. He waited for Miss Eva to turn back to the stove. "Listen to what she says," he whispered, bringing my hand to a keloid scar behind his ear. "That stove is nothing to mess with." He broke his roll in half and put it on my plate, grimacing as his fingers grazed the mess already there.

I took the bread and smiled, thinking of the scars already covering my own body. Mama wasn't nothing to mess with either. I'd take this place over that one any day, stove and all. "Thanks, Bri."

The newspaper stayed up. "Anytime."

After years of watching Miss Eva and Brian through the blinds on their way to Mount Olive Missionary Baptist Church, I was finally making the walk with them, as I'd done so many times in my mind. During revivals, I'd put my ear to the wall, listening to the music that poured over the neighborhood from their little tent. Like the mysterious talking rolls from Brian's kitchen, the people in his church could sing like nobody I'd ever known. I'd been too far away to make out the words, but I knew the tunes. There was one melody that always made my eyes water. It sounded deep down, like when Brian used to play his drum.

Sad even, like a dirge, the last word in Brian's crossword this morning. I don't know how he can hold them all, so many words, but today I wasn't a dirge. I wasn't sad. I was a happy song, like in one of those commercials where everybody holds hands over pop or something. Today, in Brian's old suit, with a belly full of good food, I was going to see God himself.

"Watch this," Brian said, with a nod in his mother's direction.

I couldn't believe it. When we got to the church steps, Miss Eva tipped right up them like a young girl. She even beat Brian and not one of the flowers on her hat even moved. I looked up at the sun, but it looked the same as always: round and hot. Still, I knew its secrets.

"She was moving, wasn't she?" Brian said as we reached the top. "It trips me out every Sunday. I forgot to warn you about that part."

I nodded. "I should have known anyway. It's the sun."

My friend looked at me like I was totally crazy. "What?"

I sighed. Brian could be so smart about things that didn't matter, but he was a dunce at the obvious. "Women. They're different at night than in the day—"

"No. It's Jesus, man. I'll explain it to you later. Come on."

Not to take anything away from Jesus, I still stood by my theory. Either way, there was no use arguing with Brian. He always won.

I straightened my clip-on tie and wondered whether or not to tell Bri that his afro, which had been a perfect circle when we left home, was drooping on the right side. Nah, I decided. Best not to mention it. Brian's afro is a big deal to him, his allegiance with the sixties "Black is Beautiful" movement. Or something like that. We joke that he was born a few years too late.

We followed Miss Eva to the double doors at the front of the church. We arrived just in time to save her from a treacherous-looking fellow with a pile of papers in his hand. Probably the programs Brian had told me about.

On further inspection of the shiny-shoed villain, I realized it was the school janitor, scrubbed until he glowed like a hazelnut. I grabbed Brian's arm, wrinkling his suit with my grip. "Is that Mr. Terrigan?"

Brian peeled my fingers off his suit and accepted a program before pulling me inside. "Yes. That's him. Those Terrigans run this place. There's a million of them. I heard they're going to put Jerry, the big one, in our class."

"The big one?" I looked around. Everybody here looked big to me: tall, strong, and smooth.

He pulled me again. "People are saying he's the one, that he'll go to the NFL. He doesn't do tests well, so they put him down a grade. You know how it is."

"Yeah." I wish I didn't know. Miss Joyce who taught dance at the rec was our teacher now, and she said I could catch up, but I didn't see how. I'd missed so many days the past few years it seemed like I'd never catch up.

Miss Eva was still behind us, lingering at the door. I looked back, shocked to see her give me a wink.

"Good morning, Miss Eva," the janitor imposter said, looking Brian's mother up and down. "I see that the Lord is keeping you as beautiful as ever. Having a son late in life must be keeping you young."

Brian elbowed my side. Our eyes met, confirming we were thinking the same thing: *Can you believe this guy?*

Evidently Miss Eva could. It took her awhile to answer, but the way she smoothed her seersucker suit with one hand and straightened her already-straight hat with the other said it all. Finally, she flashed a smile. "You go on, Deacon Terrigan. With all those children you and Ruth have, you should know." She turned to us. "We'd better get inside."

And inside we went, walking past rows of long wooden benches until she reached the second row. Front and center, Brian had warned me. That's how Miss Eva liked it. I craned my neck in every direction, taking in the climbing hair, the shiny suits and ties, Brut, Old Spice, and bacon grease tangled together into a song of smells and colors, rocking to the beat of a little girl's hair beads knocking together on the row in front of us.

Miss Eva tapped the little girl and gave her a stern stare. The girl went still, like she'd been frozen with a freeze ray. I marveled, staring at the ceiling. There wasn't any sunlight in here, but the church definitely had intensified Miss Eva's powers. I straightened my back against the rough wood, hoping she wouldn't zap me next.

A purple satin cloth with a gold cross and gold fringe dangled over the podium. Several wooden chairs perched behind it in a semicircle, with a huge one in the center like a pine tree, with armrests that jutted out like branches. I figured Jesus would be tall, but could anybody's arms be that long?

"That's where the preachers sit," Brian whispered, barely moving his lips.

I nodded, a little annoyed. Brian's the type of person who thinks he's got everything down. He figures his job on earth is to tell the rest of us fools how to get along. He's kind of right in a way, but still it's annoying. There's lots of things that he doesn't know, things

40

that can only be seen and heard from the window in my bedroom on a day when I'm hurt and alone and can't move. Things like the dirge. I didn't wish that on anybody, especially somebody who'd been eating heaven all his life.

He saw that I was a little mad and smiled at me. I smiled back. Maybe the way things were wasn't so bad—heart for me, head for Brian. Between the two of us, we had most things covered.

"Look," he said, pointing out the glass door he'd told me about.

The baptismal.

On the wall behind the pulpit were six words: One Lord. One Faith. One Baptism. Each sentence was staggered at various heights with "One Lord" above them all. I didn't quite understand why you had to count the lords, faiths, and baptisms, but it sure looked nice. The gold lettering made a nice contrast with the purple satin and gold fringe. With the shiny glass doors underneath, it was like the lipstick of the room, the only color besides the rainbow of suits and dresses. Some of the people wore no color at all: long, black skirts and tight hair buns made them look like water, all the same. I'd learn today that they weren't the same, that sometimes color can burst out of plain-clothed people without them even knowing. I'd learn it today, but not yet. Not yet.

I looked back at the baptismal, realizing that the little window was half-filled with water. It dipped a little in the center somewhere, right under "One Baptism." They'd certainly thought that through.

Brian saw me looking and took it upon himself to offer further explanation. "They just got that last year. We used to go down to the river and they'd sing 'wade in the water, children' . . ."

His sing-song voice reached Miss Eva's notice and she gripped her pocketbook sweetly and gave him the same look she'd given the little girl in front of us.

He sat back against the pew, and his voice went back to a whisper.

41

"Don't tell anybody, but I liked that better. Going to the river, I mean. That water looks fake, like they put food coloring in it or something."

I closed my eyes, imagining the people rising up out of the river like the big chair on the stage, like trees. I liked that better too. And I liked that song Brian was singing. I knew that one for sure. It always came through my window clear. Once, during a bad time with Mama, they'd been singing it and I'd dived under it like the bright blue water in the baptismal, floating through the pain, swimming around her horrible words. I took a breath and opened my eyes. This was what I'd come for—to see with my eyes what I'd felt so many times with my soul. I leaned over to Brian. "When does Jesus come in?"

"Man, I told you. He's here now. It's not like that." He gave me a look as though I were the one who had no understanding of the obvious.

I tried not to pout or stare or any of the other things I did wrong, but I wasn't doing very well with it. House of God means house of God. That much I could figure out on my own. For a guy who read so much, Brian still had a lot to learn. "Whatever." I'd find Jesus on my own. He had to be around here somewhere.

"I told you to listen last night. You don't know anything about this. Church is different. It's like, like . . . a school play that never ends. Everybody plays their parts over and over every week."

A raspberry rattled my lips before I knew what I was doing. I really wanted to do something else, but even stupid me knew that wouldn't be good to do in church. Miss Eva swatted me with a fan from a funeral home. Why would you have funeral home fans at church? Dead people didn't need God. This was past stupid and I was starting to think that maybe I shouldn't have come at all.

Brian smoothed his jacket. "You mark my word. As soon as you smell chicken, the music is going to start. Three bars of 'Amazing Grace' and the pastor is going to come out and—"

Miss Eva tapped both our shoulders. "Hush. And Brian Michael,

I hope you're telling Rodney about the wonders of Christ's love and how glad we are to have him this morning. That is what you were saying, right, son?"

I stifled a laugh. The wonders of Christ's love? Brian didn't even know what *he* was here for, let alone me.

"Yeah, Mama. Sure."

The orchid on Miss Eva's hat tipped in our direction.

"I mean, yes, ma'am."

The funeral fan went into overdrive. My eyes started to water. Miss Eva must have thought I was moved by the Holy Ghost because she offered me a tissue and told me that it was okay to cry, that sometimes the Holy Ghost just moved on folks like that. Brian looked like he was about to scream when she said that, but I paid him no mind. I was far too confused to give him attention.

They have ghosts too? I thought they weren't into that.

It was all so confusing. And then, I smelled something. It floated down the pew, smothering the lingering aromas of pressing oil and aftershave. Brian unbuttoned his jacket and gave me a nod as I recognized the scent: fried chicken.

Like a band following a scented conductor, the organist struck up a chord. Feathered hats and starched suits shot upward all across the church. The deacon who'd flirted with Miss Eva stopped to give me a sour look before seating someone at the end of our row. I dropped my head, staring at the man's reflection in his unreasonably shiny shoes. The brown double-breasted suit and light skin blurred together like an ice-cream cone. I could even guess the flavor: lemon custard. Daddy's flavor, Mama had told me once when she was drunk. My mouth tasted sour at the thought of him.

And her.

A voice like rock hitting bottom in a deep well pried me away from the ice-cream parlor I'd never been in, from the gravesite of a man I didn't remember, but a man my mother remembered all too well.

43

The voice, the one that pulled me away, rang so clear, so deep, that it seemed like the building should have been shaking; but it wasn't. "A-ma-zi-ing Gra-a-a-ce. How . . . swe-et th-e sounnnnnd . . ."

I don't remember when my mouth dropped open, but I know it did because Brian elbowed me to close it. What I do remember was when the tallest, blackest man I'd ever seen stepped to the podium. His robe billowed even though the air was still. I'm surprised I didn't stand up and run to him.

Jesus.

Right here in Testimony, Ohio, wearing a green robe with a string hanging off his sleeve and "One Lord" right over his head. And he sang the way it must sound in heaven; the way Miss Eva's rolls tasted.

I knew he would come.

"Cut it out," Brian whispered between verses. "You're staring again."

I concentrated until I heard my teeth click together. But in my head, in my heart, I was still staring. Looking into the face of God. And Jesus didn't seem to mind. My staring earned me a big smile. A knowing look. My heart leaped in my chest. It was all true. The cross, the Bible, the whole thing. I'd been pretty sure. Almost a hundred percent sure. But now, I was sold.

God knew me.

The background music faded, but the talking still sounded like singing to me. "Wel-come to Mount Olive, where Jesus makes the difference," he said in one long breath.

I smiled at the way Jesus mentioned himself like that. He didn't even blink when he said it either. I looked around. Nobody seemed to have a clue what was going on. Pretty slick. Maybe he visited a different church every week. Maybe he was at all of them right now. He was God, after all, even if no one here seemed to know it. I winked toward the podium. His secret was safe with me.

Jesus seemed very amused by my winking, which was totally

cool. I looked down at my left thumb, still a little crooked from a broken bone that never got set. Being here with Jesus was worth everything, even that.

"All visitors, please stand," he said, taking his eyes from me and looking around the church.

I knew I should probably get up, but I didn't. I couldn't.

A man, his wife, and three daughters stood to the left of us. I'd seen a couple of the girls around before. The older one seemed pretty serious. The younger one blew Brian a kiss when her father wasn't looking. She was too little for it to be a flirt, but that one was going to be something. The middle one stared straight ahead, holding her father's hand. When the man spoke, his big voice surprised me. Still, he had nothing on Jesus. "I'm Richard Shiloh, pastor of Shekinah Baptist. And this is my family." When he was finished, he smiled like a movie star.

I rolled my eyes. Compared to Jesus, this guy was totally lame. Somebody must have told him that church was a play too.

Brian gave the little girl a funny look and then stared at the floor, counting the floor tiles like he did at school when he was waiting for the rest of us to finish our work. He had no business in Joyce's class at all, but his temper got him into trouble. I tried to get him to join the debate team and use all his arguing to good use, but he wasted it all on the teachers, who'd finally washed their hands of him. I never understood why Brian had to always be counting or reading or thinking something. Not me. Not me. I knew how to suck inside myself, roll up, and fly away. It was staying put that was hard.

"Good to have you, Brother Shiloh. We'll have to send the choir over one Sunday. Talk to Sister Thelma after service and we'll make the arrangements."

A lady with a beige face and a brown neck waved her hand from the organ. My jaw dropped again. It was the lunch lady from school, but her face was an entire different shade than it was during the week.

Brian stomped on my foot. Lightly this time, at least. "It's makeup. Don't stare." He said the words without opening his mouth. Another of my friend's many useless talents. And Miss Thelma had some useless talents of her own evidently. Makeup was supposed to make people look better, wasn't it? Who would use it to do *that*?

A nervous-looking man with a high-pitched voice stood next, explaining his being new to Testimony and looking for a church home. Two women on the other side of Brian hung on his every word, especially when he got to where he worked. I sucked a piece of gooseberry from my teeth and took it all in. Even if Jesus hadn't shown up, church would have been . . . riveting.

I smiled at that, using one of Brian's favorite words in my head. On summer days, the back of the cereal box could become "riveting" if Brian was bored enough. I would lie then, agreeing with Brian about how scary all the chemicals sounded in my favorite cereal, but this time I meant it. Mount Olive Missionary Baptist Church was absolutely riveting.

Just like the eyes of Jesus, fixed on me now. Had I done something wrong?

Duh. He can read your mind, Mr. Riveting.

Just as I was about to apologize for all my silly thoughts, the giant black Jesus leaned over the pulpit and said, "What about you, young man. How'd you get here this morning?"

As if he didn't know. I paused before answering, wondering if God was really going to take the charade this far. When he rested back and folded his arms, I figured that he meant it.

"I-I came here to meet you. Miss Eva and Brian have told me about you and all, but I really had to meet Jesus for myself."

A savage kick bit my shin under the pew as the crowd erupted in laughter. Miss Eva's face flushed pink, her face a curious mix of shock and pride. I bit my cheek again, but not to keep from laughing. Maybe it was a school play after all. If so, Jesus was sure playing his part well. A little too well.

The man looked stricken. "Me? Oh no, son. I'm just a man, Reverend Wilkins. And we don't come to church to see people, we come to see Jesus. Right, church?"

"Yessir. That's right," Miss Eva said, her pink flush turning purplish. The fan was going so fast and hard that I dared not move or risk a paper cut.

I slumped against the pew, now totally confused. Brian was right. As always. This was a horrible version of *Masterpiece Theater*. Only scarier.

The music drifted in again. Soft at first, then louder as a line of kids our age trailed in, wearing the same robes as Jesus-who-wasn't-Jesus had on. At the front of the line was a tiny girl who had to be Reverend Wilkins' daughter. An hour ago I would have said she was an angel. I didn't even bother to try not to stare. She was beautiful, like walking music. And not the on-the-top-of-the-water music either. She was the low notes in the deep end.

Brian was staring too and I wanted to kick him for it. He'd probably seen that girl a thousand times. He only wanted her now because I wanted her, and I usually let Brian have everything he wanted. Except for the rolls. And this music girl with a kid body and old woman eyes. "Wade in the Water" eyes.

"Who is she?" I whispered, the way Brian had done earlier. It came out quiet and cool just like he did it. Any other time, I would have paused to reflect on the wonder of the feat, but this wasn't any other time. I'd watched Brian fall for girls since fourth grade, but I'd never found one that I really liked until now.

Brian had a dreamy look on his face. "I can't remember her name, but I'm going to marry her."

I lost it then, right on the front pew. I grabbed a handful of afro and tugged with all my might, letting go only when I remembered where I was. Brian's eyes doubled in size. He looked like he wanted to punch me. We'd only fought once since kindergarten, but this morning would probably be the second time. And I didn't care.

47

I gritted my teeth and waited for Miss Eva to knock me off the pew with that fan, but she didn't. Nobody even looked our way anymore. All eyes were on her, watching, waiting for her to begin.

When she did, I knew that I'd had it wrong. She didn't look like an angel. She sounded like one.

Brian was not impressed. Though no one seemed to hear us, I could certainly hear him. "You are going to regret that, fool. You watch. My hair was perfect. Perfect!" He hissed the word through his teeth.

I tried to scream over the music and tell him that his 'fro had been totally sideways since the second strain of "Amazing Grace" but I had no time to play games with him.

My wife was singing.

"She's mine," I said, hoping my face conveyed how crazy I felt. Crazy scared Brian more than actual fighting. That's why I'd pulled his hair.

The youth choir stood to sing the next verse. In the back row was the tallest kid I'd ever seen. Although right now Brian was looming pretty large over my shoulder. His 'fro was turned down at the edges now, sweated out like a floppy hair hat. I was glad he couldn't see it. This was war as it was.

Brian dug a hymnal into my side. "She's yours? Zeely? Man, please. She's like a foot shorter than you and she's not even your type. If you think Rev is Jesus, she's Jesus' daughter. For real. Them Wilkinses is crazy."

Still wrapped up in her singing, I didn't respond. Zeely. What a wonderful, beautiful name. It fit her perfectly. What didn't fit was Brian's angry reaction and his speech patterns. He was out of control, but I could play that game.

A foot shorter? I stared at her, sizing up her small frame, then looked back at Brian's eyes. I realized then that he hadn't been looking at my Zeely at all. His eyes were fastened on a big-boned girl in yellow on the top row, her afro bigger than Brian's by a good inch. A serious feat.

Oops. "So you're not looking at Zeely?"

Brian took a deep breath. "Of course not. We're not even friends. They're too good for me. And you too. Things are bad enough without you pulling my hair and all like you're nuts." He squinted at the tall girl. "Everybody always treats me different. Like something is wrong with me. But not *her*. I thought she'd moved away."

Zeely came down off a high note. So did I. "Who moved away?"

My friend was growing tired of me. "Her! The dance—"

He almost finished his sentence, but Miss Eva's fan crashed down on his head and knocked the last letter out of his mouth. Brian looked like he wanted to cry.

If it were anyone but Brian, I would have laughed. Mama hit me harder than that to make me turn off the TV.

Zeely finished her solo. Everyone clapped but they stopped after a few seconds. Everybody but me. I gave her a standing ovation.

Brian yanked me down by my jacket pocket. Well, it was his jacket pocket actually, but still . . . I hit the bench so hard I was thankful that the pockets were the fake kind. Just flaps. Eva's fan fluttered like a butterfly on the other side of me. The choir fought through their giggles to start the next song.

Until Brian's hot breath hit my ear, accented with rage and spit, I probably would have never stopped clapping. "Will you quit it? See that big guy on the top row? The one with the big head and the really white teeth? *That* is who Zeely is going to marry. I think it's crazy, but their parents have already agreed."

That shut me down. I scanned the row again. That dude looked like a grown man. He did have some nice teeth. Nice tie too . . .

"Stop staring."

Okay, they had me there. I looked away, but not before making my first church vow. It sounded like what they made me say in family court, but I meant every word.

If he wants her, he'll have to beat me to it. So help me God, she's mine.

49

5

Zeely

"Zeely, this has gone on long enough, sweetie. It's time to stop. You're just playing with fire and I wouldn't be a good mother if I didn't put a stop to it."

I knew it would come to this eventually. I'd gotten too lazy. Grown too bold. Ron had moved back up to the front row, joined the choir. People were starting to talk and we were starting not to care. This was the day I both dreaded and prayed for every morning.

"Mother, I'm seventeen now, grown up. I think I should be able to pick who my friends are." My breathing stayed steady. I pushed back on my bed, shoving Ron's letters into my pillowcase. He wrote things for me in the morning and passed it to me at lunch. The next day was the reverse. Sometimes, when I couldn't stand it anymore, I risked it all and brought my notebook home.

Our notebook.

Lately, that'd been every day. I thought once that a page was torn, that my marker was out of place, but now I wondered if someone else hadn't been reading it, tearing pages as they flipped through. I swallowed hard now, praying that my mother hadn't read it, that she didn't know what fire burned beneath my long skirts, what passion roughed my unmade face. The way she looked at me now—and the way my father didn't—told me the truth I didn't want to face.

They knew.

My mother pressed her hand to her throat. It was Saturday night and her nails were already filed into perfect ovals, long, full, and covered with clear polish. Once she'd worn a light-colored polish, a dusty rose that someone from her job had given her. Mrs. Terrigan and the other women from the church they'd grown up in had expressed concern that her worldly behavior might affect the younger women. If only they knew that we were already affected and not by some old-timey nail polish either. Daddy had complimented her on it several times, but didn't say anything when she threw it away. Neither did he say anything now.

"See, that's just it, Zeely Ann. You think that because you're getting older that you can choose, that now is the time for you to be making the big decisions of your life. It isn't. Now is hormones and emotions, nonsense that you'll forget when you settle down with Jeremiah and start your family. We have a plan for you—"

"Doesn't God have a plan for me?" I was on my feet now and my voice was loud and high, like when I sang the Negro spirituals at church. Daddy didn't like them much. He said they were too painful. Those songs were like books to me. When I sang them, I saw those people torn away from love, from life, and trying to create it new in a place that made no place for it. No place for them.

I closed my eyes for the slap sure to come, waiting for the sting. My mother didn't tolerate backtalk. "Rebellion is as a sin of witchcraft," she would say and she'd beat the devil out of you. For my brothers and I, the remedy had been total and permanent, and then came a skinny white boy to sit in the front row of church and give me a standing ovation. It's been over two years and he hasn't stopped clapping. If I'm honest, I haven't stopped singing. Only now, it's a new tune: Why? That's the focus of all my thoughts these days. None of the rules I once accepted about what I can wear, who I can love, where I can be seem to make sense. It seems to me now that maybe the God in my Bible and the god in my house are not the same. I don't want to do wrong, Lord knows I don't, but they aren't making it easy.

I'll talk to your father. I'll do anything. I just want to marry you.

I'll die if I don't. Please, don't give up on me. We can find a way. God will make a way.

If my mother had read our notebook, what had she thought about that? What did God think?

My parents glared at each other as if they were trying to answer the same questions, only without saying any words. There was anger in my mother's eyes, accusation. Gentleness in my father's. Forgiveness. I wondered if it was for himself or for me.

Both.

She stood, pointing at me. "You see what you've done to her? This is your fault, you know. You've encouraged it. Letting her go over to that heathen dance class—"

"There's nothing wrong with that class and you know it. Joyce prays with those girls every practice. Their performances are all based on the Word."

My mother shook her head then, raining plastic rollers down on my bed. Pink, yellow, mint green, they showered down like oversized candies. "I don't care what she prays or what she says, I know what she is. You see what happened to that other girl, the Dixons' daughter? That's not going to happen to mine. You hear me? You shall know them by their fruit. Saved girls don't need to be dancing anyhow. Dating either. I'm not going to let this boy use her up, knock her up, and then leave her for the first blond he meets in college. I'm not! And if you won't protect her, I will."

I sat down on my bed, letting their angry words float over my head. How could she talk about Diana like that? And Miss Joyce too? There was no point in trying to tell Mama anything. She could only hear what she wanted to hear. And Daddy? His voice only seemed to work in church.

"The boy just wants to spend time with us, to see if things can work out between them. You can't protect that girl forever. You're pushing them too hard. They're kids. Just let the boy come over for dinner after church tomorrow."

My heartbeat was all I could hear. Ron had never said anything about talking to my father. Maybe they hadn't seen my notebook at all. Maybe they had seen something even more telling: Ron's heart. Maybe there was a chance for us.

In seconds, I knew better. My mother threw her head back and laughed and not because anything was funny. It was mad laughter, like Macbeth or some other Shakespearean head case. Every woman has her limits and somehow, my father and I had just surpassed hers. There was no point in stopping now.

"No," she said, half screaming, half laughing. "Noooooooo!"

"But, Mama, just give him a chance. He loves me—"

The slap came then, forceful and unexpected. I knew from the look in her eyes that it was meant to knock what she thought was the devil out of me, to shake me to my senses. As I wiped the blood from my mouth, I thought that my senses were more awake than they'd ever been.

My father moved quickly, quietly, pulling Mama's hands behind her back. He spoke into her neck with his preacher voice. "Don't hit her again. That's enough."

She twisted in his grip and worked one hand free, reaching for me. "It will never work, don't you see? It never has. His mother will spit in your black face. Eva should have never brought that boy to the church in the first place. She knows better than anybody how folks are around here. Look what they done to her boy! That white girl said she loved him too."

Daddy jerked her back then, hitched his arms under each of hers and began to pull her from the room. Before he shut the door, he looked back at me, and I blinked back the tears threatening in my eyes. Tears I knew would never fall.

"Forgive your mama, Birdie. And forgive me. I should have never let her go this far."

I fell back on the pillow and closed my eyes, clutching the notebook inside the cloth to my face. Birdie. Ron called me that too, even before he knew it was my nickname. What would happen to us now in this town where race was the invisible elephant in every room, even after so much time? I could hear Ron's answer in my heart, quiet and clear: If the elephant won't leave, then we'll ride him . . . all the way to our wedding.

Laughter kissed my bloody lips. Daddy was right. It never should have gone this far.

6

When the letter came announcing my scholarship, everyone cheered. I was too tired, too broken, too empty to celebrate. It had been a long, hard year, each day like sandpaper on a wound, love in short supply. Mama and Daddy were both determined now to plan my future: for her, wedding; for him, my graduation. Ron was preaching now and then, trying his best to avoid my eyes. Our secret love was now broken open before everyone, weeping everywhere we went like an open wound.

I never knew what they said to him, did to him, to make him turn from me, but I knew him well enough to know it hurt him deeply. Cut him to the bone. Only once had he said anything to me, in the hall after choir practice when everyone else had gone.

"Can you see the scar?" he'd said softly.

"From what?" I asked, as if I didn't know.

"From you," he said, tracing my face with his finger. "From where they cut us apart."

There was movement then, on the stairs. Someone coming for sheet music they'd left behind. We turned and ran in opposite directions and we'd been running ever since. Tonight was different. We were older now, both eighteen. Eva was frail, dying, and Ron had found a place of his own. I wondered how Brian felt about that, but I'd probably never know. My mother and some of the other families had never been kind to him. People said things but I never passed them on. Life was hard enough, I was learning, without other folks' problems.

My own mother was sick tonight, too sick to protest when Joyce had thrown all of her students who'd earned scholarships, which really meant all of us, a party. The DJ was playing something that I'd heard when cars went by on the block, but nothing I knew the words to. Nothing I'd be singing in church anytime soon. Ron seemed to know it. I wasn't surprised.

"Dance with me?" It was more a statement than a question, more an inevitability than a command. While other couples started for the dance floor led by a hand, Ron steered me with his body, pressed tight behind me. He stopped at the edge of the carpet and waited, spiking the front of his hair. "I'm sorry. I shouldn't have. I should go." Contradicting his words, his hands touched my hair, his lips to my eyelids.

Our classmates pushed us back, edging us onto the carpet, shielding us from the eyes of chaperones and church mothers. My arms strained to circle his neck, despite my last-minute growth spurt. He bent down to shorten the distance between us, which wasn't any distance at all.

I waited all night for him to give me my first and only kiss, but he didn't. Instead we danced slow and close, even on the fast songs, mourning our lost love.

"I hope he's good to you," he whispered finally. "I told him to be."

Ron choked up some then. I did too.

If my mother had been there, she would have been worried how I might look to Jeremiah if he came in. "No prince wants something wasted," she'd said days before on the night of my graduation. "Virtue is all a girl gets in this man's world. Spend it wisely. You can never get it back."

At the time, her words were like some kind of torture device, ripping back and forth a piece of me desperately trying to heal. Later, I would see the wisdom in those words, the love in her motivations.

Much later.

Tonight, I only saw the forbidden and the required, both pulling at me with deadly force, striking me dumb, making me numb.

"I will miss you," I told him.

In truth I'd always been missing him, since the first day I saw him, long before he'd come to the church. He and Brian had been racing at the Charles C and a child's bike was in the way. Brian hurdled over it, but Ron stopped and wheeled around the corner to the sound of a little boy's cry.

No one else saw but me.

And now it was me crying, only no sound was coming out. We danced for four songs, but it seemed like forever. At the end of the last tune, a bone-deep Anita Baker ballad that even a church girl like me knew the words to, we let go, biting our lips and choking back everything that could have been.

And then I saw him.

Jeremiah, half drunk and wearing his letter jacket even though it was June. In one hand he held a beer, in the other, the thigh of the homecoming queen of the school across town. She'd made the cheerleading squad at Central State, where he'd be playing football, first string. I made it too, but not without a fight from Mama. Too much temptation, she said.

She gave in eventually, urging me to stay away from Jeremiah as much as possible. I even had a bishop's daughter for a roommate to keep an eye on me. Not that I needed to be watched, my mother said when making the arrangement. It was the boys she worried about. Always the boys.

I backed into the shadows as Jeremiah dropped his beer and attended to things with both hands. My hands, empty now, covered my mouth as my future stared me in the face. No matter how hard I tried, I just couldn't win.

When the first punch landed, I heard it but didn't know what it was. But the words that came after couldn't be denied. Though he weighed less than Jeremiah, Ron used his quickness. His heart-break too.

"I told you not to . . . I told you!"

Jeremiah's high crashed down and he held Ron back. He argued at first, but then they both fell in a heap of frustration. They'd become close now this last year with Brian slipping away, turning into some angry cloud ready to burst at any moment. These two had prayed together, played together, talked about anything and everything.

Except me.

Jeremiah banged his head on the wall. The cheerleader slipped from under him and disappeared into the crowd, straightening her skirt as she went. I didn't know whether to hate her or admire her. Whatever this game was, I was certainly losing.

Jeremiah couldn't keep score either. "Man, I don't know what I'm doing. Everybody has a plan for me. God wants me to preach. Mama wants me to marry Birdie. Daddy wants me to play football. I'm losing it, Red. I just want to do something because I want to, not because I have to."

Ron started to say something, but I ran out before he did. I couldn't bear to hear how I'd wrecked his life too.

Jeremiah tried to grab me when I passed by, but I slipped through his hands. Ron wouldn't let me go so easy. He dived and caught me just as we fell through the front door.

He took his time with me at first, there on the floor of his almost empty apartment. Wouldn't even let me in his bedroom so I could see his only furniture—a twin-size bed and a black-and-white TV. He kept saying he was going to get the TV set or take me home, he couldn't settle on which. All I could see was his eyes. I'd never seen them this close in this much light. Or with this much love.

Ron's Adam's apple bobbed up and down as he kept swallowing

it down, that love, trying to carry on a conversation. It was hot in there, but he kept on his jacket.

I took off my shoes.

He closed his eyes then and I knew that he was praying. I wanted to, but I didn't know what to pray. I'd been so sorry for so long that I didn't know what to be sorry for. I just wanted to sit here with Ron and look at his eyes.

"Put your shoes on, Birdie," he said, taking off his jacket. "Please."

I heard him, but by then I didn't see my shoes. I saw Mama and Jeremiah and Miss Eva's dead son who had fallen in love with a white girl and drowned in the shallow end of the public pool. A pool where if you looked real close when you were under the water, right near the bottom, you could still see the words WHITES ONLY, words that people said northern towns didn't have. I saw Ron's fiery hair and his generous eyes. I heard his steady, silent applause for my every achievement, desired his earnest love that my mother said would be the death of me.

Mama, I think I'm dead already.

And before I left this world for good, I only wanted one thing: to be kissed by a man who loved me, a man who loved God. Before tonight, I'd accepted that it would be enough for the man to love God, but now it wouldn't have been enough. Jeremiah would have never kissed me like he had kissed that cheerleader. I wouldn't want him to kiss me now anyway. There was only one man I wanted to do that.

I only had to ask once.

It was beautiful, that kiss and all the ones that came after. We laid there, quiet, knowing there'd probably be no more of this. Perhaps that was best. He got up and went to the door. He even got my purse.

"I don't want to sin against you, Birdie. Let me take you home."

That's when I began to sing.

7

Brian

I wanted to play the djembe when my mother died, to beat it up high and down low: palms, knuckles, the sides of my hands. I wanted to strap it on my belly and go barefoot by the pulpit. I wanted to scream.

They wouldn't let me.

Not that I could blame them. I'd gone a bit crazy by then, the kind of crazy that I was always scared of. Strange even. Not that it surprised anyone. Ron still came around, gave me our secret handshake, shrugged his shoulders when people raised eyebrows at me, told them, "Oh he's all right. Don't be like that."

But I wasn't all right. I hadn't been. Not for a very long time. Not since a Sunday in my junior year when Mama was too tired to come to church and I came alone. For the first time, alone. The deacon gave me a thin smile at the door. The whispers that I'd always thought I'd heard before, the ones that Mama told me were my imagination, echoed in my ears like screams.

"Eva's down sick, they say. What is that child going to do now?"

"Chile, I don't know. He's always been a bit grown, but everybody needs a mama. Now that's a fact."

"Mama? Please. Eva ain't that boy's mama. Look at him with red hair and those crazy eyes changing all which of ways. He looks more like that white boy they bring than he does Eva. Naw, that boy ain't none of hers. I remember the Sunday she brought him in, still wrapped up in a blanket from the hospital. I kept waiting for somebody to say something, but nobody never did. Some girl got in a mess with a white boy, most like. You know how that goes . . ."

I don't remember much else about that Sunday, but I'll never forget those women's words. Never forget sitting there and thinking that everything I was, everything I knew, was a lie. Although it cut me deep, the news was almost a comfort since I'd always known that something didn't fit, that somehow I did not belong.

One of the Africans who taught me the drum—there were four of them, from Ghana, Congo, Senegal, and Mozambique. One of them led a song with the other men, a sad song of a lone warrior who hunted, fought, and died alone. Sometimes at night, I still play it on my belly, still remember what the tallest of them said to me when we were done.

"An African with no land is like a never healing wound. An African with no people is like a ghost."

At the time, I'd been afraid of his words, but a time came, after Eva's funeral, when I was all alone with no people, not knowing where I'd come from, that I welcomed those words, that I became an apparition seen only at night, red-eyed and weaving through wisps of smoke.

I met X then. Not the famous Malcolm of the same letter, but an overgrown boy who thought himself a revolutionary. X wasn't much older than I, but on the street we were decades apart. He led two lives, middle-class days with his mother and street nights with his father, who lived two blocks or so away from me. Two blocks doesn't sound like a lot, but it was far enough away to be a whole different neighborhood, another world.

The first time I followed him there, I remember how the rose-bushes ended and the window bars began. I wasn't sure at first what that meant, but I learned fast. Since Eva left the house to Ron and me, people thought I had money. Sometimes I had some cash back from a financial aid check or something, but there wasn't much to speak of. Nobody from the church came by anymore to see if I was all right or if I was coming back to church. They all seemed relieved to be rid of me. The feeling was mutual, I guess.

Ron still came around, but his nose was wide open for Zeely, and I got sick of hearing about how much he loved her, how much he loved God. If he wasn't gushing, he was preaching at me, and it all got too much to bear. Didn't he see that I was dying? I saw it when it was him. I pressed my face to the window and watched for his mama, always came to get him after. Nobody was watching on the wall for me. Nobody until X. What I didn't know then was that he was watching so that he could take me down, not pull me up.

Joyce was the one person who never changed, never preached, never asked any questions. She and Miss Thelma from across the street would come and cook for me and clean the house. Joyce would drill me on Latin conjugations she'd taught me years before and sniff my breath for alcohol. When she found the scent—and she often did—she said nothing. Only kissed my cheek and turned away. Like X, my life was split between day class at Wright State in Dayton and nights drowned in forty-ounce increments and card games I didn't remember.

X had a younger sister too, half sister, I think. She always looked scared, like something was going to fall on her head. She looked like I felt. I tried to be nice to her, but the other guys treated her bad. His daddy treated her worse. That was when I started realizing that place probably wasn't the best place to be. As usual, I thought too long and ended up in a mess. I often wonder how my life would be now if Joyce wasn't there with her strong hands to save me from what would have happened.

Maybe God was still watching over me after all.

8

He called me a punk. That's how it started. Went on about me and Ron and how I would always be soft no matter how high I got. Said I'd never have heart enough to do something big, be somebody real.

I got my jacket then, a gold silk that all of us wore with our names sewn on the back, and went for the door. I didn't have to take this. Things were growing thin between us by then, fraying at the edges. I wiped the beer from my moustache and shook my head. They'd moved on from drinking in the past few months: weed, coke, crack.

They were getting crazier and crazier. They'd held me down one night when I was drunk and held my nose shut and put a pipe in my mouth. I thought I was going to die. I probably should have. At least I wouldn't have been back here again.

"I'm going." My hand was on the door. So close to escaping the whole mess.

X waved a hand at me. "Go ahead and go. Where you going? To your mama's grave? Oh, that's right! You don't have no mama. No daddy either. Nobody wants your crazy—"

My fist crashed into him. Knocked him off the chair. He became all the prying eyes, the school reports that had landed me in Joyce's class, all the labels tagged to me, weighing me down.

Distant.

Antisocial.

Deficient communication skills.

Withdrawn.

Angry.

Dangerous.

Mixed?

Mixed up.

For the first time, I became all of those words, all those things that people saw in me that made them turn away. The way they looked at me when I tried to get my real birth certificate, told me that the adoption was closed, that there were laws now and I had to have the birth mother's permission to have the file opened. That made me laugh. Why would a woman who didn't want me care whether I had my records.

She wouldn't.

She didn't.

Nobody wanted me, I thought as I slammed into X again and again.

He was laughing at me. "Go ahead. Finish me. It'll be the end of you too. I already called the police."

Fists in midair, I stopped, looked at his eyes, this boy-man who'd said he'd be my family, be my friend. "What?"

"Yeah. Somebody tipped on us selling over here. Pointed you out as coming and going. They're supposed to do a sting tonight. When they come, I'm going to be the boy from across town caught up in addiction. The boy beat down by his vicious, crazy dealer. So come on. Keep it coming. It'll be more convincing."

I looked around at the other guys, all leering at me now. I hadn't noticed that none of them had moved to break up the fight, that they'd moved away from us instead of toward us. As I took in the room, I could see why. Everything around had my fingerprints on it. There was the pipe they'd forced into my mouth, cigarettes I'd smoked, bottles I'd drank from . . . The room was spinning and they were laughing at me, all of them except for that little sister, who really wasn't so little, but she always seemed like it.

"Go to the back," she said, kissing me on the cheek. "Go to the back and run."

For once in my life, I didn't ask any questions. The guys swarmed me: punching, kicking in every direction. Somebody came at me with a needle, but I slipped through them and into the filthy kitchen, out the back door.

Behind me, I heard sirens, the crash of front doors, feet pounding down the back steps, fear running in every direction. Not wanting to be caught up in the herd, I made a quick turn back toward the rosebushes. I looked up and saw the cross atop Mount Olive somewhere over the crest of the hill. If I could reach it, something told me I might make it.

Tires peeled behind me.

Maybe not.

"Get in!"

It was Joyce, wearing a Santa hat and red gloves. I climbed into her yellow Camaro and closed my eyes as she pulled away. A stack of Bibles pinched my side and the backseat smelled of turkey and gravy. It was Christmas Eve. I'd somehow forgotten. Lost track of the days over the break.

"Thank you."

She didn't respond. Her eyes were fixed on her rearview mirror and the police coming up behind us. Joyce pulled over as easily as she'd pulled off, as easily as she told the officer that I was one of her students. Didn't he remember that I'd served him at the Law Enforcement Appreciation dinner. Yes, I attended Wright State. On a scholarship even. No, I didn't need a breathalyzer. I didn't know anything about any drugs. We were going to hand out dinners to the needy, take toys to the children in the projects behind the Charles C. Merry Christmas to you too, Officer. Merry Christmas to you too.

By the time my heart stopped racing, we were over the hill and passing the church. I turned back in my seat and said a short prayer, fixing my eyes on the cross.

Just below it, sitting on the roof, I saw something else. Someone else.

X.

And he was waving.

PART 2

HARMONY

2005

9

Grace

I should have buried it. I was good at that. So far I'd buried my father, my husband, and myself. It would have been best to bury what the package and its contents would resurrect. It would have been easy.

Instead, I stabbed at my front yard with my fingers, raking back the top layers of the soil. The young weeds gave up with a tug. The others, only among my good plants, of course, played tug-of-war with me. With the last one in my hand, I sat back on my heels, panting. Praying about bitter roots and old hurts.

I tossed the last weed on a pile of others like it and opened the envelope on the ground beside me. Hands shaking, I began to read.

Diana Grace,

I pray this finds you well. I have been better myself, but I would never admit it in person. I led Zeely's dance class last week and the ladies moved with courage and spirit. No one danced like you though. I don't know if anyone ever will. I know that you are hiding there in that empty house full of memories, but I am mourning too. Mourning the loss of you. I've included the notebook you kept after leaving Ngozi. It's taken me all these years to find it, but it was worth every second. Read it. Read the teaching contract that

I've also enclosed. My school and my students need
you. Let me know when you will arrive. If you ever
loved me, please come.

In Christ's service,
Joyce Rogers
Principal, Imani Academy
P.S. You dance in my dreams.

I hugged my knees close to my chest and closed my eyes, but the tears wouldn't come. I'd had no tears at my husband's funeral either. Some people thought that callous of me, though they'd never say it to my face. Even my mother, who'd never liked Peter when he was alive, seemed disturbed. "You should show some emotion," she said. "Even if things weren't the best between you, cry or something."

Something was what I chose and not because things were bad between us either. Things just . . . were. Peter was a good man, strong and steady in his own way. We had some things in common: a love of good books, long trips, and fine wine. Faith was not something we shared. I'd even debated over having his funeral in a church, but it felt right. And now with a dirty envelope in my lap and dandelions in my hair, I wondered if anything would ever feel right again.

I heard a car pull up behind me. I forced myself to stand, just before a kiss landed on my neck. Strong arms circled my waist.

"I waited for you. You didn't come," he said.

An uninvited tear slid down my face. I clutched the envelope to my stomach, not knowing quite what to say. Explaining to Malachi Gooden, my boyfriend-fiancé or whatever he was, never quite worked out the way I planned. Like my mother, he was a fast talker.

"I forgot."

It wasn't true exactly. Before the mail came, I'd flat ironed my hair and put on my good girl skirt. My shoes were sensible but sexy and my eyelashes curled. I'd forgiven all the times Mal had canceled on me and grabbed my wedding notebook, grateful that he'd taken the time to finally set a date.

Then, the mailman came and here I was, bushy haired and barefoot, wondering what would happen next.

He came in closer, his smooth cheek against mine. "Grace? Are you all right? And what are you doing out here anyway? Pulling weeds? I told you I'm paying someone for that. He just hasn't made it over—"

"I'm okay." I shook a leaf out of my hair, no longer shiny and straight, but curled tight and held back with a scarf from a vintage store in Beverly Hills. I'd packed it away with some of Peter's things, but this afternoon had sent me digging through my house. And myself.

Malachi stood up too, for once speechless at the sight of me. "Are you going to a costume party or something? Some neo soul club?" He stared at my feet, decked with toe rings instead of their usual safe French manicure.

"I'm not going anywhere today." I turned from him, anxious to get the envelope inside the house, under something. I needed somewhere to hide myself too before Diana showed up, wings and all. Mal would hate her. Peter had too. Grace was easier to deal with. Peter had been the one to suggest that I go by my middle name. In my heart, I would always be Diana, even if it had taken until now to admit it.

He stepped over my piles and tools and followed me inside. It was time for this. If he was going to marry me, he had to know it all. I really wanted to run to my bedroom and bellyflop onto my bed, but that would be too easily misconstrued. Malachi spent his nights as a youth pastor and his days teaching junior high. Sometimes I thought their hormones rubbed off on him. I certainly wasn't up for playing octopus tonight. There were other things to be done. To be said. I put the package in a basket by the door and headed into the kitchen. While I forced a mango through the juicer, Mal riffled through my mail.

"Please don't do that." I spoke quietly, but firmly, the way I did with my students.

He went on, picking up another piece of mail, a postcard this time, in response. I closed my eyes. It was an invitation to lead a group of children in a dance piece at the Black Cultural Festival on the riverfront. "I thought you were done with this?"

It was my turn not to respond. I poured myself some green tea from the refrigerator and stirred in the fresh mango juice. It was Mal's favorite and I should have offered him a glass, but it's hard to be hospitable when someone is looking through your mail. He put down the postcard, but kept what mattered most—the envelope with my old notebook inside.

I sat down, my drink on the bar between us. "I thought I was done with it too, but evidently God isn't done. He's not done with a lot of things."

My bare feet had left footprints, I noticed. Only the toes showed up, like a young girl on tiptoe. Perhaps that's just what it was. I grabbed the envelope and pulled. My boyfriend's shocked look made me smile. "I'm not who you think I am, Mal. Nobody is. You know me as Grace, but in this envelope is Diana, a part of me that I have silenced for a very long time. The part of me that's missing."

It must have been his turn to surprise me, because he sat down, right there in my dirty footprints on my kitchen floor. He was wearing his favorite pants. Mine too. He didn't seem to care as he motioned for me to join him on the floor.

I did, but not before offering him some tea. He declined.

"Tell me then. About Diana, I mean."

And so I did that too. Between sips of mango tea, I told him about how my ballet teacher and my mother had plotted to starve me (he laughed), the leaves and the bus stop (he cried). I even went

a little further, to my time in the psych ward (he looked concerned).
It seemed best to stop there.

Thank God I didn't tell him everything.

He hugged me, but it was more polite than passionate. "I'm so
sorry, Gracie. Or should I call you—"

"Grace is fine." I'd long since gotten over the confusion of my
fractured identities. One day there would be someone who could
see me for all I was, Diana Grace Dixon Okoye. Until then, there
was Jesus. "And I'm sorry that I stood you up. Maybe this was
supposed to happen. We can still do our planning though. Let me
get my binder."

He hung his head. "Maybe we should just pray on it some more?
We're getting married. I love you. It's just . . ."

His declaration of love sounded like he was trying to convince
himself too. It took me a minute, but I caught on. Mal had been
looking for a running mate as well as a wife. Someone to grace
his arm in the next few years when he got his own congregation.
Yesterday, I'd fit the bill, before the mailman came.

We got up at the same time. I waved away his explanations. I
didn't want to hear them. I grabbed a travel cup from the cupboard
and made him some mango tea, knowing it would likely be the last
I'd give him. He took his time with it as though he knew it too.

Outside, we held hands as I walked him to his car. He didn't
talk. There was nothing to say. He'd fallen in love with who he'd
thought I was. The real me, however, scared him to death. What
he didn't know was that she scared me too.

I smiled and waved goodbye before plunging into a patch of
Indian Blankets with both hands. Transplanted from where I'd
gently picked them on the shoulder of Interstate 75 one day when
my car went dead, the flowers had never quite taken to their new
surroundings. I watched as the man who had been my future pulled
away, probably calling a new woman from his B list on speakerphone as he went.

73

That made me laugh as the petals slipped through my fingers, bright and fragile, like all the lies I'd told myself. Another part of my life was over, and after five years of mourning one man and two years of playing games with another, I resented all of it. The meanings would come clear eventually, but right now I needed answers, and preferably not the obvious ones. The only comfort came in my heart. A verse that I memorized after losing Peter.

Return to me, for I have redeemed you. Your husband is your maker, whose name is the Lord of Hosts.

I grabbed a pot and started to pull up the bulbs, careful not to disturb the root system. If I worked quickly, maybe they'd make the move intact. I wasn't getting another man. I'd had men enough. This time, God was giving me a mission: to change the lives of children the way Joyce had changed my life.

I'd lived many places, moved many times, but this time, I was going home.

10

Ron

Broken beer bottles and overturned carts formed the trail to the Strong and Jones Market. I jogged along the path, careful not to cut myself, but just as eager to get inside. The parking lot had been a maze in itself, packed tight with the luxury cars of suburbanites in need of soul food ingredients and local wrecks driven on fumes to try to cash a check with no ID. Kool menthols and Cuban cigars crunched under my tennis shoes as the bell rang over my head. I grabbed a cart with urgency, knowing that nothing would be left but ingredients for side dishes and desserts. I'd come to get some greens.

After spending part of the summer on a mission trip to Mexico, I knew God could provide what I needed, even if it wasn't what I wanted. That was a lesson it seemed I'd be learning all my life. At least I was free of my tie and suit, if only for the weekend. The taped-up glass door opened and shut behind me. It occurred to me that there must have been another break-in since the last time I was in. I hadn't heard about it, but they didn't often report crimes over here anymore. If someone broke into a house in my neighborhood, SWAT would be dropping out of the clouds. If it wasn't so messed up, it'd be funny.

No matter how many times the store got robbed, we'd keep coming. The outside of the building left a lot to the imagination, but no finer ingredients for down-home cooking could be found for thirty miles. At least. The thing was, you had to get here early when the farmers drove in their produce fresh. And that was on a regular day. It was Labor Day weekend and I'd neglected that important detail.

The line for the produce section snailed down the cramped aisle. I glanced at my watch. Four fifteen. Who was I fooling? Refusing to give up, I waited my turn, hoping against hope while knowing the greens were probably picked clean by noon. Three bunches of wilted mustards awaited me. I tossed them in the cart as if they were weeds.

At the meat cooler, I netted the last ham hock—if you could call it that—shriveled like an oversized dog treat. My stomach growled while my mind churned with other menu possibilities. The greens and cornbread dinner I'd planned definitely wasn't going to happen. Cabbage could work if I put a little ham in it. Maybe some macaroni and cheese . . .

I shook my head, knowing I'd settle for some nasty hamburger again. If only they had a drive-thru window for my troubled mind too. I leaned over the cart and rubbed my temples, praying that the headache trying to bloom between my ears would wither and fade. More often than not, I felt like this: chest pains, headaches, nights without sleep. My doctor had no explanation and I didn't offer one, even though the cause of my pain was neither new or unknown to me.

Despite making more money than I'd ever imagined and serving God in ways I'd always hoped, there was still one thing in my life that didn't line up: the woman I dreamed about every night wasn't the one I was planning to marry.

"If you wanted greens, you should have been here this morning," a female voice spoke behind me, tinkling like a bell.

Without turning around, I knew who it was. I ground my teeth, realizing that I'd really waited so late to come here in hopes of avoiding her. And here she was anyway.

Zeely.

A quick pivot brought us face-to-face. I leaned down to give her a quick hug, but once I had her, I didn't let go. I bit the inside of my cheek, trying to ignore her perfume. Beautiful, the same one she'd worn that summer so long ago. It described everything about her.

"Hey, Zee." I'd almost called her Birdie, but thought better of it. It hurt to even think it.

She cocked her head and smiled up at me. Her dark skin was flush with the last bit of summer's heat. She had the look of a chocolate bar just before it melts. She wore pink today, from her baseball cap to her coordinating sneakers, sweat suit, and nail polish. Unlike me, she was always all put together.

I was falling apart. I knew that for sure when I realized that I'd lifted her off her feet. This realization came by way of a pinch. I eased her back to the floor, hoping it hadn't looked like it felt.

Zeely didn't let on. "It's me, Red. Or what's left of me. You were squeezing me to death."

Red. It pained me to call Zeely by her nickname, but she had no problem throwing mine around. I stood back and chuckled low in my throat, trying and failing to mask my embarrassment. She had a way of stripping me bare. Sometimes I thought she even enjoyed it. Still, I hadn't meant to hold her that tight. Or for that long.

"You want me to finish the job?" I asked, motioning to hug her again. I tried to laugh, but it sounded false. Hollow.

She swatted my hands away, managing a few genuine-sounding giggles herself. "I saw your silly behind zooming through the aisles with those crazy pants. All those pockets . . . like a little kid. I should have known it was you."

You should have.

"And I saw a pink Cadillac outside—without a Mary Kay sticker. I should have known it was *you.*"

Maybe I had known, but I just didn't want to admit it. I didn't want to think about it. My headache was breaking through, sending the first shoots of pain behind my eyes.

She balled up a fist and waved it under my nose, poked at my chest with an airbrushed fingernail. It was all I could do to keep from kissing her knuckles. Maybe she felt it too because she pulled back her hand as I lifted mine.

"Be serious for a second. Do you really need some greens? I got four packs this morning when the truck came. I came back for some sweet potatoes."

"Let me get some greens, if you don't mind." I pulled out my wallet.

She looked offended. "You don't have to pay me. You know that. Do you want me to cook them for you? I have to do mine anyway."

I sighed, remembering the first time I'd sampled Zeely's cooking. Flaky biscuits and scrambled eggs cooked just right, eaten on a bare, stained carpet.

"Ron! Do you want me to cook them or not?" She shook her head. "You're just like Jeremiah. All off in never-never land." She looked away. "Have you talked to him lately? How's he doing?"

My dreamy smile disappeared. I'd wondered how long it would take for the conversation to turn to my old friend. How was Jerry? From the looks of the guy, not too good. His divorce and move back to town had hit him hard. I saw him at church functions and we talked a lot, but we never really *talked*. "I should probably be asking you how's he's doing. We hang out, but I don't really know what's going on with him a lot of the time. You probably know more than I do."

She clucked her tongue. "Not really. We went out quite a few times last year, but lately I haven't talked to him much at all."

Good, I thought and immediately hated myself for thinking it.

"How are things at Imani? I heard there was some trouble over there while I was gone this summer."

Zeely nodded. "Yeah, you missed all the fun. You get to travel while the rest of us have to work. Must be nice."

78

I wanted to remind her that I'd mentioned it to her too, that she'd paid her deposit and pulled out at the last minute, that if I'd known she wasn't going, that maybe I would have stayed home too, but that wouldn't help anything. Things were what they were. Besides, Mindy and I wouldn't have gotten close, gotten engaged, if I had stayed home. "We dug holes, Zee. Built a church. No toilets. No cars. I'll pay your way next time if you're interested."

She frowned. We weren't supposed to talk about real things when we saw each other. Only this playful chitchat was allowed. I was pushing too far. She had missed me and I was trying to actually make her say it. That wasn't fair. I nodded in agreement.

Her smile returned. "I was just kidding. Lighten up. We've had some trouble at the school. Ever since spring semester. Had to kick out a few kids, wannabe gangsters, the Golden Boys or whatever they're calling themselves this week. Who told you? Brian?"

Don't I wish?

"Joyce. Brian and I don't talk much. He's so busy—"

"Doing what? Moving back to Africa?"

"Be nice. You know he's always over at social services."

"Which makes no sense. He's got a job." Zeely stared at the greens in her hand. "And a brother. I just don't get you guys. You're supposed to be family."

My mouth felt dry. While she was talking about me and Brian, I knew what she really meant, what she was really upset about. Me and her. We were the family she was mourning. I felt her pain, at the back of my neck, wondering not for the first time how things had turned out so different than we'd thought they would.

"Awesome God" rang out from my pocket. My cell. I held up one finger, as much to catch my breath from the pain in my head and in my heart as to take the call. "Just a sec."

She nodded, tossing my greens back in the bin.

I fumbled with the phone, watching Zeely disqualify the items I'd chosen as though she could cook them with her eyes.

79

I'd like to put her on a plate. God help me.

She looked better every time I saw her.

"Jenkins," I said, finally lifting the phone to my ear.

"Are we still on for tonight?"

I smiled at the familiar voice and the irony of the caller's timing.

Zeely gave me a frown reserved only for my girlfriend, Mindy, and whispered into her cupped hand, "Is it your woman?"

With a smirk, I handed Zeely the phone. Mindy was spending her holiday with her rich daddy somewhere I couldn't remember. They'd invited me, but when I mentioned greens and cornbread, she wasn't interested. I stayed home. Now I wondered if I wouldn't regret it.

"Nope. It's your man."

11

Zeely

The phone was small, but it felt heavy, like a rock in my hand. Ron's words, half joke and part accusation, weighed on me even more.

It's your man.

It was like a joke with no punch line. If it didn't hurt so much, I might have laughed. Jeremiah Terrigan was a man like many others, but he'd never been mine, no matter what anybody said.

Ron's starched T-shirt brushed my skin as he draped one arm over my shoulder, trying as always to stay somehow between Jeremiah and me without really getting between us. It had been years since he'd gone this far, to come this close. His sweet breath warmed my nose as he leaned in acting as though he was trying to listen. I inhaled deeply, thankful that his oral hygiene hadn't changed: Cinnamon Bianca Blast was still his habit. Sometimes I bought it for myself just to taste it, but it was never the same.

Never.

I smiled and pulled away, not wanting to make a fool of myself in the store any more than I already had. Half the choir would be calling Daddy by the time I got home. My father would never mention it, though others would. I loved him for that.

The phone felt slick against my cheek. "What's up, Jeremiah?"

"Nothing much. Ready to get back to school?" He sounded tired, as usual.

Crisp cotton brushed my waist, right where my jacket stopped but before my pants began. I tried to put down my arms, but it was too late. The cinnamon was back again, spicy and sweet as Ron rested his temple on mine, still trying to hear our conversation. His hair, auburn and wavy this summer, fell down and touched my cheek. I tried to remember Jeremiah's question, but I couldn't focus, couldn't think. Everything but Ron's closeness poured through my mind like rain.

"Did you hear me?" the voice on the phone asked again.

"I'm sorry," I said, pushing Ron away with a half-threatening look. "Your friend is acting crazy over here."

A nervous laugh echoed over the line. "You guys have fun. I'll talk to you later. Tell Ron I'll see him in a few. Bye."

"Bye." I closed the phone and passed it to Ron.

He raised one eyebrow, then finally accepted it. "You guys through? I've got free weekends."

I nodded, wondering if I had enough sweet potatoes for two pies. "We're done."

Ron dropped the phone into one of his many pockets. Crimson flushed at his throat. "Jerry and I are going to a concert tonight after your school orientation. It's at Shekinah. The Shiloh Sisters. Want to go? He said that you two have the early session."

Alone with the both of them? This was bad enough. "I'll probably head home after. My friend Diana is moving into Myrrh Mountain today. The unit near me that I tried to get you to buy."

He sighed, looking as though he regretted not going through with the purchase, among other things. "That's a nice one. I'm sure she'll love it."

I started to ask him if he remembered her, but Diana was all top secret and everything and I didn't need any drama. She worried that people would remember her for the wrong reasons, that they'd know what had happened to her. I didn't want to tell her that her biggest worry should be if they forgot. I'd learned that the hard way.

I tapped my foot. "You can come by after the concert. I'll put the food up for you and call when it's warmed up."

He looked pained, but didn't move. "Just me? Or Jerry too?"

Ron knew the answer, but he just liked to hear me say it. Jerry and I had gone out, but he never came back to my house. It just wasn't wise. "Just you."

That got a smile out of him. "Call me before if you need some help. With the moving, I mean."

"I'm pretty much done. She was supposed to meet me, but something must have happened." I rolled my neck. "Probably got a late start on the road. I took a break to come up here before they closed."

Ron had me again, almost off the ground. I tried to say more, something sensible and appropriate, but I choked on something. A scream, I think.

He set me down quickly. "Are you okay? Did I mess up? I figured since Jerry was single now, you two were back together."

I lifted my sweet potatoes out of the child's seat of my cart and hugged them to my chest, swaying like only veteran choir members can. "That's just it, Red. We were never together in the first place."

12

Grace

Daddy has a new job and he couldn't take me to
dance. I had to take the bus. I died before it came.

Diana Dixon

The ninety-minute trip to Testimony from Cincinnati seemed like a time warp. Despite the new buildings and lots of bright signs shiny with promises, a dread that I'd long forgotten pressed me down as I pulled into town. People looked happy enough. They certainly dressed a lot better. But there was still something old and foul, an invisible thickness of race and class that had only retreated, not disappeared. Maybe it never would.

My mother told me Testimony had started out as a place where slaves came to start over, a plain settlement with kindness and sacrifice. Then they found the gold. In a crag of hills past the Indian mounds, a few smashed gold bars were found along with some jewels. Most folks said it was booty some slave had brought along and hid until a good time so as not to make themselves obvious. It's the soundest story of many, but whites in neighboring counties and towns refused to believe it.

The Quakers thinned, easing out of the county as the greed moved in. Fear came next, carrying night torches and speaking in whispers. There were too many Negroes coming in and with the possibility of treasure, the influx had to be stopped, they decided. So they instituted the *testimony*, five hundred dollars per slave, an amount some people couldn't pay today to be free of the things that hold them captive. An impossible amount in those days for a walking, talking piece of property to pay. Or so some people thought.

Some came up with all the money and little explanation. Others passed over from Louisiana mulattoes or Virginia freedmen, with their wheat-colored hair and hazel eyes, to Ohio whites, living a shadow life far from any sunlight. Some from plantations in Georgia or Kentucky disappeared with the Indians only to be seen again with a papoose and a vacant look. Freedom was precious in those days with men and women on every side praying to a God with the same name: Jesus.

Only the midwives truly knew who was what—white, black, red, or a little bit of all—they saw the babies whose fingers turned brown around the cuticles, who showed their color on the backs of their ears, the children whose hair curled tight like question marks. In later years, some of those children would disappear or be given to the family maid, according to local lore. As a child, I only knew that my fair, light-eyed father didn't mind being out after dark anywhere in town. My brown, smooth mother regarded the setting sun with haste and concern, determined to be home before dark.

There were other towns like ours above the Mason-Dixon line, sleepy little places who'd sent their sons to fight for Dixie instead of Lincoln, towns that somehow managed to keep a black school and a white one in spite of integration. Places with churches who taught that love came in many colors—as long as those colors were all the same. While I'd detested my ballet class, I learned later that I'd been the first and last black girl to ever dance at that school. It closed up not long after.

I could see now that there was more diversity, but it was still a heterogeneous mix, with each group distinct and separate while sharing the same space. I'd seen the same thing most places I'd lived, but usually there was some part that gelled in the center, with no start and no end. It didn't happen often or for long, but when it did, it was glorious. For all my faith, I doubted it would happen here if it hadn't in all these years.

And yet I felt hopeful, despite spending most of the morning on the phone with Mal, fending off his feeble apologies and lackluster prophecies. He was right about one thing though: God had a plan, one I was determined to discover. The day had begun as every day had since my showdown with Mal—with the notebook Joyce had sent me and all the beauty and hurt it contained. My musings had ended with me on a packed highway zooming toward Labor Day traffic, a blur of green mile markers and sometimes bumper-to-bumper cars. Other drivers got off at the exits with skyscrapers and neon signs. I'd kept going, with my transmission protesting all the way.

As I pulled off exit 83, promising food, gas, and fun, I thought about those Testimony ex-slaves, tired and afraid but willing to lose everything for what seemed like freedom. Now I felt some deceit in the air, as though I'd fallen for the same trick.

Mal had gone so far as to call Testimony hopeless. He quoted rising crime statistics and plummeting test scores. He'd heard they were planning to close the projects and remove the rusty play-grounds and the people whose children played on them—both eyesores, as far as some were concerned.

Everyone would go along, he said. Everyone would give in. They had no other choice. Then the street would be dug down to the historic cobblestone to draw tourists to a make-believe town where no one could afford to live. It was a sound and cruel plan with one flaw, underestimating Dr. Joyce Rogers.

If you ever loved me, please come.

The lady drove a hard bargain. Unsure of the exact distance to my new place, I pulled into the first gas station I saw. An attendant approached quickly.

"Filling up, sweetheart?" he asked.

I nodded, noticing immediately a difference between the tight-lipped courtesy of Cincinnati and common flirty talk of Testimony. He pumped the gas quickly and cleaned the windows before I could protest.

"There you go. Come back soon with your pretty self. Anytime."

Too stunned to speak at first, I stared at him for a long time. "Right . . ."

Looking into the rearview mirror, I pulled away slowly. I remembered him. He'd been homecoming king at my high school in my freshman year. His hair was still blond and his shoulders square, but the years had not been kind to him. In many ways, time hadn't been my best friend either.

The fallen king hadn't recognized me, but already I knew that this might be harder than I'd thought. Especially the driving part. My car bucked under me like one of those electric broncos. I escaped just as Mr. Homecoming started toward me, no doubt to offer his shade tree mechanic services and perhaps his undying love. I turned onto Main Street, thinking I might be in need of both before this was all over. Probably not. Love had caused me enough grief. Or was it the other way around?

It didn't really matter. This car had brought me this far. Now I just needed to make it home.

Home.

That seemed strange to say, but it came to me naturally, even when I drove past the neighborhood where I'd once lived. There were two guards working the gate now. I tried not to think about what that might mean. Instead I took in the new chain supermarkets and fast-food joints.

I found my place pretty easy with a final turn. I passed Zeely's condominium and stopped in front of mine, unit eighteen eighty-two. There was a stack of flattened boxes at the curb. My front door was open. Music streamed out the door. Zeely's music.

In seconds, I was headed up the sidewalk. Zeely met me at the door. We shared a tight, fierce hug, and went inside. I purred almost like a cat when I saw it. It looked the way I'd always wanted my house to look. Eclectic. Honest. I gave her another squeeze for putting everything together. "I can't believe you pulled this off all by yourself. I just meant for you to air the place out."

My furniture, the first I'd picked out by myself, looked perfect against the desert-colored carpet. A black sofa with kente accents graced the left corner of the living room with a coordinating rug. A Japanese table I'd had in storage for years caught my eye as well as the Nigerian art and mudcloth throw blankets. Flowers and candles cascaded above my biggest piece of art, a framed black-and-white of a Sudanese mother holding an infant's shoe. A streak of blood, the only color in the scene, stained the hem of her clothes. In spite of the scene, there is hope in her eyes.

Though I'd seen it many times since buying it, once again it took my breath. "It's exactly straight. I never could have gotten it like that."

Zeely reached for her ankles and did a cat stretch. "I let the furniture guy in and the rest is history."

I gave a knowing nod. Unlike friendships built on chitchat and frequent interaction, Zeely and I had a sisterhood that picked up wherever we left off. And we left off more often than not. In my years with Peter, we'd survived off cards and phone calls, then came email, which made things easier, but still wasn't the same. Now here we were, face to face, friend to friend. We'd spent more time together in the last few weeks than we had in years.

The hard thing was that Zeely hadn't changed at all and I, it seemed, had changed completely. Zeely had a knack for getting her way, which was how I'd gotten such a choice place to live on such short notice. Still, I knew that most times I didn't meet up to her expectations. Most times I wasn't sure I even understood them. And yet, we both longed for the friendship we'd shared as girls. Whether it was unattainable now, neither of us was willing to concede. Living on the same block would either make us or break us.

Zee wiped sweat from her brow with the back of her hand. It was the only evidence that she'd been working. Her pink sweats, matching T-shirt, and hat looked as though she'd just put them on. "It really wasn't that bad. You had the layout on your boxes. That's the only reason I kept going. You had it organized. You know I can't stand a bunch of mess. You know . . . prayer plus planning—"

"Equals progress."

Another of Joyce's many proverbs she'd drilled into us. If only I'd listened as hard as Zeely to all those sayings, maybe things would have been different. Maybe I would have been different. I hoped not. I'd just started to love myself again, to really enjoy being me. It'd be a pity to waste all that love.

Zeely checked her manicured toenails for cracked polish. "It's amazing how we can still remember all that stuff Joyce used to tell us. Sometimes I find myself saying Joyce-isms to my students. It's crazy."

That much I could agree with. "Isn't it?" Zeely also had Joyce as her teacher at school, so it was no wonder that she remembered the Ngozi sayings word for word. It wasn't the words that I remembered so much but the dancing. And the beat. Lately, I'd been hearing it, seeing it in my sleep. My short time in Ngozi had changed my life. I had no doubt that Imani would do the same.

Imani. Faith. How appropriate. It had taken all the believing I had and then some to get here. All Joyce's believing too. Where she'd gotten so much faith I never could figure it, but she'd always had it, bidding us leap when we could barely stand. "The school. Tell me about it."

"You'll see it soon enough. You know Joyce. She hasn't changed." Zeely patted my thigh. "Let's talk about you. You look good. Better than the last time I saw you. You must be dancing again." She pinched the back of my arm. "But still eating the house down, I see."

I shrugged. Counting things and going to gyms wasn't my thing. I walked, climbed, ran, but never anything steady. Without dancing, my body didn't operate very well. "I did do a dance actually. Not long ago. On the riverfront with a class of kids. It was amazing. Those kids were totally into it. I don't think I was ever like that."

Zeely rolled her eyes at me. "Oh, you were into it."

Another shrug. "Maybe." We were going into were-was territory, the land of things that happened but didn't happen. It was a rocky, dangerous land.

I chose to focus on her compliment. I smoothed a hand down my jeans. "I'm still hanging on to a little muscle mass from climbing that rock wall last year, but not much."

Zeely stretched out on my couch and raised an eyebrow. "I remember that. It sounds just as crazy now as it did then. Didn't your mama tell you black folks don't do stuff like that?"

No, my "mama" hadn't concerned herself with what black folks didn't do. Even now, my mother prided herself in doing the unexpected. After I'd climbed the wall, she'd driven down a van full of her Bible study friends and done it too. "All kinds of people do all kinds of things. You'd be surprised. . . ." I joined her on the couch. It was even more comfortable than it'd been in the store.

Zeely cracked a knuckle. "Well, it won't be me. We both know that."

We both laughed. Zeely's fear of heights and planes had squashed many of our travel plans over the years. Before Peter, I'd been like that. I'd been twenty-two probably when he taught me how to drive. Back then I was scared of everything. Now I was just trying to feel, well, anything. Either way, I knew how it felt to be afraid of something. "I understand. Sometimes I still feel afraid of things, but after Peter died—"

It was Zeely's turn to shrug. "I know. I know. Tomorrow isn't promised and all that. Are you still keeping that hundred-things-to-do-before-I-die list?"

I was surprised that she'd remembered. "Yes. I'm up to thirty-seven. Wearing my hair natural." I drug a hand through my hair, curly since that day when the envelope came. A few strands floated to the floor. I'd always wanted to do it and now that there were no men to consider, I'd made my choice. Now if I could just figure out how to keep it from all falling out. That was number thirty-eight.

Zeely frowned. "I'm not even going there about the hair. You know what I think. I have to give you props for being different though. You are something else, Di—I mean, Grace. Sorry. That's still weird sometimes."

I looked up at the woman's eyes in the picture over the couch. Peace. It'd been God's gift to me. It was my job to keep it. "It doesn't bother me. It might be a bit strange here. Joyce calls me both."

"I'm not as flexible as Joyce. I liked Diana." Zeely got up and poured herself a glass of water. I noticed for the first time that she'd unpacked the dishes too.

"I hated it. It always made me think of the princess. Peter always called me Grace. When Princess Di and Peter died, I started to go by it."

"I still love Diana. I always will. Right now, though, it seems I need grace more than anything."

I held the glass up to my cheek. "Don't we all?"

We looked at each other, but neither of us spoke. The silence swirled around us, knocking off scabs neither of us wanted to acknowledge. Sometimes, the only way to clean a wound was to rip it open. Not today, though. I had enough to deal with just getting situated.

I got up and walked to the window. Sage and lemongrass seedlings lined the windowsill. I wiped my eye. That spoke more than anything Zeely could have said. I picked one up and sniffed it. All the tension rolled down my spine. "Thanks. For everything."

Zeely headed for the door. "Forget it. Call me when you're ready for orientation at the school. I'm doing the early part of the program and leaving, but you're welcome to ride. There's some teriyaki chicken in the fridge. Oh, and there's some boxes in the attic. The stuff that couldn't fit. I can help you go through it later if you want."

I hesitated. "Sure. Later." It should have occurred to me that some things wouldn't fit. A house can't fit into a condo no matter how much you toss out at the last minute. This move would probably squeeze a lot more out of me than those boxes upstairs.

What am I doing here?

My answer wafted to the ground like a sleepy leaf. Number thirty-eight on my life list, a strand of hair I was struggling to keep. I'd come here for Joyce, there was some truth to that, but I'd come for myself too. I'd come to find the weed still growing in my heart, the thing that was eating me—from the roots up.

13

Daddy keeps asking me why I'm so quiet. Secrets don't leave much room for words.

Diana Dixon

I drove my own car to orientation. It probably ticked Zeely off a little, but I wasn't quite ready to carpool yet. At least not for this trip. Zeely mentioned that she'd probably leave early anyway, after the "Everything you want to know about Imani" session. There was no sense in her driving back to pick me up. Though I'd never been to Joyce's school before, I knew that it was on South Side. I figured this was a ride I probably needed to take alone. I couldn't have been more wrong.

It was all still there. Mount Olive Missionary Baptist Church came first, where Zeely's father still preached every Sunday. She still sang in the choir, probably wearing her robe from high school. The sight of Strong and Jones Market made me smile. Daddy's favorite pork chops had come from there, right up until the week he died. Mom came back to town for church events and reunions but she never sets foot in there.

I slowed a little, checking the address Joyce had given me, following the numbers until I saw . . . the Charles C. They'd painted it and spruced it up, but there was no mistaking it. On the side of the building a blue and gold banner hung high.

Imani Academy. Where we believe in you!

No wonder Zeely hadn't wanted to talk about school. I felt a little sick turning into the lot, but there was nothing to do now but my job. And if the packed parking lot was any indication, there'd be plenty of work to do.

Circling the lot for the third time, I watched Zeely go inside. She gave me a long I-told-you-so stare before going in. Fair enough. Next time, I'd listen. Maybe. For now, I just needed to find a parking space and neither my car nor the crowd was helping me out.

Across the lot, a white van pulled out of a space and limped out of the lot. I went for it, praying my car would come through for me one last time.

I'll take you in Monday, baby. Promise. Just let me get in here.

It would have been a great coup, grabbing that space and running inside right on time, if it weren't for that black import with the same idea. I didn't see it until it was too late.

The metal made a horrible crunch. This couldn't be happening. Almost hysterical, I laughed to keep from crying.

The other driver didn't find it funny. He tapped on my window. I stared at him for a few seconds before rolling it down. This was not Mr. Homecoming from earlier. This was a grown man wearing a dashiki that wasn't made in China. He had the kind of locks in his hair that were somewhere on my life list, though they looked better on him. Until he started talking anyway. "Are you crazy?"

"Not technically. I have issues, but I'm working through them. You?" I could be a smart aleck when I'm nervous, but this was ridiculous.

Before I could apologize, he pulled my door open and extended his hand. When I got out, he gave my door a good slam. He shook his head at the state of my ride. "I'm surprised the door didn't fall off."

Me too.

He smoothed his beard a few times while I tried to figure out what color it was exactly. His skin was definitely honey. Or maybe ginger . . .

After looking me up and down, he asked if I was okay. When

I said I was, he asked—with skepticism—if I had insurance. That made me a little mad. Sure my car wasn't in the greatest shape, but I wasn't totally irresponsible. Sometimes things just got away from me. Usually the best things.

He scribbled down all his information in the biggest Daytimer I'd ever seen. Then he shook my hand and told me his name while I tried to act unaffected. "Dr. Mayfield. Nice to meet you, although the circumstances could have been better. I guess that's what I get for leaving home later than I should have."

"No, it was my fault, Dr. Mayfield." His name felt familiar in my mouth, liked I'd said it before, seen him before. But I doubted that. I would have remembered. He wasn't the kind of man that a woman forgot. He had presence like someone who usually ran things—and liked it. "I'm Grace—Grace Okoye."

He really looked interested then. "You're Nigerian?"

"Something like that." I sighed, not really wanting to get into my late husband's genealogy with a stranger, especially not if he was one of those deep back-to-Africa brothers that could talk you to death. I was late enough as it was.

The police saved me from having to explain more. I made a mental note to look out for Mayfield kids in any of my classes. Boy or girl, any child of his wouldn't be hard to find.

When the policeman left (who the good doctor had known by name, but whose name I'd forgotten already), Dr. Mayfield pointed to the boxes still in my backseat. "New in town? Or coming back?"

"Both." I grabbed my purse from the car. Poor guy. He would have to meet me when I was in one of these moods. Oh well. "Let me know if I owe you anything else," I said before straightening my dress and stepping around him.

While he'd seemed to be in a big hurry too, my last vague comment must have taken him over the edge because he grabbed my hand and spun me toward him like in some kind of black-and-white movie. I tried to duck when he—and his lips—moved closer to my face, but he was too quick. While I cringed, he planted a quick kiss on the top of my hand.

"That'll cover it," he said, before walking away, leaving me staring after him.

11

Brian

"A custom program for at-risk students . . ."

That's how the Imani Academy radio spot began. Judging from the crowd, the advertising campaign targeted the right market. *At-risk.* I hated the phrase. It was worse than a torn-up umbrella in a downpour—no help and something else to carry. It wasn't just the students who earned the label. It was the parents too. At risk of losing their jobs, their marriages, and sometimes even their minds.

Right now, I felt at risk of going crazy myself. Maybe I already had. I ran my thumb across my lips and slid into my chair at the registration table. While I processed a grandmother with a kind smile and the six thugs in matching outfits who turned out to be her grandsons, what just happened outside turned over in my mind.

I couldn't make sense of it any way I turned it, so I just let it go. Or pretended to. Women approached me all the time, but nothing usually came of it. Especially not lately. In the past year, I'd just been . . . hesitant. Until tonight.

If I could find that Okoye woman again, I'd apologize, but that might just make things worse. I hoped I hadn't gotten myself into a mess. These days, a man couldn't be too careful, litigation being such as it is. I warned my male students every day. Look, but don't touch. Now here I was doing the opposite.

A corporate couple signed in next, pulling along their son, with hair spiked like a porcupine and snakes tattooed around his

97

neck. The father looked unsure, but the mother, briefcase in hand and Bluetooth in operation, had a set, determined line across her mouth.

Next came Mr. McKnight, a man whose blood pressure was high and his tolerance for foolishness low. I'd picked that up the first time I'd met him. I think they sent him to anger management class over the summer too. We'd both blown up over his son Sean, a former student of mine who'd made some bad choices and landed me in a mess of trouble. As usual, Joyce had neglected to tell me that the boy would be back.

"This was mandatory, right, Dr. Mayfield?" Mr. McKnight didn't look up from signing his name.

"Yes, sir," I said, glancing at the V-shaped sweat stain bleeding into his embroidered nametag. I'd worked those kinds of jobs in undergrad and knew what happened when someone left early: a short check and less hours next week.

Sean's two-hundred-dollar sneakers told the rest of the story: a child spending money faster than a man could make it. And from the look on the boy's face, his attitude hadn't changed since last spring when he'd gone from being an honor student to a trouble-maker. Whatever teacher got him this time around would have their hands full.

Mr. McKnight stared me down. "I know that Sean has made some mistakes, especially with you, but he's sorry. I know you stayed on him because you cared. Can I trust you to keep an eye on him again?"

The impulsive man who'd twirled a woman in the parking lot was gone. Left behind was me, cold, calculating, and definitely keeping it real. Then I looked at that sweat stain, thought about how hot his day had been, how much hotter it was working under a car.

"Yeah. I'll keep an eye on your boy." I shook his hand. "Come see me on your next day off. My car might not be on the lot, but I'll be here. Somebody hit my car tonight."

Sean's father smiled a broad, full smile. "Now that I can help you with, bruh. Bring it by Monday morning. I'll take care of you."

He shook my hand and gave Sean a pat on the back before turning back for the door. I wasn't surprised to see him go. He'd probably come to talk to me more than anything.

Sean waited for his father to leave and then joined another group of boys with no parents, some who looked too old to even be in high school, but they all had registration forms in their hands and were listening to the orientation. Still, I planned to keep an eye on them.

Everyone was signed in now and Joyce had started her presentation. The crowd was something to see—the "smart kids gone bad" crowd interspersed with the "last stop before jail" crew. Their arms were crossed and their eyes steely, the look of most first timers. It was going to be another long year, but I wouldn't miss it for anything.

Just as I realized I was hungry, I smelled cedarwood and lime. I pushed back my chair and stood to my feet. Only one of my kids smelled like that. Quinn Rankin, my favorite student.

He'd grown. I could hardly believe it. Quinn and I stood almost eye-to-eye, with him looking down on me just a bit. He must have grown five inches over the summer. "Boy! What happened to you? What are you, six-two?"

"Six-three." Quinn laughed and put his plate down on the table before giving me a firm handshake.

Unlike other students who invaded my personal space trying to hug me, Quinn knew I wasn't up for all that. If I was going to hug a student, though, it probably would have been him. His white satin scholar jacket stopped several inches above his wrists.

Three years ago, I'd been a professor at Ohio State, a bestselling author and international lecturer. Quinn Rankin was a pimply faced beanpole who could barely read. Joyce convinced both of us

99

to come to Imani. Seeing the polite, intelligent young man in front of me, I was glad she did.

While many students balked at my sometimes unorthodox teaching strategies, Quinn reveled in them. Despite his deficits in learning, by the end of the first year, he was near the head of the class. This year, he was expected to be valedictorian. Something about him seemed different tonight, though. I couldn't quite put my finger on it.

"Well, I'm headed out. I just came to get some hookup with the cook up, if you know what I'm saying. Wanna split with me?"

I was no good at sharing things, especially if it was something I really wanted. "I'll get my own."

Quinn waved goodbye. "Okay, but hurry up. Miss Thelma is shutting it down."

He didn't have to tell me twice. While Joyce prattled on about the Imani vision, I slid into the last place in the burrito line. I stepped in front of Miss Thelma with a smile and a tray, hoping she'd be in a good, but quiet, mood. I wasn't up for the sermons tonight.

"Two supremes, please. And a sweet tea with lemon." The sugar would give me a headache after so long without it, and the beef and dairy would deal its own blow. Between the woman outside and Sean McKnight showing up, I just needed to get something to eat. Might as well go all the way.

Miss Thelma gave me a suspicious look. "Done with the vegan thing?" She looked down at the food.

"For now." I left it at that. She'd let me know when to talk, just as she had in the years when she'd served me lunch every day at school. In the evenings, in her house across the street from where I'd grown up, she spooned up wisdom as well. No doubt, she'd have an extra helping of advice for me tonight.

Thelma patted her face with a napkin, soaking up the foundation, two shades too light, pooling under her chin. She adjusted her hairnet and pushed back her gloves at the knuckle. "What you need is a wife—"

"Don't even go there," I said. "I'm still recovering from the last time you set me up."

"Lottie?" Thelma ladled cheddar sauce onto a mound of meat. "Give her another chance. She's a little rough around the edges, that's all." She handed me a plate and a cup with a lemon wedge on its rim.

I took my plate and gave a snort. "A little rough? She cursed like a sailor and drank like a fish. We went to a nightclub. Can you imagine? That is so played out."

The older woman shrugged. "You won't come to church and meet a real woman, so what can I do?"

I grabbed the last pack of nuclear taco sauce and lowered my voice since Joyce was raising hers. That was her way of saying I was too loud.

"I'm going before you get me in trouble," I whispered before turning away.

"You're already in trouble and don't have sense enough to know it." Thelma's voice carried across the room.

Without bothering to turn to face Joyce, I knew that was probably the last straw. I took a bite of my burrito, knowing she'd never let me finish it. The food was good, but a little too greasy to enjoy on the run. I tried not to think about the nutrition facts or lack of them. I tried not to think of that woman with the African name and an Ohio accent. I tried and failed at both.

All that pretty hair.

I took another bite and wiped my mouth with a napkin before tossing the rest of it. As hungry as I was, I couldn't stomach that stuff. I was starting to make myself sick, in more ways than one.

Let it go. Anger management has made you soft.

In truth, it'd just made me more angry. No matter how happy I was when I arrived, after an hour of "so tell us about your anger," I couldn't help but get mad. That, of course, meant another session. Eventually, I caught on. Told them what they wanted to hear. My mother issues and all that mess. In the months since, though, I'd wondered how much of it was actually true.

Just as I was checking the door for an early escape, I heard my name over the mike.

"Most of you now have probably heard of our next staff member or seen him on television. We're thankful that, though he could do many other things, he's chosen to stay with us another year. Please welcome Dr. Brian Mayfield."

So much for early exits. I made my way to the microphone.

"Why didn't you tell me about Sean," I whispered through my teeth, quickly recovering with a smile.

"Let the Lord handle it, baby," she whispered back, dropping her head so low that a salt-and-pepper curl tumbled down into her eyes.

She knew how to get me in place, but I had signals of my own as well. Another word from Joyce about God and we'd both be in a place that neither of us wanted to visit. Especially not tonight. I said my piece nice and easy, with my TV voice, the one they wanted to hear, that made them think we'd be able to do all Joyce was promising. I needed to hear it myself.

Zeely Wilkins had the microphone now, talking about plans in the math department for another great year. I tried to listen, but I'd heard it all before. Or at least I thought so . . .

Joyce took back the microphone. "Thanks, Ms. Wilkins. We're almost done, everyone. Hang on a little longer. This part will only take a minute."

I looked behind me for a chair. I didn't go to church anymore, but I knew that the Bible said that a thousand years is like a day to God. Well, for Joyce, a minute meant at least an hour.

"The two women I want to introduce next are both special to me for many different reasons. The main reason is that they accepted my last-minute invitation to join the Imani Academy faculty. Give a hand to *my* Bantus as both these ladies were once my students."

Two women stood up. One with neon pink lipstick and a matching miniskirt. The other, a few inches taller than the first, wearing a mustard yellow dress with wine-colored flowers that I hadn't been able to see clearly outside.

Grace Okoye.

The introductions didn't go well, probably because we'd all met under less than the best circumstances.

Joyce started with Lottie first. She looked even crazier than when I'd seen her on our last date. In her fashion, Joyce introduced her as though she were a queen. "This is Charlotte Wells. She'll be teaching art. She's done some wonderful murals and some local exhibits. Perhaps you've heard of her?"

I coughed into my fist. "We've met."

"I know Dr. Mayfield quite well," she said, taking a step closer to me. "I know his answering machine even better."

Here we go.

"Right. Well, you know how it is getting ready for school and all. Busy." I fumbled with something, trying not to think about what kind of year this was going to be.

Joyce released Lottie's hand. "Thank you, Charlotte. Please continue your orientation. I look forward to seeing you on Monday."

Lottie nodded at Joyce.

She winked at me.

I stared at Grace, who looked away just as Joyce wound an arm around her waist. My mentor beamed like a proud mother as she made the introduction. "This is my butterfly. A chrysalis I saw emerge before my own eyes. You probably don't remember it, but you were there too. I get chills sometimes just thinking of it."

Though I'm not one for the emotions much, a shudder of memory prickled my skin too. It was her. *The* dancer.

Joyce laced fingers with Grace. "This is Dr. Mayfield. He was the drummer for that first Ngozi class you came to."

It was Grace's turn to stare. Her look, and the fear streaking through it, made me remember how she'd never shown up for our recital. How I'd drummed for Zeely but it wasn't the same because her legs were shorter. Or at least that's what I told myself then. Now, seeing her again, I knew that it wasn't the same because it wasn't her.

I reached for Grace's hand and spoke in a voice much lower than the tone I'd spoken with outside. It was as if talking too loud would break the moment, shatter the memory. There was something here between us, something I'd felt that first day when she danced right up to my drum, something quiet and easily frightened away. "You had another name then," I said, forgoing any pleasantries.

She smiled, but with another flash of fear. "Diana. It's my first name. Grace is my middle. I go by Grace now."

"Right." Her hand was big for a woman's, with long, tapered fingers. It fit perfectly in my palm. No woman's hand had ever fit there before, not even my wife's. I'd thought that when I found a woman's hand that fit in mine, it would have been my mother's. Instead this dancer, this Grace with her unexpected perfume and innocent drape of her dress, had the hand that fit. I forgot myself and brought it to my lips.

Again.

I countered by kissing her knuckles and taking a deep bow, welcoming her back home in a stammering monologue that made no sense. In just a few minutes, she'd reduced me into a shy, angry boy again, one who'd wondered for longer than he should have where she had gone back in 1985.

Grace's eyes fluttered closed. Only when I leaned in closer did I hear the short, breathy prayer.

"God help me," she'd said, hardly speaking at all.

Amen, I thought before I could reason it away. *Amen*.

Joyce gave us a puzzled yet satisfied look of her own. Perhaps she'd realized that Grace had accomplished in a few minutes what she'd been trying to do for the past five years: getting me to acknowledge and approach God. I maintained that I didn't believe, but she knew me better than that. What she didn't know was that until a few minutes ago, I hadn't known myself better than that. I'd believed in my not believing. It was easier that way. Much easier than this.

I let go of Grace's hand, but she linked my pinky. I tucked both our hands behind my back, which only brought her closer.

"She hit my car today," I said for no reason in particular, stiffening with the words as if expecting another impact.

Joyce shook her head. Grace and I were laughing too, just a little with our lips barely parted. Still it was something, just enough to make me wonder if Grace would ever dance for me again. I saw it in my mind, her dancing that first time, then Joyce spoke and turned everything upside down.

"I'm not sure what happened in the parking lot, but it must have broken the ice because you two seem to be getting along. That will be a great asset this year while you're teaching together."

That made me let go of Grace and latch on to my anger, held in check by a thin leash. Joyce remained still, her collarbone rising and falling fast above the scoop of her silk shell. I'd upset her, but I couldn't help it. Did she think I needed a babysitter? Was this about that McKnight boy? I kept asking but she wouldn't budge. No answers.

Grace moved as much as Joyce stood still, crossing her arms and recrossing them, staring off behind me as though she saw something we could not. I didn't turn around to check. I'd seen her dance. She could definitely see things I couldn't. For now, Joyce's words were enough to handle.

105

Joyce delivered her explanation with a look of finality. The facts were these: Grace was to be my partner, not an observer. I hadn't done anything wrong, this was nothing personal.

My eyes eased back to Grace in her mustard yellow wrap dress and earrings as big as fists. Looking at her, I knew that Joyce had never been more wrong. This was all too personal.

Grace didn't look too happy about being my partner either. She didn't look anything at all like the mouthy flirt who'd hit my car in the lot. Well, maybe she did, but there was something else there too, someone else.

Diana.

That name, her real one, fit her better than that dress. Well, at least just as well. I'd planned for a lot of things this year, but this arrangement, this woman, wasn't on my agenda. I should have accepted Joyce's decision, but I couldn't. Not like this.

"Does this have to do with that investigation into the test scores? I thought they were over that."

For the past two years, our kids had scored higher than any public school in the county and even beat out a few private schools. The first year, we got kudos. The second year, we got complaints. With our budget, staff, and resources, what we were doing was impossible, they'd said. Someone had to be cheating. That allegation had almost given me an ulcer, but I'd thought the state board of education had left it alone.

They hadn't.

Joyce scratched her freshly waxed brow, still slightly red and raised from the procedure. "We've been given this semester to prepare for a new proficiency test. I've requested that we get another full year due to new students being at different levels. We'll see. I got the call today." Joyce swiped her brow.

I closed my eyes, counted to ten. This was part of what I hated about education. The politics. If we were some prep school, no one would say a word. But we weren't. My presence at the school had brought enough bad press. The first year, the media thought it was some publicity stunt for another book. Why else would a bestselling author and speaker go to teach high school English to a bunch of kids everyone else had given up on? The reason stood in front of me with silver hair matting to her temples and fire in her eyes. I'd do whatever she asked of me. And she knew it.

"Okay," I said, reaching again for Grace's warm, soft hand. "Okay."

I watched her face, my new teaching partner, to see what she'd say, but she was still looking behind me, still staring through my chest to the back of the room. Intrigued, I turned to look too. What I saw was Sean McKnight and the group of rough-looking boys I'd seen earlier, now blocking the main door. Sean gave me a quick nod, the kind that usually meant "what's up" or "hello." This time it meant something else, something I felt all over my body.

Run.

15

I grabbed both women's hands and started to move. Grace stayed with me, understanding somehow that we needed to go.

Joyce hadn't come as easily. "What is it?" she said, twisting around and trying to see.

"Trouble," I answered. We were almost to the door.

And then she'd seen who it was, what I'd meant. Joyce let go of my hand and gone toward them, toward Sean, just as shots rang out, peppering the ceiling, shattering the overhead lights. I tried not to think about what that might mean as I listened for her scream. It never came.

Other screams made up for it. As the room darkened, I focused on keeping Grace safe, believing that Joyce would land on her feet as she always did. Another of Grace's breathy prayers warmed my ear as our stomachs hit the cafeteria floor. This time I didn't join in, but it definitely seemed like a good idea.

"Where's Joyce?" Grace whispered.

"I don't know."

A male voice echoed through the room before we could say more. "This is a warning to all y'all who think you can leave the gang and come over here. This school can't help you. You belong to us."

I sighed, disgusted. Was this foolishness still going on? The name of the gang had changed since I was young, but the tactics remained the same. These boys were threatening to destroy what could save them. As an author and a speaker, my main message was about understanding and empowering black boys. Only one kid out of hundreds had ever made me so angry that I'd set my strategies aside for rage. Now my one failure might cost many people their lives. Even Grace.

I tightened my grip on her wrist. "I can't believe he'd do this."

"Who?" Grace whispered, sounding much like Joyce had earlier.

"Sean McKnight. Former student. Joyce kicked him out last spring. I thought he was coming back, but I should have known better. Sean's a hothead, but he's too smart for this."

"The Golden Boys own this town," the voice shouted again. "Nothing comes through here unless it goes through us. That includes this stupid school. Y'all better recognize."

I recognized, all right. I recognized the need to get out of here. I scrambled to my feet, pulling Grace along. "We've got to move."

It'd been my idea to stand, but Grace took the lead. We stumbled over lunch tables until we found the wall on the west side of the room. Though it was too dark for her to see it, I gave her a nod of approval. Good thinking.

Apart from the crowd, I fumbled for my cell phone on my belt, then shook my head. I'd left it out in the car after calling the police about the accident. That was one of Joyce's orientation rules. But Grace was new. She might have one. "Got a phone on you?"

"It's outside. Dead."

Neither of us said anything then, especially not what we were thinking, that we hoped we wouldn't end up dead too. I decided then that I couldn't let that happen. That we'd come out of this alive.

Then I heard Joyce's voice from somewhere way across the room. "Sean, honey, is that you? Please let this go so that we can continue your program. You need this education. All of you do."

I raked a fist across my beard. Joyce was going to eat a bullet playing with these kids. No matter how I tried to tell her that times had changed, kids had changed, she refused to believe it.

At least Grace has the good sense to be quiet.

Joyce called out again. "We can work this out, son. You know we can. I told you that back in June. It's not too late. That's how we work here. Right, Sean?"

"Stop calling his name," a deeper voice cried. "You don't know us!"

"Of course I know Sean. He was one of the brightest students we've ever had. If you stop this so we can talk, I can probably help you too."

"Enough talk." A third voice, even older, spoke. Another shot into the ceiling.

Tables and chairs screeched across the floor as people ran again, this time toward us. Bodies slid along our wall too, turning our safe haven into a trap. We were pinned on every side. I pushed Grace behind me and spread my arms to cover her, but it was too late. They were already pushing us apart.

Grace lunged for me, but only managed to hook my pants pocket. I reached back for her, clenching the neckline of her dress in my hand. The crowd prevailed until all I had was the tag and then . . . nothing. Just the tag in my hand. I reached down to the hole where my pocket had been. I felt the silk of my pocket, still in Grace's hand, brush my face before the crowd parted us totally.

And then, when she was gone, I heard it: Grace screaming my name like she'd always known it.

"Brian!"

I couldn't move. Cell phones and lighters flickered everywhere now, allowing me to make out my position, but elbows and arms held me captive. I wanted to run and tackle the kid with the gun. He didn't look more than twenty. He probably outweighed me by about thirty pounds, but I could tell by the look of him that he was slow. Soft. The other guys, the ones who had his back, looked different: veins popping from their foreheads, muscles cut and pumped. They looked itchy and I didn't want to be their scratch. Not until I found Joyce and Grace anyway.

I managed to get out from under two big-bosomed women and dropped back to the floor. Joyce had gone quiet since the last shot, but I knew it'd take more than a bullet to take her down. At least Quinn had gotten out safely. He probably would have been with Joyce, trying to talk Sean out of the whole thing. The two boys had been Imani scholars together. That seemed like a lifetime ago instead of last year. I wondered about Thelma too. Had she made it out or was she somewhere praying?

Itchy hair slid across my fingers as I inched forward. In the glow of a cell phone several feet away, I saw a woman crawling with a hairnet and crooked wig dangling from her neck. Thelma. She paused and squinted, as if trying to focus her eyes as well. A peculiar stench, a blend of cold fear, raw onions, Ben-Gay, and wig glue, swirled around her.

At least she was okay.

I reached for her, but she crept forward, unseeing, praying as she went.

"The Lord is my shepherd, I shall not want . . ."

I closed my eyes, soaking in the words, my mind stretched toward heaven against my will.

"Though I walk through the valley of the shadow of death, I will fear no evil . . ."

Something deep inside me agreed with her. Faith, not fear, would lead me and everyone else to safety. Somehow, Thelma's psalm pulled my broken beliefs to the edge of consciousness. What I was supposed to do with them now I had no clue. Prayer seemed like a good idea, but how does a man talk to someone he's forgotten exists? Best to make it short.

"God, help me end this before someone gets hurt," I said. "Especially Grace."

Thelma paused, adding an amen before crawling off. She never changed, no matter the circumstances. I had to give her that. Squinting myself now, I watched as the boys with the gunman argued with each other. I watched as their hands went up with the volume of their words. Empty hands. No guns.

No time to figure it out. I had to make a move.

I flung myself across the mound of bodies, praying not to step on anyone's head. People brushed against me without warning. Eyes. Arms. I pulled in my hands wondering for a second if maybe I should have just stayed on the floor where it was safe. I heard sirens, but they were still a ways off.

I stopped moving. The police would be here soon. I'd probably never get through all these people to those crazy boys anyway.

All things are possible with God.

That thought made me trip over my own feet. This was the strangest night I'd had in a long time. Though I thought I'd blocked out all the Scriptures and sermons that had once been my daily food, in this place, in this moment, it all came flooding back. Four lepers against an army. The choice? Die or die trying. Their decision? Go for it. I had to do the same. So I started again, stepping, stopping, and stepping some more. I couldn't see the boys anymore, but I could hear them.

Just as I pulled up short to listen, someone's weight shifted in my direction. An elbow landed in my throat. I fell back, but didn't cry out. She came next, knocking the rest of the wind out of me. Hair tickled my eyes instead. Lots of it. I grabbed the woman and covered her mouth, thankful she wasn't a screamer like so many here tonight. I held her still, craning my neck to hers. There was a rip at the back of her dress.

On another night, I might have smiled. "It's me. Brian," I said.

"I know," she whispered. Her thumb burrowed in my side. "Look."

Blue and red lights reflected against the walls then faded, but not before reflecting the two boys standing above us and the piece of steel between them.

The gun.

16

Ron

"The food is ready if you are."

Hoping I hadn't been too obvious when I dropped Jerry off and declined his offer to come in, I licked my lips, pressing the phone to my face. I'd called Zeely as I turned onto my street. If the concert had been at my church, I could have gone straight on, but this was a church sing with the requisite church clothes, which I hated, despite being a lawyer.

"Oh, I'm ready. Let me change and I'll be there," I said, trying not to sound winded as I tugged off my shirt and tie and yanked my favorite pair of jeans off a hanger. I wondered now if I shouldn't have insisted on Jerry tagging along. I'd felt pretty big earlier about going to Zee's house alone, now I wasn't so sure about it.

Since Jerry's divorce, things were all mixed up. First we'd prayed for him and Carmel to reconcile—okay, so I was still praying for that—but Jerry's ex-wife had made it clear that there'd be none of that. In case we didn't get the message, she'd started dating a doctor to hammer the message home. Jerry still sort of lumbered between his two jobs looking like a truck hit him. More than once, I'd lent him my couch for one of his how-did-this-happen-to-me episodes. All I could do was be there for him. I wasn't sure how any of this had happened to any of us, including myself.

And then, in the middle of the school year last winter, Jerry and Zeely had been forced to share a classroom after renovations closed off a wing of the school. For the first time since the divorce,

I'd seen Jerry laugh again. Smile even. It didn't take much for me to figure out why. He spent more nights on the couch, only this time I heard about his new twisted personal theology of how maybe his marriage had fallen apart because of how he'd treated Zeely. We'd both had enough seminary to know it didn't make sense, but I knew well enough what happened when your sins start winding a story of their own.

A "what if" story.

As far as the east is from the west, so far has He removed our transgressions from us.

Twenty questions never was a fun game. There was no way to win, really. Carmel only called Jerry when she needed money or when it had something to do with their kids, kids I knew Zeely desperately wanted but thought she'd never have. We were a mess, all of us, especially me.

Sometimes I blamed Carmel, thinking that if she'd just taken Jerry back, this would all be over once and for all and we'd all be safe—my own relationship issues notwithstanding. That wasn't how it was with me, though. God gave me rescue but not safety, no matter how much I sought it.

As for Zeely and Jerry, was something going on between these guys or what? It seemed I'd spent most of my life trying to answer that question.

"So what games do you want me to bring?"

I downed the stairs now, a little slower than I came up, stopping to tuck in my shirt. I ran to the hall closet in time for her reply.

She made her decision easily. "How about Bible Trivia? That was the bomb last time. I've been studying."

That should keep things honest. "Think you can beat me? I was starving last time and I still whipped you. This time you don't stand a chance." Neither did I. When I grabbed the game from under a stack of sweaters, a pack of cards fell too. Those went in my back pocket. Until a few years ago, Zeely had never played cards in her

114

life. She played a mean game of spades now though. "You can avenge yourself at cards."

"Can we play Five Hundred this time?"

"Sure." Outside now, I rounded the truck and shut the tailgate before climbing in. I eased out of the drive, keeping the tone light, casual. "I guess I have to let you win something."

"Let me win? You say that every time," Zeely said.

I laughed then. "I mean it every time. Believe that. Be there in a few."

She laughed too. "You're so predictable, you know that? We both are."

I closed my eyes.

We sure are.

"Speak for yourself, Birdie. I'll be there in a minute."

My F-150 bumped over the curb near Zeely's condo. So much for light and casual. I straightened the wheels and eased back even farther from her driveway. I never parked there. Not that I felt guilty or anything. Jerry said all the time that he didn't care if I was over, though I did sense some jealousy that he wasn't given the same invitation. My girlfriend never came on this side of town anyway. Maybe it was too many years of living under the noses of church ladies, I wasn't sure. It just didn't seem right.

I kicked one of my truck's tires before going in, mentally correcting the alignment. When had I rotated them last? It didn't seem that long ago. Maybe I needed a new car after all. Mindy would love that.

Zeely opened the door after the first ring; and she wasn't alone. Scents of onions, garlic, and hot, seasoned pork danced out the door like quarter notes and teased my nose. There was something else too, something sweet and warm: chocolate. She held the door

115

open, but I didn't come straight in. I leaned down, pausing at her ear and took a long sniff.

"Mmmm . . ." I didn't know what dessert she'd made, but I knew for sure that chocolate was in it. And as good as she looked, she could have stirred some of herself in a bowl and had the same effect. She'd changed her perfume to something light. Spicy. I pressed my lips together and gave her a hug. "Taste and see that the Lord is good, huh?"

She shut the door behind me before walking to the stove. "Come on in and get comfortable. I'll be out in a minute. I see you brought the game."

I shook my head. *Here we go.* "I did."

Thankful for the distance between us, I pulled back a chair at the dining room table with its four place settings perfectly arranged with a coordinating linen napkin as usual. Today's theme was sunflowers with bright yellow dishes. I peeked toward the kitchen and checked the curtains. They'd been changed too. Everything was apples the last time I'd visited.

I could see her leaning over the range to check a pot on a back burner, ladling cheese sauce into her mouth. I almost ran back to my truck. I'd prayed for casual and light, but that was killing me too. She'd dressed down tonight with her hair up in a clip, a little MAC gloss on her lips, a T-shirt, and a pair of jeans with a zebra cuff at the bottom. I stacked the games on the table and wondered if I didn't need to start reading the answers to some of the Bible Trivia questions for spiritual backup.

"You can't hide in the kitchen all night, you know. Let's eat now so the punishment can begin. I'd hate for you to be hungry *and* humiliated." I was up now and entering the kitchen.

"We'll see who gets humiliated." Zeely lifted the lid on the largest pot on the stove, releasing a cloud of all the goodness I'd smelled on the porch. "Bring me one of those plates off the table."

"At your service." I bowed once before passing the Pfaltzgraff her way. When she tried to take it, I held onto the edge, pulling her closer. "I can make my own food, you know."

She frowned. "Let go of it, mister."

I let go of the plate and watched her heap it with macaroni and cheese. From the hurt look in her eyes a minute before, I knew a speech was coming. I hoped she'd make it short. She was even cuter when she was mad.

"Have you ever made your own plate in this house? I take care of my guests. Even the ones who don't want me to." Greens chocked with ham hocks came next, then black-eyed peas and a chunk of cornbread. She set the plate on the table, turned back toward the stove to make a smaller plate for herself, and then followed me to the dining room.

My prayer was simple, all I could muster while reaching around the sunflower centerpiece and holding her hand. Thanks for the food and the friendship. I could have easily added forgiveness, but that was an unspoken verse that blessed all our times together. When we lifted our heads, we looked at each other for a long time. Too long.

I pulled back my hand and went for the cornbread before I lost it totally. It was scratch with a little Jiffy mix, I could tell, the best kind for crumbling. I mixed it with my greens and doused it with hot sauce, while Zeely shook her head.

After my first mouthful, I was shaking my head too. It was so good that I had to pause for a minute and let it sink in. A lesser man might have cried. In our little dinners together, I'd always made the greens. It's a wonder she'd eaten them at all.

"Girl . . ." I grabbed the hot sauce again, trying not to talk with my mouth full. "This is crazy good. How'd you get the greens so tender?"

My eyes started to water from the hot sauce before she could answer. She disappeared, only to return with a glass of blue Kool-Aid, my favorite. I took a gulp. Perfect.

She acted like it was nothing, but I knew she was pleased with my reaction. If she only knew.

"I washed the greens seven times. Mama used to put hers in the washing machine, but I'm not up for all that. A pinch of sugar in the ham water. Vinegar too. A splash of olive oil—"

I held up both hands. "What? Slow down, girl. A pinch of this. A splash of that. This isn't the Food Network. I need a recipe!" I pulled a paper towel off the roll in front of me. She'd known I would need them.

"Recipe? Can't help you there. You'll have to come over and watch next time I make them."

My fork froze in midair. I'd like to watch her do anything. Breathing even. "I'd be honored." I noticed that the plate in front of her was untouched, her silverware still arranged. "Aren't you eating too?"

"I'll eat it later. I took Dad his already. I'll send most of this home with you. The rest will last me the week."

She was sending most of it home with me? It'd been way too long since I'd been over. Mindy considered it generous if she got up to bring me a glass of tap water. I probably needed that now to cool me down and not because of the hot sauce either.

"Oh, I get it. You're trying to fatten me up while you stay fine. Make me sleepy with the food while you know all the answers. Hmmm . . . sneaky, but I like it." I took another bite.

She rolled her eyes. "Oh be quiet. I don't need a strategy to beat you. I can do that all by myself. Besides, you never gain weight. You thickened up some since high school, but it looks like all muscle from here." She squeezed my bicep to accentuate her point.

And destroy any remaining cool I had.

I pulled off another paper towel and mopped my brow. We both went quiet as if knowing a time-out was needed. I wiped my lips next, never taking my eyes off hers.

Zeely shot up from her chair, a saucer in hand. "Ready for the cake?"

Nice save.

I pushed my half-full plate aside and reached for the game. "No cake yet. It's game time."

She rubbed her hands together. "It's on now. I'll try not to be too rough. This time you'll realize that I can take you."

My body settled into the chair. On nights like tonight, I wished she'd take me forever.

17

Jerry

It'd been a good weekend, but a long one too. Work, school orientation (other work), work, church, work, church concert, and now there were a few hours to sleep before going to my second job.

I tossed my keys onto the table and headed for the recliner instead of the bed so I wouldn't be so comfortable that I'd oversleep. That definitely wouldn't be a problem in this chair. I lowered myself into it gently, hoping it wouldn't choose tonight to break completely. As I sank into the threadbare seat, my ex-wife Carmel's face floated before my eyes. Too tired to blink her away, I meditated on the face of the woman who I fought with so often now, wondering where things had gone wrong between us. We hadn't married under the best circumstances, but we'd loved each other once.

Maybe we could love each other again.

Maybe not, if her new boyfriend had anything to do with it.

Every time I thought we could work things out, Carmel pulled another stunt, leaving me with my finger on the trigger. A stack of bills teetered on the coffee table, anchored by the fattest envelope, the one weighing heaviest on my mind. Another of Carmel's tricks, authorized without my permission, but left for me to pay for.

A frustrated sigh brought me deeper into the recliner. It creaked beneath my weight. It was hard to believe that three years ago I'd been a sportscaster, coming home each night to a happy wife and a house full of custom-made furniture tailored to fit my large frame. That was before for the new baby, the old bills, the mess we couldn't clean up . . .

The birth of little Justice had shaken us in ways I didn't expect, especially Carmel's faith in my love for her. Like a man in midlife crisis, she went over and over the details of how we'd gotten together and whether I would have married her if she hadn't been pregnant.

"Be honest," she'd said, and so I was. Big mistake. Everything that had been an obstacle became a wall, and before I knew it, I was back in Testimony, broke, divorced, and unable to offer any explanation. Carmel moving home too and taking up with a doctor from the hospital she worked at was just extra. She said it was for the best, and at times I believed her, but my life was wearing thin.

My patience too.

I picked up the thickest letter from the bottom of the pile and slit the seam with a toothpick. The pronouncement was the same one I'd find on the other letters, with the same urgent, red type. The phrase that summed up my life:

Overdue.

One flip landed it back on the pile, now scattered across the table. I was overdue all right: overdue for a blessing; overdue for a nap. The latter came without invitation, cut short by the whir of a Pontiac fan in my driveway. I sat up and wiped my mouth, ashamed and awed by how quickly sleep came upon me these days. How deeply. I knuckled the grit from my eyes, trying to remember the schedule. It wasn't my night, I knew that much. Not that it would mean anything to Carmel. It never did.

A fist pounded against the door. When I got up, my eyes caught on my 7-Eleven uniform draped over a chair a few feet away. I'd stayed awake during the concert tonight. I'd promised Ron I'd go months ago and I was trying to do better about keeping up with friends. This was as far as I could stretch without sleeping. Any longer and I'd have to call in.

Again.

I cracked the door. "Who is it?"

Four rhinestone-covered nails curled around the door. They were worn at the edges and long overdue for a fill, but from a distance, they caught the light from every direction. My ex-wife stood in the doorway with a baby on her hip. She looked almost as tired as I did.

"Here," she said, pushing the little girl into my chest. She lifted a leather tote inside the door. "There's enough milk and diapers in there to hold her a few hours. I've got to get some sleep."

I tugged at her sleeve as she turned to go. "Come inside and let's take turns. Seriously. I've hardly slept in two days. Let me sleep for two hours and I'll let you sleep for two . . ."

My voice faded but Carmel's response was like smelling salts. For the moment, anyway.

"You don't get it, do you? In two hours, I have to be at work and pretend I'm happy that some fourteen-year-old is having a baby. Tell her that everything will be all right."

The baby wailed, startled by our loud voices.

"And it won't be all right, but it's all I got. I'm sorry, Jerry. I never meant for it to be like this for either of us." Carmel tightened the belt of her jacket and marched to her car.

I stared behind her until she pulled off. Another cry brought me back to reality and back inside the house. I patted the baby's back. "I never meant for it to be like this for you either, little mama."

I closed the door and rested on it, the baby's head under my chin. After a few tickles, we headed for my bed with the diaper bag in tow. With a prayer of thanks for family, for legacy, I called in to my job and prayed for as much sleep as I could get. Somehow, I had to get this girl to lie down.

18

Brian

The muzzle of a nine-millimeter swept an arc over us and back again with every word the gunman spoke. The floor was hard under us and cold, but we lay still. My thumb was pressed to Grace's lips, her head against my chest. The police were pulling in now, we could hear them outside.

The boy waving the gun seemed desperate. We heard him pop the ammunition out and back in again.

Grace didn't speak, but her tears soaked my shirt. That took me over the edge I was already peering over, made me want to sweep the guy's legs out from under him. I slid my hands from under her head. Just when I was going to make a move, the other boy flicked a lighter. Sean McKnight. The kid who'd almost cost me my job and now maybe my life. It was too late, but maybe he'd come to his senses.

"What are you doing, man! Turn that off."

The light flickered off. "This isn't how you said it was going to go down. No guns, remember? I want out," Sean said with a strained voice.

It was all I could do to keep quiet. Now Sean wanted to use his head, when he was about to go to jail? For all the difficulties Sean and I had gone through, I hated that things had come to this.

"Shut up," the gunman said. "Don't worry about getting out. You ain't getting in. It's staying alive you got to be worrying with now. Just follow us and keep your mouth shut. What's that lady's name? The principal—"

"Nobody. She's nobody to you," Sean whispered. As police flashlights lit up the room, Sean and I locked eyes.

"Police!" The shout came from the hall. The doors creaked open, flooding the room with light.

As the boys started to run, I grabbed for the gunman's leg. Once he was down, I tried to push myself up, but someone yanked me back. Grace. She was stronger than she looked. A policeman rushed past us and finished the job, clicking the handcuffs on the gunman in a flash.

She sagged in my arms, her words rushing out in one breath. "Thank you, Jesus."

I shrugged before pulling my new co-worker to her feet. I still wasn't feeling the God thing, but I'd almost said the same thing myself. What Grace didn't know—Joyce always omitted it from her new teacher invitations—was that several teachers in the district had been critically injured by students, one even killed. At Northside High, once the suburban school of choice, a twenty-five-year veteran teacher had been gunned down after school for giving a student a failing grade. Imani's own vice principal had broken his arm breaking up a fight during summer school and retired soon after. Last year had been a rough one for the school district, and this year might not be much better. And yet, here was Grace, standing tall with her Jesus.

One of the detectives I knew from around town gave me a quick nod, pointing out Joyce gathering parents together across the room. He'd gone to Imani himself.

"She wants to say a few words to the parents. I'll give her five minutes to clear the room. Will you keep her straight?"

I nodded, turning to tell Grace what was going on, but she and her mumbled prayers had already blended into the crowd.

My emergency faith melted away as I watched amazed while a

few parents righted their clothes and gripped the hands of their children and stayed five more minutes when everyone else had run out as quickly as they could. The five minutes was long gone now as Joyce had done a quick dash to the parking lot and guided three more parents back into the cafeteria.

"Thanks for staying. I know it was scary tonight, but I'm glad you saw what happened tonight. This is exactly why this school is needed," she said. "We have to reach these kids. Help them discover their destinies." Joyce marched by, waving for me to follow.

I frowned, but followed, righting overturned chairs as I went. The detective gave me a tense look, but I held up a hand asking for a little more time. Joyce couldn't be anything, anyone, other than herself.

Neither could Grace, whose flowery scent still mingled with my sweaty one. Instead of leaving like I'd thought, Grace had joined Thelma in helping some of the older people to their cars while Joyce dealt with the media. There was talk of giving rides to those who'd missed the last bus, but I talked both ladies out of that, leaving it to the police and myself, if necessary. Lottie was nowhere to be seen.

I tuned out Joyce's weary optimism as she talked to reporters. Instead, I watched through the doorway as a policeman walked Grace to her car. I'd liked to have done it myself, but she walked on without looking back. Despite her ripped dress and bare feet, she still made me shift my feet. I even thought of my late wife, Karyn. "You can't run from God forever," she'd said to me before she died. As Grace's pitiful excuse for a car pulled away, I wondered if she hadn't been right. For the first time in a long time, none of my philosophies rang true.

Tonight it'd been me calling out to God in the darkness. I'd been in dangerous situations before, some worse than this. Tonight though, I'd wanted—needed—God's help. And I'd gotten it. Where that left me now, I wasn't sure.

"Get off me!" someone yelled in the hall.

I turned and saw Sean McKnight struggling between two officers. Earlier, I'd put in a word for him, probably only because of Joyce. The officer, my former classmate, didn't say much, but he kept Sean behind the others being hauled off to jail. I hoped Sean, only seventeen, would get time in juvenile detention instead of being tried as adult. I clutched my gut, sore from the kicks and prods of the crowd. The sight of a student in handcuffs, even a kid who refused to live up to his potential, turned my stomach. No matter how I tried, I couldn't save them all. Joyce couldn't either. I signaled to her one last time to shut it all down. She ignored me.

"Dr. Mayfield and I will stand with this community to make changes one child at a time. We were all afraid tonight, but we all stayed, we all prayed. Things come against us, but we will prevail. This *will* be a good year." Joyce spoke softly, but I knew that she meant every word.

We all walked to the door together. I reached out and took Joyce's hand, which, unlike Grace's, felt like a child's against my own. I felt her body rest against me as the school door closed behind us. After locking it and giving the key to the officer, I kissed her cheek. She'd been doing this a long time and for all her love, all her patience, she was tired. I was too.

I offered to drive Joyce home but she refused, opting instead for a police escort following behind her. I reached for my car keys, slipped into my remaining pocket hours earlier.

Was that tonight? I wondered. A satin tag fluttered to the ground as I pulled out my keys. Once I was inside the car, I read it. Slowly.

Virtuous Woman. Size 16.

19

Grace

Morning air poured in my car window on the way to church. Though Testimony was landlocked, the breeze had a salty taste, like tears warmed with the last fever of summer. Or maybe my own tears still lingered on my tongue. Home after the mess at orientation, the tears I'd been waiting on for so long finally came. I wanted to believe that it would be the last cry for a while, that today was truly a new day, a fresh mercy.

You are a new creation.

I kept driving, past Zeely's empty driveway—she'd left hours ago to sing in the choir at first service—past Imani Academy and right up to Mount Olive Missionary Baptist Church. I did a quick scan for a black Jaguar. It wasn't there. I only had the questions to battle with as I climbed the church stairs, only the words in my head that had robbed my sleep:

You can't help those kids.

That man doesn't want you. Nobody does. Nobody ever will.

Who do you think you are?

God knew who I was, what I'd been through. He knew who he'd created me to be. He'd be with me through this, whatever this was.

Are you sure? He left you once.

"No," I whispered as I took hold of the church door. Whether I understood it or not, God had been with me.

Even then.

I took a seat three rows of hats back from the pulpit. Mount Olive looked different: padded pews replaced the wood benches and shag carpet blanketed the once bare floor. A new organ even jazzed up the old songs. Still, something, everything about the place was painfully familiar. The hurt I'd buried years ago in the downstairs choir closet crawled up through the floor and into my soul. Each word from Reverend Wilkins hit the rewind button on my life, leaving a confused teenager in a woman's body.

"Everybody has a cross—a place where something died. Sometimes we run away before the resurrection. Sometimes we linger long after the body is gone." The Reverend's voice boomed from his slight frame.

I studied the cross above the pulpit. It looked the same from the front as it had from the youth choirstand where I'd sat on my last visit. My eyes waded through the suits and sequins to the bus stop outside, the scene of my destination, the debut for which I never arrived. The bus had come eventually and dropped off its passengers. If only I had been one of them . . .

Don't play that game.

"You can't outrun God. I see it all the time. Folks cut the rug out of here and come back dragging one arm, three kids, and a parole officer—"

"I heard that!" someone said. Laughter rumbled through the church. A tall man across the aisle jerked awake and added a chuckle before nodding off again.

The sermon went on, floating around my head. Until everyone stood for the offering. We flowed into two columns in the center aisle, with each side of the room making the appropriate turn to get back to our seats. When it was my turn to put in my offering, I paused before the aging deacons and smiled, dropping more money than I could afford into the bronze plate. I remembered too late that Mount Olive had as many as four offerings in one service and could be counted on to call someone to the front who was in need of a little extra help. As I walked back to my seat, Zeely gave me a proud smile and approving glance. I stared at the floor. I wouldn't be able to give her a repeat performance if I wanted to eat until my first paycheck.

Back in the pew, I reached for my Bible and opened up to Psalms, marked with a flyer addressed to "Occupant" at my new address. The word "God" sprawled across the page in a neon blur. I paused to read it as everyone made it back to their seats.

Need a fresh start with God? Stop by anytime. Tender Mercies Church.

I crossed my legs, careful not to run my last pair of hose. Calculating how much to give on the next trip around the room, I wondered how many offerings Tender Mercies had. I stared out the window at the stone bench and withered trees, watching as a bus pulled up and released a group of laughing teens at the corner.

My hand tightened around the bills tucked in my palm. I stood slowly and headed for the back door, holding up an index finger like my mother had when she got sick of things—most times of my daddy. I didn't falter, even when Zeely narrowed her eyes. It didn't matter if the other church took up ten offerings. Being here was like worshiping next to a grave.

20

Brian

Midnight heroes made a sorry sight the next morning. And if I wasn't sure of that, pain blazed from my ankle to my thigh every few minutes, ensuring that I didn't forget. I tossed back a glass of apple-carrot juice, hoping the nutrients would sooth something. My mind would be a good place to start, especially after the fax that had just come buzzing out of my machine with both mine and Grace's names on each page. The more I thought about that, about her, the less I thought it was a good idea for us to teach together.

I reached for the phone, both hoping and doubting that Joyce would be home from church.

"Praise the Lord," Joyce answered in a tone that let me know she didn't appreciate the Sunday call. Well, I hadn't enjoyed the Saturday brawl either. We'd both have to deal with it.

"Morning, Doc. Can you talk?"

A sigh came through the phone. "Dr. Mayfield, you know I rest on the Sabbath. This better be important."

Dr. Mayfield? She was plenty mad. My leg hurt so bad that I didn't mind pushing back a little. "Sorry to bother you, Joyce, really, but it's this joint teaching thing. After last night, I don't know if Ms. Okoye needs to be in the proficiency test class at all." There was more to it of course, but there was no need to get into it.

"If you can't work with her, you can't work. Don't call me back either, sweetheart. See you Tuesday. Have a nice Labor Day."

Despite the warmth in her words, a click on the line denied me any chance of further appeal.

I lowered the phone, accepting Joyce's words. In my office, I collected the class roster. Its pages had escaped the paper tray. Many of the names I knew from years before, retakers mostly. A few kids were kids I'd met at orientation. There were also names I didn't recognize, probably kids who'd heard things about me and signed up out of curiosity. My tresses and my temper had earned me a strange fame at Imani, although the man usually disappointed the myth.

This whole thing called for some music, the easy, thinking kind. I aimed the remote at the sound system, and Wynton Marsalis's trumpet obliged. For the first time this morning, I felt myself relax. I might have even gone back to sleep if the fax machine hadn't started buzzing with a fresh transmission. Why Joyce didn't get a computer at home and send email like normal people totally evaded me. I'd even bought her one and set it up, but she just used it for the neighbor children to play reading games on.

Since she'd just told me it was the "Sabbath," it surprised me to be getting all this from her. I shrugged and rolled my chair away from the desk. It snagged on a piece of paper that I'd missed, tucked under the rug. There were only a few names on this sheet, all handwritten in Joyce's flowing script. The last name almost made my eyes cross.

DeSean McKnight.

I wadded the paper into a ball. Surely it couldn't be *the* Sean McKnight. I'd seen the police cart him off with my own eyes. He was taken last, sure, but still . . . I'd given Sean everything I knew, everything I had, long before now. There was nothing left for me to teach him.

All things are possible with God.

The thought came to me in Joyce's voice, which bothered me all the more. I couldn't deny my mentor's ability to move mountains, even in the criminal justice system, but this was insane. She loved too much sometimes. Risked too much. I did too, even though the two of us showed our love differently. I'd had my share of trouble growing up, but I'd been tricked into my mess. Sean had walked into it. Right now, the only kind of love I'd have to show him was a size 12 up the behind. It wasn't a pretty thought, but that anger class had said to be honest with yourself, even if you couldn't be honest with others—and a lot of other things that seemed ridiculous at the time. Not so much now.

I limped into the kitchen to find my Palm Pilot and another glass of juice, recalling the ridiculous tenets from anger management as I went.

Focus on the positive.

Release what you can't change.

Allow others to be who they are, where they are.

As corny as it sounded, the words made good sense. I picked up my stylus and tapped my palm file for the number to the body shop where Mr. McKnight worked. Maybe Ron could follow me there Tuesday morning. The paint job shouldn't take more than a few days.

Too bad they can't knock the dents out of me too.

21

"I was surprised to hear from you." Ron looked over his coffee at me, quite pleased to finally have me in the cab of his raggedy truck. He'd rolled the window up on my hair three times before I finally punched him like he wanted. What I refused to do, however, was get into a detailed explanation about why I hadn't called until now. Or why I *had* called, for that matter.

From the look on Ron's face, he couldn't have cared less why. He was thrilled by it. Finally, I needed him, even if it was just for this.

I apologized anyway. "Thanks for following me to the body shop. Sorry for the last-minute call."

"Things happen. That's what friends are for." Ron wanted to say that's what brothers were for, but I appreciated him for not saying it. Friends was a good place to start. The truck hit a bump, making the jarring music seem even louder.

I tried not to wince at the sound. "Can you turn that down?"

"Sure. I need a little jump start some mornings. Sorry."

That made me smile, thinking of the times when Ron had begged me to play the drums for him while he got dressed in the morning. Mama—Miss Eva—had thrown shoes at us, but she'd tapped her foot when she came to get them. In some ways, Ron hadn't changed a bit. "I know how you are, especially when it starts turning cold. Go ahead with your music. I'll survive. It's your car."

Ron smiled and turned down the volume. "It's okay. We're almost to my firm and I know you're going to turn it to jazz or something when I get out."

He had me there, although I had found myself nodding to the beat a little as I strained to make out the words.

"Rugged soldier, this rugged brother told ya, 'I love Jehovah' . . ."

I felt like throwing up. Christian rap. What would they think of next?

Reciting the lyrics word for word, Ron looked like he was going to bop right out of his seat. As he pulled up in front of the law firm where he worked, he turned to me with that nostalgic look in his eye.

I groaned.

He held up a hand. "No, seriously. Do you remember when we went to our first Christian rap concert? T-Bone, I think. Maybe Disciples of Christ. Karyn was with us. It was before your righteous black period. You were back at church then."

"I don't think so." I cut off the music and the conversation. A ride to work was one thing. A ride down memory lane was another. "What time should I pick you up?"

"Five. And watch the bumps. The tailgate pops open sometimes." He slammed the door. "Oh, and watch the tires too. They need an alignment. I'm taking it in tomorrow."

I slid into the driver's seat, trying to remember all the truck's ills. "Are you serious?"

"Quite."

My disbelief got a big smile from Ron, but I wasn't amused.

"When I get my car back, I'm coming to get you, okay?" I made it sound like a question, but he was coming with me, either way.

"Oh, my. A date. Where are we going?" Ron batted his eyes.

"Car shopping. This makes *no* sense."

More laughter. "Whatever. See you tonight." Ron slapped the truck and a more serious look eased over his face, into his eyes. He looked back at his job, where that crazy girlfriend of his was probably waiting. He gave me a quick nod before running inside. "You're right, man. Some things make no sense at all."

Ron definitely needed a new car. My body had been tight before the ride, but now I felt tied in knots. As I walked to my classroom, I lifted my arms over my head and stretched out wide. Better. My limp was almost gone too.

My first task was to turn on a fan in the wide, windowless room that had once been the crafts center of the Charles C. Now it was my classroom. I'd made macramé and lopsided pots in here during the summer, but minds were sculpted here now. In the morning like this, before the kids came with their own smells, I could still catch a whiff of the terra-cotta dust lingering in the cracks of the floor. Joyce had kept the kiln too, even though we never used it. Maybe Lottie would do something with it.

My thoughts turned to my new teaching partner. "Ms. Okoye," I said to myself. That's who she was and that's how I had to start thinking of her. Her name came out in a husky tone that I'd once reserved for teasing my wife. That scared me almost as much as the answer from the desk behind me.

"Yes?"

I almost dropped a book of poetry on the floor. Keats, I think. Grace must have slipped in while I was sniffing for pottery dust. The fan was loud, but my radar should have caught her scent at least. With a smile, I sifted through the notes of her scents, essential oils from plants instead of a chemist's vial. The strongest notes came to me easily: jasmine and lemongrass. Sweet and tart. It was fitting. "Good morning."

She looked up from the book on the desk in front of her, but not for long. "I hope you had a good holiday. Rested up from the other night and all," she said, her eyes already back on the book in front of her.

"I'm as ready as I'll get, I suppose. Not rested exactly . . ."

If this morning was an indication, I'd be up tonight too. I'd thought Grace beautiful before, but today she looked . . . smart. For some reason, that turned me on more than ever. Her twists were pinned into an updo and her glasses rested not quite on the tip of her nose. Her blouse was crisp and her makeup simple. She wore suede sport shoes, which meant she planned to be in motion. She'd attracted me the other night, but now she had me interested.

Too taken with her book to look up, she gave me a grunt of agreement.

I wanted more than that. Some eye contact or something. "Have you been here long? I had to take my car in this morning."

That caught her attention. She paused, fingers still on a gold-edged page. "About that. Please send me the bill. I insist."

As she spoke, I read the caption: *Isaiah*.

The Bible.

So much for flirting.

"No, it's fine. One of our parents works at the body shop and he used his discount." Or at least I hoped that's what he'd done.

"Okay, well, let me know if there's anything else. Please." One of her twists escaped its hairpin. She tucked it behind her ear.

"Thanks." I was distracted now, caught up in reading her high-lighted verse over her shoulder.

Remember ye not the former things, neither consider the things of old. Behold, I will do a new thing; now it shall spring forth; shall ye not know it? I will even make a way in the wilderness, and rivers in the desert.

"It's fine. We'll work it out."

Sean's father had been elated to see me. When I asked for a quote, he just kept talking. I wanted to tell him that he had Joyce to thank for getting his son out of trouble. I'd put in a good word, but if it were up to me, Sean would never be back in this school, let alone my class.

136

Grace had already left me again, absorbing the words on the page in front of her. I knew then that there'd be nothing between us. Every woman I'd ever loved had been a Christian, but I'd been a different man then. If you weren't a convert or husband material, you were a waste of manhood. Since I didn't plan on being dragged back to the fold or the altar anytime soon, I just watched her read with her sensible shoes and heady scent. She acted as if I wasn't even there. I decided this might be a good thing. There were enough people in my life trying to preach to me. I didn't need another, no matter how pretty she was.

Besides that, from the way things looked, Grace already had a man—Jesus Christ. I'd learned the hard way that nobody can compete with that. Still, she was the most interesting woman to cross my path in a very long time. Her brave simplicity intrigued me much more than Lottie's flashy beauty. She might not be dancing anymore—I'd ask her about that later, once we got to know each other better—but she was definitely that same girl I'd thought about so many times over the years. Even Karyn had reminded me of her, though I didn't realize it until now. She'd had braces before, but she must have had them removed early because as she turned the pages, her tongue peeked through the gap between her teeth.

I had a thing for gaps.

And because of that, I had to warn her.

I pressed my hand onto the desk beside her. "I hate to interrupt, but I need to tell you something."

She closed the book. "Go ahead."

"I don't know how, but I think Sean might show up today."

Grace clutched her Bible with both hands. "Thanks for telling me. I hope he does come."

Perhaps she didn't understand. I sighed. "Remember the boy who started all that mess the other night? The one who had us crawling on the floor? That's who I'm talking about."

The bell rang. "That's who he was on Saturday. Today, Sean's just my student."

I let my locks down. All of it. I'm not sure why, as it ended up all over the place, but while the class entered the room, I reached up and let them down. Having Grace in the room made me nervous, I guess, and that made me angry. Why should I be nervous about teaching a proficiency class that I created? I could do this in my sleep.

As always on the first day, too many kids had signed up for the class. The seats went quickly. The aisles filled next. Grace had a powerful presence in the classroom, and already everyone was looking at her, whispering, trying to figure things out. Usually I would have scolded them, but I was trying to figure things out too. I welcomed them instead.

"For the returning students, welcome back. For the new students, welcome to Imani. For those of you without a seat, please move to the back for now until we see if everyone is in the right place. I'm Dr. Mayfield. And this is Ms. Okoye."

A boy in the front row gave Grace a quick nod, winking in her direction.

She didn't even blink. Instead, she motioned for me to continue and walked over to her young admirer and whispered something in his ear. His eyes went big. He sat up in his chair.

"I'm sorry, Miss Okoye. Please don't call my mother."

Someone laughed in the back, but when I mentioned that they could be added to the home-calling list as well, things got quiet again.

Maybe this joint-teaching thing was a good idea after all.

Next, I asked how many people were retaking the proficiency test from last year and sent out the students who weren't.

Six students hoisted their backpacks and gave up their seats.

"Passed that in middle school," a squat girl with glasses said as she headed for the door.

"Good for you," someone spat as the door closed behind her.

"That's a start," Grace said. "Cross your name off the roster as you leave and go to room two-ten." She turned to me. "Right?"

"Right." Somebody had been reading the manual over the holiday. Nice.

I passed out the class roster and a syllabus for the first nine weeks. "If your name is on the list, initial it, so we'll know you're here. If not, add yourself. Any questions?"

A girl with a nest of blue braids raised her hand. "I've got a question. What's the doctor's phone number? His dreads are 'bout to make me faint . . ."

It was my turn not to bat an eye. "Only honor students get my phone number."

"Forget his number. I want to know about the hair," a boy with a tall cap, worthy of a Dr. Seuss book, called out.

The hair. Always the hair. I'd joked at Ohio State that if the way to a man's heart was through his stomach, the entrance to Black America was through the kitchens—the curliest hair on the back of its neck. Dreadlocks were in again, so I always got questions. I pulled another stack of papers out of my briefcase. "How many are here because of my locks? Raise your hands."

Eight hands crept up. I wasn't convinced. "C'mon. We're wasting time."

Six more hands hovered in the air. I passed a page to each of them. "This is my hair handout. It's all I know, which isn't much. The tips went blond on their own." I stared at Grace.

"Yeah, right." The cat in the hat sounded quite disappointed.

"Try lemon juice. And mark through your name on the way out," Grace said in a velvety voice that made the boy smile.

It made me smile too. With the aisles clear now, we settled into our first beats together as teachers, speaking with eyes and hands, making the students laugh and often laughing ourselves. As the bell rang, ending our first ninety-minute block, I felt something in my gut that I hadn't felt in a while . . . the ache for a woman.

This woman.

22

Zeely

Jeremiah looked bad. I hated to think it, wouldn't dare say it, but it was true. I straightened my first-day-of-school suit and looked down at my new, freshly done nails. He was off his game as much as I was on mine.

He towered over me as he whispered good morning. His breath smelled like hot garbage and scrambled eggs, and his clothes looked like they'd been balled up in a pillowcase and run over by a car. The edge on his haircut was overgrown and the bags under his eyes looked big enough to swim in. It was all I could do not to climb a chair and tuck in the tag poking up from the neck of his shirt. I didn't want to embarrass him, not like he was embarrassing me. And yet, he didn't look concerned at all.

Men have the luxury of letting themselves go, of knowing that someone will always want them. Need them. Women are expected to look like airbrushed movie stars, all while giving birth and cooking dinner. Oh, and while working too, because if you're a black woman, looking good isn't enough. You need sixteen degrees, a house, and your own church, school, or other charitable organization. And that was just to get a date.

Jeremiah distributed math pre-tests as though he was dressed in a tuxedo. As he passed me, he gave me his superstar smile, the one that I'd once taken for something more than a good camera angle. Besides his faith, that smile was the only thing about Jeremiah that remained from the man I remembered. In fact, his walk with

Christ seemed to have grown where his hygiene diminished. We had talks about God now that we never could have touched back then. Still, if I had a choice, I would have preferred his former appearance with his newfound spirituality.

The thing was, I didn't have a choice. Not anymore. We'd all made our choices. Now we had to live with them. Though Jeremiah was stingy with the details, his marriage to Carmel had chewed him up and spit out the remains. He looked like I'd felt that night when I saw them together the first time.

Only it wasn't their first time that night.

It was mine.

A boy in the front row raised his hand. "Big Dog? You got a calculator?"

My head jerked toward him, a disheveled pixie stick with matted icicles of hair pointing in every direction. The nerve of these kids. "That's Mr. Terrigan to you."

My partner smiled and gave me a thumbs-up. His touchdown code from college. The other girls always wondered how I knew to start the right cheer.

Except for Carmel. She was always right with me.

Right with him.

The memory ran down my back like ice water, forcing me straight up. Erect.

Jeremiah stood over the boy, smiling at me and then at him. "I have a calculator, son, but today I want to see what your mind—your calculator—can do. Technology is a tool, but you have to dig by hand first, you know what I'm saying?" He curved over the desk like a life-sized question mark.

The boy shrugged and wrote his name on the paper. A few seconds later, he walked to my desk and turned it in. Blank.

Now in my chair, I crossed my legs at the ankles, resting one snakeskin pump behind the other. Wrinkled or not, Jeremiah could still take down anybody with his charms. I had the wounds to prove it.

23

Jerry

Just watching Zeely made me hungry. Hungry for God. Hungry for the youth I tossed away, the promise I gave up to satisfy my lust. Just looking at Zeely, picture perfect in that orange sherbet suit, made me want to break and run. I wouldn't though.

The last time I'd followed my impulses with regard to her—the pounding desire to do something, anything, to be free—I'd run into a brick wall with big hips and brown eyes. A wall that I'd never been able to climb over, not even after I'd been thrown down from its heights. My wife.

Now I was back, wounded and weary, trying to figure out how this all started in the first place. These kids wanted things easy. A calculator. Open-book tests. Life wasn't like that. The things that seemed easy were so much harder than they appeared. Things like the way Zeely looked at me when I'd come to work this morning, the question in her eyes: *What happened to you?* It stung, like an openhanded slap.

What was worse was the question that she never spoke, never even expressed with her eyes: *I waited . . . for this?* Everyone in town had the same question on their faces when I gave them change at 7-Eleven or nodded off in church.

"Isn't that the Terrigan boy? The big one who used to sing in the choir? I thought he played football somewhere. I saw him on TV once, long time ago . . ."

Zeely had waited for me and I'd betrayed her in every way. Even worse, I'd come back in worse shape than I'd left, broke and broken with nothing to offer her. I'd spent all of myself, leveraged my soul, and still I was in the red. There was only one thing I'd kept. Something ticking in the safe-deposit box at Winter's Bank like a time bomb. The one secret I'd kept from my wife, the one vow I'd made to my mother.

This is for Zeely Ann and no one else. No one else.

Mama had left no room for failure, no space for the devil to get a foothold and climb into my life. And yet, I'd failed her anyway. All I had left now was a sparkling reminder of all the promises I'd broken. It wasn't much, but I still had that. I still had something.

Throughout the day and all the days that would come after, I moved through the class with a plastered smile, trying to pretend that I was leaking through my worn-out shoes. Every now and then though, a kid like Sean McKnight would come in and catch my pass, blazing through problems like a terror on his way to the end zone. Every now and then, I'd get the look of approval, acceptance from Zeely, a sharp nod worthy of pom-poms. In those moments, I'd throw back my shoulders: shoulders that had carried Zeely after a victory; shoulders that had hovered over Carmel after a loss.

Zeely had kept her promises to God and he'd kept her, held her up for all this time. After all the pain I'd caused her, she was still here.

Still whole.

Still offended when someone addressed me by one of my many nicknames: Big Dog, Omega, OJ. She'd hated them all. *Don't answer to just anything*, she'd always told me. *Next thing you know you'll be taking anything. Doing anything.* She'd been so adamant about it that I sometimes thought she was talking to herself too. She wasn't though. Didn't need to. The only label anyone had ever given Zeely that she didn't choose was her mother's.

And mine.

Mrs. Zeely Ann Terr-i-gan.

My little sisters used to sing it to tease me. I'd hated it then. I mourned it now. My hand eased across the chalkboard, scribbling down the order of operations:

"Please Excuse My Dear Aunt Sally. Parentheses, Exponents, Multiplication and Division from left to right, Addition and Subtraction from left to right . . ."

The words kept coming, my hand kept writing. My mind stood still, stuck on the way Zeely's spine had snapped straight when I'd given her a thumbs-up this morning. The last time I'd seen her stiffen like that was in a run-down church in Xenia decked out with Christmas lights in June.

My wedding.

24

Grace

Daddy won't say it, but he knows. I hear Mom crying behind the door, but she's not talking to me at all. God talks to me, though. I just don't tell anyone.

Diana Dixon

It was too late to bury it, too late to run. Each entry in my old notebook brought me closer to the girl waiting quietly, patiently for me to reclaim her. The girl that had cost me so much already. Every day at Imani, I saw other girls like me; girls with secrets.

And then of course there was Brian. There was no point calling him Doctor anything now. Just as it had been so long ago when I danced and he drummed, we flew together in the classroom too, finishing each other's sentences, quoting each other's favorite poems. It was too late to be afraid of him, so I was starting to be annoyed instead. The few talks we'd had about religion let me know where he stood.

Off limits.

The Bible said God didn't tempt anybody, but if this wasn't a temptation, it must have been a trial. Each morning I marked off another school day on my calendar. The last day of school would be my last day in Testimony. That much, I knew for sure.

In the meantime, there was our class.

Brian came early most days now, wrote down a word on the board for the class to contemplate quietly while I took roll. The proficiency track divided its time evenly between our class and Zeely's, with the electives required for graduation filling in the rest of their days. Today's word made me wish I'd taken my prayer walk this morning. He was planning to go deep. As if to dispel my doubts, he walked back to the board and underlined the word:

Griot.

"Anybody know what that means?"

"A storyteller." The boy who answered had started out in the back of the class, but moved a little closer to the front every day, usually on my end of the row.

Brian gave him an approving smile. "Right. In West African culture, where most African-Americans originate from, the *gree-oh*, not *gree-ot*, was the storyteller of the village." He tapped the board. "Each time we meet, I will choose a griot to recount the previous class material. You can present it any way you choose—rap, poetry, story, whatever. All I require is an effort and the correct information. And brevity of course. If you don't know what that means, check your vocabulary list."

Two girls continued recounting a fight they'd seen the day before after school as though Brian wasn't even speaking. Before I could correct them, he gave them a sideways glance.

"The assignment will be a tall order for some of you, especially when you won't stop talking long enough to hear it."

"How many points for the griot thing?" Jodi, a stern brunette who took furious and copious notes every time Brian spoke, held her pen ready to take down his answer.

Brian smiled. "The griot *thing* is one test grade. So make it good. Review your syllabus when you get home. It's all in there. You don't have to write this down."

Everyone else dropped their pencils. Jodi eyed Brian suspiciously and scribbled on. It was my turn to smile then. The girl had her challenges—her past academic record and a two-month-old baby among them—but she'd go far. I did wonder what, if anything, had happened to keep her from trusting anyone's words. I didn't want to think the worst, but one thing my life had taught me was to listen and watch. My hunches often proved true.

Except about Brian.

When he'd twirled me around in that parking lot my first night back, I'd felt violated and humiliated all at once. I knew him well enough now to know how big a deal that was, that and everything that had come after it. That evening, he'd held my hand like we'd been long-lost lovers, but he kept his distance from me these days. Now and then our hands reached for an eraser at the same time or one of his locks wandered over his shoulder and tickled my cheek. If it bothered Brian at all, he never let on. I hoped my calm façade came off as well as his. I doubted it.

Brian nodded to me for my part of the lecture.

"Another part of the class is the Daily Challenge. Every day I'll ask several questions related to art, music, history, or culture. If anyone can answer all of them for a week, which has never happened in my other classes, you'll get five dollars—"

The door slammed behind me. A boy with a huge afro covering his eyes slipped into an empty desk, all hair and squeaky clean sneakers. Sean McKnight. He leaned over his seat and asked the girl next to him if she'd brought a comb. I'd taught middle school enough years to know that when I saw Sean after lunch he'd have a fresh set of cornrows. From the look on Brian's face, though, the boy might not live long enough to get them in.

I sent a cautious look my partner's way. The look, brief but powerful, smoothed his creased forehead.

"Take it easy," I mouthed before going on, but it was too late. Brian was already headed for Sean's seat.

"What's the matter, Mr. McKnight, couldn't outrun the police this morning?"

The Honeys, a cluster of pretty but unmotivated girls in the center of the room, burst into laughter.

Sean slid down into his desk. "Whatever, Doc. Whatever."

My eyes locked with Brian's, and in that moment I saw why he'd been sent to anger management. I also saw what it was in Sean that made Brian so crazy.

Himself.

And he was trying to protect me from the both of them.

"Christians," Brian had said when I hadn't been upset about Sean being in our class. "Always the first to judge, the last to arrive at the fire. I know you think you know these kids, know this school, but it isn't as simple as you think. I wonder what you'll think about Sean when he snaps in here and starts shooting somebody. I hope we'll both live to tell our sides of the story."

"All right, everyone. Settle down. Let's do our first daily challenge. An easy one. I'll even pay." I crossed my arms.

Jodi's desk scraped closer.

"What African nation claims the Blight of Benin, where thousands of slave ships received their prisoners?"

Silence buzzed in our ears. "This country also has the largest population in Africa."

I wasn't surprised by this response. I'd told Brian my thoughts about starting with an African question. Even honors kids rarely knew the answers. In most schools, the most Africa they saw was the edge of Egypt on a map of the Middle East. I guess I thought that since some of them had taken Brian's class before, they might have known something. At least it had gotten the attention off of Sean. Best to end it quickly. "Okay, you guys are killing me with the quiet here. Dr. Mayfield? Would you like to answer and get this over with?"

Brian chuckled and the kids oohed and aahed as though I'd challenged him to a rumble. I realized too late my folly, especially when he took the rubber band off his wrist and put up his hair. It killed me when he did that.

And he knew it.

From the smile on Sean's face, it was no secret to anyone else either.

"Nigeria," Brian said softly. "That's where your last name is from, right? Have you been there? Care to tell us about it?"

"No and no." I tried to strain the edge out of my voice, but wasn't successful. Probably used to such exchanges at home, the kids started to raise their hands. Brian rattled off answers to a few questions about Africa and then passed out timed writing prompts. I faded behind my desk. I wished I could get out of the room.

When the bell rang, no one wasted time heading for the door. They'd packed up their things long before.

"Great job, everyone. See you tomorrow," Brian called out too late for anyone to hear.

Sean, the last student to leave, looked back at us and shook his head.

"They got it bad," he whispered to the girl walking behind him, who was already combing out the ends of his hair.

If only you knew how bad, I thought as the lemon juice and tea tree oil Brian used on his locks registered with my nose. He rarely got close enough for me to smell it except when I was trying to pry him away from lingering too long at Sean's desk. Now he was too close.

I looked into the hall where Sean had disappeared. I wished I was leaving too.

It was our planning period, but if I got away quickly I could still meet Zeely down the hall for what remained of breakfast in the cafeteria. It should have been easy to make an excuse and get away. Joyce had left a note for me to see her after this class, while the kids were in art with Lottie. It should have been easy to go, but we hadn't been this close since we didn't have a choice. Somehow, I found my resolve, rediscovered my legs.

"Some class today, huh? I'm going to run downstairs and get some food. I was dragging a little this morning and didn't eat. And Joyce, I have to meet with her. If you need me, just send a student for me—"

He took off his glasses and licked his lips. Not his whole mouth. Just the corners. He wasn't going to make this easy.

"No problem. You go on ahead. I just wanted to collect my payment."

For a moment, I was confused. "For the Daily Challenge?"

He nodded. Slowly.

"Okay, but my purse is locked in the desk and—hold on, I'll get it."

Brian shook his head. "I don't want your money."

I swallowed hard. "I don't understand."

He licked his lips again, all over this time. "I think you do."

This wasn't feeling fun anymore. This had happened before on other jobs, with other men. Once I'd almost had to press charges, but the guy was fired. Brian and I had something between us, but that's just where it belonged—between us. He was taking this too far. As I took a step back, he looked stricken.

"What's wrong? Are you mad? I'm sorry. I was just kidding. What I really wanted was to know why you got so mad when I asked about your name. About Nigeria. Ibo tribe, right? I recognize the name. And there's that football player . . . I was just curious. Didn't mean to hit a nerve. Can we talk about it later?"

"I'd rather not," I said, not sticking around to hear more.

"Wait. Grace!"

I didn't wait. I couldn't. For some reason I couldn't explain, I did pause just long enough to say one more thing. "Okoye was my married name and not the football player. A physics professor. He's dead. I hope that's enough information for you."

"Oh, Grace. I'm so—"

My feet carried me away quickly so I wouldn't have to hear the rest. I appreciated people's sincerity, their condolences still made me sick. He'd never known Peter. He had nothing to be sorry for.

Except me.

And I'd had enough pity to last a lifetime. Lost in a pack of students headed outside for PE, I fought all my fears, all Mal's predictions. Last month's open door now seemed like a deep pit, poised and waiting to swallow me whole. I was out of breath by the time I made it to the cafeteria, and while I'd left Brian behind, he was still with me, still invading my private, precious space. Space I was still trying to guard when I ran into Zeely, rushing from the other direction.

"Y'all big people are going to be the death of me. Watch where you're going, girl. You 'bout knocked off my wig. I tried to call you to pray this morning, but you didn't answer and I didn't see you out walking. I got your text. What's up?"

"I'm going through some things." More like someone, but I was fresh out of explanations. Like the slaves who'd arrived at the downtown square with their testimony price, I just wanted to go in peace. A little quiet wouldn't hurt either.

Not that Zeely was about to let me have any of that. She pulled me toward the trays, waving for the lunch lady to wait for us before throwing out what remained of the food. "I know we haven't been able to talk much since those kids cut the fool at orientation. If you'd rode with me, you wouldn't have been there for the madness, but that's beside the point . . . Don't let it worry you. This school isn't like those little private academies you taught at before, but it matters, you know? It counts for something. For a lot of these kids, we're their last stop. So hang on. It'll get better. They settle down in the second nine weeks. The spring is murder, but we'll cross that bridge when we get there."

I shook my head while Zeely paid for our meals. She didn't bother to ask if I had any money. My obvious distress must have given me away. "It's not the kids." True enough, what had happened in this cafeteria my first day in town still pulled at my mind sometimes, but right now it was the man in that class who had me in a whirl.

The lunch lady patted my hand as we passed by. I stopped to return her smile. I remembered her now and not just from the orientation. She'd been the pianist at Mount Olive when we were kids. Her makeup made my mother boo and hiss behind her hymnal every Sunday.

I took the last fruit bowl and followed Zeely to the pancakes, then the sausage and the eggs . . .

My friend rested easily on one of the orange disc seats connected to the lunch tables, which looked much bigger without fifty kids jammed around it. She carved her pancakes kid style while I eased onto the seat, hoping it wouldn't give out under me. Finally comfortable, I speared a piece of pineapple and sipped its juice.

"So, was he looking that good this morning?"

I almost choked.

"What?"

Zeely swirled her fork in syrup. "If it's not the kids, it's him. We don't have much time, so let's just be real about the thing. What'd he wear today?"

There was nothing to do but laugh. And tell. "Remember those African suits Peter used to wear? He had on one of those. Cornflower blue. Remember that crayon?"

She sipped her milk and nodded in agreement. "Brian isn't my favorite person, but the man can wear a suit. But you didn't almost knock me down because he's fine. That's old news. What's the drama?"

What was this, the Spanish Inquisition? My defenses started to rise. "I don't think Dr. Mayfield is the issue. The catalyst perhaps, but not the issue. For some reason being around him makes me—"

"He makes you want a man. Just admit it." Zeely smiled before biting into a sausage link.

She was having way too much fun with this, not to mention being wrong. I'd chosen my singleness this time, the moment I'd told Mal my story. Brian had a lot going for him, but he was just something else for me to pray over, walk through. Nothing that would last. "No offense, Zee, but I was married long enough to remember that it isn't as easy as it looks. I don't know how Mal talked me into almost marrying him, but that whole mess has liberated me from the pursuit of men: praying for them, waiting for them to call, trying to figure out what they're thinking. I just don't have that kind of time."

As the words left my mouth, I knew I'd said too much, traveled too far into my friend's private space.

Zeely pushed away her plate after tasting everything. "I'm not offended, *Diana*. Sure, I want a husband. Kids. I'll admit it. But I'm still here: working, worshiping, being a good thing. If nobody chooses to find me, it's his loss, 'cause I'm as good as it gets." She wiped her mouth.

I closed mine. She'd cast a blow of her own with the way she spat my real name, reminding me that husband or no, I wasn't any different from her. And I wasn't. We both had the same husband now: God himself.

She dotted her lips with a napkin and applied a fresh coat of lipstick. Flawless, even without a brush. "You can deny it all you want, but Brian woke you from the dead. Acknowledge it or you're setting yourself up for the fall."

Falls? What would she know about them? Zeely's life had been a steady stream of success after success. Her father had never looked at her as though she were a stranger. She'd never had to make sure everything was perfect before sneaking off to church. Man or no man, she still had her virtue and the respect of everyone in town. I only garnered their pity, even from Brian. I checked the clock, wondering if Joyce was in her office. "After all those years with a man who wouldn't step foot in a church, and almost two years wasted on a man who wouldn't step outside one, I think I'd rather keep things just like they are."

Zeely stood, inspecting her reflection in her compact like some of the girls in my class. "You know I'm not paying you any mind, right? Get mad at me all you want, but WE both know that just when you think you've got something figured out, the Lord will move in another direction. If you didn't know that, you wouldn't be here." She turned and patted the back of my skirt like a football player after a huddle. "Now go fix yourself up and get back to class. You know your man is back there waiting on you—"

"Will you hush?" I flicked Zeely's shoulder, looking around to see if anyone was listening. Miss Thelma had leaned over so far that she could have flossed my teeth. One thing about schools, gossip travels like fire. I'd been burned by enough of it. "I have a meeting with Joyce, if you must know, and no one is waiting for me. Trust me."

"I'm just teasing you. Believe me, I'm not worried about Brian pushing up on you. He can hardly handle a staff meeting, much less a relationship."

"Ain't that the truth." It was Miss Thelma, heading past us to the kitchen. Was there anywhere in this town where someone wasn't watching? Listening? Probably not.

With a sigh, I waved goodbye and turned in the opposite direction of Zeely's laughter. A few feet from Joyce's office, I pulled her note from my pocket and threw up a feeble, final prayer:

Please, Lord. Have mercy.

Come to the office on your break. Joyce's note had said, Nothing more. I paused at the open door, marked Intensive Care, trying to imagine what she might want to talk to me about. Was it something about Brian? Had he asked for me to be fired? Transferred? The note had been in my box before school started, but still . . .

"Are you going to stand out there all morning?"

So much for my hallway reflections. "No, ma'am." She had me. Nothing left to do but go on in.

The office, which looked smaller from the hall, bustled with books from floor to ceiling. There were pictures too, plastered on two bulletin boards like the display in an obstetrician's office, all the children she'd helped to give birth to themselves. I knew if I looked hard enough I could probably find the yellowed picture I'd tossed into the box with the others at practice one day. I knew, so I didn't look. For now, it was enough just getting through that notebook from my past.

A church scene of black figurines lined the edge of a cramped, but organized desk and overflowed onto the bookshelves behind her. Joyce sat in a winged-back office chair, leaning over her Bible. I knew from the things she'd said over the loudspeaker this week that she was in Colossians.

"Chapter three. Guidelines for holy living." She answered my unspoken question and set the Bible aside. "Sit down."

I perched on the edge of the couch across from her. When talking to Joyce, it was best not to be too relaxed.

She got right to the point. "I need a favor from you."

"Oh?" I crossed my arms. This was how I'd ended up back in Testimony in the first place—Joyce's need. I wasn't sure that I had any more to offer. Not just yet.

"For some time, I've been praying about Ngozi."

"The dance troupe?" I pushed back on the sofa now, needed its support behind me.

"Yes. I'd like to see it going again. These kids need the arts more than ever. The city is cutting things left and right."

I fumbled with the belt to my sweater. "Do you want me to talk to Zeely about it? Help you recruit someone?"

She gave me an admonishing look. "No. I want you to teach it."

The room spun. "Me? I can't. I'm out of shape. I'm—"

"You're here. Sometimes that's all God needs. All I need. Clean and available. Don't look at me like that, like you can't do it. We both know you can. You pray on it and get back to me."

Joyce seemed sincere about my prayerful consideration, but her tone sounded final.

I stood and extended my hand, trying to sound like the grown woman I was. "Okay. I'll think about it, but why not Zee? She's already teaching dance—"

Joyce clutched my hand. She squeezed. "The gifts and callings of God are without repentance. You are the best dancer I've ever met. Better than Zeely. Better than me. I wish I could have given you more, loved you longer, but I tried, didn't I?"

I nodded, trying not to cry.

"Well, all right then. I know this isn't comfortable for you. For Zeely, either. But to whom much is given, much is required. Ask me how I know. My flame is fading. It's time to give it to somebody else. These people need a trailblazer, a water-walker. I think that's you."

By the time she let go of my hand, I was struggling to breathe. While I'd thought reading that notebook was breaking me down, this was a hundred times worse. Here, in the irises of Joyce's eyes, I'd seen it all: my admittance to the psych ward on the day Joyce had arranged a special audition with the junior branch of the Dayton Contemporary Dance Company. She had believed in me then and I'd crumbled. My head told me that I was stronger now, but my heart wasn't so sure. Something told me that I'd have to find out the hard way.

Slipping back into her role as my employer, Joyce handed me a tissue and did a time check of her own. "Wipe your face, baby. It'll be all right. Sometimes we have to reopen wounds to clean out the infection. It hurts, but it's the only way to heal it for good."

For good? I wondered. Every time I thought it was done, over, somebody came and ripped off my scabs, usually the woman who I was talking to now. This was one cup that I didn't look forward to drinking from. I prayed that God wouldn't make me have to.

I picked up one of the collectibles on the desk, a chunky little angel with two afro puffs. I held her for a moment before putting her back, wondering if that's what we'd become to Joyce, toys acting out a scene. "I'll pray about it."

"That's all that I ask."

Ngozi. Blessed. I sighed. My last year in the dance group had been anything but blessed. "I'd better get back to class."

Joyce reached for my hand one last time. "Yes, but before you go, I need to tell you something, ask you for one last favor."

I stood quietly and listened to it all. I don't remember when I started crying, but once I did, I thought I'd never stop.

25

Brian

I hadn't meant to hurt Grace, but I'd managed to do a pretty thorough job. Prayer, the thing I still related to best from my church days, came to mind. It probably didn't mean the same thing to me now as it had meant then. Today seemed a prayer in itself, each breath a plea. And still I'd missed it. Joyce was probably downstairs praying for heaven and earth to slap together, as Reverend Wilkins used to say.

I sure hoped so.

With Joyce and my students on my mind, I went into my office and opened a drawer that always stayed locked, retrieved an envelope, flimsy from much handling. Inside was a class roster with four names added to a typewritten list in Joyce's flowing script: Zeely Wilkins, Jerry Terrigan, Brian Mayfield, and Ronald Jenkins. On the next page was a memo, one that I sometimes read to my classes for inspiration. Today, I needed it just for me.

Ms. Rogers,

For reasons determined by the counseling department, the following students have been identified as at-risk for re-matriculation. You will be responsible for training them for basic life skills until the special education department is fully developed. We apologize for the change in your assignment.

The Administration,
Paul Lawrence Dunbar High School

In a few places, round spots blurred the words, tearstains that had poured from Joyce's face as she read the note to us. Some people had been scared by her anger, her passion. Not me. I'd inhaled it, understood it. Not for the first time, someone had declared my failure, gathered my life into columns, black-and-white bubbles on testing forms.

I'd wondered, along with the rest of the class, if she was for real, if she really cared. Later in the year, when she invited the principal to our class to hear our Shakespeare recitation and volley of Latin verbs, I felt ashamed for having doubted her.

I was even more ashamed of that principal. It still hurt to remember how he'd waved us off in the middle of our Whitman and Hughes, frowning at Joyce as though she'd made a terrible mistake.

"Don't get their hopes up so. It'll just make things harder. Give them some crayons. Do this right and next year you'll get first pick of the students. Cream of the crop."

We'd all been written off before, but we'd never been there to hear it. Years later, in graduate school, I'd met up with that man again, this time as his student in Cross Cultural Education Techniques. His first line of the semester had changed my life: "Africa is lost forever." I'd left the room determined to prove him as wrong as Joyce had with each of us. After that, the principal was never invited back. If more memos ever came about us, we never knew. After that, we became a family.

When Joyce shut the door after that man, the class was silent. She told us to take off our shoes, to come to the center of the room. Said that since that man told us what he thought of us, it was only fair for her to tell us what God thought about us too. And so she did, in a sermon more eloquent than any preacher I've ever heard. She lined us up and blessed us, dared us. In that moment, Imani was born, seeded through one woman's faith, birthing doctors, lawyers, teachers, and preachers.

She gave us all notebooks and told us to carry them wherever we went. "You are a book, a story that people will read in everything you do and say. Your words and your actions count now. Later, you will see how all your stories come together into one story—our story, The Imani Chronicles. Each of you, every student in my dance class, every person I have taught, is part of our tale. I can't wait to see how it all ends."

We didn't know it then, but Joyce really did want to see where we'd all ended up, and whenever she could, she did find out and send an invitation to become an Imani teacher. No one could teach the system like those who had learned under it, she said. Not even her. I wasn't so sure about that.

Over the years she taught us, we were graded daily for having our notebooks, and when one had been filled, we started another just like it.

"Each day write down something. If nothing comes to mind, copy down a good poem or a bit of the Bible. Record your worst days with your best words. Later, when it hurts less and means more, you'll be glad that you did. When I'm old and have my own school, I'll find you and ask you to come and teach my children how to be a story, a dance, a song . . ."

Few of Joyce's pupils ever returned when she sent them the letter, gave them the call. I wasn't even sure how I'd ended up here myself. Was I really doing for these kids what Joyce had done for me? Before now, I'd thought so, but the more time I spent with Grace, the more I felt like I was still the one in need of rescue.

Behold, I do a new thing.

Ach. I was going to need an antacid soon to keep back the tide rising in my belly, the rumble that once led me into a cold, swift river to be baptized. Determined not to give in to the feeling, I scanned my shelf for Nietzsche or some other infectious, intelligent fool. Before I found the right book, my lips betrayed me, my heart tore in two.

"God, I doubt I'm on your list of people to call back, but this is not really for me. It's for Grace. For all of them. Help me with this boy, Sean. Help me to see in him what Joyce once saw in me."

When I opened my eyes, Grace was standing in front of me.

And she was crying.

She said they were happy tears, but I wasn't so sure. Joyce had asked her to start Ngozi up again. That surprised me, but it shouldn't have. Joyce was always up to something. I hoped that Zeely would be okay with it if Grace decided to take it on.

Grace seemed worried too. "Do you think she'll be upset?"

We only had a few minutes before students filled the room between us, and I'd played enough games with her for one day. "What do you think?"

"I know. What should I do?" Her beautiful eyes went shut.

The bell rang in time to save me. Six months ago, I would have spouted instant wisdom, told her about energy and power. Today, I had nothing. As we moved through the next class block—vocabulary, spelling, reading comprehension—I saw that Joyce's request had shocked Grace more than my brashness this morning. I hoped she hadn't mentioned it in her meeting, but I couldn't blame her if she had. I was out of line. Maybe I'd finally come up against something that was really beyond my capacity.

Diana Grace Dixon Okoye.

As quickly as I thought it, I'd mentally added Mayfield at the end.

I was cracking up for sure.

When the period went by without Joyce buzzing in, I knew that either my boss was going to leave me to figure this out on my own or Grace hadn't said anything. Either way, I was going to have to set up some fences around myself. Boundaries. I started with righting her greeting.

"Thank you, Mrs. Okoye," I said, when she passed me a set of folders.

She didn't look amused. I couldn't win for losing.

A teen suitor on the second row was quick to raise his hand. "So she's married?"

Grace interrupted when I tried to tell him it was none of his business. "I'm not married, honey. Not anymore. My husband died seven years ago."

These kids were so nosy. I cleared my throat. "Not that it's anyone's business."

For the first time since first block, Grace smiled. It was beautiful, but a little too expensive for my emotional budget. "Evidently it is important. You seemed quite concerned about it earlier," she said on the way to her desk.

Touché.

The same boy—Smith I called him since I was still learning names and it was all he ever put on his papers—spoke again, this time not bothering to raise his hand. "Isn't your wife dead too, Doc? Seems like I heard that somewhere."

This kid was going to join Sean on my Most Wanted list if he wasn't careful. "Again, not that it's anyone's business, but yes, I lost my wife too." Before the boy could respond, I gave a pop quiz and settled in at my desk, putting grades into the computer.

When the bell rang, I didn't move, even though it was time to eat. I wasn't hungry. Not for school lunch anyway.

"So how long has she been gone?"

I kept typing. "Eight years," I said. "Cervical cancer." That was probably the next question anyway.

Grace took a deep breath. "Cancer is rough. My aunt died last year and my mother had a total mastectomy awhile back. If you ever need to talk—"

Again with the talking. "I won't. Not about that. I'm sorry about your mom."

163

Grace narrowed her eyes at me, told me not to be sorry. They were praying, she said, hoping that God would sustain her mother's miracle, keep her in remission.

I forced myself not to laugh. It would have been cruel. "Good luck with that. Miracles can be hard to come by." Cervical cancer was supposed to be treatable, rarely fatal. My wife was definitely rare.

Grace went silent then, raked a hand through her twists.

Best to change the subject. "I want to apologize for how I reacted when I first heard you'd be in here. As usual, Dr. Rogers was right. You've really been a big help and the kids seem to love you. I'm a little more prickly, I guess."

That earned me another smile. This time it was a lot cheaper.

"I'm really enjoying it too. I'm still catching up to speed on the scope and sequence of this track, the big picture of what you're trying to do. I'm used to more of a unit approach. I'll have to come in a little earlier one day and look everything over. Maybe we could have a little in-service on early release day?"

"No need to wait until then. Let's have dinner. Tonight."

26

Grace

"Stayed after with your boyfriend?"

I put my hands on my hips and shook my head at my neighbor. Zeely was on her knees, putting in seeds before the first frost. I should have been doing the same. I'd hardly touched my yard since coming here. I slid my shades back into my hair, squinting past the afternoon sun. "That isn't funny, you know."

"It is funny. Trust me. Go and take a nap, you look tired. Email me when you wake up. I'm expecting a call from my brother and he acts a fool if I click over to the other line."

"Right." I didn't ask which brother she was expecting a call from. Zeely had so many brothers I could never keep up. I noticed that someone had weeded my front plot. Zeely had urged me to pay the maintenance fee even though I hadn't thought at the time I'd need it, but I was thankful for it now.

"When school is in, things get crazy," she'd said. I'd had no idea how true her statement would turn out to be. I thought I'd be able to do anything I'd always done before while teaching, but this year was something totally different. So was the conversation Zeely and I needed to have.

"I need to talk to you about something."

Zeely cut off the flow from her hose. "Go ahead. I've got a minute."

"Joyce wants to start Ngozi again."

165

"Really?" My friend's face brightened, then sobered. "What's she going to do, teach from a chair? She can hardly bend over."

"She has another teacher in mind."

She turned away from me, pulled her straw hat down over her eyes. "You should try for it, Grace. Joyce always loved your style."

I took a deep breath, wishing she'd turn around so that I could see her face. "You think so? She asked me."

Zeely bent down to turn the water back on. "You'll do a great job."

"I'm not going to do it."

The flow stopped again. "Why not?"

"You were the one who traveled with the dance company. I never made it."

Zeely dropped the hose, one hand on her hip. "Look, Di, if you hadn't missed the audition, you would have made it instead of me. We both know it."

"Maybe. I still don't think I'll do it." I'd actually been stressed out by the idea when Joyce first proposed it, but as the day wore on it had grown on me. It hadn't grown taller than my friendship with Zeely, though. It wasn't a big deal.

She wound her hose around an attachment on the side of her condo. "You are always making excuses, girl. People up here killing themselves to use the little bit they have while you going on about how you don't think you can do it."

This is what I can't do, have an argument. Not today. "I'll email you later." I left the yard, but looked back over my shoulder.

"Hit me back in the morning if you don't get on tonight. I know you probably have papers to grade the way the kids were complaining today about the writing you had them doing." Her voice lightened like she hadn't just been letting me have it.

I played along. "You know how that goes."

"I do. In a few weeks, you'll be hearing the same things about their math and science assignments."

166

I couldn't get inside fast enough. Sometimes talking to Zeely made me tired. All the circling 'round a thing again and again. If only she would come out and say that it bothered her that Joyce had asked me to teach the class, we could just deal with the thing in the open. Not that I could judge anybody for hiding things.

A vase of the Indian Blankets I'd transplanted from my house brightened my kitchen. From where I stood, I could see the trail of discarded outfits and unused walking clothes I'd left behind this morning.

Clothes piled on each arm, I climbed the stairs, bypassing the computer. They didn't call it the Web for nothing. A few emails and I'd look up and it'd be time to meet Brian for dinner. After the way Zeely had reacted about Ngozi, I hadn't bothered to bring up Brian's dinner invitation. I knew what she'd say already. Don't go.

Having one mother was enough, even if we didn't talk often. Zeely would have to settle for just being my friend. I took a shower upstairs in the bigger bathroom even though I slept on the first floor. It was a strange arrangement, but any woman who'd ever tried to dry off in a tiny bathroom and ended up sweatier than she started would understand my logistics.

Refreshed by the shower, I surveyed my twists, which had been threatening to unravel since the day after I'd had them done. The hairdressers in Testimony were a little sketchy on natural hair care, but I'd keep trying.

Despite my attempts to avoid the computer downstairs, Mal was determined to reach me and started messaging me on my phone just as I finished shaking my hair like crazy and creating a new, funky style.

BrownBibleMan: Where have you been?

First my mama outside, now my daddy on the phone. We'd agreed not to act like a couple anymore, but sometimes Mal forgot himself.

167

SweetSavour: Hello to u 2. Been busy with school. Gettin ready for meeting with co-teacher.

BrownBibleMan: Meeting? 2night? I told u not to do that charter school. 2 much work.

SweetSavour: The guy is a trip but he knows his stuff.

BrownBibleMan: Guy? That's a date! Did u tell him about me?

SweetSavour: Let's not do this, OK? Talk to you l8r.

I put down the phone before he could reply. Maybe Brian was wrong for asking me to dinner, but at least he'd asked. Malachi had been content with private affections. While married, I'd declared my love to Peter audibly and often. So much that I think he stopped hearing it after a while. Or maybe it was all the preaching I did in between that drowned it out.

At the time, I'd just wanted so badly for Peter to know the comfort of being held in Christ's hands, hidden under God's wings. Now I sometimes wondered how he'd accepted my radical changes without complaint. He hadn't embraced my beliefs, but eventually he came to respect them.

I didn't want to make the same mistake with Brian. A few sprays of fresh aloe vera on my hair plus coral lipstick and brown mascara and I was headed for the door. On my way out, I paused at the mirror, shocked and pleased with what I saw.

I need to do this craziness every day.

When the phone rang, I blew out a breath and prepared a firm, short speech to keep Mal from blowing up my phone for the rest of the evening.

"Look, I told you—"

"Mrs. Okoye?" The voice was playful and even smoother on the phone than in person.

"Brian?"

He laughed. "It's me."

How did he get this number? I tucked my purse under one arm and grabbed a notebook and pen. I don't know what shocked me more, the wonder of his voice or that he had my cell number. Life was scary these days. I checked the clock on the microwave. Six thirty. "Did I get the time mixed up? I thought we said seven. I'm heading out now."

"You're not late. I just thought I'd pick you up."

I glanced around, thankful I'd picked up a little, but unsure about having Brian anywhere near my house, let alone inviting him inside. I was a Christian, not a saint. "Not to be mean or anything, but I'm freaked out enough that you called on my cell. I'm not so sure about you coming to my house. Where are you? I'll ask Zeely for the directions."

Jazz started up outside. Billie Holiday.

"No need. I'm in your driveway."

27

Brian

Grace looked like she didn't know whether to slap me or thank me. I made a mental note not to show up at her house unannounced again. She paused to check out the car before sliding in. I couldn't blame her. I'd been shocked myself when I picked it up. Sean's father had restored the Jag to its original color—who knew?—electric blue. Purple if the sun hit it right.

Not that I knew how the sun was hitting the car right now. I was too busy looking at Grace. This woman had more personas than the law allowed. I'd seen her soft and beautiful look, her intellectual administrative gear, but this was something else altogether.

This was Diana.

For the first time I knew what Ron meant all those years ago when he said he couldn't stop staring at Zeely in the choirstand. Perfect. "You look—I mean, you always look nice, but you look—"

"Hush. Let's go." She slid across the buttery leather and fastened herself in.

I got in too, with a familiar Psalm pressing against my mind. *The Lord is my Shepherd. I shall not want.*

"So how'd you find my place? My number? Did I list it in the faculty directory?"

"I got your number from there. Your place? Google."

"That's terrifying."

"Isn't it?"

"Don't do it again. Please."

"I won't."

We went along like that for miles, all our words hovering in a cloud of the peachy-vanilla-smelling something she'd generously applied. It was all I could do not to reach out and run my fingers through her hair, all loose now and flowing free around her face. Maybe I could use a few fire-and-brimstone sermons after all. My personal discipline was seriously slipping.

"I probably shouldn't be here."

True. "With me?"

"With anybody."

I liked that answer for my own selfish reasons, but I didn't understand it. "What's wrong? Are you some kind of nun?"

She shook her head at first, then cracked up laughing. "Sort of. I don't know. I just don't usually get this personal with people I work with. Or any people really. Male people. Men."

"So you can go out with women?"

"Right. Well, no, not like that. Oh. This sounds bad. Forget it. Where are we going?"

It didn't sound bad. I loved to hear her ramble. It reminded me that she was human. Sometimes she seemed too controlled. "I think you'll like it. It's called the Whole Nine. Not many people know about it, but the few who do are faithful."

"Are you faithful?" Her words hit me hard, like a kick between the eyes.

"To the restaurant?" I drove a little faster.

"To anything."

"I'd like to think so. The school, I guess. My wife when she was alive."

"That's something."

Was it? "I suppose."

The honeymoon was over, the romance officially sucked from the car. I didn't want to talk to this woman any more than I had to. I was the one who usually unnerved people. It didn't feel so good on the receiving end. She was such a wife, even though she didn't have a husband. I was confused about that part. Someone would have surely tried to pin her down in seven years. I was a man and I'd been proposed to more times in my mind than I'd like to admit. I'd spent less than a month working with her, and already I'd lost my mind. I turned onto the main road leading out of town.

"So how is it you're not married? I know I'm unprofessional and you don't have to answer, but I really am curious. Long-distance relationship? Evil boyfriend?"

She turned to the window. "Wishy-washy fiancé. Broken engagement."

"I'd call the guy a fool, but I guess his stupidity is my gain."

"You think so?"

I know so. "Don't go getting mad now. I'm just talking."

"Well, stop."

"Okay."

We were on the highway now, headed down near the Dayton Mall. The trip seemed a lot longer than the last time I'd taken it alone, and I could tell she was getting worried.

"We really are going to a restaurant. I promise. I should have picked somewhere closer, but we'll be there soon."

"I hope so. I don't want to keep you out late. It's a school night."

She made me lose enough sleep as it was. "I'll get you back."

When we were getting close, I offered to phone in our order. As she agreed, the sun dipped low. Evening sifted through her hair.

I put both my hands on the wheel.

When we stopped at the next light, a man with a bow tie and a stack of newspapers tapped on Grace's window.

She jumped, surprised.

"It's nothing. Just roll the window down and take one. He'll move on. Just brothers trying to be positive. If he pulls out a bean pie, I might have to run the light." I was kidding, but she looked scared enough. "I wouldn't really. You know that."

She didn't know that and probably wished I'd stop saying it. Despite my feeling like we'd always known each other, she didn't know me at all. Not really.

Grace was trying to say something, but I'd already let down her window from my side.

"Good afternoon, sister," the man said. He reached across Grace to slap my hand. "Brother. Take a paper today?"

She wasted no time answering. "No thank you."

I shook my head. My dinner was going to be cold. Why'd she have to go and make things hard?

The man gave me a funny look and adjusted his bow tie. His words, however, were all directed at Grace. "Surely a beautiful sister like you wants to support her people."

I fumbled with my wallet, certain the light would change any minute.

"I do try to support our people in any way I can. Thank you for all the ways that you do the same. I'm a Christian though. I can't take that paper." Her voice rose a little. Someone blew their horn behind us. The light had changed and I hadn't even noticed.

When I tried to pull forward, the guy hung on to the window. "Let go, bruh. I'm going to pull over right there." The restaurant was within sight, but I had to kill this first.

He let go of the window, but started in on Grace as soon as I pulled over. "What kind of church do you go to, sister? Some of our greatest supporters are Christians. Will you tell her, brother?" He pushed the paper inside.

I'd planned to buy one anyway, but without all this fuss. "Look, man. We're headed to dinner. I'll take a paper, but please, leave the lady alone. Respect her wishes, okay?"

The guy looked disgusted with me, but he went ahead and took my money.

As he let go of the car a final time, he shook his head at both of us. "The black man is god anyway. Everybody knows that."

173

Why did he have to go *there*? I thought Grace was going to fly out of that car and snatch him up the way she stuck her head out the window.

"Jesus Christ is my God. I pray that he blesses you with some understanding," she yelled behind him.

He walked away, still shaking his head. I tossed the newspaper in the backseat and gripped the wheel, this time to restrain my anger instead of my passion. I was ticked with both of them. We eased into our parking space in silence. I cut the engine.

"Was that really necessary?"

She shrugged her shoulders. "It was for me. Don't forget your notes. We're working, remember?"

How could I forget?

28

Zeely

The bubbles tickled my shoulders but brought no humor to them. I'd thought that a good, hot bath might numb the pain, but some things couldn't be soaked or scrubbed away. Some things stained deep into the soul. I'd watched Grace and Brian pull away without sticking my head out the window with a last-minute warning. I'd teased Grace about Brian, about letting him just pull up like that, but it wasn't any of my business. That didn't stop it from hurting though. Didn't stop jealousy from inching up my sleeves and into my heart.

"Be flexible," my mother had always said. "That's what a man needs in a wife, compromise and endurance. Endure, baby. Endure to the end." And so here I was, still stretching, pulling, holding other people's place in line. Places they didn't even want.

I slipped on a robe and padded downstairs, wondering how long it would be before I'd be helping Grace pack up again to marry Brian. I'd thought it would be different this time, just her and me, with no men between us. I should have known better. Even when it was just our fathers, there were always men between us.

I'd played this game with widows and women whose husbands had beat them, left them. Those women hung all over me: praying, talking, coming by. And then they'd disappear. After the first time, I learned not to go looking. I still saw those women from time to time: running toward the altar on Sundays or sneaking away from some nasty-looking motel. I'd taken them in, babysat for them, helped them any way I could, but in the end, if the devil himself came by and blew the horn, they all went running. Worse yet, they'd come back and try to tell me how I too could have a man of my very own.

"If you 'd loosen up a little, you could get a man too," they whispered. "You know. Give a little."

When they came out of their mess a year or two later, I'd be right in the choirstand where they left me. No putting out and shacking up for Zeely. It was too late to lift my skirt for the meat cutter because I got a little lonely. Well, a lot lonely and not just for a man.

What I really wanted, even craved, was a baby. Only God knew how much. If things had gone the way they were supposed to, I'd have had five or six children by now. At least three or four.

But things hadn't gone like they were supposed to. Jeremiah didn't give me a ring like Mama said he would. He gave me a wedding invitation instead. And my name wasn't on it.

Sometimes I allowed myself to think about Ron and all that had happened between us, all we could have been. Sometimes, but not often. It made me too sad. Too angry. I had too much to do to sit around crying and mad. Now Ron was marrying somebody else too. Somebody who looked like him.

I fluffed the napkins in the rings on my dining room table, remembered Ron's last visit. He'd let me win the game a few times, but not all. Some of the answers I only knew because he'd recited them during other games, chapter and verse. This time, he guessed the answers more often than not. Just like I was doing now. I restacked my bowls and plates out of habit, laughing at myself for doing it. My table was always set, but Prince Charming never came.

And he never would.

I was finally ready and able to accept that. Jerry was still trying to figure out how to iron his clothes again after the divorce. He only went out with me to dull the pain of Carmel and her boyfriend.

Somehow I got that and allowed him that dignity, to believe that he could still be wanted. Be needed. He was using me in hopes of keeping Carmel's love, to let her know that he was still a man. If I was honest, I used Jeremiah too. I'd always hated those women who didn't want a man but didn't want anyone else to have him either, but sometimes that's just how things end up. It's okay.

What wasn't okay was that Grace had been back in town a few weeks and already she was riding off into the sunset. Joyce had handed her the dance program that had meant so much to me but would always suffer in the shadow of the memory of its best dancer—the missing, tragic Diana.

No matter how much time passed between the two of us, one thing would never change—I was the one called to serve, but Grace was the one chosen to be loved. In a year or two, she'd be back here on Brian's arm, holding a chubby-cheeked baby. And I'd still be here stacking plates.

Don't you think you're taking this too far?

I wasn't. Not yet. I lifted one of my couch cushions and pulled out a brochure with a smiling pregnant woman on the cover.

Tired of waiting for Mr. Right? Save a baby abandoned in our freezer and fulfill your dreams of motherhood. Call today. 1-88-NEW-THING.

I pressed the glossy paper against my stomach. The emptiness caved in beneath my hand. I reached for the phone.

29

Ron

Dinner at the country club was not my idea of romance, but to Mindy it meant something, something I hadn't been giving her, not for a while. Some of my time.

So I'd suffer through, knowing she deserved better, knowing that this couldn't go on, that my heart and my head had to line up somehow. Until then, there were the chandeliers, four forks, three spoons, and wine-colored cloth napkins. Until then, there was Mindy.

"I'm so glad to see you." She seemed both thrilled and surprised that I'd shown up.

"Me too," I said, not even sure what I meant. I smoothed a napkin over my knees and blinked at the silver. They must have used an electric buffer or something.

"You haven't touched your gazpacho." Mindy pressed her hand on mine. The bands of her rings scratched against my knuckles. She lowered her voice. "You haven't touched me either." She tried to give me an enticing look, but the edges of her green contact lenses were streaked with red. The beginnings of another eye infection.

Things had been different when we first started dating. We'd done Bible study together, went on dates, even made friends with a few other couples. Things became comfortable, which for Mindy meant serious. People told me to be careful of her, said things I never told her about. She knew about Zeely, but not everything. Sometimes I thought she didn't want to know. Sometimes I wondered if she didn't have a secret of her own. I hoped not. My closet was full of my own secrets.

She slid her foot out of one of her heels. Her toes slid up my pants leg. "I know we've been pretty casual about this wedding, but what if we just forget all that and just get married?"

What if we did. That would end everything, wouldn't it? No, not at all. "Maybe. I don't know. We haven't spent much time together lately. I'd started to think we'd be engaged indefinitely, that maybe we should call things off and see where we stand."

Mindy put her foot back into her shoe. "Look, don't talk like that. It's been crazy at work for me with all the rezoning of the city and everything. And I know Daddy has had you busy. And your friends. It's just the celibacy thing. The wedding is starting to seem a long way off."

The celibacy thing. When we'd met, Mindy had been adamant about the celibacy thing. Adamant about Jesus. Lately, we didn't go to church together much anymore, and when we did, it was like a date with lunch or a movie after. She had the same far-off look during service that I saw on her face now.

She took a bite of the appetizer, freshly delivered to our table. She told me not to look at her like that, like I was so righteous, like I didn't struggle. "I'm not like you, content to play board games and cook collard greens. I'm not a virgin and I have a good memory."

Appetite gone, I stared down at my plate, then reached for her hand. I struggled all right, just for all the wrong reasons. I bowed my head and prayed . . . for both of us.

The next course came, but none of it looked appetizing.

Mindy and I sat like that, holding hands and staring at each other. I saw something in her eyes that I'd been avoiding. I wondered if she saw the same thing in mine.

"Let's get out of here. Go somewhere and talk."

She perked up a little. "Come home with me. I'll call Dad and cover for you in the morning . . ."

That made me smile, but I knew that it could be more dangerous than anything with Zeely—we would never go beyond dinner. With Mindy, it would be easy to let myself go, to let things take their course. She was better than that though, deserved more. I liked to think I was too. "That wasn't quite what I meant. It's late and things might get out of hand."

"That was the idea." She gave me a weary smile and waved for the check. "Forget it. That was my hormones talking. I have an appointment anyway."

"More premarital counseling? I'm sorry about missing the last session. Should I come—"

"No. It's something else. Don't worry." She folded her napkin and laid it on the table.

I pulled out her chair. "Sorry about tonight. About everything. I know this can't be easy for you, waiting until we finish our counseling to set a date. We're almost there though."

She wiped her eyes. "I'm sorry too. I didn't mean all that. I don't know what comes over me sometimes. It's like—"

"Putting a smorgasbord in front of a starving man and telling him not to eat."

"That's it. Totally."

We walked out together and kissed quickly in the parking lot. I was all the way to the car before I realized I had gotten away without eating a thing. Not that it surprised me.

What I hungered for wasn't on the menu.

My appetite came back—with a vengeance. One of our biggest clients had died and left her daughter a ridiculous amount of money, more than the budget for the whole city. The desk in front of me, the one in my den, was piled with plans on what to do with the cash—plans from the daughter and a newly formed foundation,

180

whose board was made up mostly of names I recognized from local politics. There'd been meetings about it all day.

When they'd first mentioned their plans to consolidate the mirror-imaged facilities and business—black and white—on either side of town, I'd been all ears. Finally this backward place was going to catch up and get over its strangeness. Or at least that's what I had thought.

"Actually we're going to change the nature of the city altogether," they'd explained finally. "Expand on the idea of having a historical area. It'll be a tourist attraction. The story of the town's name is well known. People would pay up to a million dollars to live here when we're finished."

I'd almost had a heart attack then. When I asked what would happen to the middle-class and low-income residents who couldn't afford to live in such housing, the answer blew my mind.

"We're planning reenactments throughout town. They can always play the slaves or soldiers. They wouldn't live here, of course, but the jobs would be steady."

That comment had started some conversations that had me stuck between quitting my job or being fired. Things were said that seemed so unreal that I started to take notes simply because I couldn't believe them. My boss had taken my notes and thrown them away. "What's said in here, stays in here."

That was what scared me. If I left, who was going to help Joyce and Brian with what was coming down the road? Brian's stance that every American was born a racist to some degree had always alarmed and saddened me, but after today I had to wonder if he hadn't been right. Even me. Why didn't I have Brian's picture on my desk with snapshots of my college buddies? Why wasn't Zeely's picture next to my other smiling ex-girlfriends'?

Between racism and political correctness, I'd never have any peace. And probably not any food either. It was late and I was starving and only one person was likely to have something I really wanted to eat. The one person I had no business talking to, especially after the way things had gone with Mindy tonight.

So I'd gone home instead and ransacked my refrigerator, finding nothing but condiments and lunches gone the way of weird. I gave up. Across the street, my neighbor was attacking his lawn with a weed whacker, making the most of the warm fall night.

My yard was a few weeks from going to seed. The neighborhood association had taken to leaving me friendly reminders with coupons attached so that I could take my invisible children for ice cream. If I didn't move out of here soon, I was going to lose it.

Maybe I already had.

When I snatched my phone off the base and started punching numbers, I heard numbers punching on the other end.

"Hey! Stop dialing. It's me."

Zeely's voice came in clear and calm. A little too calm. "Don't tell me. You want more greens."

"That'd be great, but really, I'll take anything." I sounded pitiful, but I couldn't help myself.

She sighed. "Did you eat it all the last time?"

"Every bite. I think I took the foil to work for a snack. Lots of icing on there."

"The foil?"

"You heard me."

Her laughter came then, full and sweet. It made the day's confusion both tighten and ease.

"Now you're really going to laugh. The people at work were amazed at my 'soul food cuisine.' I was all into it one day, hot sauce running down my mouth and everything. There they were, staring into my office. I almost choked."

She did choke. "Stop. Please. I can't take any more. I'll feed you, all right? And bring your shadow a plate if he's there."

So that was how it went.

I didn't take too kindly to the thought of Jerry in Zeely's house,

182

even with me there. Thank God he was working that other job tonight. Still, I'd take a good meal any way I could get it—even if it was meant for someone else.

"Jerry's not here. We do our male bonding on weekends and even then, not very often."

"I see."

My neighbor crossed the street and stepped into my yard. I guess he couldn't take it anymore. I didn't want to think about what I'd say to him on my way out. So I didn't think. "Don't make me beg."

She laughed again. "No need. I've got some butter beans, smothered turkey legs with gravy, and a little rice. Will that do you?"

I leaned back on the couch. That would do me right into next week. "I'm on my way. One question before I let you go."

"Yes?"

"I know Jerry isn't usually allowed at your house. How is it that I get to come over?"

"You're safe. You just want my food."

I wouldn't be so sure. "Right. See you in a minute."

I headed to the car, trying not to think about what had happened on my job, what hadn't happened with Mindy, or why I always called Zeely when I didn't have the time or energy to explain what I wanted. Maybe it was for the best that I hadn't moved into one of those condos. I'd probably be over there all the time. Jerry really needed to step up his game. Or something.

We were playing musical chairs, all of us, even Mindy. I wasn't so sure that I wanted to be around when the music stopped.

30

Grace

I longed for sleep. Working with Brian left me exhausted and confused, especially our breathless goodbyes. I hadn't felt like this since . . . well, ever. I held my hand to my face, noting the exact spot where he'd kissed it when we'd gone to dinner. When it happened, I'd breathed a silent prayer and stepped away, afraid to return the endearment. Just thinking about it had me in a daze.

Lord, you promised not to tempt me beyond my limits. Just so you know, you're coming pretty close.

Some kind of blues sang in through my thin windowpanes, an open invitation from my college neighbors to come down and say hello. Also an opportunity for Zeely to call the police. It was midnight or later, long after the time for all good teachers to be in bed. And yet, I couldn't sleep.

Retreating to my room, I grabbed my new nightgown, purple silk from Virtuous Woman. I read the tag before putting it on.

Who can find a virtuous woman? Her price is far above rubies. She makes herself coverings of tapestry; her clothing is silk and purple. Strength and honor are her clothing; and she shall rejoice in the time to come.

I clutched the tag to my chest before pulling the gown over my head. Those words explained all that I desired to be: a jewel in God's crown, strong, smart, and beautiful. It also reminded me of everything I wasn't.

I lifted my arms and threw back my head, offering the only gift I had left—the dance.

The music had slowed from the pulsing drum of my teen years, but it was still the beat of God's forgiveness that told my body where to go, told my feet how to pray. It was devotion in motion, as Zeely often said in her weekly class, and at the height of it, my phone rang and I stubbed my big toe on the way to answer it.

If it was Brian saying he was outside again, I prayed for the courage to send him home. It had been hard enough the first time.

"Hello?"

"It's me. Joyce. Please . . . come." She gasped for breath.

"Hold on. I'm on my way."

Instantly, I pulled on a pair of jeans over the purple nightgown and a sweater over my head. I forced my feet into two odd sneakers. Every time I thought I'd reached all I could bear, God threw another rock on the pile. I guess I didn't know him or myself as well as I thought I did.

31

Brian

The empty classroom crackled with anticipation. Since our candlelit dinner of strategy and scheduling and a breathy goodbye at Grace's door, things had been quite interesting between us. Though I knew I shouldn't, each morning I looked forward to seeing her. So much about her both compelled and baffled me. Her religion made her seem narrow-minded at times, but there was something beneath it, an innocent generosity that made me want to laugh out loud. Sometimes she was smug and arrogant, and me being me, I liked that too.

When I'd seen her in the parking lot this morning, she'd been neither haughty or guarded. She'd smiled at me with her soul wide open and nothing to cover it. She'd mentioned once that she prayed early in the morning. Today it must have done her good.

And maybe me too.

I couldn't wait for her to come to the classroom with all that truth on her face. Maybe for once I'd see all of her, not just her faith and her strength, but her pain. Her need. Still there was the chance that she'd switch up at the last minute and arrive all-business, like nothing had happened between us that night at dinner and all the days after. For her, maybe nothing had.

Probably not. Her smiles might have been a gracious way of covering the awkwardness, the pieces that didn't fit. As she'd pronounced to the man selling newspapers that night, there would be no compromise for Grace. And not for me either.

Though I was feeling less and less confident in the pot-bellied statue on my dresser or the altar to the ancestors beneath my bed, I wasn't planning on running to Sunday school anytime soon. Still, I found myself reading the Bible more and more. I stayed up most nights now, studying the passages that Grace read before school or during her breaks. She always left it open on her desk and highlighted the good parts bright enough for me to see from a distance.

She probably knew that I was reading the Scriptures from some of the comments that I made. I wondered now if I wasn't playing a game of my own, making her think I could be what she wanted, what she expected. Perhaps it was best to disappoint her now and tell her all the other sacred texts I stayed up with too, tell her how we might have really made something of this if she hadn't thrown the gauntlet down:

Jesus Christ is my God.

But she had thrown it down and I wasn't willing to pick it up. Praying to an unknown deity was one thing. Yielding to Jesus Christ was another.

And yet, I had to wonder why I'd never taken the "altar of the ancestors" out of its box, why I'd never been able to repeat the words to the libations at the ceremonies I'd attended. Something restrained my lips from forming a prayer to the gods that others promised would give me peace. Did the "fear of the living God," as Eva had always called it, still live somewhere in me? Somewhere deeper than all my pain and anger?

The thought of that and the thought of her gave me another kind of fear, a fear of losing control. There is still some vein of faith deep inside me, but I dared not mine it now. Maybe once I found my mother I could face God. By then, I'd have the right questions to ask. Or maybe just the wrong answers to the one question always at the center of everything: Why?

I checked my Palm Pilot for the day's lessons, willing myself to calm down. This was a dead-end street, this thing with Grace. She had no obligation to leave her safety and jump into the chaos of somebody like me. But I wanted her to. I wanted it so badly that I'd spoken her name before falling asleep and again when I'd opened my eyes this morning. Only one woman's name had ever slept on these lips before and then only after years of marriage. I'd known Grace for what, a month?

I hadn't felt swept up like that since my first read of Ralph Ellison. I could still remember the stab of those first lines.

I am an invisible man . . . a man of substance, of flesh and bone, fiber and liquids—and I might even be said to possess a mind. I am invisible, understand, simply because people refuse to see me.

Invisible. I realized in my first read of that book that this was my greatest fear—being invisible. The thought that when I died, my mother, wherever she was, would not press a hand to her throat and hold on to her neighbor's elbow saying, "My son. He's gone." But rather that she would go on talking, choking me down, blotting me out as though I'd never been at all. Though everyone around me proclaimed my accomplishments, in the end Ellison's narrator knew me best. Or at least I had known him best, until Diana Grace returned.

When I'd seen her this morning, she reminded me of a singer, someone on the hundreds of album covers I had at home. Vinyl jackets swept through my mind: brown-sugar eyes, melted ice cream, polyester hips. Minnie Riperton? Too sweet. Thelma Houston? Close. Same body for sure. I couldn't help but smile when it finally came to me: Angela Bofill, angel of the night. And in Grace's case, angel of the day.

"That's her. Straight up," I said to the spider fern on my desk as though it was listening.

The plant wasn't listening of course, but someone else was. The door creaked open behind me, and I clenched my fists. How long had she been standing in the hall? Was she feeling as awkward and anxious as me? Why didn't she say something?

Calm down.

Her footsteps stopped right behind me. Too close. She smelled different today. Overpowering. I'd cataloged the scents. Patchouli. Clary Sage. I turned to face her. As I did, two slim wrists plunged into my neckline. Braids brushed my face. I knew without looking at the face that it wasn't Grace at all. It was Lottie Wells.

"What's the matter, baby? You forgot old Lot now that there's fresh meat on the block? You never call me." She went for my neck, attaching like a vacuum until I managed to pull her away.

I flung her arms from my shoulders, and nudged her back. "Act like you've got some sense."

Lottie pulled at my shirt again.

This time I pushed. Hard. Probably too hard, but she barely budged. She was worrying me now. "Get off me. And stop calling me too. I know that's you hanging up all the time."

Lottie pressed herself onto me, her arms around my waist. "You don't fool me," she said. "You want me."

I sighed. Why had I ever dated this woman? These types were always more trouble in the end than I could see at the beginning. I generally enjoyed dating a few times a year, like eating Thelma's burritos. Now I wished I'd never taken the first bite. I had to hold her off with one arm, while moving toward the door.

She lunged forward and clawed at my arm as I stepped aside, leaving her to sprawl on the floor. What a mess. I felt bad not helping her up, but I didn't dare touch her again. I didn't need any trouble. "Enough. Please go."

Lottie scrambled to her feet. "Never," she said, just as Grace walked in.

I had to close my eyes. I wanted so bad to see Grace, but not like this. I watched as her eyes swept the scene—Lottie's sideways skirt, the button missing from my sleeve. The mask lowered over her face. Her eyes repeated the word spoken a moment before—*never*.

32

Grace

There's something in my belly. I can feel it fluttering,
like a butterfly.

Diana Dixon

I didn't watch while Brian scrubbed pink lipstick off his hands.
It wouldn't come off easily—for either of us. My faith wanted to
believe all things, to bear all things, but my mind wasn't having it
as he arranged his shirt and wiped his hands before approaching
the office where I'd retreated.

"Come in." I sounded cold, like Joyce before an expulsion.

Brian inched toward me, pushing around the kiln to get to my
desk. "What're you reading?"

"The usual." I held up a squat paperback with a neon pink cover
titled *The Message*. He groaned. He probably wondered how many
Bibles one woman needed.

From the way my hands trembled as I turned the pages, maybe
I needed a few more. Brian kneeled beside my desk.

"That wasn't what you think. She came in and jumped all over
me . . . At first I thought it was you—"

My lips tightened into a smile. A fake one. "You don't have to
explain." *But I want you to. I really want you to. I just don't think*
you can.

Brian sucked his teeth. "There's nothing *to* explain. I just didn't want you to think I was—like that."

My false smile twisted to one side. I let the book, the Bible, slip from my fingers as I stood, staring into his eyes.

"Uh-oh," he whispered.

He'd gotten that much right.

"In your own words, it will be a rough day, so let's get to work. I brought some of the books we discussed the other night." I took my tote from the back of my chair and dumped a stack of paperback classics onto the table.

Brian nodded as he found his feet and went to his own desk. "Right. Thanks."

"Oh, and Dr. Mayfield?"

"Yes?" His eyes lit up.

"If you'd like, I can loan you some foundation to cover that *thing* on your neck. The students have enough to gossip about as it is."

A few minutes later I hid in the bathroom, beating myself up for having gone out with Brian at all. How could I have been so stupid? Malachi was right about one thing. A single woman wasn't safe, not even in the workplace.

Brian's words reverberated in my mind: *I thought she was you.*

Not wanting to think about it anymore, I went back to the classroom, straight into the office. I took a deep breath when Brian wasn't there. And then, smelling of almonds and honey, he was there. I acted as if he wasn't.

He pressed into the desk as though his arms were his only support. As he did, a patch of red crept over his buttoned collar.

He touched my arm. "You ready to get started?"

I jerked away, heart pounding. Suddenly I was somewhere else. He was someone else. Someone dangerous.

191

"Grace! Are you afraid of me? Come on now. We talked for hours the other night."

What a waste of time. "I remember."

"Do you? Look, I realize you don't know me well, but that wasn't what it looked like. I promise."

I didn't respond.

He crossed his arms. "We'll talk more later. Let's just get through the day. Here's what we discussed. The history lesson? I do it every year. I know you said we'd be doing it today, but we can do it later. If you're still working with me, that is." He placed a stack of papers on my desk.

He made his point. And it was my fault too, mixing business with pleasure in the first place. I adored Joyce, but this had been an unwise placement from the first. Now I had a choice: sit at this desk and sulk or do my job. It was difficult to consider either without knowing what was really going on. If it was something mutual, consensual, it was none of my business. But if it was something else, something violent, then that changed everything. Maybe I should have asked Lottie to stay, let Brian explain . . .

Perfect love casts out fear.

Though I loved the Lord, I wasn't so sure about this one. I'd taught on that verse before, using fishing line as a prop. *Cast* meant to throw far, like a fisherman pitching a line. I'd have to fling my suspicions all the way back to Cincinnati to get through this. A woman had to have some common sense. I'd learned that the hard way.

I watched through the doorway as Brian mounted a timeline of the Middle Passage, the longest and deadliest part of our ancestors' trip to the New World. The display was laminated and colorful like most teaching aids, but intricate in its detail. I looked closer at the words beneath each image. Brian's firm hand and block letters gave him away as the artist.

I walked hurriedly to the doorway. "You made that?"

He smiled cautiously at my presence. "I like visuals. Helps them to remember."

I nodded, remembering the morning's events. Some visuals were unforgettable. "What about the hands-on project you put in the lesson plan? Aren't you going to do that too?"

Brian's smile widened. "I didn't think you were up to it. Help me move the desks. If we work fast, we can still pull it off."

Once the desks were out of the way, we rolled a giant poster across the floor. A life-size ship. Dotted outlines indicated the slaves' positions. From the looks of it, Brian had drawn that out too. *Incredible.*

I stepped close to it, careful not to rip the shiny paper. "I've never seen such a big poster."

"Go ahead, walk on it. It's laminated."

With one step, I was transported to the cramped quarters . . . women huddled with their infants, men sandwiched together in ways that brought them shame. Such closeness and no bathroom. It hurt to even think about it, and yet I must, we must. This town was confused enough as it was.

I covered my mouth, then turned to Brian. "What now?"

Eyes wet, Brian leaned over and rubbed his hand down the length of one of the outlined bodies. "Now we put the desks on top."

I fell in place beside Brian, pushing the desks across the room. I tried to be wary of him, but as the time to start class grew near, my passion for the lesson displaced my fear.

He climbed on top of some of the desks. "This is the deck. We'll pack the kids in the 'hold' below. Head-to-head. Just like it was. Do you remember the Swahili from Ngozi?"

"Some."

"Good enough." We rehearsed the words, with Brian explaining the meanings as he went along.

After testing the hold to be sure, I held my breath. The ship, scaled from an actual slaver, was quite convincing. I remembered my earnest tears after reading the ship scenes in *Roots*. I'd thrashed and wailed, balled up in knots. I'd carried on until my mother took the book away, declaring it too much for a nine-year-old, especially one with such an overly emotional personality. That had only brought more tears and a secret copy I left in my desk at school.

Even now, Mom dismissed my passionate nature as a defect, a problem. "Please don't start it. Don't get yourself worked up. Anger killed your father, you know. Anger and pork chops," she'd say on the phone when the conversation reached a conflict. Only in dance could I release the emotions restrained first by my mother and later, my husband. My version of art "wasn't acceptable." They'd both made that very clear. A young lady, a good wife didn't wipe up the floor with herself or do poetry readings in the bathroom. A good woman sat still and quiet, rotting in her own skin.

The two of them had interpreted my creativity as something sensual. Sinful. My mother had even implied that my free spirit caused the theft of my womanhood. "You have a slutty way about you," she explained. How an overweight teen with braces and glasses could look slutty I still didn't understand. Peter too had scolded me for being "too friendly" with people. He encouraged me to be detached, uninvolved. Like him.

Even now, there were times like this morning when I had to run to the bathroom whispering Maya Angelou's "Phenomenal Woman" under my breath, running from the beast lurking in my own skin. Until now, until seeing Brian again, I'd always been able to force down the monster when it resurfaced, to keep myself calm. Safe. But now it was harder, watching as he strapped a set of drums across his shoulders, his eyes lit with the same fire, the same beast of emotion lurking behind his gold-green eyes.

"You're getting into it, aren't you?" He patted the biggest drum in the front a few times playfully, then tapped the smaller ones on the sides.

I looked at the door, not expecting this. "You still play?"

He unbuttoned his sleeves, folding them up to his elbows. "I'll let you answer that when I'm done. The question is, do you still dance?" His palms molded to the drums' canvas. In seconds, the air filled with his pulse, extending through his hands—and into me.

The beat tackled my senses. I might have forgotten most of my Swahili, but my body remained fluent in rhythm. Still, I really hadn't planned to dance. I wasn't dressed for it. I hadn't prayed about it. I crossed my legs, sucked in my stomach.

Hold it in, girl. Hold it in.

He hit the drum with the heels of his hands and backed up to face me. He gave three short beats before starting in hard and fast—the signal for the solo I'd never danced.

He hadn't forgotten.

I wanted to ask Brian to stop, but his eyes were closed and my feet were already moving. My slip-on shoes were replaced with the cold floor under my bare feet. As the drums talked back and forth, male and female, I shuffled forward. Shimmied back. I rose and fell.

Brian was sweating now and swaying too. Crouched low, he played each note truer than the last. His arms were stronger now than they'd been all those years ago. His soul was bigger too. I danced on, slowing as the female drum screeched to a climax. The full-bellied male drum called back, daring her on. Joyce's voice whispered in my head. *Head up. Shoulders back. Now let it go . . .* I leapt at the crescendo, landing in a sweaty heap, cradling my knees.

Unexpected applause poured in through the doorway as the drumming broke off and Brian and I crashed through the surface of ourselves. I was shocked, vulnerable, and quite speechless.

Brian had no such problem. He wiggled out of his drums and climbed onto the nearest desk. *"Habari Gani!"* He welcomed them in Swahili, continuing in dialect for several sentences before paus-ing. The students looked to me for help.

I translated. "Welcome! You have been sold or captured. You belong to me. Do not try to escape." I pulled back a chair. "Ladies enter here. Boys there."

Brian waved the boys to the other side.

The logistics proved more difficult than anticipated. One girl was as tall as she was wide, and another seemed a little too eager to be sandwiched between her classmates. I motioned for Brian to move things along. The beauty queens were wilting and the boys were plotting to crawl over to the girls' side.

He relented and directed the kids back to reassemble their seats. "Think about what you just experienced. You'll be writing about it at the end of the period. Who will be our griot today?" Now warm and red-faced, Brian freed his top button and stroked his beard.

My eyes widened. I tried to get his attention, but several stu-dents were already waving their hands. One in particular found the sight of Brian's neck so funny that he twisted around in his seat to smack hands with a friend behind him. He was doubled over with laughter.

Brian didn't look as if he found anything funny. He pointed at Sean. "You. On your feet."

All the class laughed then.

Brian reached for a yardstick in the chalk tray at the board. He tapped it on the floor, demanding silence. He pointed to Sean again. "Come on, Mr. Griot. Tell us what we learned yesterday."

An uneasy hush fell over the room. Everyone realized now that Brian wasn't in one of his kidding moods.

Sean didn't look worried. "Don't worry. I got this." He took a step toward Brian. "I don't remember what we learned yesterday, but I'll tell you what I learned today: you and Miss O aren't as uptight as y'all try to act. From the looks of your neck anyway—"

Brian crossed the space between him and Sean in three strides. "Sit down."

The braver half of the class, the students in the back with less to lose, resumed their laughter. The other half looked at each other and then at me, unsure what to say or think. Regret rose in my throat. I'd had such a sweet time of prayer this morning. How could a day with such a blessed start unravel so fast?

Brian recovered quickly, giving excuses that sounded too much like the ones he'd given me. He had the students in his hand again, telling a story about some trip he had taken, some king he had known . . .

I heard it all and none of it too. I had to get out of there. I needed some air.

"I'll be right back." I went to the door without waiting for Brian's reply. I paused in the doorway, where the morning took a dark turn. Pushing the memory away, I stepped into the hall and ran into Joyce.

My boss stepped in front of me. "Where you headed?"

"Bathroom."

"Stick around." She led me right back into the room. She smiled at the students. "Hello, Bantus, how are you?"

The students answered in chorus. "Excellent."

Brian's chalk squeaked against the board. He turned, his face as red as his neck.

"How are things going this morning?" Joyce asked next, looking first at Brian, then the students.

"We're fine," Brian said, his eyes on Sean.

Joyce didn't look convinced. "Good. I need to speak to you and Ms. Okoye in the office for a moment."

He looked annoyed. "Sure. Everyone go ahead and start your paper about our activity. Five paragraphs. Sensory details. Approach it from any angle you like. I'll be right back if you have questions."

I led Joyce into the office. Brian followed with clenched teeth.

Once inside, he took the lead. "Look, I'm glad you came by. Something happened this morning."

"So I've heard." Joyce pushed back Brian's collar and inspected his neck.

Brian looked at me with resignation and betrayal. He changed the subject. "It's not just that either. It's McKnight too. I still don't think I should be teaching him. I'm not sure that boy wants to change."

Joyce grabbed his other collar, pulled him down an inch. "Change is hard for all of us. Wouldn't you say so, Grace?"

I nodded, surprised to see Joyce so angry.

She let go of his shirt. "Now for the real reason for my visit. I'll need to see both of you in my office during lunch today. Separately. It's imperative."

Brian hoisted a box of books from the floor and onto the desk. He took his keys out of his desk and punched through the gap in the cardboard. "Can't you just tell us what you need now? I don't have time for another five-year plan. Not today."

Joyce took a deep breath. "Fine, we'll stick with a one-day plan then. Charlotte Wells has accused you of sexual harassment. She's named Grace as a witness. If you can't make time for me, I can bring in the school board."

33

Jerry

"What's the opposite of a negative?" I asked the class.

"A positive."

I turned to the second row and smiled. Sean McKnight again. That one was really changing, getting back on track. I tossed the boy a chunk of bubble gum. A perfect pass.

Sean opened his hands in the shape of a dove. "Only one piece?"

I laughed. "Just one for now. And don't leave the funny papers on the floor. I find them all over the building."

The prizewinner slouched in his seat, chuckling. "It's my modus operandi, Mr. T." He wiggled his fingers. "I'm sticky." He ripped the gum open and plopped it in his mouth.

Zeely caught the paper before it hit the floor. "You're going to be sticking to a jail cell if you keep talking like that." She started for the trashcan with the same angry look she'd had all morning.

I tugged her sleeve as she passed. "Are you okay?"

She ignored me, turning to the class instead. "It's time for group work. Here are the problems." She tossed a packet to the students at the head of each row. One of them dropped it.

"Sorry," Zeely said before moving on.

When she returned to the desk, I tapped her shoulder. "Are you sure you're all right? You seem a little tense."

She pushed her belt low on her waist. Yanked a thread from her sweater. "Tense? You seem a little lax. This is high school, not kindergarten. You shouldn't reward them for doing the basics. Nobody else will." She whispered the rebuke.

Not this again. "They certainly won't get any breaks from you. You won't give yourself any either. I'm just trying to get them interested—"

"Phone call for Mr. Terrigan." The intercom swallowed her response.

I frowned. Carmel again, no doubt. How many times had I told her not to call the office, but to call my cell instead? "Can you take a message?"

The secretary cleared her throat. "The caller insists on speaking with you. Something about a debt—"

All eyes were on me. Especially Zeely's. "I'll take it on one."

Zeely waved her hands. "Group one, are you done? I'm coming back there to check . . ."

I lifted the phone to my ear, stretching the cord around the corner. "This is Jerry Terrigan."

"As you know, today is the last day to remit payment."

"I sent two thousand by Western Union this morning—"

"Only full payment is possible at this point. You've forfeited all your payment arrangements."

I wound the cord and the accusation around my finger. "Actually, my wife made those arrangements."

"You signed the form."

Did I? Or had Carmel signed my name? It didn't matter. We got into this together. "I'm sorry."

"We are too. Your daughter is one of our top students. I planned to recommend her for a Harvard interview next year. Is there anything you can do?"

I sighed. "We sold our house, our cars. We even moved home to cut expenses. There isn't anything else." To hear the doctor tell it, I'd pawned my health too.

"No stocks?"

"Sold."

"Bonds?"

"Turned in."

"Jewelry?"

I sucked in a breath. *The ring.* It would be worth three thousand at least . . . They didn't make jewelry like that anymore. I stared at Zeely, paused in the doorway. They didn't make women like that anymore either. No matter what happened, my mother had intended it for her. It wasn't mine to give away. "There's nothing else I can do."

A whistle on the line. "What a shame. Such promise. We'll be forced to withdraw her effective immediately."

Immediately? "Okay. We're a couple hours away and my ex-wife is working today too. We'll pick her up tonight."

"Correction, sir. You'll pick her up now."

The trip took longer than usual. I'd tried to get Carmel to come along, but she had the night shift and her boss wouldn't let her go. So Justice and I set out for Rose Hill Academy. Monique, my older daughter, was packed and waiting when we got there. We hadn't said much on the way home.

I rubbed my forehead with one hand and guided the steering wheel with the other. Justice wailed in the backseat. "Can you give her the pacifier, please?"

Monique turned around to reach the backseat, her fingers rustling against the baby's jacket. "The pacifier isn't on her coat. The day care people must have put it in the bag."

Day care. Carmel and her bright ideas. The extra sleep had been nice, I had to admit, but the extra hours to pay for it often cancelled that out too. I switched hands on the wheel and fished behind my seat. I pulled up Carmel's leather backpack. She was too old to carry a diaper bag, she said.

Too cute, more like it.

"Here. Look in there for it. Does she still feel warm?"

Monique reached back and touched the baby's head. "She's a little hot. A fever, you think?"

I nodded. "They probably won't take her tomorrow. I'll call Joyce. Maybe she'll let me bring her."

The baby whimpered again, followed by a sucking sound. I chuckled. "You found it. Good. I've got a spare pack in here somewhere." I turned into my ex-wife's apartment complex, a few blocks from my own. "Do you still have your key? Probably not, huh? You're not here much."

Monique nodded, looking past me to the convenience store uniform hanging behind my head. "I've got my key, Daddy."

A tear coursed down her nose, into her mouth. She sobbed, taking short breaths. "I'm sorry about Justice. The day care. The school. You and mom. I'm sorry for messing up everything."

"Things were messed up for a long time, honey. It's not your fault." I grabbed two napkins from the glove compartment and gave one to Monique. With the other, I blew the baby's nose. "Come on now. Blow." A honking sniff. I smiled. "Good girl."

I got out and opened the back door, unfastening the car seat. By the time I unbuckled Justice, Monique had disappeared inside. Now she reappeared in the door with a strange look.

I sighed. "What?"

"Mom left a message. She has to stay until eleven."

I stared at the uniform in the car. I'd already taken off most of the day on one job. Now she was going to have me missing again on the other. And when there wasn't enough money, it would be my fault.

Monique seemed to know just what I was thinking. "We'll be okay. Go on to work, Daddy."

"S'up 'Nique?" A dark-skinned boy in a skullcap sagged around the corner. "I thought you only came on the weekends."

My daughter gave the boy a sly smile. "Hey, Ced. I'm here for good."

The boy nodded slowly, like he'd just had an idea. "For real?" He walked to the door.

I had an idea too. This wasn't happening. I left the baby seat on the sidewalk and was quickly in between them. "Go on home, son. And don't come back."

Monique looked embarrassed. "But, Daddy—"

I shook my head. I knew exactly where this was going. I saw it every day at school. I saw the results of it now—bright and beautiful on the sidewalk with a binkie in her mouth. This time I knew not to take any chances.

It couldn't happen again. Not on my watch.

"Get in the car, Monique. You're coming home with me."

34

Brian

I sat in the dark classroom, staring at the door, the portal to disaster. I stretched myself over my drum set, licking chalk dust from my lips. A knock sounded at the door. I looked up at the clock. Three thirty. School had let out long ago. I'd watched Grace peel out of the parking lot right after the bell, so it wasn't her. Whoever else it could be, I didn't care.

"Doc? Open up. It's me. Quinn."

"Go away," I said from somewhere in the pit of myself. I couldn't be a mentor now. Role model either. Breathing was challenging enough.

"I ain't," Quinn said. He forced the knob and entered the room, feeling along the wall for the light. A basketball bulged under one arm. He fingered the drums lightly before striking out a melody of his own. "Middle Passage, huh?"

My grunt was the only response, but Quinn wouldn't give up. When I walked into the office and plopped into my chair, hair overflowing my hands, Quinn dribbled in behind me. "Brooding? You know I can't let you get away with that. Pity is the doorway to excuse and excuse the entrance to ignorance—"

I growled into my hand. There was nothing worse than having your own words used against you.

Quinn laughed, reaching into a box of books with comic strip drawings on the cover. "*The Black Holocaust?* I thought they cut the funds for books. How much these set you back?"

Too much to discuss. I peeked out from under my hair. "You remember it?"

"Remember it? Man, I bought my own copy. Still have it at the house. Why are they still in the box? Don't you give them out after the Middle Passage?"

He remembers everything. If only I could forget.

"Things don't seem to be following my lesson plans these days." What an understatement. A few months ago, I had life figured out. I'd stay single and pour my life into these kids, kids like Quinn. Next summer, it'd be back to Africa and one day, maybe for good. Then I met a woman . . . one who'd likely never talk to me again.

Quinn pulled up a chair. "The thing with Miss Wells getting you down?"

"You know?" I paused. "I guess it's best. I'll probably lose my job anyway."

Quinn balanced the ball on his finger and gave it a spin. "Many are the plans of a man's heart, but the counsel of the Lord shall stand."

I retreated under my hair again. The Lord? This was ridiculous. By the time I got around to God, there'd be nothing left.

Quinn dribbled around my chair. I sat up, slapped the ball to the floor.

Quinn jogged after it. "You're such a pessimist. Don't worry about Miss Wells. We all know what's up with her."

For such a quiet student, it was amazing all that Quinn seemed to know. Sometimes I forgot that when he showed up at Imani three years ago, he'd come right off the streets. Literally. I didn't want to figure out what Quinn meant about Lottie, but I knew what was up with her, all right. He knew what was up with her too. "You know her well?"

Quinn made a snorting sound. "She used to run a summer camp at the rec a few years back." He stared at the floor. "I know her better than I'd like."

I just stared at the ceiling. Though Quinn's recent spiritual epiphany had caused a bit of a rift between us, I'd been closer to this boy at times than a lot of the people I called my friends.

If she did something to him, I'll . . .

Quinn passed me the ball. "You down for some ball or what?"

When I pressed my thighs to check their condition, pain met my touch. "Not today."

"Hamstring?"

"And quads. Comes and goes. I got a little crazy with the drumming."

Quinn sat across from me, hugging the back of the chair. "New teacher's chair? Smells good."

I leaned in too, drawn by the faint sweetness wafting from the fabric. I smiled as Quinn sniffed deeper. In spite of his becoming a Jesus Freak, I often wished Quinn were my son.

"The young set told me she was fine. It'll be hard to top Miss Wilkins though. I'm a senior and I just stopped sweating her over the summer. Sounds like Ms. Okoye has potential. What do you think of her?"

That was one question I didn't intend to answer, especially not to a student. I reached for my bag under the desk and slipped out of my shoes, exchanging the leather slip-ons for a pair of sneakers I kept on hand for basketball emergencies. "One quick game. I've got somewhere to be."

Quinn raised an eyebrow. "Can't even talk about her? Sounds like you've got it bad."

"You know me well, don't you?"

"Know you? Doc, for a long time, I wanted to be you. I studied your every move."

That's scary. "What did I do to change your mind?"

"Nothing. I just found another hero." Quinn picked a Bible up off the floor and placed it on the table. "Ask your girl. Looks like she knows him too."

35

Grace

*We went to King's Island. I rode all the rides that said
don't ride if you're pregnant, but nothing happened.
It's still in there. I can feel it. When I got home, I
climbed up the banister and jumped down to the
landing three times. Nothing. I'm sore, that's all. The
women on TV always lose their babies when they fall
down the steps. I'd fall off a horse if I had one. No one
will ever love me now.*

Diana Dixon

It had been a long day. A long life. And though I'd danced my
heart out with Brian today, dance was the river I chose to drown
my sorrows in. I'd agreed to attend Zeely's dance class at the new
and beautiful John Glenn Recreation Center long before now, but
the day's tension had made me sure to keep the commitment. The
women all seemed to know each other and embraced me easily,
telling me how good I'd do after a few classes, how fine I'd be.

That made me smile, especially since I didn't really care about
how well I would do or how many inches I'd lose, I just needed
to let my body go so that I could listen with my spirit. So I could
hear God.

"I haven't been coming and I can tell," the woman in front of
me said, frowning as her shorts rolled up, exposing fat around her

knees. The rest of the women, all shapes and sizes, nodded with agreement, their faces sparkling with expectation.

I smoothed my vented tank and cotton shorts and offered a tired smile.

"Don't worry about it. They'll be loose by Christmas," I said to the woman. If Zeely's classes were anything like her personality, we'd both drop some weight for sure.

The lady sighed, nodding. "Yes, Lord. I receive that."

"I'm gonna gonna serve-a Jesus Christ-a . . ."

Reggae music blared, but Zeely was nowhere to be seen. Just as I considered leaving, my friend appeared, wearing a gold sarong and matching head wrap. Zeely's eyes met with mine and turned away. A man with a set of drums came in next, his eyes honed in on me. I gasped.

Brian.

Zeely clapped her hands. "Say hello to Dr. Mayfield, one of my co-workers. He's our live entertainment today."

"I hear that. He's entertaining me just standing there." A woman with gray curls elbowed me in the side, her headband slanting sideways. A grin split the lady's face from ear to ear.

I really tried to smile back.

"Also say hi to my friend, Grace. For my first recital I was her understudy, so you know she's no joke. Hey, girl." Zeely waved.

I waved back, my mind collapsing under the weight of everyone's stares. Then Brian's hands met with the goatskin. My body started to move, almost against my will.

If I survived this, Zeely was getting a beat down.

I made it through the class, but not by much. I limped into my apartment on rubbery legs. What the squats and lunges didn't do, Brian's sideways glances had taken care of. Zeely followed me inside without being asked. She dropped on the futon, guzzling water from the mesh bag slung at her side before turning to me.

"I can't believe you didn't tell me Brian would be there."

Zeely looked regretful, but not guilty. "If I'd told you, would you have come?"

"Well . . ."

"You wouldn't have." Zeely walked to the kitchen, tripping over a bag of trash. She shot me a questioning look before gathering the plastic handles in her fingers. And she wrinkled her nose at the smell.

The mess I'd made this afternoon was substantial, more than some clothes thrown around on the way out the door: a sticky bowl and a half-melted quart of Häagen-Dazs, a worn copy of Nikki Giovanni's *Ego Trippin'*, a notebook with tattered pages. There was the usual too: three outfits and two pairs of shoes.

Zeely picked up the ice cream and tossed it down the disposal. Then she lifted the trash bag outside the door. "What gives?"

I didn't even want to get into it. "It was an ice cream kind of afternoon. That's all I'm going to say."

She reached for my hand. "Yeah. I heard. I'd already invited Brian and it was too late to back out on the invitation. And honestly, I didn't think you'd show."

Me either.

I didn't want to talk anymore. I didn't know what to pray. I kicked off my shoes and spread out on the couch.

"Oh no you don't. Get your sweaty self off that good furniture. It'll be all slick and nasty. Come on. Get up to the shower. You'll feel better after."

Too tired to argue, I mounted the steps.

As usual, Zeely was right. When I returned from releasing my sweat and tears into the steaming shower, Zeely had picked up and vacuumed. Candles burned in the oriental lanterns along the wall. I stopped at the last step and drank in the smell. Blueberry cobbler, my favorite scent.

My friend wiped the counter in the kitchen. "I know you're all into that aromatherapy stuff, but that won't cut it today. I had to put some of the goodies in the attic to use." Zeely pointed to the sky blue pillars extending an inch above their glass containers. "If those don't work, I'll run home for the sugar cookie. It's the psych ward after that."

It won't be the first trip.

Zeely put a hand to her mouth, but went right on cleaning. Some things were just better left unsaid.

And some things had to be dealt with.

I laid my head on the Formica counter. "Maybe we should drive on over to the head shop, especially after that workout class. You almost killed me."

"You'll live and I'm not taking you anywhere. They'd admit me first. All you need is a good dinner—well, scratch that since you dogged that ice cream—and a nap." Zeely put on her coat.

"Maybe." I fingered my sleeve. "I know I need something."

Zeely froze, one hand on the front door. "There. You said it. You need something. It's a start. Enough for me to stay. I'll just shower here. This is my bathroom, anyway, right?" She walked back to the couch and stroked my hair.

That made me laugh. That bathroom wasn't big enough for me to turn around in, let alone shower. I showed her the body wash and scented lotions I kept in there for the other skinny visitor who had yet to show up—my mother. No, I hadn't talked to her much lately outside of a few rounds of phone tag. I told Zee before she could ask. Mom was still mad about me moving here. Going backwards, she said. In truth, I knew she didn't want me uncovering the skeletons she'd buried so carefully. Or at least she thought so. She'd call when she was over it and not a minute sooner.

Zeely said her daddy did the same thing, but she and the Reverend were so close that it was hard for me to imagine him being mad at her. About anything. Her relationship with him was the opposite of what Daddy and I had in the end. She said her father never could make it until lunch without calling to apologize. I smiled. That was the Reverend Wilkins I knew.

She disappeared behind the door and poked her head out a few seconds later. "Pearberry. Now this is me! I know you say the chemicals will kill me, but at least I'll die smelling good."

I had to laugh then.

"I love you, girl. I'm glad you're my friend," I whispered beneath the roar of the water so that she couldn't hear. Would she still love me the same when she knew everything? Not just what had been stolen from me, but what I'd given away? Until now, I'd been too afraid to find out. Maybe I still was. I got up to cook to clear my mind.

"I'm going up yon-der to be with my Lord . . ." Zeely's singing boomed through the bathroom door. Her voice massaged my mind as my knife sliced through the gold-green peppers on my cutting board.

Zeely emerged wrapped in a towel, strutting as though it were a mink coat. She slid onto one of my barstools looking like her song had sounded. Her shoulders shined like wet satin.

I looked at her with wonder. "I think we've got it turned around, you and me. I say I want to be single and you say you want a husband. You don't need anybody. You're defined, completed. I'm the one who needs to be rescued."

Zeely adjusted her bracelets. "Me, completed? No. That's what loneliness—aloneness—does. You have to get real with yourself. Get used to yourself. There's nobody else. There may never be."

I stopped dicing. "Of course there will be somebody. Look at you . . ."

She put a finger to her lips. "Don't. It hurt to hear it at twenty-one. I despise hearing it at thirty-five. I spent my entire life preparing.

Becoming the best woman I could be. Struggling to keep myself. To maintain."

Water cascaded over Zeely's collarbone, like tears. "But good men, Christian men, don't want women like me. They want to save somebody. I don't have any kids for them to watch, no drug habit for them to free me from, not even bad credit. That's too boring for them."

It was funny how she said it, but it was all too true. Everybody loved an underdog, even when it turned and bit them. I scratched my forehead. "Don't feel bad. I don't have anything to offer either."

"Please. You have it all and won't even work it."

I dropped the vegetables into the wok, now bubbling like a volcano. With my other hand, I measured two cups of basmati into the steamer. I had no clue where Zeely was going now, but I'd traveled enough for one day. I was going to sit this one out.

"See? That's it exactly. That innocence. That naïveté that says, 'Somebody has looked out for me, protected me. I'm a wife.' It's how you reach for your cell when the tire goes flat, and I reach for my jack."

Grease popped up and almost got me as the peppers danced in the oil. Zeely had obviously given all this some serious consideration. "And I'm supposed to work that? I don't even know I'm doing it."

"You can't control where the chips fall, but you can arrange them. Pray on that and let the chips fall where they may. That's all I'm going to say."

I was still confused, but I nodded anyway and reached for the tamari, making sure it was the organic one. It was. For Zeely, I bought the regular soy sauce. She distrusted anything that resembled health food except for fruits and vegetables.

We were quiet for a while, but I knew it wouldn't last. Zeely gave in and tried to break down what she was saying, using herself as an example. Dark like her daddy and small like her mother, she didn't need bulky clothes or big hair—though sometimes she liked it. God had made her a black cat. A panther. So she didn't try to be anything else.

When I looked at Zeely, sitting there with no makeup and my worst towel and her toes curled around the chair rungs, I had to agree. She looked exotic. Interesting. And I believed that because she did. I steeled myself, knowing that a commentary about me was coming next. I wasn't disappointed.

"You, on the other hand, aren't sure who you are. You've got an earth woman thing going with the flowers and herbs, but you're not sure about your body. Your clothes. You married Mandingo when you were still copying hairstyles from magazines and shopping at Lerner."

"Cut the Mandingo bit, okay? He's the only husband I'll probably ever have." I lifted the lid on the steamer and checked the rice. Hard as a rock. I walked to the fridge and dug out a pan of leftover brown rice. I had to get sister girl out of here. I loved her, but I couldn't take much more of this.

"Sorry."

I dumped the cold rice into the wok and stirred. It pained me to hear it, but I knew Zeely was telling the truth. I had an identity crisis, one that started with that pink leotard and Miss Fairweather back in the day. I'd reclaimed parts of myself along my journey, but it was stitched together in crazy ways. Even if it wasn't the best time, I had to move forward from an identity crisis . . . to Christ.

The food smelled good but something was missing. I grabbed a clove of garlic from the wire basket on my counter and peeled it quickly before sticking it in the press by the stove. I tossed it in. Yeah. There it was. And Zeely already had two plates down from the cabinet, the square ones that drove her nuts.

She looked at the food with suspicion. "You know they sell this stir-fry stuff already made. You just throw it in the microwave."

I gave her the slant-eyed are-you-crazy look. Her cheeks puffed out. Mine did too.

"Cancer!" we yelled in unison, doubling over in laughter as we always did at the mention of my microwave, a wedding gift used only as a clock. Peter had had been determined not to die of cancer, which had affected several people in his family. His number one no-no? Microwaved foods. I'd never even turned the thing on. Why I'd brought it with me instead of just buying a clock I didn't know either. What I did know was that old habits—and new heartaches—died hard.

"Girl, you haven't changed. Always scared of something. Mostly yourself. You almost had me fooled with that mountain climbing mess." Zeely poured two glasses of water from my filter pitcher in the refrigerator. "What was your blessing?"

"My blessing?" I spooned the stir fry onto the dishes. This time, she had me for real. I had no idea what she meant.

"You know, the stuff that Joyce told all of us. You weren't in Imani, but I know you have one. If you didn't, you wouldn't be here."

My lips clamped around the fork. The phrases, words I thought I'd forgotten, lined up in my mind, pressed against my lips. My voice lowered to a whisper. "'You are a dancer. A mover. A shaker. In Him, you move. In Him, you have your being.'"

"Do you believe that?"

I hadn't believed it. Not for a long time. But here, now, a part of me was breathing what I thought had died a long time ago. "I want to say yes, but I'm not sure it's true . . ."

"Then start with that." Zeely wiped her lips, staring down at her empty plate. "Okay, you know that I'm a carnivore from way back, but you did your thing with those vegetables. You're going to have me cutting up some." She rewrapped her towel, tucking in the corner. "Thanks. I'd better get dressed and get home." She got up from her chair.

I grabbed her arm. "Wait. What did Joyce tell you?"

Zeely snatched her arm back and walked toward the bathroom. Her voice rang out behind her. "You don't think I came up with that black cat junk on my own, do you?"

There is a laughter so deep that it can cleanse things, purge the residue of sad, fearful days. A laughter that makes you collapse onto kitchen counters and dance in your underclothes. That's what came over me then.

When it was over, I sat on the floor heaving and spent, and I laughed some more.

36

Ron

The pastor's office smelled of oranges and cinnamon, cloves and cardamom. I stared at Pastor David behind the desk, dressed in a black shirt and matching pants. If I hadn't heard the man's sermons myself, I might have mistaken the minister for a hit man.

"Melinda. Ronald. I'm glad you could make it."

Leather squeaked as Mindy shifted in her chair. She touched the desk. "Sorry about the last appointment. I was—tied up."

I sniffed and crossed my legs. She was tied up a lot these days. Not that I could really be mad about it. We both had our issues.

Pastor David reached for a leather notebook beside him. "No problem." He flipped through several pages. "Let's see. Last time we discussed physical intimacy. There seemed to be some conflict there."

Mindy frowned. "I don't remember any conflict."

The pastor smiled, but his gaze, leveled at me, remained serious. "No communication means conflict. You're hiding something from me . . . or from each other. Two people in love should have something to say about sex. Especially two Christians." Pastor David turned his chair slightly. "Ronald, you look troubled. Is there something you'd like to say?"

Forget the whole thing.

"Not really." I checked my watch. Brian would be picking me up at six to look at cars. He'd probably take me to Rolls Royce. Oh well. Any place would be better than here.

216

Brian didn't disappoint. He showed up on time and we test-drove several frivolous vehicles. In the end, he took me to the Ford dealership, but they were about to close. Now, for the first time in I don't know how long, we were at his place. Just hanging. Or as much hanging as you can do in a house that looks primed for a layout in *Architectural Digest*. I was trying to stop staring at my reflection in his stainless steel refrigerator when I accepted, not for the first time, that Brian and I saw things from different angles. What man would buy appliances that he had to polish? I couldn't imagine. I lifted a jug of milk from inside and set it on the counter. "You actually shine this thing, B?"

"I do. It's pretty quick." The cappuccino machine buzzed. Brian pulled a mug of steaming chocolate from the burner. He pointed to another pitcher inside the enormous fridge. "There's cream in there too. Farm fresh."

I frowned, pouring a white stream into the puddle of brown. I shook my head. "Homogenized suits me just fine."

Brian laughed. "Always has. I'm surprised you still have a colon after all that cheese . . . I've been eating pretty funky myself lately."

We both took a sip, looking up at the other for a reaction. I tried not to look the way it tasted. I don't care who ground it or grew it, nasty was nasty to me.

He laughed. "I see you haven't changed."

"You neither. You're still nuts."

Brian whipped around, all locks and laughter. "I'm crazy? How many cars did we look at tonight? Twenty? I can't believe you didn't like one of them."

"The Nissan King Cab looked good, but I told you to go Ford first. I've gotta do me."

Brian rolled his eyes. "Take you to Ford so you can buy the same truck again? No way. You've had what, three of them since that first one? Three identical cars in ten years, and I'm crazy . . ."

I pressed my lips together. "Actually, that was the same one for most of that time. Paint job."

"You're kidding, right?"

I grinned, all teeth.

Brian made a sound worthy of a wounded superhero. Obviously my choices pained him deeply, but I couldn't help but laugh. In response, he reached over and grabbed two keys from a red, black, and gold hook mounted on a cutout of Africa.

"Here."

"What's this?"

"Keys to the Saab. That's the only car I've owned that you liked to drive."

I handed them back. "Can't take it."

Brian took a sip from his mug and reached in his pocket. "Okay. Take the Jag."

I folded my arms. "Me? In a purple car? Come on."

"Good point. The Saab then." He pushed the first set of keys as far into my pocket as they would go. He left the room.

I followed him down the hall. Brian turned sharply and shut the door. I knocked. "What are you doing?"

"Going to bed. Today was murder."

I heard.

In a town like Testimony, there was no such thing as a private matter. Everything but bodily functions was well discussed around town. And then it'd show up in the newspaper for good measure if you weren't careful. Or worse yet, someone's pulpit. Sad but true. Keeping my own secrets hadn't been easy.

"Come on, man. Are you really going to stay in there? How am I going to get home?"

Music clicked on. Handel's *Messiah*. "Drive your car. I'll change the title tomorrow."

37

Jerry

I'd not only missed a night of work. I'd missed a night of sleeping too. Monique would be starting at Imani the next day and had a whole new life, starting with motherhood, to adjust to, almost overnight. I'd offered to keep the baby with me through the night, both out of habit and need, I knew now. Monique, ever the smart one, had declined. "We need to get to know each other, Daddy. It's time."

And maybe she was right. With Monique home from her boarding school, some of the financial pressure would let up, but there'd be other pressures now, the crush of people knowing that Carmel and I had not only failed as husband and wife but as parents too. As the springs of my sofa bed stabbed my back and the thin mattress chilled my skin, I tried not to think about it.

I was up spreading the comforter underneath me when a pair of headlights flashed though the curtains. I shielded my eyes, running to open the door before Carmel could knock and wake up the house.

Carmel sagged against the doorframe. "Sorry I'm late. Full moon. Lots of deliveries. I don't want to fight. I'm here for the girls."

I took her hand, pulled her out of the cold. There were some things even a divorce decree couldn't erase, common courtesy being one of them. "The girls are knocked out. And you don't look in any shape to be driving. Take a nap. I almost fell asleep at the wheel last week. With all these bills, neither of us can risk it."

Though I expected her to protest, Carmel nodded, toppling onto that pitiful mattress. She pulled the sheet up to her neck and patted the void beside her. She never was one to sleep alone. "Come on. I won't bite. Just don't steal the sheet. I'm freezing as it is."

I swallowed hard, eying the broken recliner in the corner. The last time I'd slept in it, my neck was stiff for days. I walked to the other side of the bed and slid in, moving close enough to borrow some of Carmel's heat, without starting a fire. The landlord had promised to see about the heating system, but so far my calls hadn't gotten any results. If I'd known I'd be having a houseful of women tonight, I would have pressed the issue. Instead, the girls were sleeping comfortably with my only space heater while I prayed we wouldn't have a fire—Carmel sighed a little—of any kind.

I doubled the pillow under my head, pinched my eyes shut. I could try to squeeze in with the girls, but Monique and I together would break the bed. She took after me in the big and tall department. Besides, I wasn't so sure that I wanted to leave where I was. Even though this was temporary and artificial, I'd spent some of the best years of my life beside this woman. One more night wouldn't hurt.

Or so I thought.

Carmel threw her leg across me like she had on so many other nights in our many years together. Before it would have barely earned a smile. Tonight, it was a match on dry tinder. I could have turned away just about anything at that moment, anything but that. Hoping not to get slapped, I turned to her, kissing her shoulder, checking for her reception. If she pushed me away, I'd just roll over and catch a cold. I'd endured worse from her when we were living under the same roof.

I'd made up my mind that it was okay if she played sleep or said something to trouble me, but she didn't push me away. She turned over slowly, sat up on one elbow, and pulled me in. Her lips opened wide for me. Inviting. I shivered, but threw off the sheet.

There was more than one way to get warm.

⁓◎⁓

Carmel lay still as I moved around: to the shower, to my closet, to the kitchen to warm a bottle. She was stirring slightly, moving the covers a bit, so I finished quickly, not wanting her to wake. If she woke up, she would say something and I didn't want her to. Maybe the space heater I'd gotten up to buy at the all-night Meijer was warm enough for her to stay put. I should have been freezing myself, but I wasn't.

I'd forgotten what it felt like to be beside Carmel. Inside her.

Even now, with Monique's mess and Carmel's doctor boyfriend out there somewhere, I felt like we could win. We could be a family again, even if it wasn't the family we'd planned on. Then I'd heard it. So soft that I almost didn't make it out.

"Jerry . . ."

I knew that tone and I didn't like the sound of it. I'd do everything I could to quiet it so that my dream could last a little longer. I walked over to where she was sitting at the edge of the couch and leaned over. My cheek, freshly shaven, slid across hers. I felt like my old self, back from a long trip. "Want some breakfast?"

"No thanks."

That didn't deter me either. I kissed her neck, put one arm around her waist. I mumbled something about her being my breakfast, starting with a kiss.

"About that."

"What?" I closed my eyes and kissed her shoulder. Right on her birthmark, I knew from the way she sighed. It sounded so good it hurt. Her words would hurt too. I never should have asked her to stay.

She covered her face in her hands. "Last night. I shouldn't have— we shouldn't have—"

Hurt burned my eyes. "So what are you saying?"

"I think you know."

I got up. I knew it would go down like this, but I'd wanted to

221

believe that somehow I'd gotten through to her. I guess that other man had left a mark on her I couldn't undo. I'd tried not to think of it last night, like I'd thought about it so many other nights, but in the end that's what it came down to. She didn't want me. She never would. "'I don't bite,' you said. I should have known better. This is how it always is between us."

It was definitely how it would be from now on. Carmel held a finger to her lips, motioning for me to be quiet so the girls wouldn't hear. What did it matter if they heard? It was their lives in this too.

She pulled the sheet around her shoulders. "You're right. We make good love and bad spouses for each other. We did it for a long time. Only, I'm not a cheerleader anymore, Jerry. And you're not a running back. There has to be more to us."

My head dropped back. "Get up so I can close the couch."

"That's all you have to say?"

"Does it matter what I have to say? You've got the keys to the kingdom. You lock the bank to me anyway."

"Jerry."

I got up, pulling the sheets with me. I closed the couch, slamming each cushion in place. "Don't Jerry me. I've given up everything to make this family work. Everything."

Carmel gave me a look of pity, one that made me want to be anywhere but here. I'd seen it before and hated it then. It was like she knew some secret, something about me that I couldn't figure out.

"What!"

She closed her eyes, folded her hands in her lap like she was trying to cover something. Like I was. "You haven't given up everything for this family, Jerry. You haven't given her up. You never will."

"What? Who?" Now I was totally confused.

"Are you really going to make me say it?"

All the warmth seemed to go out of the room. I paused for a

second before I spoke, wondering if my breath would fog up in front of me. I almost hoped it would. We were going to a bad place. "Zeely? I haven't been near her. Outside work, we hardly even talk—"

"You called her name last night."

There it was, bleeding and ugly, but out in the air. There'd been a whisper of it when I woke this morning, echoing in the room like a ghost. I'd drowned it out with my eggs and aftershave, my joy. And yet, here it was. I stumbled to the recliner and dropped like a rock. It crunched under the impact. The footrest flipped out. I felt like my heart was going to come out too.

"I didn't."

"You did."

"I didn't mean to. I wasn't thinking of her. Really. I don't know why I—" Well, I did know why, or at least I had an idea. I was alone again, a grown man living like a teenager or a college student. In my adolescence, Zeely was the only name on my lips, the only name I knew. Maybe some nights while I tossed and turned knowing Carmel was in Dr. Rick's bed, I'd unwittingly invited Zeely into mine. How it'd come out when I least expected it, I'd never know. "Honey, please—"

She shook her head. "We had something beautiful last night. Something that made me remember all that was good between us. And yet, in the best of it, Zeely was there, as always. She is your dream. She always has been. I was just the flesh you practiced on. It's taken me all this time to accept it, really accept it, but I give. I thought at the beginning that I'd beat her, but the victory is hollow. Meaningless."

"No, baby, no. It's not like that. It was never like that. Please . . ." I was begging like crazy now, up out of the recliner and back on the couch next to her.

She gave me a smile that broke my heart. "I won't keep waiting to see if you can really love me—and just me. After last night, I accept the truth. I cut in on a God thing and this—" she nodded to the bedroom where the girls slept—"all of this has been the price."

"Honey . . ." I held her face in my hands, letting her tears mix with mine. "No. Please don't do this." Her eyes answered, giving me a look that meant the end, that honey was only good for catching flies.

"It's her you want. It's time for us both to accept it." She got up and dressed quietly before knocking on the door to my room. Monique was a light sleeper and had probably heard us, but right now I didn't care. My heart was breaking all over again.

I stared at the wall while Carmel talked to Monique and Justice . . . my granddaughter. I was going to have to learn how to say that out loud. Everyone here, including the people at the day care, thought she was my child. Maybe Carmel and I had convinced ourselves of it too. Well, she wasn't mine. Ours. Not like that. It was time to stop playing house on all fronts.

"Girls? You dressed? Come and eat," I said, adding that they should give Mom a kiss, but I couldn't look at her just then. Even after the divorce, I'd always seen Carmel as my wife. Now I knew that she'd really never felt like I was her husband. In her mind, I'd belonged to someone else all along.

38

Brian

The buzz of the metal detector and the shuffle of students' feet sounded like music to me—even the complaints. After the mess with Lottie, I'd decided to focus on what I was here for, to teach. Anything else that was going to happen, good or bad, was out of my control. It was hard to admit, but freeing somehow. There was just now. Today. And this morning I was manning the new media-finding machine. This would be fun.

A sophomore leaned across the table as I tossed her pearled Nokia into the pile: six phones, two handhelds, and a music player. Not bad for the first morning.

This girl wasn't going down without a fight though. "You can't take that. My boyfriend bought it—"

I chuckled. "I hope your man has a good job or your mom comes to get it quickly. Talk to Principal Rogers. Next!" I motioned for the next person to step through the machine.

"So no phones? Since when? This is outrageous."

"Isn't it? You have to listen up to those announcements. You got the new policy in homeroom a few days ago. Everyone signed them. Parents too. Just have your mom pick it up. It'll be here." I hoped so anyway. Personally, I thought the policy a little silly and totally unenforceable, but it provided just the distraction I needed today.

As phone girl walked away, I caught a whiff of her. Plumeria. Though I loved it on Grace, it smelled horrible on that kid.

Her boyfriend should pick up some new perfume with that next phone.

"Good morning." Head shaved and wearing clothes clean and pressed, Jerry made me do a double take. A tall girl holding a baby stood behind him. I smiled at her as the pieces came together in my head. She had her father's big bones with Carmel's hourglass proportions. Her hair curved just below her chin, then hung in layers past her shoulders. I didn't envy Jerry the job of trying to look out for her in this place.

She'd been a toddler the last time I'd seen her. The baby news had definitely been left out.

"Is that Monique?"

Jerry nodded reluctantly as though prying the last layers off their secret. "She's grown up, hasn't she?"

That was one way of putting it. There was no sense beating around the bush. I lowered my voice. "They're going to be all over her."

"I know."

Monique pulled a chair from the hall and sat down with the baby asleep on her shoulder. No wonder bruh had been looking so rough. Life was sure something. "Your girls. Do you need to drop the baby off somewhere? I can cover." Joyce had laid a plan for an in-school nursery, but so far the funding and licensing hadn't come through. I wished now that I'd shaken the town trees a little harder to hustle up the funds.

"They're both staying here. Thelma is going to watch Justice and Monique is transferring from Rose Hill—"

My head snapped then. "Rose Hill Preparatory? *The* Rose Hill?"

Jerry nodded. "The one and only."

It was my turn to sit down. I'd sent plenty of kids over there to smooth their way into the Ivy League. Even Quinn. Not one of them made it through the interviews. And the money? More than most colleges. "That place has to be twenty grand a year. How on earth did you manage—"

"We didn't manage it. That's why she's here."

Monique looked away, patting the baby's back.

Realizing that I'd stepped into a place reserved for family only, I reached into my wallet and held out a twenty to Monique and her baby. "Go to the cafeteria, honey. Miss Thelma is in there. Your dad and I can take your books up."

She looked to her father for approval, and when he nodded, she left looking glad to get away.

When she was out of earshot, I could hardly remain calm. "Are you really going to enroll her here? We have a few honors classes, but Miami Valley would be ideal. I went to grad school with a guy over there. I could give him a call." I felt desperate to help, to keep Monique's time at Rose Hill from going to waste. I didn't know what her best subjects were, but if she had Jerry's knack for math, she'd have a free ride anywhere.

And where will the baby go?

It was a question that I didn't know how to answer. Evidently, Jerry didn't either. He seemed to feel good about this choice. As much as I loved Imani, I wasn't so sure. Some of these young cats were just . . . trouble.

"We're going to make this work for now. Sometimes you have to make the best of things. Even bad things. You know?" Jerry's eyes narrowed.

I did know. I stared at the floor, wishing I had something to offer besides another problem. The hall cleared momentarily, leaving the two of us alone. What he said next rocked me back on my heels.

"I heard what happened."

I tried not to act as shocked as I was. Had there been a feature on the six o'clock news or what? "Who hasn't heard?"

Jerry gave me a look from his football days. "What were you thinking, man? You were the one who warned me to skip the drama, remember? Grace is really special. Don't let Lottie confuse you. You'll . . . regret it." His voice faltered.

"There's nothing between me and Grace. I barely know her."

Jerry's whole body shook with silent laughter. "Please. You've talked more in the last week than you have in the past year—and every word of it was about her."

Was I that obvious?

"I'm praying for you. Just be careful."

Now I was a little offended. "I didn't touch her. Have a little faith, will you?" I wanted to gobble the words back into my mouth as quickly as I'd said them. Faith was the last thing I wanted to get this guy going on. He'd never shut up.

Jerry waved to the security guard outside the front door. "I believe you, but it's going to be a tough ride. I'll be praying."

"You do that, O.J."

As if energized by his nickname, Jerry headed for the cafeteria.

Before he disappeared around the corner, I called to him. "Hey!"

"Yeah?"

"I know you and Ron talk. Would you mind not telling him about this? I'd like to tell him myself."

Jerry flinched. "That'll be hard. He told me."

It shouldn't have bothered me so much that Ron had known and said nothing, but it did. It was hard to make out now with all the pictures of my former students crowding my desk, but a picture from my own graduation sat there too, jammed up against the wall. The snapshot was mostly tired smiles, mortarboards, and tassels, but in the midst of it all was one white face, one pair of questioning eyes. The lawyer-eyed picture, Eva had called it. I searched for it now and took a swing at the wrought iron frame. It tumbled to the floor, cracked across the middle. I picked it up with regret.

It wasn't Ron's fault that he'd known, but he should have said something. And worse yet, who had told him? Zeely? Not exactly her style, but possible. Joyce. It had to be.

Grace came in with a stack of photocopies and a dreamy look. She leaned over to look at the picture, broken in my hands. "Look at you! Is that high school? Oh yeah. I see Zeely back there." She picked away the glass as she spoke, leaving the open frame and the photo inside. "There. That will do until you get another frame. That's a priceless shot. Who took it?"

I couldn't remember. "My mother maybe. Or Zeely's father. Maybe Joyce."

My mother? I hadn't called Eva that in a very long time. And yet, that was what she'd been. feeding me, clothing me, loving me. That other woman, the one who was both never and always with me, had only offered her DNA. It seemed rational when put that way, but DNA was a curious, irrational thing. Perhaps it was my mother's part of me that made me take this thing with Ron to heart, even when I knew I should let it go. I think I just wanted someone to be mad at.

"If you don't mind, I'm going to run down to Joyce's office for a while before our first class. Will you need me for anything?"

"Not that I can think of." She looked relieved.

"Page me over the intercom if you need me."

"Sure."

My shoes skimmed the hall like a tap show as I passed the attendance desk headed for Joyce's office. Long before I reached her door, I heard voices, especially Joyce's. Odd. She rarely raised her voice, and from the sound of it, she was talking about someone—another rare event.

Embroiled in a phone conversation with her back to the door, she didn't move when I came in, but she gave me a sidelong glance recognizing my presence. Instead of trying to make out her sparse, graveled words, I picked up the book off the top of the pile on the corner of the desk.

What Every Woman Should Know about Menopause.

I dropped it back to the desk with a thud, wishing I'd bothered to read the spine. There were some things I'd rather not know.

Joyce turned a little farther toward me, her words now louder, more clear. "No. She will go through with it. You know why. I know why. Neither of them has a clue."

Every muscle in my body tensed. It sounded like she might have been talking about me, but I knew better than that. Not right in my face. I searched the room, looking for something to focus my mind on. I noticed her purse first, a designer bag I bought for her two Christmases ago, but had never seen her carry. Next to the purse, an array of bottles lining her file cabinet, many of them the same ones as in my bathroom at home, caught my attention. The difference was Joyce actually took hers. All of them.

Alfalfa, astragalus, B-complex . . .

Joyce continued as she turned a little more, almost facing me. "The body is a temple even when the altar has been abandoned. Sex is church. Worship. And you know what happens when you take a woman to church. She wants more. Much more."

I got up. Whether she was talking about me or someone else, I didn't want to hear it.

She motioned for me to sit down.

I took my seat, shocked by what she said next. "I tried to tell him about her before. He said there was nothing to it. Do what you can, Red."

Red. Ron. Not only did he know about Lottie but he had the nerve to be talking to Joyce about it behind my back?

And to think I gave him my car.

I straightened, expecting Joyce would cut the conversation short. She kept talking while looking me right in the eyes.

"Yes. The main thing I need you to do is pray. This is all heading somewhere and only the Lord knows where that is. She could do a lot of damage. Especially now. You know what I mean. I love you," Joyce said before hanging up.

And then with a slow deliberation that made me crazy, she rearranged her desk, then clasped her hands.

"Is there something I can do for you?" Her lips curled, but not into a smile.

There were a lot of things I could have said: Stop talking about me, be honest with me. My answer surprised us both. "Fire me."

She looked away. "You don't mean that. I'm doing all I can—"

"You're doing too much. Calling Ron about me? Come on. We're not kids anymore. He's got his own problems. I don't need him to fix mine. You either."

Joyce tapped her computer mouse. A document appeared on the screen. She hit a few strokes on the keyboard. Another tap of the mouse. The printer hummed. She eased up from the chair, retrieving the document from the printer. "Sign here. Have your things out today. Tell Grace to take over the class until I find a replacement."

I wadded the paper into a ball. I didn't want to quit. I just needed some understanding. "Don't tempt me, Doc. I don't have to be here—to take this. I could have stayed where I was."

"Maybe you should have." My former teacher walked around to the front of her desk and sat down on it with her ankles tucked beneath her.

She pointed to the file cabinet, the bottles on it. "Olive leaf extract. Hand me that, please."

I obeyed quickly, watching as she dropped two capsules into her palm and swallowed them dry with little effort.

"I'm sorry. I didn't mean it. Any of it."

She stared over her glasses at me. "No, you were right. Your coming to Imani was a mistake, both mine and yours. You thought you could change me—"

"That wasn't it!"

She held up a finger. "I thought the students would change you."

My voice betrayed me. "They did change me."

"I know. You're worse. Before, you thought you knew everything. Now, you're sure you do." Joyce put down the bottle and pressed her palms into the desk.

More analysis? Everybody wanted to shrink me.

"That's not it at all. Perhaps I'm still adjusting from the aptitudes at the college level to the aptitudes here." It was my dissertation voice and it sounded as wretched and false to me now as it had back then. Some things couldn't be defended, my motivations among them.

Joyce grabbed a dictionary from somewhere on her desk and flipped quickly through the A's. "'Aptitude . . . Talent. Capacity for learning.' There is no adjustment needed for that. These students have the same aptitude as the ones you taught at State. It's your attitude that needs adjustment. You think this job is a joke. And it shows."

A vein popped at my temple. This was too much. "It shows? You want to see my lesson plans? My student files? I know more about them than their probation officers, than their parents!" If I'd known I'd be the defendant instead of the judge, I might have prepared better. As it was, I was going down in flames. I felt a little sick.

"That's just it. You know everything about them, but you don't *know* them. It sounds the same, but it's worlds apart. As far as life is from death." Joyce retreated behind her desk. The leather headrest hissed a little as her head pressed into it.

Death. What did Joyce know about it? Everything I loved died. Everyone. "They don't need me to be their friend, Doc. They need tools. Resources . . ."

Joyce cupped her face between her fingertips. "Is that all I gave you? Resources? If so, I'm also to blame."

That knocked the wind out of me somehow, like someone had hit me with a wrecking ball. I stood and leaned onto the file cabinet, trying not to think of all that Joyce had given me. Her voice echoed across the years in spite of me, refusing to be silent.

You're brilliant. Better than just going to college. Good enough for a doctorate.

I stared down at my shoes, tracing the square toe with my eyes, traveling back over the path of my life. Those simple words had survived all my failures, all my hurts. There had been good books and great learning; Joyce had given more than that. She'd taught us all to believe. The one thing I'd been trying to forget.

Her words moved across my forehead and settled around my eyes. I held onto the file drawer to steady myself in case it was a bad one. Tension headaches, my doctor called them. Ron had them too. Joyce's bag fell from its perch.

I caught it, but lost the contents. When I bent down to retrieve her things, the floor was thick with secrets.

Joyce's eyes never left me as I took in the view: seven pill bottles, upended and rolling in different directions, peppermints, wig adhesive. The fattest vial read DCOP. *Dayton Clinical Oncology Program.* I knew that stamp all too well. I shoved everything back into the bag and put it back on the file cabinet. I tripped over my feet on the way to my chair. She'd told me to sit down. One day I'd learn to listen, even when I didn't feel like it.

Joyce's voice cracked. "You got it all?"

I stared at her, hungry for some evidence to disprove the theory I'd just seen outlined on the floor. As my gaze skimmed across her—a tendril of arm, a slip of neck held high over two bony hollows that were her cheeks—my eyes widened, choking on something familiar. My knees buckled even though I was sitting down. "Cervical? Ovarian?"

"Blood now. Leukemia. I had it in both breasts before you came. I made it through that. I hoped you would get in the yoke with me, take some of the stress."

I leaned way forward, almost off the chair. "Why didn't you tell me? You said you were sick before, but not this. Never this. I would have—"

233

Joyce shook her head. Slowly. "You would have what? Made the budget meet? Searched for new teachers? Bailed students out of jail? No. If I have to tell you to do something, you're doing it for the wrong reasons."

The past five years tumbled through my mind like dirty laundry. Meetings I'd missed. Memos I hadn't read. The summers in Africa. That irritating urgency in Joyce's voice. I'd lost all the women I dared to love. This couldn't happen again. "How long?"

Joyce crossed her legs. "Not long enough for us to waste time discussing it. I picked out my casket last Christmas."

I slid to my knees.

"It's that bad, even if I'm just starting to look it. My bottles of friends over there have been a great help, but things are speeding up. Or maybe I should say slowing down. I've been running forever, it seems."

I was in the right position to believe, but when I looked up at Joyce, I didn't see the healing I was praying for. I saw her in a casket.

She frowned. "Don't look at me like that, Brian. I'm just dying. You're already dead."

39

Ron

My office looks down from the tenth floor of Freedom Tower, home of the courthouse, City Hall, and as of six months ago, Bentek and Associates, founded by Mindy's father, my current employer.

From my desk, I can see things up here that are easily missed on the ground: a businessman leaving the homeless shelter with a small boy, wiping his breakfast on the back of his sleeve; a woman wearing clothes out of season, her whitewashed shoes mended too many times. Things that make me watch and pray, speak into my voice recorder; add to my list of things to do. Things to be.

"Inquire about volunteering at homeless shelter. Stop."

It hurt sometimes to look down from Freedom Tower and see hungry confusion instead. After so many years, the fee of testimony was still required to live free in this town. Now more than ever.

Even I wasn't immune. I had a stack of wedding invitations on my desk to prove it. Though I wasn't starving or homeless like some of the people passing by below, I longed to be free. I knew though that by freeing myself I would be sentencing many of those people to a life of bondage. God had made a way for me, created hands to pull me out of that house on the hill. Though I didn't like it or want it, I'd been put in place for such a time as this. The pages in front of me were proof of that.

Lottie's complaint against Brian.

Why she'd come to us—to me—I wasn't sure. Despite an internship in criminal law, it wasn't what I or my firm was known for. I'd tried to downplay it to talk her off the ledge, but the others had stoked the fire, hoping my friend would easily burn. He had it coming, they'd said. A bigmouth who had finally showed his hand. I wondered how much Bentek had to do with this—Brian was his nemesis at city council meetings. And no matter how much I squirmed, pleaded that it wasn't my specialty, they didn't budge. In a town like ours, there were no specialties. The family doctor often served as dermatologist, gynecologist, and every other "ologist" needed. It looked like things were about the same for lawyers, outside driving to the next town.

So here I was, trying to do my job, love my friend. The hardest part was Lottie. She'd been thorough: pictures, witnesses, everything. When she showed up, I hardly knew her either. No makeup or short skirts. She played the victim well, but she played the gardener better, planting a seed of doubt so deep that even I found myself wondering. A lot had changed. I wanted to say that I knew how far Brian would go, what he would do, but I wasn't sure.

Are you talking about yourself or him?

Probably both. At one time we'd boasted that we knew the other as well as ourselves. These days, that wouldn't be saying much on my end. Still, there had been all those messages from Lottie when I'd gone to Brian's house. Things he'd said about her months before. A picture she'd had taken of them at a club.

Little things, bones and teeth.

Skeletons.

They tumbled out of closets at the oddest times, stacking odds and threatening jobs, friendships, lives. And then there was God, who'd caused even the dry bones to dance before me.

My assistant's voice came through the speaker, just as I lowered my head to pray. "Sir, there's a Mr. Mayfield waiting to—Sir! Wait! You can't—"

I heard the door burst open behind me. I lifted my head and looked out the window, watching a pigeon on the ledge take flight. Free as a bird. "What took you so long?"

"Why are you in my business?" Brian's words were cold. Cutting.

I'd wanted to talk to him, but not like this. "Maybe if you'd handle your business a little better—"

"Don't even go there, okay?"

Brian was next to me now, and I looked up to see his anger dissolve as his eyes roamed over what was spread out on my desk: Lottie's pictures, obviously taken moments after the incident; another snapshot of her looking like a wholesome art teacher in a long denim skirt; Grace's name and number scrawled on another piece of paper.

The truth must have hit him like a bullet. He collapsed into the chair behind him. "I didn't do this. You've got to know that."

"We can't talk about the case."

"I just need to know that you believe . . . in me."

"Always." But I knew he could see things behind my eyes. Questions. That seed of doubt I was battling to uproot.

My receptionist's voice came through the speaker. "Mr. Jenkins? Call for you. Line two."

"The little woman?" Brian rarely mentioned Mindy Bentek or the wedding plans he and I no longer discussed. He stood and started to pace.

My finger lingered over the blinking light, then pushed another button instead. "Can you take a message please? Yes, I know she'll be disappointed. Tell her I'll call her at lunchtime."

I turned to him, swallowed hard. "Let's get it over with. You didn't come here to talk about the case. This is about Joyce. You're mad and we both know it, so let's just do it."

"Why are you all in my business? Calling Joyce about me. And did you know that she's dying? Did you?" Brian's words were sharp again, but they were cutting both ways.

I got up, looked him eye to eye, something few people dared to do. "Your business came to me. And about Joyce, yes, I knew. I saw she didn't look well and I asked. It took a lot to get it out of her—"

"Whatever. You can call her, gossiping about me, but you can't call me to tell me something important. You haven't changed."

"And neither have you." I was amused for a second, but just as quickly, I returned his hardened look and held up both hands. "You done?"

"I guess."

"All right. I have an appointment waiting, so I'll make this quick. First, I called Jerry regarding the case I'm working on."

Brian just glared at me.

He wasn't putting it together. This was starting to feel like charades. I swept a hand over the pictures on my desk. "Read between the lines."

It suddenly registered on his face. "Why would she come to you? You don't even do that kind of law."

Okay. He figured it out. That was as far as I could go. It was my turn to be quiet. "I can't discuss this with you."

"Bentek is probably loving this. They've got it in for me over here, a lot of those guys. I go to the city commission meetings and ask questions they don't want to hear. They'd love to smear my name." Brian moved toward the door. When he reached it, he looked back over his shoulder. "There's no way out for me on this one. We can't legally prove we're related so you won't get off it. Don't go down with me. Save yourself." He paused before turning away. "Just let me fall."

I closed the distance between us and put my hand on his shoulder. "If you're innocent, I'll do what I can to prove it."

Brian put his hand on the door, but I didn't let go of him.

"But if it comes to that, we'll both fall," I said. "Together."

"You don't have to, you know. You could just walk away."

I did it before. We both have. My grip faltered. "I know."

40

Monique

After two weeks the school's media ban had been lifted and I saw things I'd never seen in a classroom before: headphones, crazy clothes, and chaos. At first, I'd been a little scared and taken my place at the front of the class, never daring to look back, but each day brought me back another row until I could see the vacant eyes of my peers. Their faces were blank, unconcerned. Though I knew I'd have to move back up sometime, switch to another school, today I just wanted to blend in, to be someone other than the math teacher's daughter. Once people heard my name called the first time, everything changed. I could see it on their faces. So I raised my hand fast, never allowing any teacher to get to my last name.

This math class wasn't a class at all for me really but some kind of community service hour where I'd tutor students studying to take the proficiency test. My schedule—peer tutoring, leadership seminar, Latin—still read like Daddy was hoping for Harvard. I wasn't. I'd tossed that dream out the window on the way home from Rose Hill. Now I wasn't sure if it had ever been my dream in the first place. Now, I just wanted to fit in, to belong to something.

The class filled. The purple-haired girl I'd seen the first day sat beside me. She had her phone back and took it out frequently to text someone. Finally, she looked my way with what I mistook for a smile. Like a fool, I grinned back.

She leaned back from me like I had the plague. "What you looking at, Moesha?"

"Nothing." I said, fingering my new braids, vowing to judge smiles more carefully next time. She'd have to try a lot harder than that to offend me. I'd been the only black student at Rose Hill for two long, lonely years.

My dad came in next, which I wasn't expecting, followed by a dark-skinned woman in a pink suit and matching shoes. I knew without asking who she was. My mother had told me about her many times. This was Zeely, the woman my father had planned to marry instead of my mom. The woman I'd kept him from by being born, the woman I was still keeping him from. And she looked so good that I didn't know whether to hate her or ask her for fashion advice. At the sight of her, any hopes I'd had of our family holding together slipped away.

A coat brushed against my face as a tall boy with freckles shoved into the desk beside me. I turned away before he had a chance to blast me. These kids were so rude. I opened the math book I'd been given, turned to the section for the day.

"Sorry," he said, pulling the book down.

I swallowed hard; now close enough to really see him, especially his eyes gold in a ring of green.

My daughter's eyes.

I gripped the desk.

I'd never known the boy's real name, so I hadn't been lying when I told everyone that. We'd talked online for a while, biding time until I'd made it to Testimony one weekend to meet relatives. He'd had a party that, despite the other people there, I eventually realized was planned to celebrate me alone. After that night, I'd never seen or heard from him again. He had deleted his MySpace and changed his cell number.

He looked different now with a 'fro instead of locks. He'd grown some too. Sometimes I'd wondered if I hadn't made him up altogether. But now he was here, leaning close, kissing my hair.

"Doll, is it you? What happened? I lost my phone. My mom

went loco about the MySpace. You look so good . . . Why did you run away from me?"

I looked up front at Zeely and my father, thankful for once that his attention was occupied. My hand pressed against his, a feeble attempt to stop him from caressing my shoulder. My fingers found my lap again. There was no use.

He'd found me.

41

Grace

I talked to the baby today. I told her I was sorry for trying to kill her. I think she understood. It's a girl, I think, but I hope I'm wrong. Being a girl is a difficult thing. Men don't have to think so hard. Or at least I don't think so, although Daddy thinks too much. I told her to just keep quiet and try not to get too big while I try and think of something.

Diana Dixon

"Who was that girl with Jerry in the hall?" I loaded salad onto my fork, staring at the baby in a travel crib next to Thelma. She had beautiful eyes, that little girl.

Zeely nibbled on a french fry. "That was his daughter, Monique."

"She's striking. And so tall. She could model easy."

My friend pointed a potato stick toward the baby. "She's his too."

"Wow. Such cute kids."

"You act surprised. It's not like he's ugly."

It's not like he's cute. "No, but I wouldn't have expected those girls to be his."

Zeely shrugged. "They look like him to me."

"I guess." I opened another pack of salad dressing, immediately wishing I'd brought my own from home. I puckered.

"Nasty?"

"Too much vinegar."

"Want some of mine?" Zeely pushed her cheeseburger across the table.

"No thanks." Zeely's size six cheeseburgers would become solid fat on me. "Let me ask you something."

"Shoot."

"A guy left a message last night. A lawyer. Brian's brother? Maybe he said friend. Ron Jenkins. Do you know him? He sounded . . ."

"White?" Zeely pinched off a piece of the sandwich. She bit half and put the other part back on the plate.

I pulled down my bottom lip. White. Did my old college roommate describe me as black? Or Kim, my old prayer partner from church? What about Jackie, my neighbor before I moved away? I looked over at Zeely, a darker version of all three women—they had the same personality, painfully blunt. Would my friends say I was black? Absolutely. "Yes, he sounded white."

"He is." Zeely picked up the whole burger this time and took a bite.

A trail of vinaigrette dripped onto my shirt. I thought of the picture in my drawer, the one I'd seen this morning. "Is he the redhead in the graduation picture? Between you and Brian?"

"Yep. That's Red."

"Red? I remember you talking about him, but I just didn't see him as . . ."

"White?" Zeely laughed this time.

"Yes, that. Real light skinned maybe. Light enough to make you wonder. Like Joyce."

Now Zeely seemed irritated. "So now that you know, does it change anything? Does it matter?"

"Not to me. It must matter to you though."

Zeely sat up straight. "Why do you say that?"

I dabbed my shirt. "Because you never mentioned it before."

42

Ron

"Good afternoon, sir."

"Hello, Dee. How are you?"

I couldn't help but smile as the coat checker reached for my coat at the Sterling Club. No matter how many times I came here, my best times were usually spent as I checked in my coat. I pushed past the woman's outstretched hand and hung my coat on the first hanger.

She looked around, both worried and delighted. "Here's your ticket, Mr. Jenkins. And please stop hanging up your coat, you're going to get us both in trouble."

The things I'd looked down on from my window lately played through my mind. It pained me that of all things in town for anyone to worry about, they would waste their concern on whether a grown man hung up his own clothes. "Okay, I'll tell you what. Next time I'm here, I'll come in and toss my coat on your head and storm to my seat. How's that?"

She shook her head. "We'll both get fired. They'll know you're fooling. And when I don't sling it back at you, they'll know I'm fooling too. You know I don't mind what you do, but I have to be careful. You should too. They already think . . ." Her voice faded as she rearranged my jacket on the hanger, just for effect.

Considering that what seemed frivolous and even enjoyable to me might cost Dee a much needed job, I apologized. I knew what people at the club thought of me. The trick of it was that they had no idea what I thought of them. I stepped away, whispering something Dee already knew—that I'd much rather have had lunch with her than any of them.

Except Mindy, of course.

Of course.

Dee patted her salt-and-peppered afro and said she understood but I should try and have a nice lunch anyway. Eat something. Said that she'd told the fellas in the back to put a little twist on my plate: sweet potatoes instead of white, hot sauce hidden in my greens, and cornbread instead of yellow cake. Most of all, she said, I should smile. Mindy looked to be in a good mood.

I doubted that, but thanked her anyway and passed the maître d' to Mindy's table—soon to be our table. I couldn't help thinking of Brian as I approached. He'd sop this place up like butter, both reviling its luxury and reveling in it at the same time. Though he wasn't going to church anymore, Brian still had something honest at the core of him. Something true. My life had turned into one big lie.

"On time? That's a first." Mindy stood to greet me. I didn't realize until she rested her hand on my arm that my whole body had tensed in preparation for a barrage of kisses or some unexpected spit in my ear.

I'd seen her briefly at the office, but she looked different now, both better and worse. Her face seemed radiant, but her eyes were streaked red, cried wide. I tipped her chin up. "Getting enough sleep?"

She sniffed and not from a cold. "You know how it goes, surfing the Net for research and next thing you know it's 2 a.m. No sleep, Min weeps." She offered a weak smile.

I'd come to say something today, to do something, to try to be honest and true. Mindy's tears hadn't been part of the equation. I could deal with a lot of things, but watching a woman cry wasn't one of them. Still, if I didn't speak up now, there'd be a lot more tears in the years to come. It was now or never. "I need to talk to you about something."

My intended waved for the waiter. She gripped her elbows and leaned forward, pushing the tablecloth out of place. If I'd heard something at church, it wasn't true, she said. People could be so jealous. Didn't I know that? Didn't I love her?

Before I could answer, the waiter arrived with sparkling cider. Astute enough to sense the tension, he suggested house salads and moved quickly away. I wanted to tell him to wait for me, but there could be no more running. This was it.

I rolled back the foil and popped the cork on the chilled cider, commenting again at how much the bottle looked like champagne.

Mindy sighed. "I wish it was."

"Why?"

Her eyes looked even redder than before. Wetter. "To celebrate us and whatever good news you have to tell me."

She wasn't going to let me off easy. No way. "You don't know what I want to talk about. What if it isn't something to celebrate?" There was no sense in boosting her hopes. This was a day of reckoning.

Mindy pushed back the cuff of my shirt and rubbed my wrist with her thumb, in small circles. "I guess I was hoping you'd say that you've changed your mind about that silly case. I know Daddy wants to take it, but it's all wrong for you and for your career."

My career? I had no idea she'd been pondering it so closely. Interesting. I also had no idea that her father had told her about the case at all. I let her know as much.

She said that he'd let her know and that at first he'd been excited at the opportunity to do justice for a gifted member of the community. "Lately, though, he says you've been distracted and perhaps you're too close to the case to do a good job. He thinks it could be a mistake in the long run, especially if you damaged your ethical reputation. He explained it all to me."

So that she could explain it all to me, no doubt. "There's a lot involved, I admit. I'm praying about it. I want to do my best for the client, and yes, I'd be lying if I said I didn't have some concern for my brother too."

She pushed back from the table then, all diamonds and teeth. "He's not your brother, okay? Please give that a rest. That's the other thing Daddy wanted me to talk to you about. I know you had a rough childhood, but if you want to move up, you're going to have to move on. Like it or not, there's still a color line in this town, and your friends are on the other side of it. You're a lawyer now, not some trailer trash in the 'hood."

I hadn't known before then that it was possible to choke on water. Probably went down the wrong pipe when I opened my mouth so wide. My eyes went pretty big too. For several seconds, I said nothing, gasping for breath instead. The waiter, who'd been always nearby, but never close exactly, asked if I needed a doctor.

I shook my head, thinking of all the times in my life when I'd needed a doctor but hadn't been able to afford one or get to one. Instead, I took light shallow breaths and deep, silent prayers. As my pulse slowed, words came. "So I'm supposed to move on, huh? To what? You?"

She twirled the carat solitaire in her left ear. "Yes, move on to me. To us. Our children."

We hadn't ordered yet, but my plate arrived when the waiter brought the salad. It smelled right on time. I gave the guy a nod and a fat tip. "Can you box that for me?"

Mindy looked horrified. "This isn't some chicken shack. Are you kidding me?"

I wasn't. The waiter grinned from ear to ear. "I'll be right back with it."

Good. I hoped he did come right back, because what I had to do now, say now, wouldn't take long. Even though this would hurt her, going on like this would hurt her more. I took both her hands in mine and willed myself not to get my coat and walk out without another word.

I'd done it before.

She didn't resist my touch.

"Melinda, we won't be having a family. I came here to ask you to postpone the wedding, but you've cleared up everything for me. The wedding is off."

"You can't do this to me." She dragged her hands to her lap and stared down at her engagement ring.

Amazing. "Keep it."

Mindy shook so hard even her spritz-stiff hair moved. A bead of sweat ran down her face. "You think it's this easy? You think you can put me down and go back to your little ghetto life? I'll destroy you. And them. You'll never practice law in this state again." Desperation seeped through the cracks in her voice.

I started laughing. "No more law? Good. I'm pretty sick of it."

Mindy picked up her fork. She was in a composed rage now, stabbing at her spinach, chasing down tomatoes to skewer them too. "You're a fool. You're not one of them. You'll always be outside. You told me how things changed in college when they could go to their all-black schools and clubs. How they told you to go back to your own. They don't love you. None of them. Especially not that Zoë or whatever her name is."

Maybe not, but I planned to find out. The waiter returned with a Styrofoam container with a Wet-Nap and a plastic fork. He offered to get me a Coke too, but I shook my head, stood, and put my napkin down lightly lest I dive across the table and strangle Mindy with it. There was nothing worse than giving yourself to someone and having them beat you up with your own stuff. Maybe she was right, maybe Brian or Zeely hadn't really loved me. If not, then they were in good company, because Mindy certainly hadn't loved me. Of that much, I was certain.

On the way out, I did not reach over the counter to get my coat.

I held out my ticket instead. Dee took my number and gave me my jacket before handing me a card of her own:

Mount Olive Missionary Baptist Church. Where Everybody Is Somebody and Jesus Makes the Difference.

"Stop by some Sunday," she said.

I grinned, forcing my arms through the sleeves one at a time so I could hold on to my lunch. "Don't be surprised if I show up sometime. Don't be surprised at all."

43

Mindy

My reflection in the ice bucket reminded me of day-old bread; stiff and pasty. My resolve felt much the same. I'd gambled everything and pushed Ron too hard and now all these months of preparation were gone when I needed them most. I needed a place to go now, a place to hide, and my last chance had just walked out the door. And I knew from the look on his face that he wouldn't be coming back.

And now, I had to play my last card.

The Joker.

I took the bottle of cider Ron had opened and started toward the car. The club would bill everything to Daddy's account anyway. Once outside, I reached into the pocket of my knee-length mink and pressed 1 as I pulled out my phone. It only rang once before someone picked up.

"Daniel? It's me."

There was laughter on the line. Cold, mocking laughter. "Why, Melinda, I'm surprised. Booty calls so early in the day? Your daddy will know something's up when you can't walk at dinner."

I squeezed through cars in the parking lot. Probing eyes. If only it wasn't day. Too many people my father knew had seen what happened at lunch, had watched me walk to the car. Daniel's sarcasm just made it worse. I knew Daddy had said horrible things to run him off. Terrible things. Still, I needed him to hear me. This wasn't a joke.

"I need to talk to you."

"About what? You know we talk best without words."

At my car now, I climbed inside and locked the door, lowered my mouth so that no one could read my dry, cracked lips. "I'm pregnant."

He didn't laugh, but the silence was worse.

"So why you telling me? Tell your preacher man. I'm sure he'll be thrilled."

"It's not his. He's celibate. We never—" My Corvette seemed to close in on me. There wasn't enough room. I didn't have enough words.

Daniel was out of character now, sounding a little like he had two years ago, before Daddy found out about us. There was a small melody in Daniel's voice when he was hurting, imperceptible if you didn't know him well. "Get real, Mindy. You, go without? Not even for your little choirboy. You kept going until you broke me down."

The cider went down easy, both warm and cool somehow. "Danny, please, don't be like that. You know I've only been with you. Ever."

"Right. That's all I'm good for. Not good enough to be with you in the daytime. Or meet your friends. But you think a baby can change all that, huh?"

I dare to hope so.

"What can Daddy do now? He's against abortion. He'll have to accept this. It isn't how I wanted to do it, but maybe this is the only way."

The only way left *now*. Ron's face, so calm and strong an hour earlier, seemed fixed in my mind. He could have gone through, given both of us an easy way out, but he hadn't. He'd chosen love. He'd chosen Zeely. I wanted to hate him for that, for being strong enough to choose her, but I couldn't. Somewhere, under all the hurt, I was proud of him. "I'm sorry I let my father hurt you. Hurt us. I'm sorry I didn't take your side. I'm ready to do that, to make it be about our family. Let's get married. Today."

"Too late, Mindy. I told you when you started coming around again not to expect anything from me. I'm through with God and I'm through with you."

"Don't say that. Please. Maybe God is in this somehow, even in our mess. My father won't deny his own flesh and blood. He can't." I didn't sound very confident despite my sure words.

Daniel really laughed then, almost split my soul in two. He said that maybe one day when I was pushing a little black boy down the street and someone crossed their white daughter to the other side, maybe I'd understand. He'd do anything for the baby, even raise it if I wanted to keep my safe, white life, but as for my father and I, we could both go to the same place he was headed—hell.

The phone clicked in my ear. I rolled down the window and screamed, no longer caring who could hear. With my last bit of energy, I tossed the cider out the window, closing my eyes just in time when it returned to me as a shower of sweet, sharp glass. I dropped back in my seat, too numb to cry.

There'd be no celebrations now.

Not ever.

44

Grace

Fall's first freeze crunched under my feet, leaving green footprints on my white, sparkling yard. Zeely had offered me a ride this morning, and for once I was going to take it. She'd called a few minutes before, saying she'd be down as soon as she got her dinner in the crock pot. Me, I couldn't even figure out what I was having for breakfast. That woman should be a Girl Scout leader.

While I didn't have dinner settled on, I used the time to check on my latest garden experiment—summer bulbs fooled into blooming out of season. The gardener on TV had insisted that getting plants to bloom when and where they were planted wasn't easy. Considering how many times I had done it myself, I figured it couldn't hurt to try.

I was wrong, of course. I'd picked daffodils, of all things, and buried them in my side yard. The TV gardener had advised keeping the bulbs at a constant forty degrees with plenty of moisture. The numbness in my toes read forty and falling. The ground felt like an icy rock. When I turned on the hose, water spurted out of it. Since it wasn't frozen, I figured the daffodils and I had a chance. I hoped so. I could use some color in all this cold.

A horn sounded in the driveway.

"Just a minute!" I walked in a circle, drenching the ground. Maybe the blankets and extra dirt I'd buried the bulbs with would hold the heat until I got home. That was the theory anyway. Instead of winding it up on the side, I walked around the back of the house

253

and tossed down the hose under my bedroom window. I'd bring my container plants out back and water them when I got home. Near the S-shaped imprint the hose made in the snow was something that had no business being there.

Footprints.

I looked up at my bedroom window. The screen was gashed in two, one side peeled back. Zeely beeped again, but she didn't need to. I was already running toward her car, kicking up a storm of white behind me. I tried to tell her what had happened, but the words, my screams, stuck fast in my throat. Thank God for my eyes.

Zeely gave me a strange look. "Quit playing and get in. We'll be late."

I shook my head, willing the words to come. "The—the back window. It's cut. Footprints—"

"Cut? Did they get in?"

"No. Well, I don't know. Nothing really looked different this morning. That window is at the foot of the bed. It was chilly. You don't think . . ."

Zeely opened her car door and shoved me inside while tapping out 9-1-1 with her knuckles. "An attempted break-in at Myrrh Mountain, condo eighteen eighty-two. Possible entry. A bedroom window."

She clicked the phone shut and gripped my hand. "They're on their way."

With each minute that passed, the snow filled in the evidence, each flake suggesting a different scenario, another intruder. I stared down the road. "How long has it been?"

Zeely got up from my front porch. "Twenty minutes. Let's go to my place. We'll see them pull up. I already called the school." She led the way, fumbling for her keys.

After a silent walk, we huddled inside Zeely's condo, gobbling the heat.

I rubbed my shoulders. "It had to be by chance. I don't know anyone." I knew better, even as I spoke the words. Violence was only random when it happened to somebody else. When it happens to you, it's always personal.

Zeely snorted. "Girl, you don't have to know anybody. People are crazy. You know that stringy-headed boy who lives on the front row? I've seen him walking around here at night . . ." She nudged the thermostat a few degrees to the right. "Want some cocoa?"

"Sure."

Hot water poured out of Zeely's teapot, scalding the names of other suspects into my thoughts. A rush of images came at me then: a ski mask, a tall tree with leaves going everywhere, screams no one wanted to hear. I'd learned later in self-defense class that it's best to scream "fire" instead of "help." People aren't too willing to offer help, but they definitely don't want to see their things go up in flames. If I'd screamed "fire" that day, I wouldn't have been lying. The memory burned me still.

I held onto the sink as the flashback became a vision. I hadn't had memories like this in a long time. And when I'd come out of that storm, there'd been a lot of debris left behind. I had to get in touch with God, before this thing got too strong on me. Before it pulled me under.

Too late.

I grabbed my mouth as I smelled the stench of the boy's liquored breath, heard the sound of his zipper . . .

Zeely rushed to my side. "You okay?"

"I need to sit down." I pushed past the barstools and onto the couch. The room fogged into more sights and sounds: gunshots from the school orientation . . . the crunch of metal between my car and Brian's . . . the sound of ripping clothes from that day, that horrible day . . .

"In the name of the Most High God, I ask peace for Diana. Peace and protection. May nothing come nigh her dwelling. I thank you for her sound mind, Lord God, in Jesus' mighty name."

I blinked, emerging from the flashback to see Zeely's praying hands in front of me. "Bible." It was all I could say.

Zeely had never been with me through any of the traumas that had come raging back at me, yet she seemed to understand. She pulled a book out of her purse. "Psalm ninety-one?"

I nodded.

Zeely's voice jogged across the page, rushing me to Jesus in record time. Just as I was really getting there though, she slammed the Bible shut. "You know what? It might have been that other boy. The one who just moved in with his dad . . ."

I took the book from her hand. "You know what, Zee? I've got this. You go on to school."

She frowned. "Are you crazy? What if he—if they come back? There's no telling when the police will get here."

"I can't let this spook me. Besides, it's broad daylight. I don't think anyone is going to do anything to me now."

Zeely didn't look convinced, but she put her coat back on. "Keep your phone on. I'll call you every few minutes until I get to school. They should be here by then." She straightened her bracelets.

"Right. I'll be there too, before you know it."

Five minutes later, when I was outside alone with only the howling wind for company, I regretted sending Zeely away. The truth I'd squeezed in between brushing my teeth and getting dressed this morning returned to me when I needed it most:

Do not be afraid of their faces, for I am with you to deliver you, says the LORD, *Jeremiah 1:8.*

I tried to wrap God's presence around me, only the cold shivered through me. Today I needed to feel God's love through human hands. I needed Jesus "with some skin on," as I'd heard children in my old Sunday school class say before.

I needed people and yet I'd pushed them all away. Zeely, Mal, and even Brian, who despite my best efforts seemed to be every- where I turned. Mixed with all the bad flashbacks this morning, one person, someone who made me feel a different kind of fear, stood out against the rest: Brian.

Police lights painted my thoughts as the long-awaited officer made his appearance.

After a quick survey of the scene, the officer reported his findings. "It could be a kid, although I'm not sure why they cut the screen with you in sight. Do you have any enemies?" He dared to say what I was trying not to think. "No enemies. I just moved here."

The officer paused and made a note on his report. "It's probably kids then. We've had a couple calls this year around here. Other- wise, I would suspect personal. It's as if someone wanted you to know they'd been here."

I grated my teeth as the officer told me to be safe and offered to escort me to school. My stomach churned as I accepted his offer and got into my car and drove to my job. All I could do was wonder who had watched me last night and whether they'd caught me sleeping or come early enough to catch my nightgown ballet, meant for God alone. As I turned into Imani, I decided maybe it was better if I didn't know.

Do not be afraid, for I am with you.

After the first few weeks of school, Imani's straightforward schedule had changed a little, allowing for a daily morning assembly. Now in the second quarter of school, both the students and many of the teachers looked forward to it. I strained to hear the end of Joyce's uplifting words as I hastened to my classroom. I paused to pray when I passed Zeely's room and dipped my head when I went by Lottie's class. She'd be changing rooms with us for the second semester so that she could use the kiln sitting in our office, unused except to remind me that each day was another firing on God's pottery wheel. Sometimes, like now, I felt like he shattered me to the floor and then fired me up, starting all over again.

The assembly let out just as I reached the classroom and headed for my office. It wasn't long before Brian appeared, his face pale and strained. It took all I had to keep from running into his arms, burying my head in his chest. I dug my nails into my palm.

It could have been him, fool.

The students were filing in behind him, but he came straight to the office. "Are you all right? Zee said something about a Peeping Tom."

Shaken by his genuine concern, I forced myself not to pull away. "It's nothing. The police think it was a teenager. There have been a few other calls they said. Zeely and I overreacted."

"You're not staying there tonight, are you? Zee said—"

"I'm fine. And I'm sorry for being late. How's homeroom? Morning assembly?" I took my chair.

Brian remained standing. A little too close. "Fine. I hate to ask, considering your morning, but did you decide on the books for English? I have something planned if you'd rather I lead today, but I'm trying to go by the schedule we worked out."

The mention of work was a welcome change. "No, I appreciate that. I think that teaching today will help keep my mind off things. As for the books, I decided to use a theme list instead of choosing individual books."

Brian shrugged. "Sounds good. What's the theme?"

"I figured since you're covering slavery in first period, I'd look at writers who expressed their culture's tragedies in literature."

He picked up a box cutter from the corner of his desk and slashed the corner of a box of books we'd ordered. A perfect instrument for slitting a screen. Best not to think of it.

"Showing them the sin of man, are we?"

258

My eyes fixed on the blade. "I wouldn't have phrased it quite that way, but yes, I think they need to see what we're all capable of, if given the right motives and enough power. They also need to see what it takes to overcome the worst of circumstances."

Brian removed the books by the handfuls and stacked them on the desk. "Nice premise, but your 'We shall overcome' stuff might not fly here as well as you'd like. For most of these kids, this is the end of the road. And along that road, they've seen more than you could imagine. More than you'd want to."

"That's why I want them to read these books. They need to know that this school, this class, can be an end or a beginning. The choice is theirs."

Brian crushed the box flat. He shook his head. "Whatever. Your idealism won't help them when they get pulled over for getting a soda after midnight."

"Maybe not, but it might keep them from becoming hateful and hopeless like some people. Bitterness dulls brilliance." Who was I now, Jesse Jackson? Brian just brought this kind of stuff out of me.

Brian stumbled back and bowed at the waist. "Okay, Princess, go for it. Just don't be surprised if you don't get your happy ending."

Princess.

Growing up, I'd heard that word every day, spoken with a tone of fatherly pride. Despite my mother's list of criticisms, nobody was as smart or pretty as Trey Dixon's daughter. Or at least that's how it was. A day came when shame swallowed Princess and left Diana in its place. But Daddy's eyes were the worst. So hurt, so disappointed. The counselors tried over and over to tell me that it wasn't my fault, but when Daddy came to visit and I looked into his eyes, I knew I'd never be anyone's princess again.

The kids loved it. Once the last student had gone, I could still hear their excitement choosing their own books for the literature unit. The day's griot had recorded the books everyone had chosen, leaving me to laugh at the comical remarks. Brian didn't say much during class or now, one seat over, tapping away on his PDA.

Knowing I'd end up regretting it, I struck up a conversation anyway. "The kids were something today, huh?"

He didn't look up. "Yes, they were in rare form, but you're a great match for them. I didn't think it would go over well, but I was wrong."

"Is that an apology?"

Brian turned to face me with those laughing eyes of his. "Yes, I apologize." He blew me a kiss and bowed his head.

I pretended that his gesture had no effect on me, while praying he'd repeat it both immediately and never again. "Apology accepted."

"They really respond to you." He settled back into his chair. "I'm surprised you didn't have any children of your own."

I went for my best smile, the super fake one that I used whenever this came up in work situations. As I suspected, I couldn't quite pull it off with Brian. I pointed to the empty seats around the classroom. "All those children are enough, don't you think?"

He pressed on, undaunted. "So you never wanted any kids?"

"More than anything. It just didn't work out." I paused, thankful for a moment of silence to flip the script. "What about you?"

His eyes glossed over. "Me? I wanted three, but Karyn kept putting me off. After a while I knew better than to ask. When she changed her mind, it was too late."

I had to look away then. I knew how it felt to have the hope of a family dashed. Three miscarriages and a vasectomy had ended my dreams of motherhood. "I'm sorry."

260

"Me too. I used to pity those guys with baby's mama drama, but there are times when I wish I'd picked up a kid with somebody."

"You don't mean that." I frowned.

"Okay, so maybe I don't. I do wonder what it might have been like."

I shrugged, hoping this topic was coming to a close. Hadn't I just stood outside my bedroom in someone else's footprints? Enough for one day. Still, Brian wasn't going to give up until I finished this once and for all. And so I went for the heart, both his and mine. "Who knows? Maybe you do have a child out there somewhere. Stranger things have happened."

He pulled his locks into a ponytail. "Nah. I was too busy studying to leave any kids behind, but if I did, the woman would have told me. She'd need child support and all that."

I shook my head. "Sometimes situations force people to do things they wouldn't normally do. A lot of women raise children without any—"

"Let's drop this, okay? Even though I know it's impossible, the thought of my child growing up without knowing me . . ." He stared out the window. "The man I thought was my father died before I was born. Unless I find my mother, I'll never find my real father."

This was going way deeper than I wanted to go. I'd remembered him saying something about finding his mother before, but I'd never pressed him. I had enough baggage of my own to try to carry his. I didn't say anything, but once again, my eyes gave me away.

"You didn't know? I didn't mention it because I figured Zeely had told you. It's a small town, you know. No secret is safe here."

Except mine.

I cringed, imagining how close I'd come this morning to spilling my own secrets into Zeely's ear. And now, in the tenderness of Brian's honesty, I could have easily told him my story too. All of it, even what I'd left out when I talked with Mal. I swallowed the words whole. "I hope you find your family. I'm sorry if I rubbed you the wrong way with the kid thing."

"It's okay. If I ever have kids, I'll be there for them. I don't understand how anybody could cast off their own flesh and blood. Especially a mother."

I dropped my eyes. On my desk was a notice from the Equal Employment Opportunity Commission asking me to testify at a hearing—on Lottie's behalf. After the day I'd had so far, I'd chosen to ignore it. Until now. "Like I said, sorry."

"No problem." Brian looked down at his desk, where a similar notice awaited him. "My past doesn't worry me as much as the present."

After staying at Zeely's for a few nights, I came home to find a note saying that the new window had arrived. The original wasn't exactly damaged according to the repairman, but I'd requested a new one anyway. At lunchtime, I'd gone out to one of the new shops in the pseudo-historical district that seemed to be taking over Testimony and bought some things for my moving-back-in party, of which I was the only name on the guest list.

Zeely seemed a little salty that I'd be missing exercise class, but I knew it was also because I wouldn't be sleeping over anymore. We'd had fun and I'd enjoyed it, almost enough to give up my place and move in. Not quite though. Now, inside my bedroom, shoving open my new window so that the cold could kiss my new curtains, I knew that I couldn't let anyone run me out of my house. Zeely and everyone else I knew would have freaked to see me in front of the window like this, but I needed some air. I'd had enough fear to last a lifetime.

The phone rang just as I got the tiebacks on straight. I hesitated before picking it up. Mal hadn't called in a few days, but he usually waited for evenings and weekends. Only another teacher would call in the middle of the afternoon. With Zeely at dance class and Joyce in meetings downtown, that only left . . . my mother. I checked the caller ID and picked up the phone with a prayer that I would hold my tongue and lend my ear instead.

"Hello?"

"It's me, dear."

"Hey, Mom." Though I never would admit it to her, I felt comfort at the sound of her voice. This call could mean a lot of things. Either she'd made peace with my move or she meant to go to war until I moved back—which I wasn't. I wound the kitchen timer beside my phone, where I'd placed it soon after moving in, knowing this call would come. I set it for fifteen minutes, the only safe window of time when dealing with Mom.

"You sound tired. Are you okay? I heard about some mess at your school."

Even in Cincinnati, my mother didn't miss a trick. Best to let her tell me what she knew, rather than spilling my guts. "Uh-huh."

"Well? Are you going to tell me about it or what?"

"There was an incident with the police at orientation. You know how it is, even in a small place like this. High school is just different now."

"You never should have stopped teaching middle school over here. You don't have to be so difficult about telling me what happened either. I'll call Zeely. My soror will tell me what I need to know. How is she, anyway?"

It begins. In any conversation, my mother never failed to mention the sorority to which she and Zeely belonged. I'd passed on pledging in college, but Mom thought I still had a chance at becoming a real woman by pledging the graduate chapter. I'd considered it a few times—I'd never tell her that—but never felt a peace. Keeping up with Jesus was more than enough for now.

"Zeely's fine."

"She hasn't gained any weight, has she? I have some skirts for her. I would have bought you some too, but they didn't have your size."

Not that she'd checked. My mother wouldn't be seen on that end of the rack. "No problem. As for Zeely, not a pound. In fact, I think she's lost some."

The voice on the phone changed pitch. "If you were that size, you'd be married. I just don't understand you."

Halt. Do not enter.

Like a fool, I raced past the mental warnings to respond. "Zeely's still single too, Mom. And I'm not looking for a husband." I ran a hand down my hip. Contrary to my mother's opinion, I looked pretty good these days. If Brian's reactions meant anything, real good.

"Zeely would be married if she weren't so picky. Before the African died—"

"Mom." In all the years I was married to Peter, my mother had rarely spoken his name. It was always "the African."

"Anyway. I introduced her to a nice fellow. His wife left him with a new house and she didn't ask for a dime. No children. A perfect opportunity."

I smiled, remembering Zeely's frantic phone call detailing the incident.

My mother's account continued. "She spent the whole evening interviewing the man. Was he a Christian? What church did he go to. On and on."

I giggled. *That's my Zee.*

"That boy's daddy has been a deacon for thirty-five years, and his mama is the superintendent of Sunday school. Zeely acted like he was a heathen."

I checked the timer on the stove. Almost done. The last three minutes were the most dangerous. Especially on my end. "No offense, Mom, but what do his parents have to do with anything? He's a grown man now. You act like faith can be passed down or something."

A blowing sound came through the phone. "See, I can't talk to you. You are so negative and judgmental. Ina Mae was right."

Here we go. No conversation was done without Aunt Ina being thrown in my face. "Mom, I didn't mean to hurt Aunt Ina's feelings. The Lord put it on my heart—"

"Don't go bringing the Lord into it, Miss High and Mighty. Writing my sister letters on her deathbed about how to become a Christian. As much as she did for you? The nerve."

I thought the same thing the whole time I was writing it.

The timer sounded.

"Mom, that's why I wrote it. Aunt Ina did so much that I wanted to share with her the best gift in the world."

"You are so sickening. We were singing in the choir before you were even thought about."

And long after I was forgotten. "I love you, Mom. I've got to go."

"Don't you hang up this phone. You think you're so holy. At least I was a grown woman before I had a b—"

I closed my eyes and rested the phone in its cradle. "Lord, forgive me, but I just can't take it. Not today."

45

Ron

"So where've you been?"

I stared across the restaurant booth at Zeely, not sure how to really answer her. I'd been nowhere and everywhere at the same time. I'd tried to call her before leaving, but in the end, I just had to go. "I took the Greyhound to Florida. I had some coupons for a free hotel stay. Once I was there, I decided to stay for a few days."

She picked up a rib bone and nibbled one side. "You should have turned your phone on at least. And Greyhound? That's insane."

"It was nice actually. I read quite a bit. Stared out the window and thought about some things. I forgot how nice it is to think."

Zeely spooned baked beans onto my plate from the Styrofoam cup on the table between us.

"I hope you didn't think too hard. You were messed up enough before." She smiled, a spot of barbecue sauce at the corner of her mouth. "Speaking of messed up, what did your lady friend think of your disappearance?"

"Good question." After our last encounter, she was probably relieved. I still had her father to deal with, but at this point, I didn't care about that either.

Zeely poked a hole in her napkin as she wiped her hands. "I'll leave that alone." A serious look replaced her smile. "I'm glad you emailed to say you were okay, but I was worried."

That was nice to know. "Look, I'm sorry. I bungled the whole thing. I invited you here to make it up to you."

"The Rib Hut is supposed to make it up to me? You've got to cook to make up with me, mister."

I'd known that she'd have wanted that, for me to cook for her. I'd planned a menu, even bought the ingredients. And then I'd looked at that empty space in my dining room where Mindy's curio was supposed to go, that bare stretch of carpet that would have been behind Zeely's chair. I thought about it so long that I settled on the Rib Hut and went for a walk. I was going to have to get over that. She'd have to come over sometime. "No problem. I'll cook for you. You can even pick the menu."

"Deal." She pushed back from the table, tugging a sweater dress away from her curves. She put her tray into the trash. "So what are we going to play tonight?"

I tossed my stack of bones too and hugged Zeely as I passed her, expecting her to wiggle away as always.

She didn't. "For real, what are we playing?" Her voice softened. She relaxed in my arms.

"Monopoly." I smiled down at her, hoping she'd pull away before I did something even more stupid.

Zeely tapped my chest. "Monopoly? That's a switch."

The first of many.

Her perfume crept up my neck. I loosened my grip—for both our sakes. "Do you mind playing something else?"

She shook her head. "I like Monopoly. I just wondered why you chose it."

"Tonight, I need to own something." I pulled my house keys from my pocket and grabbed her hand. "Come on, my place for dessert."

46

Grace

The secret is out. Mom saw me naked. She kept me home from school today and took me to a clinic for them to kill it. There were three girls with their fathers and some women with wedding rings. I don't know why a married woman would want to kill her baby. I wanted to ask somebody, but it's probably another one of those things that women are just supposed to know.

Diana Dixon

"Miss O, you looking good today. Not that you don't every day—" Sean stood in the hall, trying to salvage his compliment.

"That's okay. I know what you mean." I took a second look at him. A low afro had replaced his usual fuzzy cornrows. No earring. Was he standing up straight?

"You don't look too bad yourself."

"So I've been told." He walked away like a prince.

A brown tree of a girl, all eyes and hair, turned the corner. Jerry's daughter. Sean nodded and walked to meet her. I shook my head before starting my own journey. Relief washed over me at the sight of Brian's empty chair. We had an assembly today, so he and I had two free planning periods this morning. Maybe he'd stay away as long as he could.

I hoped that he would and prayed that he wouldn't.

For the last few weeks, I'd been on the losing side of a war between my heart and my spirit, and Brian was the spoils being fought over. I didn't need to see him now, no matter how much I wanted to. And yet, he'd appear before long.

This weekend in Thelma's at-home beauty shop, with a straightening comb sizzling through my hair, I'd sat and listened to the old ladies unashamedly telling their tales as their hair smoked and sizzled into precision. When they got to me, I said a little about Mal and they laughed, waiting for more. I couldn't get the words to go past my lips, but I watched with wonder as they aired fifty-year-old laundry and cut through family dramas as though they were chicken bones.

"You remember when my Joe used to slip around with heifer Sally on Kentucky Street?"

"Yes, Lord. That Negro had his nose wide open, didn't he? Well, we prayed him right up, didn't we? Got snowed in over there. Frostbit and all. He don't even walk on that side of the road no mo'!"

The ladies under the dryers strained to hear, pressing their plastic rollers against the hoods until there were bobby pin imprints on their foreheads. I tried not to listen, but it was impossible.

"And oh, remember when Toot went out there to meet the white side of her family?" someone said from under the dryer.

Miss Thelma paused to look up without disturbing the bobby pin between her teeth. "She went and found her white folks. Walked right up to 'em. Ain't her people the ones that own part of that bank downtown in the Tower? They was one of the first ones to pass. You know they wasn't gone claim that chile."

"I know that's right," someone else said. "The mayor is my cousin. His daddy still comes to my grandmother's house on New Year's to get some chitlins."

Thelma commenced her pinning. "Girl, that's how they do. I know plenty of folk passed over. I see one of 'em every time I go over to Columbus to do my insurance. You should see the man looking at me all crazy like I'm going to out him. I walk by like I don't even know him, but when the white folks turn away, I pass him some pound cake and hug him close. It was his mama that made them do it. You should have seen her husband and 'nem when all those black folk showed up at that woman's funeral. They probably still confused . . ."

And on and on it had gone like that: secret babies, secret husbands, secret lives. I'd always thought Testimony was slow and boring, but now I saw that below this slow, easy river of a town ran a sweeping current of secrets. And I was the main one being swept along.

"And who are you, baby?" the loudest, largest woman asked.

Thelma eyed me while I considered my answer, but she didn't say a word. There were many things I could say, but the most obvious was the last thing that I wanted to say: Trey Dixon's daughter, that girl who . . .

"Me? I'm Grace. A new teacher at Imani Academy."

The woman, Nita was her name, stared at me for almost a minute before accepting my response.

"Joyce Rogers' school. Oh yes, they do a lot of good things for the blacks over there. Them Latinos too. Even white children. That Mayfield boy is still over there, right, Thelma?"

I'd squirmed a bit at hearing Brian called a boy. He was anything but.

"Yes, Nella. And he ain't nobody's boy, especially yours."

"You got that right. Don't nobody know whose boy he is. That's what's wrong with him now. He's right handsome though, 'cept for those worms all over his head. I always used to watch him when he was on TV. Did you see him on *Oprah* that time about black boys? Powerful, I tell you. Liked to make me cry . . ."

I had cried. Under the dryer with a plastic cap over the conditioner on my hair and hiding behind a ten-year-old issue of *Ebony*, I'd bawled like a baby. And not just for Brian. Most of it was for me, a grown woman too scared to say who she really was, to tell what she'd been through. At some point, I was going to have to do what I feared most—tell the truth. Give my real testimony. It'd been so much easier to do this, be someone else, when I was away. It was the one way I could overcome all the things going on in my head.

And they overcame him because of the blood of the Lamb and because of the word of their testimony . . .

Resurrection was what I needed. And to get it, I'd have to bare my heart. I wasn't sure who to open up to, but when the time came, God would provide someone to partake of my broken bread and poured out wine. The memory of Thelma's home beauty shop faded and my eyes fell on Brian's empty chair again.

He'd have to come in soon. I smoothed my temples, gathering materials for today's lesson. It was Brian's day to lead, but the way he'd been acting lately—quiet and withdrawn—I'd better be ready for anything.

I reached into a stack of books from the desk and selected a volume of poems by Paul Laurence Dunbar. With Dayton, his birthplace, so close by and his work so rich, he was always part of my curriculum. Brian agreed. After making a few notes, I checked my freshly painted nails for chips and picked up my Bible to copy the passage from yesterday's sermon onto a file card to carry in my pocket. Reading it aloud three times a day for a week usually sufficed for getting the verses into my memory bank.

With a pen and index card, I scribbled down the words still ringing in my head from the sermon:

Who can lay a hand on the Lord's anointed and be guiltless?

After years of hearing the passage used to excuse church leaders from accountability for their actions, it was not one of my favorite places in Scripture. Yesterday, though, when Pastor Rodriquez taught about the verses at Tender Mercies, he'd come from another angle. Instead of a leader-follower application, he gave a personal relationship twist by suggesting that Saul had been used to refine David. It was at that point in the service that I'd dropped my pen.

"Stop trying to put out God's refining fire!" The pastor's intense gaze burned into my memory. "If you want to reach your potential in Christ, keep the home fires burning, even if the house starts burning down. If God started the fire, he can put it out."

What he'd said was true, but how long would the fire burn? I had enough scars already.

I put the Bible aside and skimmed another poem, searching for an excerpt to read to the class during homeroom. As the words blurred in front of me, a troubling concept emerged—Brian as God's anointed.

The door creaked and Brian filed in, wearing a suit the color of cashews. His mane, freshly retightened, fell to the middle of his back. He beelined to his desk, risking only a nod. He kept all his questions simple since we'd gone to give our stories to the EEOC. Maybe he felt that I'd somehow sided against him, but I could only tell what I saw, what I'd heard. Lately he didn't give me more than a passing glance, but this morning, he turned away from his desk and gave his eyes what they must have been craving—a good, long look.

His gaze slid down the shine of my kimono like a child on a slide. I looked down too, first at my knees, slimmer now since I'd been taking Zeely's class, then at my waist, my shoulders . . . My hair. He was staring at my hair. And he didn't look happy.

"What did you do to it?"

"Got it pressed. Wanted something different."

Brian looked again at my sleek updo that I'd pierced with two chopsticks for a final effect before leaving the house. It was too cold outside to be dressed this way, but I didn't care.

He seemed to understand. "It looks good. I wish you'd said something though, about wanting a new style, I mean. I could have tried my hand at it before you let Thelma get to it."

I raised a brow at the mention of Thelma. This town really was small. "So you're a cosmetologist too, huh? What happened to 'this is all natural, just take the handout' when the kids asked you about your hair the first day?"

Brian inched his chair toward me, abandoning his former reserve. "Did *you* read the handout? I know a little, I used to braid my mother's hair most nights when she couldn't do it herself anymore. I cared for my wife's natural hair. I also had a friend with braids, the little ones. I used to put them back in when they started sliding."

My smile dissolved. The only person I knew with micros was Lottie. "A friend? I'll bet you just tightened her right up."

Brian rolled back to his desk and swiveled away from me, obviously regretting breaking his new get-to-work-but-keep-quiet plan. He picked up his bag and headed for the door.

"I'll be back in a few. Long before the assembly." He got up and moved around his desk, carefully navigating the space between us.

My shoulders crumpled for a second, rising only when Brian brushed my arm on the way out. I grabbed his fingers. "Wait. I shouldn't have said that. Will you forgive me?"

Something in his eyes stirred. Hope. A spark among the ashes. I dared to keep looking, tracing the outline of the contacts around his pupils. He leaned down until his hair tickled my shoulders. "You have nothing to be forgiven for. I'm going to go now so I can say the same." He straightened.

Tell me about it. Brian's suits were enough to make this grown woman a little teary eyed. Only God could create something— someone—that fine.

"If looking good is the best revenge, then somebody somewhere is hurting. Bad." I covered my mouth. Did I say that out loud?

He turned and stared at me. "What?"

I did say it out loud. I forced my face into the book I was reading. "Nothing."

He turned and left the office, but not before giving me a sly smile. I forced my chair back to my desk. If God planned to use Brian to reveal my weaknesses, I couldn't think of a better man for the job.

PART 3

RHYTHMS

47

Brian

"What book, written in 1958, is often considered *the* classic of African literature?" I asked the class.

"*Things Fall Apart* by Chinua Achebe," Monique answered from the back.

There she was again. Real potential. I stroked my beard. "It seems this is going to be a tête-à-tête between Miss Terrigan and me this week."

Sean frowned. "That's not fair. She answered the first one."

"Maybe you can answer the next. And don't worry, Monique, you get your money regardless."

Sean shrugged. "If the question is about that book, the one she said, I'll try to answer."

This was new. "You read it?"

"Yes, Doc. I did."

"Interesting. Here's the question. In one sentence, tell me what *Things* was about." Hands went up all over. I waved them all off, pointing at Sean instead. "He's Mr. Literature today. Let him tell us."

"Yams." He said it with a straight face too.

I couldn't help but laugh. "Boy . . ."

"Okay, it's a story about white colonization, from the perspective of the son of an African chief who was converted by missionaries." Sean straightened in his chair. "And yams."

Across the room, Grace straightened her lips, removing the smile from her face. Monique looked pretty satisfied too.

"I'll give you a quiz grade for that answer, Sean." I looked at the clock. "One more. It's open to everybody. Achebe based his title on what famous poem?" I had them now. Only Monique would know it, if even she did.

Sean's hand shot up first, followed by Monique's. This was priceless. I nodded to Sean, rooting for him to get it right despite our past problems.

"*The Second Coming* by Yeats. William Butler Yeats." Sean grinned. "See? I'm not as stupid as you think."

He had me there. Sean wasn't stupid at all. I was. In that moment, as he stared at me defiant and triumphant, I saw all that he could be, all that I could have been, and the girl sitting behind him blurred in the edge of my vision. Monique hadn't been here long, but his love for her had made Sean remember how to love himself. I wondered for a moment how I might have been different if Grace had shown up for the concert that day. Beyond Sean, I saw her, looking at me too, maybe somehow wondering the same thing. Not that it mattered now.

What did matter was Sean and all the boys like him in this school, in this town, in this world. I made a note to go home tonight and read my own books, take my own counsel, remember what it was I was meant to do in the world. Joyce was right—when Karyn died, when I walked away from the church, I hadn't just stopped believing in God, I'd stopped believing in people too. I'd spent much of my career trying to save black boys. Maybe two of them—Quinn and Sean—had been given back to me to teach me how to believe, both in God and in man.

I pulled out two five-dollar bills and placed the first on Monique's desk. I stepped up a row and handed the second bill to Sean. "I underestimated you." I even smiled. "It's a mistake I won't make again."

After the class let out, I had some trouble breathing. Water didn't help. A walk in the cold outside just made it worse. Something pressed on me, squeezing, pulling . . . That same thing I'd felt at that church with Quinn. It got so bad that I did something I thought I'd never do; I asked Grace to borrow her Bible. She looked so happy I almost told her to forget it, and by the time she started in on the benefits of the different versions, I'd snatched a King James off the top of her stack and headed for the faculty lounge.

The book had a few gaps in it, secret places as Eva had called them, spots that had been read so often that the Book fell open to them without trying. I went through them all, learning more about Grace than she could ever tell me. The last time I'd held a Bible at school was to showcase it as a tool used by slave masters to keep their human property docile and civilized. I never added that, in my heart, I thought it'd been used to do the same thing to me. Eva or any of the other church people might not have meant it that way, but that's just how it went.

I did all right letting the Bible fall open until I got to the biggest break, the spot where the binding cracked, where the page was yellow with highlighter, a page creased with pain. On top of that, she'd had the nerve to mark the spot with a ribbon. Ephesians. The bright marker showed the trail that her eyes had taken. The ink in the margins showed the journey of her soul. I dared to follow.

Having predestinated us unto the adoption of children by Josus Christ to himself . . .

I grabbed the arm of the sagging couch as the verse hit me. *Predestined.* It was a word I'd once used a lot when talking to boys, telling them that they'd been created to do great things before the foundation of the earth. And now, thinking over the word and its context, I wondered what my mother really meant if this was true. If I was meant to be adopted by Jesus anyway, did it really matter who my mama and daddy were?

Daddy? You never mention him.

My breath got thick again. I'd never put much on my father because I knew the nature of men. I'd spent my life studying them. I'd convinced myself that he hadn't known about me, that my mother was the one who should have cared. It was she who I threw in God's face again and again in those years, asking why God would want me when she hadn't. I forced my eyes down again.

According to the good pleasure of his will . . .

If the first part was a blow to the head, this got me in the gut. Pleasure? Could there be anything in me that could give God pleasure? I'd pleasured a lot of women and I was a sure thing for a good interview or a quick controversy, but it was hard for me to imagine God being pleased with me.

. . . to the praise of the glory of his grace, wherein he hath made us accepted in the beloved.

I slammed the testaments shut, both Old and New. I knew that the writer, the Apostle Paul, had meant God's grace, but when I read it I saw brown eyes and big hips—my Grace. At home on my headboard was a worn piece of embroidery that I read every morning before my feeble, tattered prayers. Now this.

As if the whole bit about adoption in God's family wasn't enough, they had to go and throw in something else to mess with my head, the glory of God's grace.

And my Grace too.

Back in the office, I went at my laptop like a madman. Sweat stung my eyes. My breath was steady and her Bible was safely in her possession, but I was messed up in a bad way. No matter how many times I listed the futility in pursuing God, pursuing Grace, something told me I wasn't going to be able to walk away. After the break-in at her place, I'd spent plenty of nights watching over Grace's condo. More than once I'd seen Lottie driving through. Until this whole mess with her was officially over, I'd have to lay low. There were the students to think about too. They were teasing us enough as it was. One kid had gone so far as to ask if we lived together. I thought Grace was going to pass out. It was all I could do to keep from saying what I was thinking—I wish.

I don't wish that really though, to live with her. For one, she'd never go for it. She's old school, the marrying kind. For two, it'd be too easy for her to walk away from some live-in thing, and I wasn't up for that.

So you're marrying her now? What are you, nuts?

Pretty much.

During our one and only date, Grace had told me that she was looking for something at Testimony Social Services. She hadn't said more, but from her notes in that Bible and the way we vibed, I wouldn't have been surprised if she was adopted too. Though many of the files were now closed, my clearance with TSS—they'd given me a part-time gig since I spent so much time there—might help find what she was looking for. I wasn't sure why, but I wanted so much to do something for her, something that had real meaning. Still, it was kind of nosy and crazy and I wasn't sure how far to go.

"Brian?" Grace pulled me out of my thoughts.

I looked up at her, stuffing my feelings back into their cave. "Yes?"

"I'm going to run over to the cafeteria for a moment and see how things are going with the assembly this afternoon. Do you need anything?"

You.

I shook my head, looking away. Pretty soon, I wouldn't be able to look at her at all, which worried me with Lottie running around like the school's resident psychopath. I'd tried to talk to Joyce about it, but with what she had going against me, nobody much wanted to hear my side.

Sweat stung my eyes as I tried to think it all through, fit all the pieces together in a way that might work, but nothing was working. If I thought I'd needed God that night in the cafeteria, I knew I needed him now. A few kids with a gun seemed like nothing compared to losing Joyce, to losing everything . . .

Maybe if I found something out for Grace, she'd see how I felt without me having to show it. I listened for her boots going down the hall, then logged into the Ohio adoption database. Maybe I could find something to give her as a peace offering. Something so she'd know my true feelings even if I couldn't act on them. If I hurried, I might have something before she returned from downstairs. The wonders of technology. I almost typed in Grace at first, but then I remembered and put in her maiden name, Diana Dixon. If she'd been adopted like I thought, it could still be a longshot, but maybe there'd be something.

One entry found to match your criteria.

I glimpsed at the office door, still closed like she'd left it. It seemed like forever until the blue bar inched all the way across the screen. I held my breath and let it out in a fizz as the disappointing red words flashed on screen.

Locked by client. Contact Testimony Social Services.

Oh well. I could get the code, but I wouldn't. Besides being illegal, it would break any bit of trust Grace had left in me. At the bottom of the page, in small letters was the file's last activity and an ID code, a chain of numbers and two letters:

BM.

Birth mother.

My head fell into my hands as I remembered all the things I'd said about my mother in front of her. No wonder I'd freaked her out.

Before logging out, I clicked the date the case had been created and did a search for a couple of terms: Clark County, Black. Enter. Fifty entries flooded the screen. I skimmed the log. All births but none of them made sense.

What am I doing?

I clicked exit then, but instead of logging me out of the program, it netted me another list. One of the entries, a baby boy born in Hamilton county, stole my breath.

It can't be.

The office door creaked open, Grace's heels tapping to her seat. I blinded the monitor with the push of a button and pushed back from my desk, my head pounding. I pulled the plug from the wall.

She tapped my shoulder. "Ready to go down?"

"Down?"

"The assembly?"

I looked at the pages stacked in my inbox. Joyce was probably going to say things that I didn't want to hear, like how she might not be around next year. I'd much rather stay right here. "Right."

"Well, it's starting. The kids are going in."

"Sure. Let's go." I stood up and pushed in my chair, still trying to grasp what I'd just learned. I'd remember later thinking then that the day couldn't get much worse. I couldn't have been more wrong.

We entered the crowded cafeteria in silence and slipped in beside Zeely on the faculty row. Joyce stood slightly above us on a podium I'd made two years before. She looked good up there, as good as could be expected. The same sickening calm graced her face as usual, and her eyes had that same stubborn determination.

The second hand hit twelve and Joyce began to speak.

"Thank you all for coming." She beamed at the group. "As some of you know, and others of you are learning for the first time, I am ill. In fact, I am dying."

Way to beat around the bush.

Grace's hand attached to my wrist with a firm, desperate grip, but her expression didn't change. Zeely, on the other hand, looked as if she'd been hit by a truck.

Joyce unbuttoned her blazer. "Don't look so sad, everyone. If I die tonight, I have been blessed beyond measure—"

Someone behind us started to cry. No, wail. Grace swallowed

283

hard. Her fingernails dug into my skin. I tightened my grip on her hand, trying not to look at Lottie, a few seats down with bleary eyes, shrouded in a waterfall of braids.

Joyce lifted her hands, the way she had when we were kids. I loved to see her like that, in the pose of a loving teacher. Her eyes fastened on me as her voice welled up through the silence.

"Stand up, everybody. I want a circle of love."

The group joined around the room. Joyce took her place inside the ring, lifting her hands like a maestro. Vulnerability clawed at me as I remembered the many times I'd done this same exercise in high school. I closed my eyes, waiting for Joyce's questions; questions I was still trying to answer.

"Who are you?" she asked.

"Imani," we all answered.

"What is Imani?"

"Faith." The circle captured the word.

"And what is faith?" She whispered this part, as she always had.

"Power!" The word came out of me like a blast. This time, it was me who grabbed onto Grace.

Joyce spoke again, this time in a guttural tone. "Power to—"

"Power to create, to love, to change the world." A baritone answered from the door.

A gasp choked in my throat as the speaker, an ebony man with graying temples, approached Joyce in the center of the circle. The sound I'd swallowed came out of Grace's mouth instead. I didn't even want to imagine why. Instead I stared at him, trying to tell myself that it was somebody else.

It wasn't.

It was Malachi Xavier Gooden, "X" as he'd been called back in the day. The friend who'd replaced Ron in my college days. The enemy who almost cost me everything.

Joyce looked at me one more time before welcoming the visitor openly.

"Bantu Gooden? I've been waiting for you. Please. Come in."

I tried not to swallow my own tongue as X cut into the circle and stood by Joyce's side. When she patted his hand, I almost threw up in my mouth.

"Some of you know Bantu Gooden. He was one of us not so long ago. He's moved on to greener pastures now, but I'm thankful he's surprised us today."

My hand slipped from Grace's fingers.

Joyce continued. "There have been problems this last year, as you all know. Problems I can't fix." She lifted her head. "But God can. Dr. Mayfield will serve in my absence for the duration of the term. That's all for now. I just wanted you all to know why I might not be around as much in the weeks to come."

Grace looked away, probably searching for Zeely, who was half-slumped onto Jerry's shoulder at the end of the row. I felt Zee's pain. Mal's presence was just an added blow, like a brick through the window of a burning house.

Overkill.

I stood my ground as X—Dr. Gooden was how people knew him now, we'd met before professionally with less-than-stellar results—approached, burning my nose with his stinky, cheap cologne. He had the nerve to be smiling. I wasn't.

"What are you doing here?" I had to know if Joyce had asked him or if he'd tricked her too.

"Just taking care of my people, that's all." He leaned over and kissed Grace's hand.

God was real, I knew that then because I didn't punch him in the mouth.

Grace looked like she wanted to do it for me. "Mal? You—you never mentioned coming. Why didn't you tell me?"

That was it. I wedged my body between them, turning to Grace instead of him. "He didn't want you to know. That's how hustlers run their games."

Grace looked like the toothpaste at the bottom of the tube. Squished. She looked as horrified to see that we knew one another as I was to see that the two of them had some connection. Was this the fool she'd told me about at dinner? The one who she'd been engaged to but who couldn't make up his mind?

That figures.

Mal touched one of my locks. I slowly, carefully, removed it from his hands and knotted it at the end. I'd trim that tip off when I got home. Maybe the whole thing.

He laughed with that irritating laugh of his. "Well, I see you haven't cut that mess off your head yet. I knew they'd get tired of you at Oh-State sometime. They finally realized that even when you paint trash gold, it's still trash."

I smirked, thumping the clergy pin on his lapel. "You should know."

48

Grace

*When it was my turn, they said I was too far along,
that it'd take two days to kill the baby. Even Mom
couldn't bear the thought of that. I wasn't going to do
it anyway. Like Daddy always says, things will work
out. Somehow.*

Diana Dixon

Brian thundered away, leaving me alone with my ex and an au-
dience of empty chairs. Mal and Brian not only knew each other
but knew each other well. Something had strained their relationship, something that neither of them wanted me to know about.
I found this quite interesting since Mal had seemed so concerned
about my past.

My former beau touched my elbow and plastered a smile over
his angry look from his conversation with Brian. "Don't look at me
like that. I'll explain everything."

Right. "I'm all ears."

His smile collapsed. "Not now. I've got to hit the road to make
it back for youth revival. Soon, okay? I'll ride over early and drive
you home—"

This again? "This is my home."

"Right. I'll drive you back to Cincinnati. We'll have a picnic at
the zoo after church, just like old times."

"I don't think so."

As he turned, I saw something hanging from the chain on his neck. A ring. Our ring. In the confusion before, I hadn't noticed it. I wished I hadn't now. "It's good to see you too, Mal, but as far as that date, I don't think so."

He gave my cheek a lingering kiss. "No strings. Just talking. Aren't we still friends?"

Friendship had never seemed so dangerous until I moved here. "I guess."

After giving me a satisfied look, Mal left as quickly as he'd come. I stood in the empty cafeteria wringing my hands, trying not to think about the Cincinnati Zoo. The butterfly garden would be long out of bloom by now. After our Sunday picnics, I'd often returned there to clear my mind, get my head on straight, especially during the "hair phase" when Mal continually indicated his displeasure over my new appearance. The blunt and blow-dried style had been born in that garden. If I went with Mal again, I had a feeling that something would die.

My hair.

I stared up at the clock. There were fifty minutes until my next class and I was late for my appointment with the scalp specialist Thelma had recommended to me. She sounded encouraging over the phone. I hoped she was as sweet in person. After this day, I felt like I needed my head examined instead of my scalp.

I looked around the examination room—at the leaning stack of magazines, at the glass container of cotton balls, even the bottle of hand wash at the sink—anywhere but at the bald-headed giant smiling in front of me. This was something the doctor might have mentioned on the phone.

Dr. Stein batted her eyes, which were quite beautiful. "Tell me about your hair." She spoke steady and calm.

I wanted to respond to the soothing mother-speech oozing from this blue-eyed Amazon, but my words dissolved under my tongue.

The doctor patted my shoulder. "Would you feel better if I put my wig on? I forget how I look to the first-timers." Sugary laughter chased the bitterness of words.

"You're fine. You just caught me off guard. My hair? Well, I have my ups and downs. Loss from chemicals, thinning temples from braids, just plain rough, dry hair . . ."

The woman took notes. "Your sample indicates that your diet is fairly nutrient rich. Do you exercise? Do you sleep with your head covered?"

"Yes to all. I lose my cool with food when I'm running around too much or upset, but I do pretty well at home. The water is hard for me, but I'm up to two quarts a day now."

The doctor examined my scalp once more before scribbling again. "What about moisture? I notice your hair is straight today."

"It's pressed. I like to change up sometimes. I make my own hair butter and braid spray. I coat the ends every night."

A few hairs floated to the floor as the woman raked her fingers through my tresses. She sat back on her stool. "Is there something that you enjoy doing? A hobby?"

"I've taken up dancing again. My hair is still coming out, but it seems to help."

The doctor stopped writing. "Well, I've got good news and bad news."

"Go for it," I said, not sure if I really meant it.

"The good news is it's not alopecia, female pattern baldness, or anything like that. The change from chemically processed hair to natural hair is a difficult one for African American women. In your case, doing so probably saved your hair. Though it may seem to shed a lot, this is about right for the stage you're in. Drugs and chemicals can stay in the hair shaft for years. In time, you and your hair will adjust to each other. The bad news is that there's more than normal shedding going on. Some of your hair loss is stress related."

Makes sense. "I did just move and get a new job."

"I don't think that's it." She paused. "I'm reluctant to say this, but since we discussed our faith on the phone . . ."

I swung my legs over the edge of the table. "Just say it."

"There is something you're trying to hide, but instead, it's hiding you, eating you up, if you will. Until it's dealt with, your hair will keep coming out, perhaps all of it. When I prayed about your case, that's what came to my spirit. What I've seen here is in line with that."

No wonder Thelma sent me over here. I get church even at the doctor. Not sure how I feel about it. "No offense, but I don't think it's that bad. I've got some issues at work, but other than that, my life is going great." My voice cracked at my audacity.

Yeah, right. Everything is just peachy.

She nodded and handed me a list of directives: hair vitamins, eight hours or more of sleep a night, eight glasses of water a day, five servings of fruits and vegetables. Things I was already doing, except for the sleeping.

I lowered my voice. "Have you ever had a patient with loss like mine?"

Light gleamed off the doctor's head, accenting her eyes. "I've had one case like yours."

"And what happened?"

The doctor took my hand and placed it on her own smooth skull. Her lips trembled as she spoke. "This."

49

Brian

It made me crazy every time I thought about it. Grace and Mal? The two of them knowing each other, much less almost getting married, was enough to drive me to my second job at Testimony Social Services. The stack of case files leaning against my sad excuse for a desk would be just the thing to keep my mind off the two of them.

Only it wasn't working.

"Just leave things to me," Mal had told me the first time I landed in juvenile hall, picked up because I had the wrong face in the wrong place. He was still at Imani then, though he'd gone on to every private school around. He was the new kid at school, but a veteran of the system. He'd encouraged me to stay calm and stay quiet, ask for books, and obey all the rules. Days later, when we were both released, I'd marveled at his ingenuity. Years later, when he filled the gaping hole left by my nonexistent family, I learned the hard way that Mal Gooden was no friend.

Through the fabric of my shirt, I traced the scar his crew had left me as a reminder. If it weren't for that girl, Mal's half sister, if it weren't for Joyce . . .

If it weren't for God.

The scar, raised and hard under my fingers, was some of why I didn't get too close to people. Didn't trust them. I had tried to ask Mal once, at a symposium, what happened to his little sister or cousin or whoever that girl was who used to hang over there.

Mal had laughed in my face and walked away. Ron said that the guy had changed now, that he did amazing things with youth. It might very well be true. From the way he'd looked at me at that assembly, it was adults he still had issues with. Like everyone else, that guy was still trying to get rid of me.

And yet, I was still here.

The sad thing was that Ron and I had never really recovered from all that. Rejected by his white friends—they were horrified to see where we lived, which made me mad since Ron's own house had looked ten times worse—I had pushed my brother, my closest friend away. I'd lost track of the others too: Zeely, Jerry, and all the Imani grads. By the time I connected again, nothing ever seemed the same. I never felt welcome. Fueled by anger and isolation, I'd studied hard, earning several degrees simultaneously. Only when I saw a girl with brown, frizzy hair and smooth curves did I let my guard down. Though I'd been blessed to meet my late wife that day, I knew now that it was Grace that I thought I saw then, Grace who I'd been searching for all along. Maybe I'd been searching for the rest of them too, especially Ron. The past few months were the closest Ron and I had been in a long time. Too long.

My back arched in the chair as I closed my eyes and the last five years sped under my eyelids: talk shows, book tours, red-eye flights, and then lesson plans and research files like the ones stacked behind me. Where God had once reigned, I placed goal after goal until I settled on the unattainable—finding my birth mother. Though I continued to scour documents for clues, there was no certificate for my birth. I'd been a mama and 'nem adoption, as I called them, family taking family, friends taking friends. I didn't want to deal with it, but the secret I longed for was lodged between the pews of Mount Olive Missionary Baptist Church, and God himself would have to get it out. Still, what I'd learned the other day at school when I wasn't really trying gave me hope, even though it had nothing to do with my case.

I reached for the next file. For now, my search was stalled—locked like Grace's file—but I could still help these other people trying to put their families back together. I'd been so angry about Mal, upset about Joyce, that I'd forgotten that Grace, like these people, was hurting too. What was it she'd said in our conversation about having children? *"It's not always that easy."* Maybe it wasn't. God knows I'd simplified my own situation, made the story fit what I could handle. Now I had to accept that perhaps my mother gave me up out of love instead of abandonment. While I thought the idea misguided, I had to consider it.

And I did consider it as I updated case after case, filed the information request forms. From the things Eva had said about my mother, she'd been in her twenties at least, not some teenager with no options. When I'd ranked high on IQ tests, Eva didn't seem surprised, saying I'd come by it honestly, whatever that meant. From the quirks in my personality, it was hard to tell. She could have been a genius with no time for children or a nutcase who tried to trap a man only to have it blow up in her face. I wasn't sure that I liked either option.

The agency director, a slight man with straight teeth and a crooked smile, walked in and shook my hand. "There you are. It's great to have you back. I know you've been tied up with school for a while."

He'd probably be seeing a lot more of me. "It's good to be back. I should have this pile down some before I leave."

The man whistled. "I can't believe the dent you've put in it already. Why do you think I missed you? That stack has been on every desk in here. Nobody's made much progress."

I nodded, understanding how the documents could be mundane for people who had parents and kids of their own. For me, every entry represented someone like me: misplaced, searching. Perhaps one day the piece of information I filed would be the key I was looking for to unlock all my questions. "It's no problem. I love it."

"And we appreciate it. I wish I'd been here when you concluded your own search. We were a little sad you didn't call, but we understand these things are personal. It's good to know you'll still be with us."

Huh? I tried not to get excited. "Thanks for the vote of confidence, but I still haven't found anything."

"No? What about the lady?"

"What lady?"

He spoke faster now, his homespun Spanish mixing with his on-the-job English, something that only happened when he was excited or worried. "A black lady come here and ask for you. She ask if you find your mother. When I say no, she say, 'That's okay. She will find him.'"

My body stayed still, but my mind sped away. Would the woman I'd searched so hard for just walk in off the street like that? Maybe. This was Testimony, after all. Sweat trickled down my forehead. "Did she give her name?"

"Let's see. She had a nametag on her uniform. The sister on *Good Times*? You know, the TV show?"

"Thelma?"

The director smiled, nodding. "That's it! Do you know her?"

The folder I'd been holding slipped from my fingers and littered the floor with papers.

"I thought I did."

The car jerked with my uneven pressure on the gas. I tried to remember the list of questions I'd rehearsed for so many years, but I no longer cared about the reasons. What I wanted was the truth.

I asked myself all kinds of questions as I drove. Had Thelma moved into the neighborhood before us or after? It seemed she'd always been there. Hadn't she always treated me special growing up—extra cookies on my plate, Easter baskets, Christmas gifts . . . Was she just being neighborly or was it something more?

My old house came into view. I pulled into the drive, glancing over at Thelma's. Light glowed through her windows. Gospel music vibrated across the street. James Cleveland, I think. I put my car in the garage this time, in case our local stalker decided to visit.

No matter how many times I tried to think of a reasonable way to ask Thelma if she was my mother, my mind was blank. It was jacked up no matter what I said. I reached up and pulled down the garage door. When I felt a hand on my shoulder, I jumped.

"There you are." Thelma stood behind me in a flowered house-coat. Her head was full of rollers. "I saw you over here the other night, but I had a kitchen full of heads. Pastor's anniversary. All the girls wanted a new style."

I nodded, studying her face for some piece of me, something I could claim as my own.

She laughed. "Can't talk, huh? Well, I've got some smoked turkey wings, rice, and gravy over there that will loosen your lips. I came to Social Services awhile back to bring you dinner."

Here was my opportunity. "My boss, he told me you came by. He said you asked—"

Thelma looked around the yard. "Funny for him to remember me."

"He said that you mentioned something about my mother. That she would find me." I stepped closer, looking into my old friend's eyes. "Has she found me, Thelma?"

She grabbed my hand. "I asked him if you found your mama. When he said no, I told him that Lord willing, she might just find you first. That's all." Her words raced like a runaway train.

I stared into her eyes, still streaked with blue eyeliner from a long day in the lunchroom and a longer night at church. She knew more than she was telling, but I wouldn't get more. Not a bit. Great. Another dead end. "How would she know where to find me?"

Thelma patted my hand and looked away. "Trust me, baby. A mother always finds her children."

50

Grace

Of all the Cincinnati Zoo exhibits, I loved the World of Insects best, especially Whiting Grove, the picnic area, where I could ruminate about the monarchs and hummingbirds I'd seen. It was too cold for all that, so the Japanese maples held my attention instead. Their snow-covered branches extended like fingers ready to carry me away.

Mal had picked me up early with a call only when he was almost to town—he and Brian had that in common. Why I'd come, I wasn't sure, but here I was, shrimp salad sandwich in hand, with the nerve to wonder if Mal remembered to put in the grapes.

He'd remembered, all right. He'd even thrown in something else too.

"Ow!" I clutched my jaw.

He reached for me. "Are you okay? I guess I didn't think about that part. Oh goodness. Here I am trying to be romantic and I hurt you . . ."

I dabbed my bloody gums with a napkin and stared at the offending ingredient. A ring. And a huge one at that. Whoever said that diamonds were a girl's best friend hadn't had lunch with Mal. It was everything I would have wanted a year ago, but now it was just a piece of jewelry hidden in my lunch.

An oak above us pointed accusingly at my hands. Not only had Mal evaded my questions all morning, now he'd thrown another twist into my knotted life. I turned to face him with grapes and celery lingering on my tongue. I sighed.

Mal cracked a grin. "Speechless, huh?" He placed a jewelry box on my lap.

"Basically." What does one say after almost choking on a diamond?

"I've had this planned for a while. When I found out about Joyce, I knew the time was right, that you'd be coming home—"

Was he serious? "Are you kidding me?"

He looked offended. "Of course not. I just wanted to make my intentions clear." Malachi slipped off the bench and onto the icy ground, gathering my hands between his. Firmness lurked beneath his gentle grasp.

"I thought you'd be happy. I thought . . ." He raked his fingers through his cropped curls, sprinkled with gray.

"You thought what? That something has changed? It hasn't. I'm still the same woman you walked away from a few months ago. The woman who accepted that and moved on." My voice faltered.

He had the look of a man intent on getting what he wanted. "You make things so complicated, Grace. I made a mistake—"

"A mistake? You called off our engagement!"

His forehead creased a little. "I was confused. Now I know what I want." His fingers pressed through my wool coat. There was a lot of difference between this and Brian's light yet strong touch. Although Mal met all the requirements—saved and single—his hands felt like a death grip.

"I want *you.*"

How long had I waited to hear those words from him? If only it were true. Need. That's what this was about, need masquerading as love. I needed to get out of here. And quick. I opened the jewelry box and pushed the diamond into its slot. "Here." I pressed the box into his palm.

Malachi took it, but his eyes remained fixed on me, almost

threateningly. An ultimatum of sorts. His expression spoke almost audibly—*I won't ask again.*

Again, God's promise came to me:

For your maker is your husband—the Lord Almighty is his name— the Holy one of Israel is your redeemer . . .

"Just say yes. It's so easy."

I shut my mouth tight so that no words could escape and betray me. My head shook back and forth, saying no without words.

He ran a hand through my hair, then went silent again. Though only six years older than me, the sprinkle of gray on Mal's scalp gave away his well-masked worry habit. The rest of his body exuded youth. He loved God, looked good, worked hard, and he wanted me. What else could a woman pray for? A vision of flashing eyes and a head full of locks swept across my mind.

Everything.

Malachi knelt to gather the remaining food into the basket. He looked up at me, a determined smile creasing his lips. "I'll keep the ring until you're ready. Even criminals get three strikes, right?"

I prayed for the right words. "Please, Mal. Don't."

He slammed a loaf of French bread into the hamper. "I'm sorry for letting your past scare me away, okay? How long do I have to pay for that?"

"You're missing the point."

"I—"

I held up a finger in protest. "That day after you left, after I told you about me, God gave me a peace and a mission. I've been a little sidetracked, but I'm going to give myself to these kids. It's enough. It has to be."

Mal stood and buried his face in my hair, the thing he'd complained about most. "Sweetheart . . ."

The warmth, the closeness, threatened my sanity.

An unmarried woman . . . is concerned with the Lord's affairs. Her aim is to be devoted to the Lord, in both body and spirit.

The rest of the verse hung in my mind like a dead weight.

But a married woman is concerned about the affairs of this world—how she can please her husband.

Futile attempts to please one husband festered in my mind. Would spending the rest of my life trying—and failing—to please Mal be enough? If I was honest, I wanted more than a man with all the trimmings. I wanted something I'd never had; I wanted to fall in love.

I moved away from his touch.

Mal tossed the ring into the basket at his feet. "So nothing will change your mind?" He flipped a wheel of Gouda cheese atop the pile.

"I'm not waiting for somebody to love me so I can live, Mal. I'm ready to live now. I don't want to be anyone's wife."

"Not even Brian's?" Malachi stood, his fists in his pockets, the basket handle dangling at his wrist.

He called me out.

Still, I had to play dumb. "What?"

He snorted. "Come on. You two were wrapped up at that assembly like swizzle sticks. I saw you through the window."

I pulled my coat tighter, remembering Brian's big hands in mine . . . touches in a moment of sorrow, nothing more. "This has nothing to do with Brian, though I do find it interesting that you'd bring him up now. You haven't wanted to discuss him all day." A breeze churned up the path behind us, waking leaves from their snowy grave.

Mal's eyes bore down on me, as if searching for the meek, mellow woman he'd shared a first date with at this spot two years before. "I hope you haven't allowed yourself to fall into some delusion about Brian. He's dangerous."

Snow powdered my hair. I could almost feel the curls sprouting from the moisture. "And you're safe?"

He threw down the picnic basket. Kicked it a few feet. "I heard about those charges against him. I think you need to take them seriously. Unless you want to be his next victim, I suggest you stay away from him—even at work."

"The thing with Lottie Wells? I know about that. I was there." I stared at one of the goblets from our lunch, now shattered on the ground. I wouldn't let the same thing happen to me, not with Mal or with Brian. Even if it meant resigning from my job.

Mal motioned toward the shelter when the snow came down harder, stinging our faces. I didn't move. He wiped the white from his nose. "It's not just that. Brian was doing this stuff years ago, when we were growing up."

"He'd be in jail . . ." My voice sounded firm, even through the brewing storm, but I didn't resist when Mal pulled me under the pavilion, dragging what remained of the picnic basket with him.

He restated his case. "He was never charged, but trust me, he was guilty."

I staggered. "How can you be sure?"

He pressed the ring box into my hand.

"I was there."

I visited the new church again on Sunday, both thankful and sorry to be an anonymous face in the crowd. Monday came too quickly, bringing with it the somber mood of Joyce's announcement. Of all the students, Sean looked undaunted. Brian looked crushed.

"Can anyone give me an example of a writer from the Harlem Renaissance?" I asked.

Sean's hand shot up. "Langston Hughes."

My hands moved across the chalkboard, writing his answer. "Good. And what were some of the themes of his works? What was his struggle?"

Brian watched from the side of the room, half listening. He'd asked this morning what had happened over the weekend. Besides

300

my hair being nappy again, nothing had changed really. Nothing and everything too.

The bell rang.

I turned from the board. "We'll discuss Jean Toomer's *Cotton Song* tomorrow. Be prepared." The students moaned agreement and filed out of the room. I smiled at them. And then frowned at Brian.

Immediately I regretted it. Sure Mal had always been honest with me before, but I didn't have any proof that Brian had done anything wrong. Sure, he was even more distant since the assembly, but that didn't prove anything either.

My heart judged Brian innocent on all counts while my head told me to get away as fast as I could. It was time I admitted it, to myself and to God, that without meaning to, I'd fallen for Brian. Somehow I was going to have to get back up.

When the class emptied, I pushed past Brian into the office, trying my best not to look at him. "Excuse me."

He tapped my shoulder. Gently.

"Can I talk to you for a minute?"

I shrank back. "Yes? Can I help you?"

From the look on his face and the flip in my stomach, that was the wrong question. He let the moment pass. "I have a memo for you, but first I wanted to clear up something."

A memo? This had to be some kind of sick joke. "Put it on my desk. It's not really a good time to talk."

Brian walked into the office and stuck the memo inside my Bible. In Ephesians somewhere. I'd scour that passage when I got home, though it probably meant nothing.

As he turned back to me, he had a puzzled look on his face. "You know, things between us were fine until X—Mal Gooden showed up. What did he tell you about me? Did he tell you how he—"

The office door swung open. Quinn bounded in, then stopped

short, probably discerning the tension in the room. "I can come back . . ."

I started clearing my desk. "You stay, Quinn. I was just leaving."

Brian rolled his eyes and motioned Quinn to the chair beside his desk. He looked over at me and shook his head. Just a little, but enough for me to notice.

Quinn sighed. "Now doesn't seem like a good time. You want me to go?"

"It's okay. Come on in," he said, inviting Quinn to sit with his hands and begging me not to go with his eyes.

I left anyway.

He got rid of me.

Of all the things I expected that memo tucked in my Bible to say, learning that I'd be switching positions with Zeely was a total shock. I'd wanted to talk to Joyce about it, but I knew she was resting most of the time now. I'd have to be a big girl and deal with it. As I'd left school and set out for the store, I began to wonder if maybe it wasn't a good idea after all. This way I could get over Brian and not have to wonder what he was going to do next or whether he was a good guy playing bad or the other way around. I could just teach and go home. Easy. If only shopping were as simple.

I strolled six aisles in Strong and Jones Market and still couldn't find the Jiffy mix. It was almost November, time for a practice Thanksgiving meal. The cashier looked surprised at being asked about a boxed mix, but asked if I didn't want some cornmeal anyway. It was so much better than a mix, she promised.

To her, maybe. That was a little too back-to-basics for me. Vegetables were the only thing I cooked from scratch. I couldn't believe I'd bypassed the Kroger with a four-foot-high Jiffy display to come to this dinky little store that Zeely raved about so much. I probably should have gone to a health food store anyway, but after reading Brian's memo requesting that Zeely and I switch classes through the end of the semester, I was not in a stir fry kind of mood. And then there was the ring in my purse that I still had to send back. If it was even safe to mail diamonds, that is. Saturated fat was definitely in order.

I scanned the different kinds of cornmeal—white, yellow, fluffy, sifted—trying not to think about it. An older woman reached past me for a box of white meal and put down three boxes of Jiffy mix in its place. I snatched them with glee and inventoried my cart—cabbage, onions, a turkey leg, and a homegrown seasoning formulated by the store, selected on Zeely's recommendation. The cornbread mix completed the scene. I put the first two boxes in the cart and held up the third for inspection. A puff of yellow escaped a crack along the seam. Open.

Before I could put the open box back, another cart rammed mine from the side. The box of cornbread mix burst open. Yellow dust settled on my lips. I sucked in a breath, swallowing mush. I peered through the fallout, making out the person's face who'd run into me. Lottie Wells.

I refused to stoop to her silly level. "Lottie, watch where you're going, honey. You're going to hurt someone."

The buggy villain stepped closer, whispering like she'd heard nothing I'd said. "I know you. You fooled me with that nappy hair and a different name, but I recognize you now. I never forget a face."

I gripped the cart's handle. Was she drunk? She looked it. Just what I didn't need. "We work together. At Imani, remember?"

She blew whiskey breath in my face and wagged her finger. "I'm not talking 'bout that." Her words slurred. "Diana Dix-on. Room two forty-three."

I swallowed the Jiffy, sweet and gritty. Shock slid down my throat too.

"Say the right things at my hearing or I'll tell everybody 'bout you and that baby you gave away. Even your boyfriend, Dr. Mayfield." The contents of Lottie's cart clanked as she backed up and sped toward the register: six forty-ounces of beer, a can of butter beans, and a lifetime of secrets.

My secrets.

51

*They brought me here in the middle of the night so
the neighbors wouldn't see me. I wore Mom's old
maternity dress. It's denim with leaves. Pretty leaves.
Sometimes, when I wear it, I feel like dancing, but I
never do.*

Diana Dixon

I came in the house barefoot and hugging that raggedy, wonder-ful notebook. Until today, I'd sometimes wondered if it had really happened, that baby growing inside me, those hands coming to take it away. Lottie was the last person I thought would give me validation. She knew it all, even my room number.

My jacket was somewhere in the car. I made it into the kitchen before I totally broke down. I left the food on the counter and stumbled upstairs. In Peter's bed and under five blankets, Lottie's words screamed in my head.

I know you.

St. Andrew's Maternity Home for Unwed Mothers. To know my room number, Lottie would have to have to have spent some time there too. That explained a lot. Everyone dealt with their crazy in a different way.

I am with you always, even to the end of the age.

I burrowed in the covers, running from the voice of God. Why did he always seem to show up after everything was over? Today I was tired of praying, of pushing, swaying like a tower of game pieces, tottering but somehow standing. Today the weight of Lottie's words had tipped the balance, scattering me in a cloud of Jiffy mix. A cloud that brought whispers in my mind and pictures to burn my eyes. A cloud that could turn into a tornado if I wasn't careful.

And they overcame him because of the blood of the Lamb and because of the word of their testimony . . .

My testimony. Only the truth—and the entire truth—could really set me free. Had God used Lottie to force my obedience? No. I served a God of love, not manipulation. I peeked up from the covers, second-guessing my own thoughts. Maybe the prompt to tell the ladies at the beauty shop who I really was, what really happened to me, was meant to prevent what had happened today, not cause it.

Now I'd have to tell. Despite the way Brian was acting or what Mal said, changing my testimony at the hearing wasn't an option. I dialed Zeely's number. The answering machine picked up.

I turned off the phone and stuck it under my pillow. What was I going to say anyway? "Remember when I moved away and never came back? I left because I was pregnant and I was pregnant because one day at the bus stop, a boy threw me on the ground . . ."

I squeezed my eyes together, trying to cut off the memories. The pain. The lies. St. Andrew's. The tutors. An art class. That little girl, even younger than me, who wouldn't stop screaming when her baby came out dead. Anne. Charlotte Anne.

Lottie.

I tried to stop my racing pulse. Brian, whose mother had given him away, would probably be plenty disappointed to know that I'd done the same thing. And Zeely? Goodness. She'd thought I was crazy for climbing a mountain. Black folks definitely didn't give up their children. Aunt Ina had aborted her babies and told me proudly, "At least I didn't give them away."

Maybe it didn't matter anymore who knew . . . It would feel good to fill in the blanks at the gynecologist's correctly. To accept a corsage at church on Mother's Day. To be honest when people asked, "Do you have any children?" I scratched my scalp. I had to find a place to lay my burdens down, somewhere for my heart to rest. Maybe this truth telling would be that place. A place to lay my head.

The stink of bad pork and wilted cabbage marched up the stairs to meet me the next morning. I stared down the street at Zeely's empty driveway. Maybe I'd catch her at lunch. I cleaned up what I could and sped to school, praying all the way that I wouldn't be late. It didn't hit me until I parked that I probably wouldn't see Brian today. No wonder Zeely had left early. By now, she'd gotten a memo too, the one reassigning her with Brian.

I hope they don't kill each other.

The closer I got to the school, the slower I walked, in no hurry to face the change. The thought of teaching with someone new felt like starting all over. Would the students who loved me in Literature hate me in Algebra? Math had been my minor, but that seemed a lifetime ago. I hoped I'd be able to keep up. Armed with my own unanswered questions, I walked into the new classroom and to the front desk, still smelling of Zeely's perfume. Jerry sat quietly while the students chattered on, moving around the room out of their seats. I clenched my teeth. As maddening as Brian could be, I missed his order already.

"Morning, Ms. Okoye. Come on in." Jerry stood and faced the class to introduce me. For the first part of the class, they worked in teams to complete worksheets. While they worked, Jerry showed me the way he and Zeely organized the lessons. He did a short interactive lecture at the end of their hands-on class work. It seemed backwards to me, but I told him I'd do all I could to make it work. He smiled, saying it was all he could ask. Before I knew it, it was time for the lecture and board work.

"Anybody remember where we left off yesterday?"

Sean's hand shot up. "Um, exponents in New York or something like that."

Jerry flipped Sean a piece of bubble gum from his pocket. "That's right. A negative exponent is just a road trip. It's like this: Your mom lives in New York and your dad lives in Miami. New York is the numerator. Everybody say num-er-a-tor."

The class chanted back in a weak tone.

Jerry dropped the chalk and crossed his arms. "Sean, give me a beat."

Happy to oblige, the boy alternated his knuckles and his palms on the desk.

"Everybody say nu-mer-a-tor." Jerry cupped his hands to his ear.

I felt the beat pass through me like another pair of drumming hands, Brian's hands. My feet started to move. My mouth too. "Nu-mer-a-tor!"

"That's what I'm talking about." Jerry turned to the board. He drew a line and wrote NY on top and MIA under it. "New York is live, but in the winter it gets cold and Moms can get a little crazy, so," he turned back to them, "you have to call Pops and go to Miami, the—"

"De-nom-in-a-tor!" Before Jerry could even say it, the students waved their hands like they did on the weekends. I surprised myself, raising the roof too.

Unable to resist, Jerry answered in rhythm himself. "Somebody, everybody, scream . . ."

"Ahhhhh—"

Jerry choked with laughter, sliding one hand across his neck, signaling the cutoff. "We'd better quit that screaming. Dr. Mayfield will put us out of here. Sit down."

Again to my surprise, the students sat. On their desks. On the floor. But they sat. Brian would have gone crazy.

"All right. Here's the problem. One over X to the negative one."
No heads bobbed. No arms waved. Silence.

"Hold on now. It's just a road trip, remember? Exponents are all about attitude. That isn't a negative number. He just isn't feeling Miami." He drew an arrow on the board. "So we move him to New York, on top, and he's feeling positive. He's chilling."

Sean shifted in his chair. "Oh snap. I think I got that. Do it again."

"Nope," my new partner said, extending the chalk to Sean. "The next one is on you. Need some music?"

The boy shuffled through the desks, his pants trailing the floor. "Yeah. Y'all help me out."

The hat guy from the first day in my old class provided a beat while a girl with an afro puff added the words. "Nothing but a road trip, with the ex-po-nents. Too hot? Take it up. Take it up. Too cold? Shake it down. To the ground!"

Three more girls jumped from their chairs and followed their friend's commands. Even the most disciplined students, stiff in their desks in the front row, swayed to the side. Sean worked his body as he boxed his answer. The class looked to Jerry with expectancy, wondering if the calculations were correct.

"It's perfect." Their teacher nodded and flipped Sean more gum, two pieces this time. "That's all I've got left. And that's the bell. I'll see you all tomorrow. The homework is page one twenty-seven, odd."

"All of the odd problems?" someone asked.

Jerry looked over his glasses. "You heard me. And check them in the back, don't try and copy the answers. I'll know."

Nonplussed by the assignment, Sean folded his paper into a triangle and slipped it into his pocket. He pulled the headphones from his neck onto his ears. Dullness covered his face. I checked the clock. He'd have Brian next. Maybe Zeely could lighten things up. He flashed me a smile so quick I almost missed it. "Peace out, Miss O."

Peace. I could use some of that. "Same to you, Sean."

I looked at my new teaching partner in amazement as the class flowed into the hall. "Jerry. I'm stunned."

"At what? The kids? This is a smart group. I just wish they had a better teacher. Math wasn't my major, but I am certified in it. It was Joyce's biggest need when I came. Zeely's better with the geometry." He wiped his head with a washcloth from his desk drawer. He looked like a preacher after a good sermon.

"I can't tell math wasn't your major. Some of these kids never said one word in Brian's class. I know I've never seen Sean having so much fun."

Jerry rubbed the back of his head. "Brian is getting them ready for college. I'm trying to get them ready for life outside of here. We're both needed." His forehead gleamed.

"I guess you're right. Everyone has their purpose."

Brian seemed intent on breaking my heart. Lottie aimed to destroy my life. Everyone else just got to watch.

No wonder Zeely liked him. I rubbed my aching arms and tried to swallow the hoarseness in my throat. A day in Jerry's class felt like a low-impact version of my friend's workout. Between the jumping, shouting, and a run around the hall singing the quadratic formula, I wondered if I'd be able to keep up with my new teaching partner.

Jerry sat down with a pile of papers. "You can go home. I can handle these."

"One-hundred-point scale?" I grabbed a stack of tests and sat down.

He smiled. "Uh-huh. Thanks for staying."

I nodded and started on the exams, trying to grade the work as well as the answers. Jerry squinted up and down the page in front of him, as if hoping for correct solutions to appear. He passed me the grade book. I never took it.

310

He rapped on the table. "You all right?"

I wasn't, not really. I'd made so many wrong choices in my life, so many mistakes. I stared at the open door. Brian threw up a hand across the hall. I wanted to run for him, to tell him everything. I didn't dare. "Can I ask you something?"

"Fire away. I can do this in my sleep." Jerry flipped the third test over. "Blank spaces are easy to grade, just hard to look at."

"This is going to sound stupid, but how can you know if a man is really a Christian?"

I looked on as Jerry added five creativity points for a math poem in the margin. He laid the page across his lips. "Only God knows that for sure. We aren't to judge hearts. We're to pick fruit. When a man gives his life to Christ, you'll know, and not just by his church attendance. His words, his wallet, his woman . . ." Jerry sucked his teeth. "Every part of his life will begin to reflect Christ."

I picked up my pen and commenced grading.

"Wasn't the answer you were looking for?"

"It's not so much your answer as it is my questions. Some people do all the right things: go to church, read the Bible, pray . . . but they still *act* wrong. And then other people do all the wrong things, but their heart seems right."

Jerry frowned. "Thinking like that earned me a stack of bills and an ex-wife who isn't taking my calls. Don't follow hearts. They can't be trusted. Stick with the Word."

An unexpected guest waited for me in the hall after school. I almost knocked him over.

"Miss O?"

"Yes, Sean?"

"I just wanted to say again how sorry I am for what I said in Doc's class about you two, you know . . ."

"Forget it."

"For real? You're not going to hold it against me?"

I smiled, glad to offer forgiveness to someone. "For real. Now how are your grades doing? You seem like a totally different guy lately."

"I'm different in math because there's a different teacher. And you know, I got me a girl." He sighed, looking across the hall at the English room.

My eyes didn't follow his. Seeing Brian again would be too much. I hoped he'd gone home. "You two really don't get along, do you?"

"Nope. And we never will. I'll never be good enough for him."

I let myself look into Brian's room—it felt strange to call it that when it had so recently been my room too—and read the day's word on the board. It was simple today. *Goals.* No wonder Sean was looking so blue. "So, Sean, what do you want to do with your life?"

"Live."

"Seriously. If you could do whatever you wanted, what would you do?"

"Anything?" Sean shifted his gaze from side to side and peered over his shoulder. He spoke just above a whisper. "Music."

"You sing?" My eyes lit up.

"You could say that." He shrugged his backpack farther up on his shoulders.

"Well, what are you waiting for? Do you have a demo?"

"Naw. I tried a couple times, but it costs like a hundred bucks an hour and they want a down payment—"

"Is that all you need, money? Do you have your songs together? Tracks?"

Sean looked surprised. His voice cracked. "I got all that. One of my boys has a system. I mixed the tracks awhile back."

"All right then. Start practicing."

"But Miss O, the down payment is two thousand bucks. It's impossible."

I looked upward. "I'm not promising anything, but hey, God specializes in impossible things."

Whoever chose the teachers' lounge should have been shot. It had once been the equipment room, before the city renovated the gym. It still had that sweaty, squeaky smell of basketballs and boys. Still, it was a place to be alone. I sat down with the application I'd gotten from the guidance counselor to get the funds for Sean's project. The foundation was called Excellence in Color, and the application looked so long that Sean might have a better chance of getting into college now than getting that studio time. From the looks of things, I'd need everything short of his dental records to fill this out.

Not that I needed to be fooling with this at all. Why couldn't I just keep out of other people's lives anyway? Probably because my own life was so screwed up. I heard someone coming in the hall, but kept my eye on the pages, searching for a line I could actually fill in. So far, all I'd been able to do was his name.

"Hey." Brian's voice caught me off guard. Papers tumbled onto the floor. He leaned down to pick them up, but not before I scrambled to get most of them.

"Excellence in Color student grant?" he asked.

"It was going to be, but I don't know if I can finish it before the deadline. This application is Ivy League." I knelt on one knee, the cold floor biting through my skirt. When I looked up, Brian's lips were inches from mine. For a few seconds, neither of us moved. Then he took a step back.

He helped me back into my chair. "So, how are you doing? How's the class?"

"I was going to ask you the same thing."

Brian gave me the top page. It had been stuck under my chair. "We miss you, but everything's good. Sean and I are still bumping

313

heads some, but he's really improving. Still, I wonder if he wouldn't do better in a regular school environment. I've wanted to talk to Joyce about it, but with her sick, that puts all that on hold."

His words hit me like a brick. If I wanted to help Sean, I'd have to hurry. I shoved the papers back into their envelope. I'd call Sean's mother tonight to get their personal information.

"Right, well I'd better head out. I'll have to work on this later."

"Wait, is it for one of our kids?"

I hesitated, deciding to tell less rather than more. "It's one of ours, but I'd rather not say who. Privacy act and all that."

Brian reached into his organizer. "Take this." He offered a beige business card, similar to the one he'd given me the day we'd met but with no heading and an unfamiliar number. "Call and ask for Tiki."

Did he have the hookup everywhere or what? "Tiki? Are you serious?"

"Very. Do you want the grant or not?"

"I do."

"Okay. Tell Tiki to issue a grant for a student at Imani. Ask for only what you need for the project. Three thousand is the limit, and the kid has to write an essay afterward explaining how their life has been changed."

This guy was unbelievable. "That's all? I know you've got connections and everything, but that seems too easy."

Brian grabbed my hands between his in that heart-wrenching way that was becoming his habit. "It'd better be easy. It's my money."

It was only eight thirty in the morning and I had already run out of excuses. The studio manager—and Brian—had come through, but Sean hadn't shown up yet. The owner wanted his money either way.

"I don't know what could have happened." I clutched the envelope in my pocket. Carrying so much cash around wasn't an experience I wanted to repeat.

The studio manager didn't look concerned. "Want to sing something? You'll have to pay for the time anyway. I came up here special because it was a kid. I try to help out, you know?" He cocked his head to one side like he was proud of himself.

A discount would have been more helpful.

"I understand." I stood and moved to the open window. Nothing but snow. A bell jingled behind me.

Sean walked up, unwinding a scarf from his mouth. "There was an accident—"

If he hadn't been in an accident on the way to the studio, he would have been in an accident upon arrival—with me. "Are you hurt?"

He shook his head and stacked two CDs on the counter.

"Good." I pointed toward the booth, smiling. "Now get in there and sing."

Sean moved toward the recording area, striding at first and then taking baby steps. Finally, he went in.

The studio manager, his lips glossed with donut glaze, offered me a set of headphones. "Do you want to listen?"

I groaned. The last rap music I'd heard sounded like a root canal for the ears, but I'd come this far so I might as well listen.

Sean waved from the glass booth and mouthed the words, "Thank you."

I pushed on the headphones over my hair. "Let's do this."

The man wiped his hands on his pants and put Sean's CD into the machine. When no music played, I gave him a questioning look.

"The track is pretty clean, but I'm going to sharpen it some. Bring it out. Who mixed this anyway?"

"He did."

"I'm down to hear him sing then. This is nice. Different than what the kids usually come in with."

A melody rushed into my ears. Unlike the pounding beat I'd expected, it was a wave of sound, dipping and rising with a bass line somewhere underneath. I held the seat to restrain myself. This was dancing music.

The manager did a quick sound check. After that, Sean closed his eyes. I closed mine too, listening as Sean's voice flowed through the system like butter yielding to a hot pan.

"I am an invisible man, shaped by God's hand. Wondering who I am . . ."

The manager leaned closer to his equipment, nodding to the beat.

"I keep asking folks, but they keep walking. They keep talking. Say they don't know who I am. Say I'm an in-vis-i-ble man . . ." Sean's voice boomed now, full of his passion, his pain. I was on my feet, tangled in the words.

"I know you can't see me. I know you don't need me, but please stop walking on my head. I'm not dead . . ."

I blinked back tears.

"Watch your step. Watch it. Watch it. Watch it." The music pulsed with lyrics for a haunting chorus. Sean sang another verse as time stood still in my mind. Invisible. As the music faded, Sean kept singing, still bursting with the words he'd held inside so long.

"Lord, don't you see me? Please tell them. Oh-oh. Tell them you know who I a-am . . ."

The manager's voice broke the moment. "Cut."

Sean frowned and slid out of the box, his eyes on the ground. "Sorry, Miss O. It sounds much better at home."

I opened my mouth, but the manager beat me to it. "Better than that? I hope not or we'll be taping in your bed. You got more?"

Sean stumbled back. "I got a whole album."

The manager sniffed again. "It's going to be a long day, then. Get back in that box."

52

Ron

For a long time, my Sunday visits with Joyce had been the highlight of my week. Now that she was in the hospital, it was more difficult, but I still enjoyed it. The other thing I'd missed—then and now—I didn't want to think about. Not until I figured out for sure what to do with her. For her. For now, I'd sit here with Joyce, happy just to hear her breathing and talking, when she felt up to it. We'd had a great time reminiscing today. I smoothed back a stray hair from her forehead. She smiled in her sleep.

"Ron Jenkins, please report to the information center." I jerked at the sound of my name over the intercom.

Joyce opened one eye. "Something wrong?"

I patted her shoulder. "I'm sure it's okay. I probably dropped my wallet somewhere."

Joyce nodded and eased back into a sleeping position.

"I'll be right back."

Already asleep, she didn't answer.

I made it to the elevator just as the doors closed, riffling through my pockets as best I could without bumping into anyone. I clutched my wallet or the worn piece of leather passing for it and flipped through the sleeves. Social Security card. Driver's license. Bar association. Debit card. All there. An accident maybe?

Lord, don't let anybody hit Brian's car out in that lot.

I hated to admit it, but I was actually growing attached to the Saab. The smell as I approached the information desk made my belly howl. I tried to remember when I'd eaten last, but couldn't. I'd have to hit the cafeteria on the way back upstairs. I put both hands on the counter. "I'm Ron Jenkins. You paged me?"

A slim blond with dark roots pointed behind her to Zeely, sitting in the waiting area. She had a foil-covered plate in her hand.

The Lord knows what you have need of before you ask.

I ran and hugged her, squeezing the plate between us. "How'd you know I was here?" The foil pulled back from the edge. The aroma of hot meat and seasoned vegetables danced in the air.

"Church in the morning. Hospital in the afternoon. Not too hard to figure out." She loosed my grip on the plate. "Watch out. You're going to drop it."

"I hope not. I'd hate to have to eat off the floor in front of all these people." I motioned to the small crowd gathered at the desk behind us.

Zeely met the women's sweeping looks with a sigh. "You'd better let go of me before they call security. They're really checking us out. Probably thought I was the maid or something."

I frowned and released her shoulders. If that was meant to be a joke, it wasn't funny. Why did she always have to care so much about what other people thought?

She wants to please people. You do too.

I took the plate from her, recalling the image so often in my dreams—Jerry's hand with Zeely's. A ring on her finger. A smile on their faces. That image had restrained me for so long . . . I balanced the plate and took her hand, brown against my pale one, locking my fingers with hers. A new picture flashed in my mind. A new possibility.

"What are you thinking about?"

I ignored the question and took my hand off hers, lifted the foil. All good stuff was there: greens, oxtails, rice, black-eyed peas, plus a hunk of red velvet cake wrapped in plastic. My stomach jumped, already pleading for a bite. "I'm thinking about you and this wonderful food. Jerry is one lucky man."

Zeely's face clouded. "I never cook for Jerry. I've got to get going. We have evening service and you know how Daddy gets about starting service on time. I have a solo."

I nodded, remembering her in the choirstand, belting out God's praises as though her body were an amplifier. People at that church still laughed at how I'd given her a standing ovation, but I'd meant every clap. I'd never heard anyone sing like that before. Or since. "What are you singing?"

"'His Eye Is On the Sparrow.' I should sing it now, the way those ladies have their eyes on me." Zeely waved to the group of women still clustered nearby, rapt in a discussion about the nature of our relationship. They kept staring, but moved away, disarmed by Zeely's smile.

I leaned over and tipped her chin, lifting her face toward mine. "Don't worry about them. Keep your eyes on me." We stood there a silent moment, only a breath separating our faces, our lips . . .

I pulled back, reaching under the edge of the foil, into the plastic. I licked the icing from my finger. "This is so good, I think I'm going to cry."

She smirked. "You? Cry? I won't hold my breath."

"Good food can make even the strongest of men a little emotional." I squeezed her hand. "Especially when the cook looks as delicious as the meal." In a silver sweater dress, matching coat, and burgundy-lined lips filled with silver gloss, Zeely looked even tastier than the food.

Behind us, someone cleared her throat.

"My daughter married one of them. They've got two kids. He's nice enough. We weren't expecting it." One of the ladies at the desk spoke loud enough for us to hear. I turned. They all spun around, rustling papers. I knew that if I turned back they'd be staring again.

"If they want a show, we might as well give them one," I whispered in Zeely's ear, then leaned over, this time going straight for her lips. I stopped short, letting my mouth brush her cheek instead. Trying not to eat the food was hard enough, if I tasted those lips, I might not be able to stop.

Instead of the frown I expected, Zeely smiled, although her eyes were wide.

I shrugged. "I could have made them run with a real kiss, but you would have slapped me."

"Maybe. Maybe not." She crooked her finger, beckoning me to come closer. I came as close as I dared and tried not to moan when fifteen years of frustration melted in my mouth. I tossed the plate on the chair beside us and pulled her tight to my chest.

Her lipstick still perfect in a feat I couldn't figure out, Zeely stepped back like she wasn't making me totally crazy. Breathless, I watched her, wondering how she'd dissolved so much time, so many prayers, all with one kiss. I tried to get another while she was giving them away.

Zeely swatted my hand. "Stop. We're in public."

I laughed. "Now you want to have etiquette? You can't kiss me like that and just walk away."

"Watch me." She reached into her pocket and tossed me a five-dollar bill. She started for the door. "Here. Get yourself a soda to cool off. I know you. Don't have a hard dime on you. Nothing but plastic."

53

Zeely

I didn't wipe my lips. Not on the way out of the hospital, not on the drive back to the church, and not now on the way downstairs to change into my choir robe. The wetness would stay on my face until I could think a minute, clear my mind. It certainly wasn't clear now. I tiptoed into the choir room, placing my hands through the neck of my robe to keep from squishing my hair.

It wasn't just my hair I was trying to protect. I didn't want to brush my lips, my face, anywhere Ron's lips had been. I slumped into a chair grateful that the room was empty. Upstairs I could hear laughter that meant I wouldn't be alone for long. Across from me, a full-length mirror reflected my face. Despite my inner turmoil, on the outside everything was in place.

Gotta love permanent lipstick.

There was still that wetness on my cheek, unseen to the on-looker, but I could feel it. I touched it with the pads of my fingers, transporting it to my lips where it belonged.

Where Ron belonged.

I hugged my own shoulders, thinking of how Grace would tease if she'd seen today's action. I had two rules concerning men: never chase them and always keep them an arm's length away. Lately, I'd been breaking both of them and I wasn't upset about it.

"Girl, you're losing your mind."

My reflection mimicked my words. I kept talking anyway. This therapy was free.

321

"Times are getting so hard that you get excited when a friend kisses you. And a white friend at that."

I winced at my own words. There it was again. Color. Hadn't that been what separated Ron and me in the first place? That seemed like forever ago.

"The Bible says know no man by the flesh, Zee. Why can't we just be together instead of checking off boxes? This isn't a census, it's a relationship," Ron had said then. I'd agreed, hopeful that things would work out between us once. I was still trying to figure how it could be that it was Ron I'd always wanted anyway, but my mama's voice was still in my head, saying Jerry was the one God wanted.

In the end, I couldn't get over "the color thing." And evidently Ron couldn't either. After a surprise visit and meeting his new friends, I'd overheard his friend telling him that having a black girlfriend was a liability, that he could have me, but he couldn't marry me.

Ron didn't disagree. He didn't say anything at all.

Neither did I. The boy was right. It wouldn't work.

"And it didn't work. Not after that. No matter what Ron did, I knew how he really felt. We never discussed that day when I'd overheard him and his friend or all it had cost us. Sometimes I wondered what might have happened if I'd gotten there an hour later or a half hour earlier. Those are times when I don't sleep well because my dreams are full of red-headed babies with brown eyes.

You know what he felt then. What about now?

Now. That's what scared me. I tugged at my choir robe, wiping my tears. Could Ron's friendship with Jerry be what held him back so long? I sang my scales, warming my throat and filling my lungs with air. I didn't want to consider the possibility that I'd spent all these years waiting for the wrong man and running from the right one. What I knew for sure was bad enough. There was only one other thing that could have held Ron back all these years. Something best forgotten. But there was no way he could know about that. No way.

If I was honest, there was no way at all now. The past, the racial thing, there had already been so much between me and Ron. I put my hand on my stomach. Now I had another secret, one that he'd never go along with.

Lord, perhaps I'm yours alone.

Conversation flooded the room as the choir members piled in, smelling of buffet dinners and weave glue. Our newest member whose name I could never pronounce, with her heaving bosom and laughing eyes, pushed toward me, almost pinning me to the wall.

"I was wondering where you was. I hope you ready to sang, girl. Shekinah brought their male chorus. We're all going to get a husband tonight!" Laughter filled the small space, choking my air.

I tried to think of a response, but despair erupted from my stomach, rose to my throat. I ran to the choir closet, shut the door, and threw up on my shoes.

54

Jerry

I sat on the edge of my bed disgusted, pants wrinkled and baby vomit on my tie. I pulled a T-shirt and jeans out of the closet. It was four thirty. Too late to make Zeely's solo and too early to catch Ron. Carmel had done so well about Sundays until lately. Even if she showed now, I couldn't get there in time. Where was she anyway? The phone rang. I made a face, but picked it up anyway, not bothering to say hello.

Carmel cut right to the point. "I can't make it."

I untied my shoes and kicked them across the room. "You're doing this on purpose, aren't you?"

"Keeping you from your little church date? No. I'm working. You know, working, to help you pay the bills?"

I sighed. Church date. Was that jealousy in Carmel's voice? It was too late for that. About as late as I was for the service. I'd tried to make things work with her, but it seemed that Zeely would always be between us. She'd said so herself. Now she was mad because I was actually moving in that direction? Did I act like this when she asked me to babysit so she could date Dr. What's-his-name? I couldn't understand women to save my life. "Why do you have to be like this?"

"I was trying to be polite and call. Next time I won't."

I hung up the phone, knowing there would be no more words. Our recent conversations ended as abruptly as our marriage had—leaving me feeling the same way as I did when they served me with the papers out of the blue—confused. I'd prayed all these months for God to reconcile us, to put our family back together, but now I realized, accepted . . . it was too late.

Justice flipped over onto the bed beside me. I sniffed the air and reached for the diaper bag. After a quick change and a battle with the pacifier, she dropped back to sleep. If only she'd sleep like that at night. Against my better judgment, I leaned down and kissed the baby's head. I'd worried about waking her up, but it was me who fell asleep, in my clothes and everything. And when I woke up, there was Justice, just as cute as ever.

She was growing fast. Soon she'd be like Monique, no longer needing Daddy's kisses, trying to find her own way in the world. Monique hadn't come over this weekend. The situation with Sean was a sore spot between us, and Carmel was taking her side for some reason. I hated to lose Monique but I couldn't stand by and watch what I saw coming. Not this time. The last time I'd believed her report cards instead of going with my instincts.

Lifting myself one leg at a time, I got up from the bed and loosened my tie. I picked up the phone again, slowly punching numbers. "Hey, Zee. How're you doing?"

She cleared her throat. "I'm fine. A little stomachache is all. Daddy missed you today. I told him you probably had to work . . . or something."

"Thanks. Justice is sick again. Bronchitis. And Carmel had to work."

"I hope she feels better. I'll tell Dad. Or you can tell him yourself. We're still having dinner downstairs if you want to come."

I looked down at Justice. Her chest heaved, stopped, and then fell again. "I don't think I'll make it today—"

A sigh. Was she relieved I wasn't coming? Or disappointed? "No problem. I'll let him know. See you at work tomorrow."

"Okay. Did they tape you? I'm sure you blew the house down."

"Not quite. They didn't tape it and I'm glad. Let's try again next week."

"Great. I'll be there."

I stared at the phone. Why did it always have to be this way between me and Zeely—a chain of paper-thin promises that I was sure to break? I looked at the chubby baby as she took ragged breaths, still exhausted from a night of screaming. I didn't want to disappoint Zeely again. I hadn't told her a lot of things because I thought she deserved better, but maybe it was time to come clean and let her into my life. Maybe she *could* handle Monique, Justice, Carmel, and all my drama.

I edged the baby over on the mattress and reached for my top dresser drawer, digging for a musty velvet box. I closed my eyes and cracked the lid. A teardrop diamond, still as radiant as the day my mama got it off layaway, sparkled between my fingers. She'd bought it for Zeely, and when things took a different turn, I'd been unable, unwilling, to give it to Carmel. I'd kept it in a safety deposit box until a week ago. I'd always meant to give it to its rightful owner, just to fulfill my mother's wishes. I'd always meant to . . . someday.

Years of pain welled in my chest. Someday might never come. I was broken, and she deserved more, but I couldn't live two lives anymore—a single man and a loving father. Justice needed a family, something Carmel had decided we couldn't be. Something Monique and Sean would never be either, regardless of how bad they wanted it. I put the ring in my pocket and walked to the closet, choosing an even better suit this time.

Today was the day. I'd say the words Zeely had longed to hear and tell her the truth about my crazy life. The bills, the baby, all of it. I hoped Zeely could understand and become what she should have been all along. My wife.

55

Zeely

I lay on the couch in front of my television, munching saltines and drinking ginger ale. I'd sung like a bird, but now I was tired and more than a little sick. I flipped to the Christian TV station. A familiar evangelist was hosting a telethon, screaming for money. I turned off the TV and rolled over, my face against the cushions.

Grace had left two messages and her car was in her driveway, but I didn't feel like talking. Not yet. If I talked, I'd also have to listen, and I wasn't sure I was ready to hear what Grace had to say. Especially since the usual pattern of girlfriend confessions was that the listener follow with an admission of her own. No matter how bad Grace thought her secret was, I knew mine was worse.

And not only in the past, either. I'd wrecked things in the present too. Growing inside me was the baby I'd always wanted, but now I had no idea what to do. How would I explain to my father that I'd gone to a clinic and saved some stranger's egg? And yet, in all my fear and crying out to God, there was happiness. Maybe my dreams could still come true.

The phone rang again. I closed my eyes.

That girl isn't going to give up.

"Hi, this is Zee. I'm out and about, but leave me a message and I'll hit you back. Have a blessed day." My voice sounded sickening. Fake. I waited, knowing Grace would have plenty to say, talking until the beep cut her off like she always did.

"Zee, you there? It's Ron."

I flipped over the arm of the couch and grabbed the phone with one hand, clutched my stomach with the other. "Hello?"

"Hey. I'm glad you picked up. Can I come over?"

My eyes roamed the room for excuses, finding none. The place was clean as usual. He knew I didn't get sick much; if I told him that, he might freak out and take me to the hospital. "I'm not feeling too good. A virus I think."

"Did you throw up? I hate to be gross, but you don't want to get dehydrated. Tell you what, I'll bring some Gatorade—"

The doorbell rang.

"Can you hold on? Somebody's at the door. Probably Grace. I should have called her back earlier."

"Let her in. Call me back as soon you feel up to it. I need to talk to you. Tonight if I can. It's important."

"Okay." I put the phone on its base and walked to the door, my stomach and head throbbing. I tried not to imagine what Ron wanted to talk about.

Don't get your hopes up. Just wait and see.

"Who is it?"

"Jeremiah." The answer glued my fingers to the knob.

I pulled the door open while yanking my sweatshirt down as far as it could go. The image on the other side took my breath. Jeremiah rested against the frosty bricks in a leather trench coat and high-collared suit, with pearl buttons down the center. A matching pair of oxfords completed the look. Justice slept on his shoulder.

"Come in! Get that baby out of the cold."

He smiled and walked inside. I reached for Justice and made a bed for her on the couch. She didn't make a sound.

Jerry unbuttoned his coat. "I'm sorry I didn't call, but I might have lost my nerve."

Nerve for what? "You did surprise me. I was about to call the hospital and check on Joyce."

"I spoke to the nurse about an hour ago. She's down for the night."

I nodded and walked toward the kitchen. I wanted to run. "You hungry?"

He grabbed my hand. "Stay here."

"Okay." I folded my arms, hoping he couldn't hear my heart beating.

Jerry dropped to one knee. I grabbed my throat, then bent down too. He shook his head and motioned for me to stand. "I planned this all out much better, but here goes. We were always meant to be together, and if you'll have me, if you can put up with my family and all my drama, I want you to be my wife." He took a velvet box from his pocket.

I gasped as I noted the name on the box. Foxman's. Out of business since . . . I breathed in and out again, disarmed as he slid the ring on my finger. My mother had been right. He'd bought it. The perfect ring. I couldn't help lifting my finger into the light. Already feeling lightheaded, I crumpled to the ground beside him, in a pool of tears. "You did buy it. You did."

He held me. "Of course I did."

I threw my arms around his neck, drenching his collar.

"Is that a yes?"

I stiffened. A yes just like that? This Cinderella thing was harder than it looked. Ron's kiss at the hospital forced itself in front of the diamond. What about him? What about the "important" thing he wanted to talk about? I touched my stomach and the secret it held. I'd gone too far and I knew it. Ron would never accept it, never marry me to cover it. Jerry had his own scars, his own skeletons. Maybe we could cover . . . each other. I wasn't sure, but I didn't have time to think too hard. The clinic experiment had been successful and I'd become a mother without the love of a man. My child, however, deserved a father's love too.

Jerry noted my hesitation. "Do you need some time? I should

have planned this better. I'm not offering love necessarily. We can grow into that. To be honest, I need a mother for my children and someone to share my life. I just thought maybe if I did what I was supposed to do in the first place, God might—"

My hand went to my stomach, now turning inside out. "Yes. That's my answer."

He waved his fist in the air. "Thank you, Jesus!"

I bit my lip, as nausea eased into the back of my throat. "One thing though, have you talked to Daddy? You know how he is about stuff like this."

Jerry shrugged. "I didn't. I figured since he's the one who started the whole thing, it wouldn't be a problem."

"Just go over and talk to him tomorrow. I don't want to wait too long to tell him, but I want you to see him first."

"All right."

I looked at the ring again and then covered my mouth. I started to bend over again even though I tried not to. I staggered to my feet and started toward the bathroom.

Jerry followed. "Are you okay?"

I shook my head.

"Sick?"

I nodded.

The baby cried. Jerry picked her up. "Sorry you don't feel good. We'll celebrate later. I'll let myself out."

As the door slammed, I stuck my head in the toilet, wondering what Cinderella did when Prince Charming showed up at the best—and the worst—possible time.

56

Brian

I once thought it could never get too cold for basketball. Some of my best games had been played on slushy courts cleared with a squeegee from someone's garage. Last year, I'd played on Thanksgiving, Christmas, and New Year's, but today, after going to church . . . after listening to those songs, those words, I felt stiff. Frozen. I might hang up my shoes until spring. I must be getting old. If the score was any indication, I was ancient. Quinn was skunking me. Six nothing.

"So what'd you think of church?" My youthful opponent fired off the basketball.

I snagged the rebound, then lied. "Not much."

"I felt like that too. I never set foot in a church until last year. It still reminds me of the NBA."

"How so?" I fired off a jump shot. It clanged off the rim and back into my hands.

"The guys on the bench get paid without playing. Some of them have more potential than the starters, but they're too comfortable. They don't want to do the hundred foul shots, pack on the muscle, lose the weight . . ." Quinn jumped up and down behind me, his hands in the air.

I hooked another shot. One point.

"Check." I stepped forward with a bounce pass.

The boy dribbled slowly, still explaining. "It's too hard, too much

331

trouble. So bench guys show up year after year, happy to maintain their mediocrity."

I adjusted my glasses and held my hands high. Not that it helped. Another point for Quinn. This kid never ceased to amaze me. "What about the little players who've made it big? They're not passive."

Quinn held the ball. "Exactly. Those little guys didn't stay on the bench, though. They recognize their limitations, but refuse to accept them. They work hard every practice and obey the coaches' advice."

Quinn took a dribble and wiped his forehead. I motioned for the pass. He held the ball at his side. "The hungry players are ready every game—looking for an injury, illness—anything to get on the court. The people in church like that, they grow fast. Strong. People who've been saved twenty years just sit there and watch. Pretty soon the new cats are running things." He passed me the ball.

I tossed off a quick shot. Quinn rejected it.

Send me to the old folks' home, why don't you?

Quinn's little illustration was nice, but I wasn't even in the building, let alone the game. I ran behind the young philosopher and stopped his layup with a blocked shot of my own. Two dribbles and another quick shot. Around the rim. Circle. Circle. No good. I'd have to be more patient the next time. Let the game come to me. "Where do you fit on the team?"

"Me? I'm still on the bench. No special abilities, not much depth. Just trying to stay humble and hungry." Quinn faked left, then right, leaving me hanging in the air. He shifted again and drove to the basket.

I crashed down on my heels and doubled over, bunching my shorts at the knees. "I've got to admit, you've made some remarkable progress. Even since last year. I saw your PSAT scores. You'll make National Merit for sure. Did you use those tricks I taught you?"

Quinn held the ball again, smiling. "It's the Lord, Doc, plain and simple. Why can't you face that?"

I rolled my eyes. "This is the most talkative basketball game I've ever had." It was the most thought-provoking game I'd ever had too, but I didn't want to swell the boy's head.

"It's hard to be on the listening side, huh?" Quinn dribbled between his legs. He stepped to the next spot on the key and fired off a shot. Swish.

You know about them, but you don't know them. Joyce's words played over in my head. It hurt when she was right.

"I know more about the Lord than you think. Some things just aren't so simple." A stupid line of logic, but it was all I had.

Quinn bounced the ball into my hands. I caught it and re-shot in one motion. It swished through the net. Sweet. I passed the ball away.

Quinn squared his shoulders toward the basket and released, his fingertips extended. "There's one more group besides the starters and the bench riders. The naturals."

I watched the ball hit the center of the square and fall through the hoop. The naturals. I knew the type. There was one at every playground in Testimony. I nodded as he went for the ball. "I'm hip to that. Those brothers are deceiving. They look all crusty, with two knee braces. Oh, and a Jheri curl. They always have a Jheri curl."

Quinn laughed into his fist. "I know right! With a headband and some long socks, up to the knees. And a matching outfit, but off brand."

I doubled over and dropped the ball, laughing until there were tears in my eyes. "Yeah. Wilson down, except for the shoes, some Pumas in mint condition."

Quinn and I locked fingers, and slid our fingertips across one another in agreement. "You a fool, Doc. But for real. Those cats could beat anybody in the league, but they broke the rules somewhere. Then they walked away, thinking there wasn't any forgiveness. Now they take out their frustrations on suckers like us."

I pulled the damp shirt from my chest. I turned my back on Quinn's probing eyes. His probing words. "Sucker? Speak for yourself." I closed my eyes and squeezed off what felt like a perfect shot.

When I opened my eyes, I was up by a point and Quinn wasn't laughing.

"You're right, Doc. You're a natural for sure."

The last game fanned a flame in my hamstring that refused to be extinguished. I threw Quinn one last pass and headed for the car.

"Can't hang, old man?"

On another day, those words would have been enough to make me play through any amount of pain. But, today a fire burned in my heart as well. "I'm going to change my shoes and get something to drink. I'll be back in a minute to take you home."

Quinn shook his head. "That's all right. Just pick me up for church on Wednesday. Six thirty."

That was smooth. Who were we fooling? *He* was the natural.

Giving the ball one last bounce, I shook Quinn's hand. "I'll think about it. Church, I mean. I'm not promising anything."

Quinn smiled like he'd won an NBA championship—all by himself. "I'm not asking you for promises. Just be there."

I shuffled to the car, my mind and body both in pain. I couldn't help wondering where Grace was now and whether she was with Mal. Zeely had politely evaded all my fishing expeditions for information during class breaks. Either she didn't know or she and Grace were just that tight. It must be nice. The closest thing I had to a friend was the fifty bounced emails to Ron's account and the preacher boy on the court behind me. A boy who would soon be a man. Although I cared about all my students, I'd hate to see Quinn go.

I turned back to watch him shoot around, only to find an empty court.

57

Grace

*The chores here keep me busy. I'm making a bowl
and a vase for Aunt Ina in ceramics class. I mixed
the colors to paint the angels brown. At first, teacher
said to paint them pink, but she let it go. She seemed
surprised that anybody would want to paint a face
brown on purpose. They must not get many black girls
through here. Maybe she'll let the next girl paint her
angels brown if she wants too. There are brown angels
in heaven too. At least I hope so. My baby will need
one.*

Diana Dixon

The horizon faded as I pulled into the lot of Mount Olive Baptist,
a place where I'd once felt safe and close to God. Tonight I needed
both. As the sun tipped low, I realized the foolishness of my trip.
Surely the Reverend wouldn't be here this late. I tugged at the church
door, prepared for it to stick fast. It opened instead. I called out
toward the cross shining at the front. "Reverend Wil-kins?"

"I'm in the basement. Come on."

Amazed at both the lack of security and his presence at such a late
hour, I headed downstairs. What I saw there amazed me even more.
The minister's hands moved like lightning as he buffed communion
plates and stacked them carefully, like supermarket eggs.

"Let's see now," he said, straightening his glasses. "Diana Dixon. I've missed you a few Sundays. How you?" He grabbed a box of matzo crackers from the shelf.

How am I going to talk my way out of this one? "I've been visiting around. I'm trying Tender Mercies right now." I should have thought this through more.

"David, over at the shopping center? Fine brother. Tell him I said hello. I don't care where you go, as long as you going somewhere. The Lord only keeps one membership—the Lamb's Book of Life. Have a seat."

I looked down the hall at the choir room, stuffed tight with memories from the Buds of Promise Choir. Some of us had bloomed early and some never at all.

He laid another plate on the stack. "I was sorry to hear about your husband. He seemed to be a right fine African gentleman, if I recall."

"Yes. He was."

Reverend Wilkins reached into a basket on the table, piled high with apples, red, green, and yellow. "Have one?"

I shook my head. "No thanks. I'm not hungry."

He chose one from the middle of the pile. "Well, excuse me then. Zeely brought my dinner but I left it to the house. Too late. I don't like to go to bed on a full stomach." He spread another piece of the service out on the table. From the look of the even columns, there was probably just enough for each deacon, enough for each row.

I ran my hand across the cloth under the utensils. "Don't your deacons do all this?"

The preacher wiped his forehead. "Yes and no. They clean the dishes. I get them out to shine them and pray over them."

"Really?"

His pearly teeth parted his lips in a smile. "Of course. I pray over the pews too. I know you all do the same thing in your classrooms."

Not lately. "Sometimes."

"I thought so. Speaking of praying, I'm on my way up to the sanctuary. Care to join me? I don't figure you came over here just to chat."

"Is it okay if I stay down here?"

The Reverend slapped his palms together. "Yes sir. This here is a praying room. I've prayed through many a thing in here."

Maybe that's it. I'd been praying around my problems instead of through them. "Prayed through?"

He grabbed a broom and whisked a cobweb from the ceiling. "Yes. Through. Sometimes the Lord delivers folks out of things but most times he takes me through. I can't get over it. I can't go around it."

That summed things up well. "So you just pray?"

Zeely's father looked at me as if I'd taken God's name in vain. "Just pray? You make it sound like something to do when you can't think of anything else. That's why you young folks struggle so. Make it easy on yourself. Pray first."

With that sage advice and one last sweep of the collection plates, Reverend Wilkins left me alone. He even turned off the light and shut the door. I started to stop him, but I didn't, feeling my way around the room instead. The satin of the choir robes slipped between my fingers. There was a stack of extra robes piled across the bottom of one side of the closet. I sank down into it, ignoring the smell of pine cleaner, and closed my eyes.

I stayed there like that so long that I almost fell asleep. It was peace, plain and simple. I'd hidden here before, on my last trip to Mount Olive before we moved away. In this little room, I'd told my whole story to no one in particular, begging God without saying much.

Tonight felt the same way.

Something rumbled overhead. There was shouting too. I left the closet and climbed the stairs, inched into the sanctuary . . . There weren't any intruders, except maybe God, from the looks of things. Reverend Wilkins danced and hopped as though he were riding a pogo stick.

"Thank ya, Jesus. Hallelujah!" He circled the pulpit. "Yes sir! Yes sir! Thank ya! You're a good God, yes you are!"

I nodded. My meeting with Christ hadn't been as eventful as the Reverend's, but I'd reached the same conclusion. God's goodness surpassed my problems. My pain. Neither death, nor life or any created thing could overcome God's love for me. Not even my love for Brian.

"A-ma-zing grace how sweet the sound." The pastor circled the room, hands outstretched, not seeming to notice that I was even there. I knelt at the altar, like I'd seen my father do here so many times when I was growing up.

Reverend Wilkins touched my shoulder. "God is here, honey, if you'll enter in. It's your turn," he said, wiping his forehead.

"What?"

"I know you heard that. I heard it before you came, but I didn't know it was you. It's usually for me."

I looked around the church. Silence echoed. "I don't hear a thing."

The man of God rose to his perch and opened a Bible on the glass stand. He flipped the pages. "'Do not be afraid; you will not suffer shame. Do not fear disgrace; you will not be humiliated. You will forget the shame of your youth and remember no more the reproach of your widowhood.'"

I gripped my knees and rocked back on my heels.

"'Though the mountains be shaken and the hills be removed, yet my unfailing love for you will not be shaken nor my covenant of peace be removed,' says the Lord, who has compassion on you."

My feet moved out from beneath me towards the silent noise. The music Reverend Wilkins had heard. In the depth of my heart, I heard a beating of drums. My arms reached for heaven. I leapt between the pews, smiling back at the old man still reading in the pulpit. He heard something after all. The sound of forgiveness.

The rhythms of grace.

58

Zeely

I brushed my teeth and sat on the edge of the tub, my stomach trembling. When it finally stopped, I laughed out loud. My stomach must have been as tired as I was. I got up, starving but too afraid to eat. I walked to the bedroom and checked my clothes for the week. Five hangers, each with a quart-sized Ziploc bag attached full of earrings, hose, and other accessories. The matching shoes hung onto each hanger. It was a good thing I'd done it yesterday before I started feeling like this.

My workout clothes hung in a similar lineup at the other end of the closet, but I avoided looking at them. The thought of flying through the air didn't sound too appealing right now. I walked away from the closet, forcing back worries about the coming week, trying not to think about what I'd done, the decision I'd made so quickly after waiting so long.

Just deal with now. Today.

True enough. Today had evils of its own. I didn't need to borrow any more. Was that the bell? That Grace. She just wouldn't give up. I had to smile at that. It was good to know that somebody was looking out for you.

When my time comes, my trouble, I hope I'll be as steadfast.

I thought about opening the door without asking who was behind it, but after the last visitor, I decided against it.

"Grace, is that you?"

I pulled back the curtain. A silver sedan kissed my car in the drive.

"It's Ron."

I grabbed my stomach again. It didn't hurt anymore but I knew it would soon. My hand pulled back the knob, ushering in Ron and a furious wind. He stomped his shoes on the mat. I waited for him to speak.

"Feeling better?" He put two bottles of Gatorade and a box of crackers on the table. His hands slid from his gloves and onto my shoulders. "I was worried about you."

I folded my hands around myself, rubbing my sides. "I'm okay right now. I think it will blow over. I'm praying so anyway." I raised one hand. "In Jesus' name."

The sparkle of the diamond, forgotten on my finger, stripped the smile from Ron's face. He dropped his arms and jammed his fingers back into their suede gloves. "Christmas come early?"

"You could say that." I closed my eyes. It wasn't supposed to go like this.

Ron snorted and threw another jewelry box, one encased in salmon satin, onto the counter. "I had a little something myself, but I guess I'm too late. How much did he beat me by, huh? An hour?"

I swallowed hard, staring at the ring box, now stuck in my poinsettia.

Why didn't I wait?

My stomach turned, reminding me why. It was too late to play Romeo and Juliet. Somebody always died at the end. I had a chance to be a mother and that was worth giving up everything, even my love for Ron. Or at least that's what I was telling myself.

"Don't be mad, I didn't know. I didn't know he was coming—"

One of Ron's curls fell over one eye like a bloody finger. He snatched it back. "You knew I was coming! You knew how you kissed me at the hospital. You knew that I love you, that I've always loved you, even when you only wanted me because you couldn't have him."

340

I grabbed his arm. "It wasn't like that. It was always you. Always. From the first time you came to church all wide-eyed and goofy . . ." I sobbed. "Clapping offbeat and singing at the top of your lungs. Even before that, with that little boy on the bicycle. From the minute I saw you . . ."

He grabbed my wrist, holding my finger in the air. "Then why this?"

I snatched my hand away. He wasn't about to turn this around on me. I'd done the waiting, the hurting, not him. Never him. My stomach flip-flopped. I leaned on the ledge, to steady myself. "Why this, Ron? Well, let's see . . . you're engaged to another woman. Now you kiss my cheek and show up with a ring. It all makes perfect sense."

He wiped his chin and turned for the door. "I hope he makes you happy, makes your father happy. I never wanted to mess up what God had for you. I just wanted to love you. That's all."

"What about Mindy?"

"It's over."

"That's what Jerry said about Carmel. The next thing I know I get a wedding invitation. I'm too old to play games. My clock is ticking." I covered my mouth, wishing I'd kept the last sentence inside my head.

Ron spun around. "That's classic. Is that what this is all about? A baby? You're marrying Jerry to get a baby?"

"Not exactly, but it does factor in."

"So what am I, sterile?"

"No, but you're not stable either. You're still living off your savings after what . . . four weeks out of work?"

He sucked his teeth. "I'm back at legal aid and taking some private clients—"

Now he tells me. "You let Mindy almost swindle you into a marriage you didn't want, you're driving Brian's car, which I know you hate. And the thing you're best at—preaching—you're afraid to try."

Ron sat on the couch, his arms locked across his chest. "Just clean my clock, why don't you? It isn't as bad as all that. You're not as perfect as you make yourself out to be. Neither is Jerry. I wouldn't hold him up as some model of fatherhood. He couldn't even get Monique through high school without her getting knocked up."

I joined him on the couch, wishing I could stretch out and rub my belly like I wanted to. "What do you mean? Monique isn't pregnant."

"I hope not. Justice isn't even a year old."

"Justice? Her sister? What's that got to do with it?"

He frowned. "Justice is Monique's daughter, Zee."

"He never said a word. No wonder . . ." I rubbed my forehead. "Who's the dad?"

Ron shrugged, pushing up to his feet. "Well, I'm not sure, but—I don't know. Look, I shouldn't have said anything. No matter how mad I am at you and Jerry, it's no excuse for gossiping. My point is, if you're just marrying him to feed some baby fix, you're making a mistake." He picked up the box, my box, and put it in his pocket. "Take it from me." He turned the knob.

I grabbed his pants leg. "Take it from you? What's that supposed to mean?"

He tugged his jeans from my grasp and opened the door. The night air rushed in. Ron looked down at me with tears in his eyes. "What I mean is that I almost married Mindy for the same reason you're wearing that ring—because even though she didn't want me, she wanted my babies. Or at least she said she did." He wiped his eyes. "More than I can say for you."

The door slammed, leaving me with goose-bump-covered arms and quivering lips. I rolled over on the floor, dying a million deaths. He knew. I didn't know how, but somehow Ron knew about the baby conceived from the only real love either of us had ever known.

He knew I'd killed his child.

59

Jerry

For the first time in my life, I hesitated a little when I entered the sanctuary of Mount Olive. I'd planned on waiting until tomorrow to talk to Reverend Wilkins, but seeing the pastor's study lit and Reverend's car in the lot—I'd decided to stop. I crossed behind the organ and empty choirstand, to the minister's closed door.

"Reverend Wilkins, are you in there?"

A gravelly voice invited me to come in. Zeely's father sat in a high-backed leather chair, mopping his forehead with a washcloth. On his desk rested a shiny apple, stuck through with a paring knife on a plate in front of him.

"Omega Terrigan. A pleasure. You're my second visitor tonight. What can I do for you, young man?"

"I need to talk to you about something. Something about Zeely and me. We, I mean, I . . ."

"Sounds like you'd better have a seat." Reverend Wilkins handed me the Bible in his hand. "My eyes are tired. Read to me, will you? Give me John, the fifteenth chapter. When it comes to you, exactly why you're here, stop reading and spit it out, hear?"

I obeyed, reading three chapters before gathering both my courage and my thoughts. The pastor's amens to my reading subsided, I went for it.

"As you know, Reverend, a long time ago I was supposed to marry your daughter." I paused to check the old man's expression. Blank.

I continued anyway, words piling on top of each other. "But I didn't marry her. I was scared. Scared of you, and scared of God. Now, I think I'm ready and I've come to ask your blessing. Your permission." I let out a half whistle and sank back into my chair, waiting for the man's reply.

The pastor crossed his legs, laced his fingers around one knee.

"I can't give you my blessing on that, son. It's already been given to someone else. I can only say this—all things are permissible, but all things are not profitable."

"Someone else? What's that supposed to mean? Should I marry her or not? You're the one who started all this."

Reverend Wilkins yanked the knife out of his apple. He severed the skin, careful not to waste too much fruit. A ruby spiral snaked against the mahogany wood. A few more whittling rounds left the apple bare. Exposed. Two deft cuts left it cored and seeded. The pastor sliced it neatly and speared a piece with the knife, pointing it in my direction.

I shook my head and gripped the knobs at the armrests of my chair. If this were anyone else, I'd have lost it by now. Big-time.

The pastor shrugged and popped the fruit in his mouth. "So that's it, eh? I started this?"

I sprang to my feet, the top of my head just missing a collision with the motionless ceiling fan. "Yes. You started this." I enunciated every syllable.

"Tell me, son. What did I say? How'd I get all this going?"

I leaned over the desk, slapping one fist into the other palm. "Hello? That beloved deal? I've heard the story my whole life."

Reverend Wilkins pierced another slice of apple. "And who did you hear that from, son? Was it from me?"

I dropped back into my chair. "No. Not exactly. My mother—"

Zeely's father nodded, mumbling to himself. "Umm-hmmm. Did *I* ever tell you Zeely was your beloved?"

I looked at him as if he'd pulled out a gun. This man couldn't be serious. "Then why isn't she married? Surely you picked somebody. She's your only daughter."

Reverend Wilkins pointed the last piece of apple to a picture behind him of two boys, arm in arm, one white and the other one pecan tan.

"You're right, son, I picked somebody. Why he didn't marry her, you'll have to ask him."

60

Brian

Quinn thought I couldn't turn him down. And I couldn't, not for a ride.

"Sure. I'll pick you up and take you to church."

I didn't add that dropping Quinn off was all I'd be doing. That much was understood. The things I needed to talk to God about were best said one-on-one.

I expected for Quinn to show some disappointment when he got out of the car alone, but as usual, the boy showed maturity beyond his years. He trotted away unshaken. The way I used to be. This time, I wanted it to be different. Real. Permanent. Not some fake once-a-week ritual. What was the point in that?

I didn't advertise it or anything, but I'd been reading the Bible for weeks now. The Gospels. Ephesians. Proverbs. Psalms. Even Revelation. As he did each week, Quinn would drop off a CD of the latest sermon on my desk, probably thinking that I wouldn't listen to it.

I did.

I listened to them all. The current series topic—forgiveness—gave me even more reason to stay in my car. Coming back to Jesus, admitting who God really was, I'd thought that would be hardest. It wasn't. Loving God came easy. Loving people, forgiving them . . . that was hard.

With God, nothing is impossible.

Instead of leaving the lot, I pulled into a parking space, considering the results of my Bible reading the night before. I rubbed my legs, thinking of Quinn and our conversation on the basketball court. The naturals. I didn't want to be one anymore. I wanted to get in the game. God's game. After reading about the people of Ephesus exchanging their old lives for life in Christ, I couldn't go to bed without piling all *my* idols—altars, statues, crystals someone had given me for a gift, and all those crazy books—into the trash. Now, only one task remained: for my head and my heart to meet together; to ask Jesus to take me back.

Forever this time.

I cut off the car and bowed my head. "Lord, I know I shouldn't have walked away. You never walked away from me. You sent Quinn, Ron, Joyce, Thelma, Zee, Grace . . . All of them. To remind me."

Grace. I gripped the steering wheel. "Thank you especially for sending her. For reminding me what love is. I thought it was about her, but it was you all along. I'll try to give you my love instead.

"I'm messed up and only you can fix me. Please take me back . . ."

This was getting corny. And I wasn't even done.

"I don't know where my mother is, my father . . . Let me be your son again. In Christ's name, Amen."

I lifted my head just as Quinn's face appeared outside the glass. I turned on the car and lowered the window.

"What's up?"

"It's the break. You know, the welcome time. I had a feeling you might still be around. It's freezing. Why not come in?"

Chirping birds didn't appear. No flowers sprouted through the snow. But something changed. I felt . . . peaceful. In spite of everything—Joyce's illness, all the mess with Lottie, Grace, Mal . . . I felt free. For the moment, anyway.

I smiled at my young friend and reached for a sheet of stationery from my planner. "I'm right behind you. I need to write someone a quick note."

61

Ron

"I've got some good news, folks."

I smiled at Pastor David, perched on a stool at the front. The man had that look that meant get ready to repent.

Good.

"All have sinned and fall short of the glory of God. All. Not your brother. Not your drunk mama. Not your lying sister. Not that co-worker that you can't wait for somebody else to witness to. You. You have sinned. You have fallen short."

I stared down at the floor. That's what I loved about Pastor D. He gave up the truth, the whole truth, and nothing but the truth.

"We see the flesh. We write people off because of what our eyes see. We tiptoe around them so their sin won't rub off. Well, guess what? Those same people might be ahead of you in the throne line in heaven!"

"Umph." I shook my head.

A woman two aisles up, her blond hair stiff and wide, turned and stared back at me. Mindy. I nodded and looked away, to the doors, the ceiling . . .

"We see them as a second away from hell. God looks at them as a second away from heaven. Man sees with the eye. God sees with the heart."

The minister stood, the Bible raised in one hand, and walked to the middle of the aisle, to the end of my row. My breath quickened.

"We try to fight heavenly battles using the enemy's tactics. We come to the altar, but we drag our grudges with us, trying to pray around them. Scream over them. It won't work. You have to let it go. Right here. Right now."

A soft instrumental played. "Today is your day. If you're not saved this morning, the only sin you need to worry about is the sin of not accepting Jesus. If you are saved, but you aren't free, aren't forgiving or forgiven, you need to drag whatever you've got—a fence, a door, a wall—I don't care. Just get it down here."

I stood to my feet, remorse welling in my chest. I piled up all the stones in my mind—my mother, Zeely, Mindy, Brian? No. Not Brian. He was in worse shape than I was. I had to cut him some slack . . .

Blue fabric fanned past me, blocking my path as I stepped slowly into the aisle. A man in a flowing African robe almost trampled me on the way to the altar.

"Excuse me," the guy said without looking back.

I froze.

It was Brian. And he'd beat me to the altar.

62

Zeely

I might as well have boarded a cruise ship, the way my stomach rocked and rolled. Three days now. If this morning sickness didn't run its course soon, I'd have to find someone to teach my class next week too. The TV whispered in the next room. *Jeopardy*. I didn't know any answers, but anything sounded better than my questions. Why did Jerry ask me to take off my ring until we could talk privately? What had Daddy said to him?

You don't want to know.

I heard a bell. Was that the TV? No, definitely the doorbell. I rolled off the couch. Didn't people use the phone anymore? Email? Something? At least I could be sure it wasn't Ron. We didn't have anything left to say. Tugging at my clothes and wiping tears from the corners of my eyes, I went to the door and looked out the peephole. I tensed. Jerry. The conversation I'd avoided at work was coming. Seeing him this much was a little disconcerting. I'd have to get used to it. I cracked the door.

"Hey."

Jerry widened the crack, his jacket pulled close and a knit cap pulled low on his head. "Jack Frost is making me rethink this head shaving thing." He headed straight for the couch.

"Can you wipe your feet please? The carpet." Lord, this man-in-the-house thing was going to take some real getting used to.

He smiled. "Sure. I wasn't thinking."

Neither was I.

Maybe Grace was right. Was this what marriage would be like? Nagging after a grown man all the time? Jerry wiped the slush from his shoes and moved back to the couch. From the look on his face I wouldn't have to worry about marriage. He cleared his throat. I clutched mine.

"What's up?"

He patted the seat beside him. "I just need to talk to you, remember?" He took my hand. "Besides, I haven't been alone with you since—"

Alone? Was he going to start coming over every night? Have mercy. "Sorry about that. You know I haven't been well."

"Another reason I came by. You need anything? I didn't get the chance to ask last time. You were a little . . . busy."

My stomach rumbled. I was about to be busy again. "All I need is a nap."

"Okay. I'll make this quick." He untied the belt to his coat.

I took a deep breath, freeing my lungs to scream if necessary. "Yes?"

"I talked to your dad like you asked me to. Sunday night, in fact."

I'd talked to my father several times since then. Why hadn't he mentioned Jerry's visit? "And?"

"And he wasn't pleased."

I pinched one eye shut, trying to focus on my guest with the other. He was talking crazy. "What on earth do you mean by that?" I was up now, circling my sectional like a panther.

He didn't try to calm me down. In fact, I think he was just as mad as I was.

"I had the same reaction. Your dad asked me *when* did *he* tell me I was the one, your beloved. I had no answer. My mother always said it. Did he ever say it to you?"

I walked to the fish tank. "Well . . ." Now I was at the counter. Did he say it? Of course he had. I just couldn't remember. The table held me up now. "I-I don't know. I can only remember Mama saying it now, but—but . . ." I was back at the sink.

Dear God. Could it be true? Had I missed it all along?

Jerry's arms surrounded me. Smothered me. I wiggled forward trying to get my breath before he squeezed me to death. Literally. "So that's it? All this time and he just let me think—"

"Let us think."

I rolled my eyes, glad I was turned around, out of his view. "You didn't think anything. You had a wife. Still do, no matter what the state of Ohio says."

He let me go and turned me around to face him. "Carmel doesn't want me, Zee. She says I'll always be hooked on you, that we should just be together. She's right. I didn't think she was, but she is."

Carmel gave her man over just like that? Why now? I opened a drawer in the coffee table, reached inside, and handed Jerry a jewelry box. "Well, it looks like Carmel got it wrong too. Just like the rest of us. Go pawn this and buy Monique and your grand-daughter a Christmas gift."

"My what? You know about that?"

I shrugged. "Not because you told me. When was that update scheduled? After the wedding?"

He hugged me again, softer this time. "I was going to tell you tonight." He pushed the ring my way. "I don't want it back, no matter what your father says. My mother picked it out just for you. All I came to tell you was that we won't be able to count on your father's support like we thought."

I laid my head on his chest. Or was that his belly?

He's so tall. Great for a child to look up to.

"Since Daddy wants to play crazy, we'll have to find another pastor to counsel us. Marry us too, I guess. He won't marry anybody he doesn't feel right about."

Jerry ruffled my hair. I went stiff, wishing I'd tied it down before he came. Now I'd have to wrap it all over again. Oh well. I'd have to get used to this. A man. My man. It sounded strange even in my mind.

"I'm glad you mentioned another pastor. I didn't know how you'd feel about that since you've been at Mount Olive all your life."

All my life. All my life wasted, sitting on the front pew, wiping the noses of other people's children, singing when nobody showed, cooking when nobody felt like it, and still, Daddy had done this. Never said a word. "No. We can go wherever you feel comfortable. God is everywhere."

He smiled. "I already have a place in mind. That mixed church over in the shopping center. Quinn goes there. Ron too."

I wobbled a little. Jerry bent down, steadying my shoulders. "Are you okay? We can wait if you want—"

I pulled away. "No. That's fine. We can try it out whenever you want. Grace goes there too."

"See there! I told you the Lord was in this. We'll go Sunday, okay?"

"Su-ure." I ran for the bathroom.

63

Grace

Mom and Daddy came to visit today. They didn't stay long. People are wondering where I am, they said. Mom worried they'd been followed. Daddy looked at my belly—it's big now—and he cried. I've never seen him do that, not even when Grandma and Grandpa died. I guess watching me die is worse.

Diana Dixon

From the sound of the church tape, I'd missed a great service. Pastor David had been on point as usual. If I hadn't been so tired, I would have pushed myself to make it, but there was nothing worse than sleeping in church. When it gets like that, I need to check myself.

Since that night at the church with Reverend Wilkins, I'd been dancing most every day. In the mornings at home, developing a curriculum for the new Ngozi dance troupe, and in the evenings at Zeely's dance class or an occasional ballet class at a studio nearby. Ballet had been a nightmare when I was a girl, but now it seemed soothing somehow.

Still, I couldn't dance my way whole. It wasn't going to change Lottie's threat or stop my feelings toward Brian. Those were things that I was going to have to put as much energy into overcoming as I was putting into my dancing. The question was . . . when?

Lord, please be patient with me. I'm trying.

The Brian thing might require fleeing the locality, but the thing with Lottie could be dealt with easily by me doing what I should have done years ago, opening up my mouth. Zeely had been having company most every night this week, male company by the looks of the vehicles, but I'm no one to judge. Still, I had a story to tell and, before this week was out, Miss Zee was going to hear it.

I eased my car around the corner. There was a black SUV in front of Zeely's house. The license plate made my mouth drop: Big Q Dog. Jerry had worn a fraternity jacket with the name last week. A man at Zeely's place on a weeknight? It was a sight I thought I'd never see.

He's marrying her. I guess he's got the right.

I still wasn't so sure how I felt about that. When Zeely dropped her diamond bomb on me the last time we were together, I should have been happy. I wasn't. Something about it just didn't fit. Zeely's sad face and her bare finger since her announcement was another weird thing. I kept praying and kept my mouth shut. I had problems of my own.

I dragged my sore body into my condo, which felt emptier than usual tonight, probably because Zeely had company. And from now on, she'd always have company. Was this how Zeely had felt when I married Peter? I felt like I should go down and apologize. I didn't want to, not with Jerry there. I loved working with the guy, but as a husband for Zeely? Nah.

I thought it would have been Ron.

I'd joined Ron and Zeely a few times for their fun nights: a few board games, a good movie, a great dinner, lots of prayers. The guy had even beaten me at Bible Trivia. That didn't happen often. And the guys who could beat me were usually serious, intense, like Mal. Ron knew how to laugh, how to have fun. And he and Zeely seemed to have a lot of it. After my third time with them, I'd declined their next invitation. The two of them didn't realize it, but they were dating, and I didn't care too much for being the third wheel. Now there'd be no wheel at all.

I peeked out the curtains. Jerry's car hadn't moved. So much for late-night girl talk. I sighed and mounted the stairs. Zeely might be getting married, but I still had something to tell her. No man would stand in the way of that.

64

Ron

I dialed the numbers with caution and turned the heat in the car up a little higher. Toasty. She probably wouldn't pick up anyway. A woman's voice surprised me on the line.

"Min? It's me. Ron. How are you?"

"Okay, I guess. I see you're back in town, huh?"

"Yeah. A few weeks now."

"You didn't have to leave. Daddy still thinks you're a saint. If you want your job back—"

"I don't. I just wanted . . ." What did I want? "I wanted to say I'm sorry for how this whole thing went down and that I'm proud of you for keeping your baby and—"

There was a gasp on the other end of the line, then silence. If she was surprised that I'd figured things out, she had a quiet way of showing it.

"Min?"

"Don't be proud of me yet. By tomorrow, there won't be any baby."

She wouldn't. "What are you saying? Come on. You counseled at the Women's Center, led the Life march—"

"Things change."

"God's Word hasn't changed. Where are you? Let's meet somewhere. Talk. You can't get an appointment tonight anyway." At least I hoped not. I made a U-turn just in case. If she did have an appointment, I knew the place. Twenty-five hundred Stroop Road.

357

"I had to pay double, but they're going to take me. An evening clinic."

I revved toward the highway.

Just keep her talking. "How many times did you tell me that women who do this are just scared, unable to see their options? There are options, Mindy. A way of escape. God always provides one."

"Not this time. I'm not taking a life, I'm saving one. When my father finds out, he'll beat it out of me anyway."

I threw my head back, pressing harder against the accelerator. John Bent, my former employer, had been a jerk with me enough times, but with Mindy, he always seemed so nice. Quiet. Weren't those the ones? My mother had hardly ever said a peep in public. She saved her words for me.

"You're not a little girl, Mindy. You can move out. Move away if you have to. I'll help you. Your dad will change his tune when the baby comes. It's his own flesh and blood. He'll thank you."

Laughter, mixed with tears. "If I made it to delivery, he'd take one look at that baby and kill it right there on the table. I'm almost to the clinic. I've got to go."

The Saab roamed lane to lane, chasing a gold Corvette up ahead. Was it her? Yes. Blond hair filled the front seat. A phone to her ear. She headed for the exit. I followed.

"Wait. Is something wrong with the baby? Special needs? He'll understand. It'll take some time, but he will—"

"He won't, Ron. The baby is healthy. I saw it on the ultrasound. It's just black, and a boy just like Daniel wanted. Daddy won't stand for it. No way."

I slowed, a few car lengths behind. Black? What was she saying? And Daniel . . . It couldn't be. "Daniel Lazarus? The old worship leader everybody talks about?" I'd only met him a few times, but his voice and his walk with the Lord were legendary around Tender Mercies.

"One and the same." She turned off up ahead into an office complex. I stopped behind a van marked Medical Delivery.

She stepped out of the car. "I'm here. Don't worry. I'll be fine. This isn't my first time."

Mine either.

The van moved on and I pulled in behind her. She didn't notice me. "Does your dad know anything? What did you tell him about us, about the wedding?"

"Just that things didn't work out."

"How about we work them out then?"

"Ron . . ."

"If I married you, would you keep it? The baby, I mean."

"You would do that for me?"

It's for me too. "I would." I walked up behind her.

She jumped. "How did you find me?"

I stared down at the mound curving up through her dress. I smiled. "I know the way. I followed someone here before."

Mindy laughed, wiping away tears. "You married her too?"

"Nope. That time, I got here too late."

65

Grace

*I've got some friends now. Jenny is seventeen. She's
keeping her baby. She has pretty fingernails and a ring
on every finger except the right one. Her boyfriend
comes to visit every weekend. Kelly is from Cincinnati.
I don't know why somebody would hide out in their
own town, but I guess it works for her. Kelly knows a
lot about boys. I asked her how she got pregnant since
she knows so much, but she got mad at me. I really
wanted to know.*

Diana Dixon

My opportunity to get with Zeely came quicker than I thought.
When I went out to start my car for work, it wouldn't start. In my
rush last night, I'd left on my headlights. I grabbed my purse and
started for Zeely's house. Maybe now, we could talk.

Of course I'd have to endure the speech about why we both
didn't need to drive anyway. I felt guilty enough about it, wasting
the gas, but Zee could be all too perky in the morning sometimes.
It was a wonder she was still home now. She usually left for school
an hour to an hour and a half early. I'd started out the year that
way, but now I got there thirty minutes before school started and
was glad of that.

Zeely's engine hummed as I passed it and stepped onto her

porch. Before I could knock, the door opened. "What's wrong? No gas?" she said, buttoning her pink angora coat.

"Left the lights on," I mumbled, knowing that Zeely had never done such a silly thing in her life.

"Bummer. Come on, I'm on my way out." She grabbed her keys from off the counter and stepped outside. We walked to the car in silence. Zeely avoided my eyes and picked up her scraper, attacking a patch of ice on her windshield.

"I've got something to tell you." My voice strained over the sound of the running car.

Zeely continued scraping nothing. "The only thing you need to talk to me about is why I'm stuck listening to Brian talk about you all day."

"Brian? Asking about me?" What did *he* want to know? "You'll have to fill me in later. Right now I need you to listen to me."

The scraper screeched against the glass one last time. Zeely opened the car door and got in. I sighed and slid in beside her. Was she avoiding me? Maybe I was imagining it. I aimed the heat vent at my face, then turned to my friend.

"Remember when—"

"Whatever it is, Grace, I don't want to hear it." The car rolled back onto the road.

I can't believe this.

After all this time of trying to keep my secret, I hadn't planned on someone not wanting to know. Unless . . . I looked over at Zeely's eyes, swollen with sleeplessness. Did Zee have some skeletons too?

"Sounds like maybe we both have something to tell. You go first."

Zeely sniffed. "Sometimes it's best to leave the past alone."

My thumb ran along the seat belt as I processed what she was saying. What she wasn't saying. Whatever those tears running down her face were about was big. Too big to carry alone.

"I noticed you've been having . . . company. Is everything all right? Do you need to talk?"

"I'm not ready to talk. Just pray for me. And I'm sorry I'm not here for you right now. It's just—" She ran a hand up her neck, behind her ear. A whimper escaped her lips.

I leaned across the seat and took her hand. "It's okay. We'll get around to it. Girls' night out maybe."

"Thanks for understanding." She turned into the gas station and stopped at the first pump. "I forgot to fill up."

Maybe she was human after all. I dug a twenty out of my purse. My friend pushed it away, sliding her purse up on her shoulder. A gold envelope with black and green accents fell out of her bag and onto the seat. She handed it to me.

"Oh yeah. This came for you. Someone put it in my box by mistake." She winced an apology. "Probably been there a couple days."

The car door slammed, leaving me alone with the letter penned in handwriting I recognized all too easily. On a hunch, I lifted the envelope to my nose. There it was, cucumber melon aftershave. I jammed the letter into my bag. Zeely had got one thing right: some things are better left alone.

66

Carmel

"It's a . . . girl!"

I smiled as the young girl above me fell back to the bed, exhausted and overjoyed. I bundled the baby in a blanket and lifted her toward the new mother. The girl tried to reach up, but fell back again.

The baby's grandmother took the warm handful instead. She peeked beneath the folds. "Oh Megan. Look at her. She looks just like Daddy, doesn't she? Look at that frown. That's him in the morning."

"Hey . . ." The old man's gruff voice objected from the back of the room.

I lingered, gathering the used supplies for cleaning.

The doctor nodded to me and tossed his gloves in the trash. "Nice job. Are you on tomorrow?"

I sighed. "No, I'm supposed to be off now. This is my second double this week."

He smiled. "We all love you, that's why." He turned to the new mom and patted her knee. "You did a good job too, young lady. See you next year." He started for the door.

The girl looked at me. "Is he crazy?"

I laughed. Dr. Washington always said that to the young mothers. Reverse psychology probably. From the look on the girl's face, it worked. "Most of the girls do come back. And soon."

"Not me. I love my baby and everything, but I should have listened . . . It hurt so bad!" She grimaced and turned over in the bed.

The girl's grandmother stroked her hair. "Lord willing, we won't be back. We'll make it."

Three other nurses entered the room. The girl, transformed into a woman by the rites of labor, moaned in pain. "Oh . . . it hurts again."

The other nurses circled the bed. One massaged the girl's belly.

"Ow!" She twisted, grabbing the rails.

I walked to the top of the bed and whispered in the girl's ear. "You're doing fine." I wished I could say the same for myself. I rubbed my eyes, strained from watching monitors, anticipating the doctor's needs. I could go home now, should have gone hours ago, but this girl, this delivery, reminded me so much of Monique's experience that I'd stayed. Another nurse arrived, whisking the baby off to the nursery.

The grandmother squeezed my shoulder. "Thank you. I don't think we could have made it without you. Last night before you got here, I was sure she'd end up with a caesarean. You've been a blessing." She pulled a card from her purse.

Tender Mercies Church. The healing place.

Church. With work and not wanting to invade Jerry and Zeely's space, I hadn't been there in so long. Monique and I had visited a church in the neighborhood a few times, but we'd spent most of our time downstairs or in the hallway trying to quiet the baby. I settled for reading my Bible each day at work, listening to Charles Stanley on the Internet each morning, and praying. Lots of praying. The more Sean came around, the more I prayed.

I passed the card back with a smile. "My daughter has a baby too. We've tried to go to church, but it doesn't work so well. Maybe when she's older. Thanks for asking though."

"You have a grandbaby too? I should have known. You've been so sweet." She held the card out again. "Please come. I work in the nursery. The baby will be fine. Your daughter can go to the youth group or sit with you—"

"She'll stay with me."

The lady looked down at her granddaughter, still quivering under the sheets. She rubbed the girl's knee. "I don't blame you. The service will be better anyway. The pastor is doing a good series right now. She'll enjoy it too."

Maybe. "Okay. What's the topic?"

"Forgiveness."

Forgiveness. I could use some of that. For myself, for allowing Monique to follow in my troubled footsteps. For Monique, for being too weak last year and too strong this year. And for Jerry, for being such a good man, but loving someone else. I tucked the card in my pocket.

"We'll be there."

67

Grace

I tried to act natural in class, like Brian's note wasn't burning a hole in my pocket, like I wasn't losing my mind. It didn't work. Both Jerry and the students were too peppy for my mood.

"This little hat means the guy is crazy. Wild. What do we call him?" Jerry asked the class, pointing to the board.

"Radical!" A new girl in the back stood up to answer. A snack-sized chocolate bar sailed through the air.

I managed a smile. What would Jerry come up with next? I tried to join in. "And radicals can't tolerate what kind of people?"

"Negative. A radical cannot contain negativity." Sean leaned across his desk in the front row. He stared past me at Jerry, as if his answer held more meaning. No gum or candy flew across the room. The bell rang, drowning out the tense silence. I wasn't proud of it, but I was glad to see them go.

Perceptive as always, Jerry turned to me as the kids filed out. "Do you still need to step out for a minute? Go ahead. They've got a test next period."

I nodded. "Thanks. I'll be back in a bit." I stepped into the hall. And into Brian.

He grinned. "Where you headed?" He stepped closer.

"Bathroom." I tried to ignore the thunder in my chest at the sight of him. The smell of him. Coconut today. He must have oiled his hair. I tried not to think about that.

"Faculty bathroom?"

I nodded, starting off in that direction.

He followed. "I'll walk you down."

He's killing me and not so softly.

"Did you get my note?"

I patted my pocket and stopped at the bathroom door.

He chuckled. "O-kay. Just don't throw it away." He started back toward his classroom.

I shoved myself into the bathroom, painted an ice blue that made me cringe but would have relaxed Peter. I dropped into the chair next to a vanity, whispering thanks to Joyce mentally for the small comfort. I took the envelope out and rested it on my lap, where it balanced precariously like a bomb in a minefield. I was making way too much of it. It was probably just a thank-you for teaching with him or something else just as harmless. I ripped through the flap, revealing the gold foil inside.

> *Dear Diana Grace,*
>
> *I have something I'd like to share with you. Please honor me with your presence for dinner this Friday at 7 PM. I've enclosed a map to my house.*
>
> *Yours,*
> *Brian*
> *P.S. Bring Zeely too.*

I read the closing again.

Yours.

Had he left out sincerely by mistake? I tried to breathe. He had something to share. What was this—true confessions week? I dared not imagine what he might say. At least I'd have Zeely along.

I took a deep breath and tucked the note back into my sweater pocket, realizing that I had already decided to go. No prayer, no thought, no nothing. I was in deep trouble.

The bathroom door took more pull to get out than the push to get in. My muscles cried out as I walked back to class. If anyone had asked, I would have blamed my staggering on tired muscles, but in my heart I knew the truth: the invitation in my pocket had sucked any remaining strength I possessed.

Zeely handled the invitation much better than I did. At the end of the day, I'd wandered into the hall, where I knew Brian would be, mumbling something about how fine dinner would be and thank you and you don't have to cook, you know. He smiled to keep from laughing and thanked me for coming.

"You won't be sorry," he said. "I promise."

Another promise. Just what I didn't need. The weatherman had said sunny skies for the afternoon. Little chance of snow.

It looked like a blizzard had done its thing while we were in the classroom. Snow still drifted down now and then, as if the clouds weren't quite sure whether to keep back or give away. I wiped the cold from my face and walked to Zeely's car. Knowing that I'd lose my nerve if I waited, I handed Brian's note across to Zeely as soon as I got in.

She skimmed it quickly and handed it back. "I'm not going."

For the second time today, I stared at my friend in disbelief. "You're kidding, right?"

The engine of her pink Cadillac slowed to a purr. "I'm serious. I have . . . plans tonight. I can't get out of it." She checked her face in the mirror. "And even if I could, I wouldn't go." She turned on the main road, her car sliding toward home.

I didn't know what Zeely's drama was, but she was really getting on my nerves. "Make up your mind, okay? A few weeks ago you chewed me out for letting Brian come to my house. Now you're ready to turn me loose alone with him?"

Zeely positioned her hands on the steering wheel, ten o'clock and two o'clock. "You two defy rules. I'm sick of you both. And—"

"What?"

"Now that I've been teaching with Brian, for some reason, I trust him. Kind of."

Me too.

But didn't people always trust the friendly neighborhood rapists and serial killers? Mal was crazy, true enough, but something of what he'd said still lingered in my mind. What if all my—our—instincts about Brian were wrong? "Maybe I shouldn't go."

Zeely pulled onto our street. "If that's what you really want."

Good thing we were getting close to home. If we were in this car much longer I might strangle her.

"You know what I really want?" I went on without waiting for her reply. "The truth. He has something to tell me, so I'm going. I'm a grown woman. I can handle this."

Zeely nodded and pulled up to the curb in front of my condo.

"Just be careful, Grace," she said. "Sometimes the truth hurts."

68

Ron

I stared out the picture window beyond the desk in front of me. From this perch, I couldn't see the ground outside, but that was good. Today I didn't want to look down. What I needed to see was up high, here in Freedom Tower, clouds foaming against the winter sky, forming a cross of condensation. A cross of tears. My tears.

If only I could cry them.

"Sorry to keep you waiting." John Bent, Mindy's father and my former employer, lowered his hulk into the seat across from me. "Thanks for coming."

"No problem. How are you?"

The older man sighed, his chins flapping against each other. "I'm a lot better now that I know you and my Melinda are together again. I'd be much better if you would come on back to work—"

"Sir . . ."

Mr. Bent raised his hand. "I know I'm pushing. Can't help it, I guess. That case you took, I just didn't think it was a good idea once I had more time to think about it. Didn't seem like it turned out to be much anyway. At least not so far. I should have talked to you myself."

Communication. What a novel concept. "That might have been better, sir."

"Yes, well. Hindsight and all that, eh? Anything new with that situation?"

I shifted in my chair. Is this what he'd called me in for? To fish

370

around for information on Brian? "The woman I was representing might drop the charges. It's not official yet, but the case may be over soon."

Laughter lit Bent's cheeks, blushing up to his nonexistent hairline and back to the middle of his head. "Over indeed. You see? I knew the Lord would work it out. They didn't need you. Those people can work out their own problems." He reached in his drawer and pulled out a certified check with my name on it. A pudgy finger covered the amount, but I saw five zeros extending beyond the man's manicured nail. Bent scribbled his signature at the bottom and handed it over. "They can take care of their problems and I know how to take care of mine."

My hands remained on my lap. My eyes went back to the window. The cloudy cross remained.

"I can't take that."

"Please. Do. Melinda's had some . . . problems in the past. Some things we aren't so proud of. But I see you're willing to overlook those things. I respect that. Admire it. And things that I admire, I buy."

Not today.

I stood, smoothing my slacks. "Thanks, but I'm not for sale."

Bent tossed the check aside, reaching in the same drawer for a photo of Mindy, smiling in the arms of a handsome man—tall, dark, nicely dressed. Daniel. He propped it up on the desk.

"You may not be for sale now, son, but there are things . . . Things that a man needs recompense to endure."

I stepped back. Twice. The only thing I needed payment for was enduring this meeting.

"I put my trust in Jesus. Whatever comes, he'll get me through it." I turned for the door.

Laughter rang out behind me, this time dripping with sarcasm.

"I hope Jesus can keep her from running off. As sure as she's her mother's daughter, she will. You and I both know it."

69

Grace

When they ask me how I got here, I tell them I don't know. It sounds crazy, but it's the truth. I'm feeling bad about leaving the baby. I saw a girl come back here and leave her baby at the hospital. She carries his picture around and keeps showing it to everybody. One of the nuns told her to stay in her room and rest. I think someone should stay with her. She doesn't sound right. I wish she'd get herself together so I can ask her how bad it hurt.

Diana Dixon

I piddled around the kitchen, making a big salad. I didn't want to be too hungry tonight. Being alone with Brian would be hard enough. The phone rang. The third time in the last half hour. I stared at the spinach in my hand, trying to decide whether or not to answer. I checked the caller ID. Mal. No doubt he received his ring by now. I reached for the receiver, knowing that he'd be blazing up the highway if I didn't answer. And that wouldn't do. Not tonight.

"Hello?"

"You're driving me nuts, you know that?" Yep. It was him.

I forced a smile, hoping it would come through in my voice. "So the ring got back okay?"

"You could say that. I'm not okay though."

Join the club. "I can't really get into it right now. This is my final decision. That's all I can say."

"It wouldn't matter if he were a murderer, huh?"

"This isn't about him."

"Of course it is." *Click.*

I stared at the phone. Mal had never hung up on me before, no matter what was going on. I shrugged. That would have to be dealt with later. Right now, I had some praying to do.

70

Ron

My car followed the tire ruts carved into the black slush by everyone in town. The ride came easy, my mind busy slipping over my future father-in-law's words. Saving Mindy's baby was noble, but it seemed foolish too. I'd spent enough of my life trying to get a woman who loved someone else to love me. It hadn't worked out. In some weird way, I almost felt comforted that Mindy wasn't in love with me. It made things cut and dry.

I don't know if I want her to love me.

I rubbed my temples, turning onto my street. I squinted, stunned by the brightness of hundreds of fluorescent icicle bulbs draping the roofs and eaves of every house but mine. They must have voted on those at the last homeowners' association meeting. The Saab kept going, crawling past my house, a dark eye in a sea of brightness. I drove on, down the street and around the cul-de-sac. I turned out of "Winter World" and back into the dirty ruts that had led me home. I reached for the phone, praying for an answer on the other end.

"Mayfield."

"Hey."

"Hey yourself. Did you get my email? Zee gave me the right email address. I was bouncing because I didn't have the underline part."

"I hit you back this morning. It should be there now. You busy?"

"A little. I'm having company for dinner. Grace and Zeely. Coming

374

for your truck? It's in the garage. The alignment's fixed. I figured you'd be back for it."

I stopped at a red light, considering Brian's words. Zeely. Just the mention of her name made me nuts. And the truck of course, definitely the truck. "I'm afraid so. I appreciate your gift, but this just isn't me. And you know I need my snow tires. This thing might flip any time."

Brian chuckled. "Rides nice, though, doesn't it?"

"It does. Sounds nice too." Another few turns brought me up to Brian's gate. "I'm at the front. What's your code?"

"John three sixteen. Word then the numbers."

"I like."

"You would."

I pulled up along a lane of trees. Christmas lights twining the branches. One trunk was completely covered. Brian's house rose out of a hill on the right.

"I'm here."

"Okay, the keys are in your truck. I'll hit the opener."

"Can I come in? I need to talk."

"Me too, man. Come on in."

71

Grace

I arrived at Brian's house at seven sharp—too curious to be late, too afraid to be early. If I worked it right, I could be in and out within the hour. Forty-five minutes if I kept my mouth shut and didn't eat too much. I paused at his street sign, setting the timer on my watch. If it went off, I'd just say I needed to go. I wouldn't be lying.

I'd started thinking about the fact that this was Brian's house, with the bed that he slept in . . . I almost turned back. But then I remembered that God always provides a way of escape. If need be, I'd pull a Joseph and run out of there. Still, as I drove into Brian's gated community, I wished Zeely had passed on her clandestine engagement and come with me.

When I checked the map for the key code to get into Brian's neighborhood, I wasn't surprised by his simplicity—and his spirituality: JOHN 316. The size of the houses, near mansions from the looks of them, and the canopy overhang of trees over the entrance made wonder if I'd driven into another world. The house where I'd spent some of my suburban childhood wasn't that far away, but it was nothing like this. It was a bit more than I anticipated, even for Brian.

His steep driveway left me wondering how I'd back out. I gave up and parked on the street.

That was a mistake with my heels and the snow and all, but I kept at it, one foot in front of the other. Brian's house, missing the colonial pillars of its neighbors, sloped above in a unique and modern design. Like its owner, the home was anything but ordinary.

Brian appeared on the porch when I was almost up the hill.

"You walked up? Oh goodness. I forgot to warn you. I'm coming. Stay there."

I shook my head. "I've got it."

He bit his lip, eyes clouded with what I'd learned was concern, but those dimples were still there, held in place by a hopeful grin. His hair was down, but there was a band on his wrist that probably meant it wouldn't last long.

I hoped not anyway.

Swallowing down my fears, I finished the climb. It'd only been a few steps, but he let out a gust of relief when I stepped off the driveway. With a few strides he was there, taking my hand and kissing it softly. "Welcome."

"Thank you for having me."

He stared past me to the car, probably wondering where Zeely was. He didn't say anything. He didn't have to. If I didn't know better, I'd say that he looked as worried as I felt as his hand rested against my back, urging me forward.

I hadn't prayed hard enough. Not for this.

72

Brian

I hung Grace's coat in the closet, wishing I could stay in there too. Instead, I stood in the hall for a moment watching her, poised like a queen as she admired one of Mount Olive's old deacon benches in my foyer. Her voice brought me back to reality.

"Beautiful. Absolutely stunning," she said, stroking the wood, pointing at the African prints along the walls.

You're the best-looking thing in here. "Thanks. Just things I've picked up here and there."

She smirked. "Yeah, right. I recognize some of these pieces. You searched hard for them." Grace tucked a strand of hair back into her scarf.

I shook my head slightly, hoping she didn't notice. How could anyone be so lovely and not know it? In a fuchsia head wrap, hoop earrings, and a sweater dress, hers was an obvious attempt at a casual look with a regal result. Casual wasn't possible. Not for her.

With a wave of my hand and more careful banter, I asked the question that was really on my mind. "Is Zeely on her way?"

Grace shook her head. "She couldn't make it."

Alone? I swallowed hard and glanced up at the ceiling.

Now you know I need some backup on this one.

Clearing my throat helped me recover. "Zeely won't make it, huh? That's okay. We'll send her some food. Have a seat." While pulling out Grace's chair, I shot a few mildly angry prayers. I hadn't much wanted to invite Zeely in the first place, but I'd finally admitted to myself that it was the best thing to do. And now, God had flipped the script and left us alone anyway. Or was it the devil trying to tempt me. Either way, the answer was the same:

Lord, help me.

I disappeared into the kitchen, returning with a plate heaped with curried chicken, fried plantain, and roti, a flatbread well known in the Caribbean and India. I added a cloth napkin and a glass of sorrel tea before going back for my plate and drink. Back in the room, I sat, watching with relish as Grace took a bite.

"Oooh . . . roti? Where did you order this from? I didn't know there were any Caribbean restaurants here."

My mouth went slack. Not only did she know what it was, but she thought I'd ordered it from a restaurant. I draped an arm over the back of my chair. "I made it."

She rolled the hot bread around the chicken mixture and took another bite. "Okay, you've been holding out on me. Seriously. Is there anything else I should know?"

I cleared my throat . . . and my mind. The things that I was considering sharing with her weren't worth discussing. "I try to enjoy my time in the kitchen as much as I do my time at the table. I had some Trinidadian friends in college. My roti isn't quite up to their standard, but it's edible."

My guest didn't look convinced. "Look, I'm a fair cook and I've tried and failed to make this plenty of times. How'd you get the peas to spread all the way to the edge without breaking through the dough? You must be very observant to have learned so much just by watching."

"I notice things, especially when there's a worthy subject."

She looked away, focusing on the food instead of my words. I motioned towards her head. "That's a nice head wrap you're wearing, by the way. You hooked it up."

"Thanks. Bad hair day." Grace smiled and closed her eyes. Slowly.

I choked down some tea and wrapped one of my locks around the rest of them. It was getting hot in here. "Bad hair day isn't the phrase I'd use to describe it, but I hear you. Is your hair still falling out?"

Grace dropped her fork.

So much for small talk.

I picked up my fork, but the food went sour in my mouth. I could almost hear my chorus of women in my head: Karyn, Eva, Joyce, Thelma. *"What kind of question is that to ask a dog, Brian, let alone a woman? Have you lost your mind?"*

Pretty much.

She looked stricken, the exact opposite of what I was going for. "Is it that noticeable? I don't recall mentioning it."

I took another sip of tea, wondering if it'd be better not to say anything else. I was eating foot pot pie as it was. "Don't worry. It's not really noticeable. I'm just observant. And I really love your hair."

Her eyes widened. Another bomb.

Before I thought it through, I'd put down my napkin and reached for Grace's hand. She tensed, but let me take it. I was going down in flames.

As if things weren't bad enough, I let go of her hand and rounded the table. Put my hands on her shoulders. "I'm not going to hurt you. I just want to look at your hair. May I?"

The chorus in my head let out a scream. "She came for you, not a scalp treatment, fool," Thelma said, foundation dripping over my thoughts. The other ladies nodded in disappointment.

Just when I was about to apologize, Grace tugged at her headscarf and started to unwrap it. I tried not to gasp and sound crazier than I already did. I almost managed.

"It's even prettier up close."

Grace shook her head. "Are you on something? It's a mess."

"If so, it's the most beautiful mess I've ever seen."

She laughed. Her shoulders relaxed. "Whatever. If it keeps coming out though, there won't be much of it left."

Biting my lip, I finger-parted a section at the nape of her neck. "Of course there'll be hair left. A lot more will grow in too. The scab stage is almost over. In about . . . six more months, you'll be home free."

She looked confused. "I've never heard of that. I just sort of went for it and cut off my perm. Nobody seemed to know much. I go to some places on the Internet, but it's like I'm learning myself, getting to know myself all over again."

And you're doing a great job of it, I thought.

Karyn gave me a mental elbow. "Now that's what you should have said to her!"

"It looks great. You transitioned for a long time?"

She nodded.

"Weave?"

"No."

"Braids."

"Yes. Braids and two-strand twists. Mostly the twists. The girl did great with the synthetic ones, but when it was my hair, not so much. I do them sometimes, but it takes me forever."

Against my better judgment, I buried my fingers deeper into Grace's hair, massaging her scalp. "It'll be fine. Don't worry. You just might have waited too long to trim the ends off. I don't understand why really, but it happens. Like a plant that outgrows its pot."

She pulled away and pushed forward on the edge of her chair. I went for her scarf, but she already had it in hand and going around her head. "I did wait too long. Mal liked me to keep it blown out straight all the time. My hair was one of our biggest fights."

At the mention of Mal's name, it was my turn to tense up. If Grace's hair had been one of their worst arguments, I could only imagine what one of their other big fights had been about—me.

"Speaking of him, I need to talk to you about something—"

Grace's watch beeped to the tune of a gospel song I'd heard on many mornings but didn't know the name of. She mumbled something about setting the alarm to be safe and I should get to what I wanted to tell her because this was really difficult and on and on. It was all I could do to keep from tearing that scarf off her head and kissing her senseless.

I held a finger to her lips instead. "I know just how you feel."

"You can't possibly. I—"

"Actually, that's what I wanted to tell you. It sounds strange, I know, and I debated telling you at all, but since we're not teaching together anymore—"

The phone rang. Any other time I would have ignored it, but I was waiting for a call from Joyce's doctor. We'd talked during my last visit about her not having signed some of her forms. I'd thought Ron would have been the one they called, but Joyce had listed him on many of her forms.

"Hold that thought. I'm expecting a call from the hospital about Joyce."

Grace looked concerned, but I waved it away. "Nothing like that. Just some paperwork. Let me get this."

I caught it just when I thought they'd hung up. Out of the habit of being alone, I clicked on the speakerphone.

"Dr. Mayfield?"

"This is he." I straightened a little at the sound of a woman's strained voice. The doctor I talked to had been a man. It was probably nothing.

"This is Charles Drew Memorial Hospital. You're listed on Joyce Rogers' emergency list. She's fading fast and we can't contact anyone else. I'd suggest you come at once."

Grace let out a sob behind me.

I grabbed Grace's coat and my keys. "We're on our way."

73

Jerry

"That's it. You've lost your mind." I stood in my ex-wife's living room staring down on Sean and Justice sprawled on the couch asleep. And Monique in the chair beside them. What a mess.

Carmel's voice sounded over the hiss of ground beef in the kitchen. "Sit down, Jerry. We need to talk, but not like this."

I snatched the covers off the happy group. Sean murmured and reached for the baby. Monique opened her eyes, just a bit at first and then wider.

"Dad?"

"Me, Dad? You tell me. It seems I'm nothing around here anymore. I came over to talk to you all about something, and I find this—this boy laid out like he lives here." I leaned over Sean again, determined this time to wake him up. A tangle of basketball shorts and pajama pants peeked from under the couch. I had the same pair at home. "Is that it, Carmel? Is he living here?"

A spoon clanked against the spaghetti pot. The stainless one, my favorite. Sean sat up and wiped his eyes. He dug in the bag under the couch for his jacket, his keys. He turned to Monique.

"Baby, I'm going to dip and let you talk to your father. Call me."

I stepped back for the boy to pass, fighting the urge to sweep his legs out from under him. Baby? What gave this little chump the right to call my daughter "baby"? The fool was nothing but a baby himself.

"Excuse me, sir." Sean stepped around me, pausing at the door. "You want me to bring you back some basil, Mrs. T? It's good like that."

Mrs. T. It sounded so strange to hear Sean call my ex-wife by the name the students used for me. I took a deep breath.

Carmel put a finger to her lips before waving goodbye to Sean. As the door slammed, I exploded again.

"What in God's name is going on? Can somebody tell me? Please?"

Monique got up from the couch, her thumbs hooked in the pockets of her jeans. "Daddy—"

"Wait." Her mother, standing at the stove, shook her head while her body moved in a motion I'd seen so many times before. The spaghetti dance. Her hips swayed left and right in front of the range. Salt. Pepper. Oregano. And a pinch of sugar, just for me.

"Sit down, Jerry. Monique, take Justice into your room. I'll leave some food for you in the microwave."

"I'll lay her down, Mom, but I'm coming back. This is about me too."

After drizzling sauce in a design around the edges of the plates, Carmel filled the center with angel hair pasta, more meat sauce and two sprinkles of Romano cheese. She made a second plate just like the first. She knew just how to get to me.

"Want some?"

Of course. "No thanks."

She shrugged and walked to the table, motioning for me to have a seat. As soon as I sat down, she hopped up again for a basket of garlic bread and a tumbler of water.

"I can explain about Sean—"

"I doubt it."

"It won't be an explanation you like, necessarily, but it's the truth nonetheless. Before I start, I'd like you to tell me what you came

384

here to say. It must be important. You haven't come inside here since . . ."

I stared behind me at the bedroom door, looking for Monique. I knew exactly how long it had been since I'd crossed Carmel's threshold. Since the day she'd left me alone with a space heater and a cold bed. Since the day she'd decided that I'd be better off with Zeely instead of her.

"Monique, come on out. I have something to tell you and your mom."

My daughter tiptoed out of the room, pulling the door shut. "Shh. She almost woke up." She walked around the table to the chair opposite me, next to her mother. "What's up, Dad?"

I rubbed my tongue against the top of my mouth. How to start? "As you know, your mother and I have tried to work out our differences over the past year. A few months ago your mother, well both of us, decided that wasn't going to happen."

Carmel's fork stopped midair.

"Something—someone—came between us. According to your mother, she's always been between us."

A knowing look passed between mother and daughter. Panic overtook Monique's face. "Miss Wilkins? What about her? I thought since she moved to the other class, that maybe . . ."

I hadn't sent her across the hall. The separation just made me miss her more. "You thought what, honey?"

"Nothing. Go ahead."

"Well, since your mom and I can't work things out and she and I both agree that Zeely is the person I should be with, I've decided to make it official. I've decided to be part of a family again."

Carmel closed her eyes. "When is the wedding?"

Good question. "We haven't set a date yet. Next summer maybe. Zeely was coming over here with me tonight, but she didn't feel well."

Monique pursed her lips. "I'll bet."

I hadn't planned on this being so hard. "What do you say, Monique, won't it be nice to be part of a family again? And your mom won't have to worry about Justice and you can dump Sean—"

My daughter banged the table in front of me, her eyes filled with tears. Anger. And something else. Hatred? It couldn't be. "Dump Sean? He's the best thing that's happened to me in a long time! And what do you mean Mom won't have to worry about Justice? Do you think you're going to take her off for some other woman to raise?"

"Zeely is an amazing woman. She's waited for children for a long time. She'll make a great mother."

"And I won't? She's my baby, Dad, no matter what you say. And I don't need you or your little girlfriend to raise her. You can keep your little family. I've got one of my own."

I reached out and grabbed my daughter's hand. I lifted my other hand to her eyes and wiped her tears. "I know that you're upset, but don't talk to me that way, do you understand?"

She squeezed my fingers, talking through her tears. "Ye-es, sir."

"I know you're probably surprised about me getting married and you're saying things you don't mean. The three of us are still a family. Your mom and I will always be here for you and Justice. Zeely will too. You'll see."

Carmel walked to the sink with her plate. She changed her mind and stuck it into the refrigerator. "Jerry, I wish you all the best, but let's talk about your new family another time. I think that's enough for one night."

I rubbed my forehead. "Okay. I'll drop it for now, but we've still got to talk about Sean and what he's doing here." I got up and walked to Monique's chair, and put my hands on her shoulders. She tensed. "Like I said, you can let him go now. You don't have to make a family for Justice. I took care of it."

Monique brushed my hands away and stood to face me. "That's

what I'm trying to tell you, Dad. Sean is my family. Justice too. Your job is done."

"Honey, I know you think that, but—"

She dug in her pocket and fished out a ring, a gold band with a fleck of diamond. She slipped it on her finger. "I don't *think* we're a family. I know we are. Sean is my husband."

I slammed a fist into the concrete wall. I fumbled across the blinds and the windowsill trying to get back to my chair. I tried to breathe, but my chest hurt. Only a little air at a time. When I finally dropped into the chair, the metal made a crunching sound, yielding under my weight. "Carmel, what is she saying?"

My ex-wife stepped to the table, the other plate of pasta in her hand. She placed it in front of me. "It's true. They got married in Kentucky, with my consent."

My head dropped forward, almost into the spaghetti. "Why would you let her do a stupid thing like that? Just to make me mad? We tried so hard to give her a chance. What can Sean offer them? He's nothing to Justice, just some thug off the street."

Monique pinched her eyes shut. "You're wrong, Daddy. Sean is everything to me. And to Justice. He's her father."

74

Ron

I knocked at the door of Reverend Wilkins' study, still wondering how I'd ended up here. Of all people, Zeely's father seemed the worst choice to confide in. But tonight, I needed to talk to someone who knew me, someone who had always known me. I needed perspective.

"Come in."

I walked in and had to smile at the Reverend, one of the last guards of the old school of ministry. Even this late in the evening, the old preacher was hard at work in a shirt and tie, bent over a *Strong's Concordance*. He looked up over his bifocals. A grin spread across his face like chocolate icing. He waved toward the door. "Well, if it isn't the preacher boy himself! Come on in here, son. Where've you been? I get all those emails you send me. Good stuff."

Stepping behind the desk, I embraced my former pastor, patting his shoulders. "You look so good, Rev. Just like when I left. Taking good care of yourself, I see."

The pastor laughed. "I stopped trying to take care of myself years ago. The good Lord takes care of me. Long as I do what he tells me, things turn out all right. In the end anyway. Sit down."

I took a seat.

"What's troubling you?"

"You never were the subtle type, huh?"

"No sir. Time's too short. These are the last days. We have to redeem the time. You preached on that back when you was a boy, remember that?"

I chuckled, remembering myself hemming and hawing in the pulpit in Brian's hand-me-down suits. I could still see Eva on the front row, fanning her mortuary fan in one hand and waving her scarf with the other, amening me every other word. "Those were the days, huh?"

"Sure enough. And it ain't over yet." He took off his glasses. "The prayers of a righteous man availeth much."

I shook my head. "I told you last time. I'm not ready. I don't know if I ever will be."

Reverend Wilkins raised his hand. "I done said too much. Time for you to talk. What brings you?"

I waded through the tale, swimming around Zeely, but revealing the rest. Ending with my encounter with Mindy in the abortion clinic parking lot and my meeting with her father, I eased back in the chair. "Saving that baby is the right thing to do, but all of a sudden I'm not sure if marriage is the best way to do it. What do you think?"

Pastor Wilkins poked through the cellophane-wrapped basket on his desk. He picked a tangerine, skimmed the middle with a paring knife, and cut it in half. He flipped the seeds into the trash, and handed half of the fruit across the desk.

Nodding, I accepted and bit into the sweet flesh. Juice ran down over my goatee and onto my shirt. I looked around for a napkin.

The pastor extended a wet napkin in a plastic sleeve. "Surprised you, didn't it? That's how things are. They look just about the right size, like you can handle them, but when you bite in, more comes out than you expected."

I sighed. What was I thinking, expecting a straight answer from the Reverend? "You're not going to tell me what you think, are you?"

"What I think? Heavens, no. What good is that? You've got to get God's opinion on the thing. What I can say is that marriage is not something to be taken lightly, no matter the circumstances. If you marry this girl, you're going to have to stand by her, not just her baby. That's the part where things get juicy." He took another bite.

"Right. That's the part I'm worried about."

Another knock at the door. The pastor shook his head. "I ought to start a drive-thru, you know that?" He turned to the door. "Come in."

Zeely came in slow with red eyes and plump, plum-colored lips pushed first this way and then another. Her eyes were on the ground. "Daddy? Are you busy?" She looked up in surprise—more like terror, actually. "You have company. I'm sorry—"

"I was just leaving." I dropped my peel into the trash and wiped my fingers. I smiled at the Reverend and nodded goodbye. I reserved no expression or goodbye greeting for Zeely, stepping around her instead as though one touch would burn my skin.

She grabbed my arm first. Her voice was almost a whisper. "You don't have to go. Stay."

I closed my eyes. Stay. It sounded so good. If only I'd driven straight over instead of stopping for a card with pink roses and four simple words. *Will you marry me?* If only I wasn't still that white boy who was going to hurt her somehow. But I had stopped for the card, and in her mind, I would never be stable enough, safe enough, black enough to deserve her love. I headed for the door.

"No, Zee. I can't stay. It's too late for that."

75

Brian

My car skidded across the icy streets. I should have driven more carefully, but all I could focus on was getting to the hospital. Everything else, including my feelings for Grace, who rode quietly beside me, would have to wait.

When I'd looked in on Joyce earlier in the day, I'd thought she hadn't looked so good, but the on-call doctor had assured me that her appearance was just due to a new medication. Paperwork. That's what the guy had asked me about.

I'd lingered over her bed for a while anyway, even considered calling off my dinner plans with Grace but the nurses had shooed me away. "Don't come back until tomorrow," they'd said.

I should have stayed.

Joyce had always taught me to go with my first mind, which wasn't working so well until I got that last call. This time, nobody was going to tell me not to worry or to go home. This time I was going to stay.

If she could just hang on until I get there.

Joyce hung on . . . by a thread.

It didn't look good. Grace leaned over the bedrail and smoothed Joyce's curls, free of the wig that covered them so long. Tubes extended from Joyce's body in every direction. In between her labored breaths, Joyce took a pause that made the both of us want to cry.

As the hours passed, I prayed more than I had in a very long time. The nurses seemed surprised when they came to check and found her still breathing. Her eyes were closed, though. Her pulse thready and weak.

Lord, please. Don't take her. I'll do anything . . .

"Brian?" A hoarse whisper came from the bed. Joyce's eyelids parted enough for me to see her pupils. They looked tired, those usually fiery eyes. Very, very tired.

"I'm here. Grace is here too."

She closed her eyes again. "I'm glad you're both here. It won't be much longer."

Something inside me snapped. Perhaps Joyce would choose now to be wrong about something. Grace took Joyce's hand.

I followed her lead and took the other hand. The coldness of her skin surprised and saddened me. I tried not to let it show. "I'm the one running out of time, remember?" I rubbed my hand on hers, trying to warm her up.

Joyce smiled before the pain sucked her under again. I reached for the nurse's button.

In an effort that took what remained of her strength, Joyce reached for my wrist. "They can't do anything else. I'm tired. Let me go."

Grace gave me a helpless look. She was obviously conflicted.

I wasn't.

I didn't want to begrudge Joyce her dying wishes. I knew what Grace was trying to say with that face she was making—that Joyce would be with Jesus. I got that. It was me I was worried about. I was man enough to admit it.

"I picked a name for the dance troupe. Rhythms of Grace. By the time you get well, we should be ready," Grace whispered in Joyce's ear.

Joyce angled her finger toward me.

"He's a good man. Stubborn, but good. He'll love you forever."

Grace gasped. I stared. If she wasn't dying, I might have screamed. She just called me out. Totally.

I pushed the call button. "We need meds in here—"

Joyce shook her head. "She's a good woman, but she's scared. Don't let her run you off."

Grace's legs buckled, but she managed to stand on her feet. She wouldn't look at me.

Joyce sighed as I pulled the sheet up to her neck. "I wish you hadn't called them. Oh well. Bring Thelma with you next time."

With that Joyce slipped into what I prayed was sleep. A nurse stalked in, responding to my call. "There's nothing we can do. She's refused any more meds and signed a Do Not Resuscitate form. It's her right."

Grace nodded. I frowned.

"Did she move at all?" the nurse asked.

"She patted my hand—"

"And she squeezed mine."

The nurse seemed surprised. "Are you sure? Anything else?"

I pinched the bridge of my nose. I felt a nosebleed coming on. "She talked quite a bit."

What an understatement.

"She spoke?" The attendant checked Joyce's reflexes. No response. "The doctor wrote unresponsive on her chart an hour ago. When her vitals started dropping, I called the people on her list. I guess I'm not totally surprised. Patients sometimes rally like that before the end."

I didn't know what to make of the woman's words.

. . . before the end.

Or Joyce's.

He's a good man.

Why had she needed to make sure Grace thought well of me? I eased into a chair in the corner. Joyce would wake up again, I felt sure of it. And when she did, I had a few questions of my own.

76

Carmel

I wiped up the last of the spaghetti sauce from under Justice's highchair. Sean held the baby on his lap, wiping her face. He kissed her forehead and held her tight, the same way Jerry had done with Monique years ago. Too long ago. Too much water under the bridge. Water that would soon be flowing in another woman's direction. And I had guided it there. "Any luck finding a place, Sean?"

"Not really. Mr. Trent, the man down at the studio, saw a place and left my number on their machine. We're also on the waiting list for housing."

I had to draw the line there. "Let's not do anything drastic. Monique's father won't go for that. I'm off Sunday. We'll go to church, grab some lunch, and see what we can find."

Monique raised an eyebrow. "Church? Do you remember what happened the last few times we tried that? I don't think I can take that again, Mom."

"It's okay. They have a nursery. I know the lady who'll be watching her. Real nice. I was in with her granddaughter when she delivered. She's about your age."

Sean carried Justice to the playpen and sat her down. "What'd she have?"

"A girl. Real pretty."

Sean slapped out a beat on the table. "I'm down to go to church. Sounds good to me, you know? God's been blessing me left and right. I got a good woman, a sweet baby, school is going well, and my music is booming. I still can't believe Mr. Trent gave me a job."

I stared at my son-in-law, hoop earring dangling from one ear and his fresh cornrows touching his shoulders. I hadn't seen his tattoos yet, but Monique assured me they were there. I couldn't believe he'd landed a job either. "You make sure you keep it. Don't be late."

"Don't worry. I love it. He's showing me how to mix better. How to record. Everything. God is good."

Monique frowned. "God this. God that. When did you become a holy roller?"

"I always believed in God, girl. He brought me you, didn't he?" He leaned over and kissed his wife's cheek.

My stomach turned. I'd tried to accept the decision they'd made—that I'd made with them—but I still felt like scolding them whenever they expressed affection. This would take some getting used to.

I hope signing for this marriage was the right thing to do.

Oh well. They were going to run off if I hadn't done it. At least I still had them all here where I could keep an eye on them. "I know what you mean, Sean. I love the Lord too, even though I haven't always done what he says."

The boy nodded, the ends of his cornrows brushing his shoulders. "Me neither. I've done a lot of things wrong. But this is a new start, right, babe?"

Monique smiled. "Right."

"And when I blow up and my record goes platinum I'm going to get up on the Grammys and thank God in front of everybody. But not like everybody else be doing. All fake and everything. I'm going to mean it."

I closed my eyes. Again with his music.

God help us all.

"Did you look at that career planning survey I brought home?

395

I think both of you should do it and see where your interests are, what kind of thing you might want to major in when you go to college."

Sean nodded. "I'll do it, Mrs. T, but I already know what I want to do. Sing. It's all I ever wanted. I'm not stupid though. I'm going to take up business so nobody can steal my money, you know what I'm saying?"

"I hear you, baby." I stared over at the card hanging from a magnet on the refrigerator.

Tender Mercies Church. The healing place.

We were definitely going Sunday. All of us. Especially me. After the past year, the past month, the past week, I couldn't hold on much longer. Not without some divine intervention.

77

Brian

"Sir?"

I lifted my head to meet the unfamiliar voice. A male nurse had replaced the first. All sleep left me. I sat straight up in the chair.

I glanced at the bed. Empty. My breath shortened. "Is she—"

"She's stable. They've taken her for a treatment. I don't know what you and your wife did—"

"She's not my wife." I answered too quickly. As though I didn't wish it were so. Grace. Where was she?

The guy smiled, like any of this was funny. "Really? You two aren't married? I just assumed from the way she watched you sleep . . . Anyway, after she walked with your mother to her treatment, she went down to get you something to eat."

Grace had saved the day again. I stood to stretch my legs.

"Do you have any questions?"

None I wanted this guy to answer. He seemed a little too happy that Grace wasn't my wife. I decided not to tell him that Joyce wasn't my mother. I managed a weak smile and shook my head.

"Okay, well, why not go down to the cafeteria and find your . . . friend. You've both have had a long night. We've got things under control."

"Are you sure that it's okay to leave? She seemed so . . ."

"We'll call you if anything changes. And your friend. We'll call her too." He scanned a page in Joyce's chart. "Grace Okoye, is it? We have her number listed here."

And the joker looked ready to punch it into his phone.

I narrowed my eyes. If looks could kill, that guy would have been headed for the morgue.

More than twenty-four hours after we raced to the hospital, Grace and I left in the freezing twilight of uncertainty. Though I wasn't a big sleeper, exhaustion had taken its toll on both of us. Grace's car was at my place. Out of practicality, I headed there first, hoping that she wouldn't try to drive her car home tonight.

"Don't worry. I'll sleep on the couch," I said in a weary voice.

"I'm going on home," she said, looking out the window in a voice that made me wonder if underneath all her strength, Grace wasn't just what Joyce said—afraid.

The car slid as I made a U-turn. "I'll take you then. I can have Ron follow me with your car tomorrow."

She shook her head. "That's okay. Zeely can follow me over." She paused. "Thanks. For everything."

"Sure," I said, wishing I could put my hands on her shoulders again, slide my fingers in her hair. I wished I could go back before Joyce had bestowed her words upon us like some kind of twisted fairy godmother. But when I thought about it, maybe that's exactly what she was. She'd been bringing us together all along.

Still, I hadn't been able to share what I wanted at dinner, to tell Grace that I'd given my life back to God. Not that it would have changed things between us, but I desperately wanted her to know. Maybe she did know. We'd sure prayed enough last night to rival any church meeting. But I knew Grace well enough to know that wouldn't be enough for her to know anything. And yet, even now, when she wasn't saying a word, I felt like she knew everything.

It was good that she'd decided to go home. Joyce's life was fading away and our little fairy tale romance was dying with it.

BRIAN

"I kept hearing your phone ring when you were asleep. Was that Zeely? Or your other friend—"

"Ron? No, I got him when you were in the cafeteria. Those other calls were hang-ups. Just somebody playing games."

At least that was what I hoped. In my gut, I thought it might have been Lottie, but she was the last thing on my mind. What worried me was that the calls went back to 7:00, when my cell had been on vibrate.

When Grace had been at my house.

The thought of Lottie following Grace or even watching me was too much for my brain. I didn't dare mention it to Grace. Despite my stupidity about hair comments, this I knew for sure.

"Games, huh? Somebody must have been really confused. It seemed like a lot of calls."

I nodded. "You can never know what people are thinking, but I think it was a genuine mistake. I probably set something wrong as flustered as I was about Joyce."

She turned back to the window. "Could be. It shook me pretty bad too."

Grace's condo appeared all too soon, but I knew I needed to get home and sleep, process the past few days. I'd forgotten how exhausting constant communion with God, let alone women, could be. And almost losing Joyce? Forget it. I'd thought that knowing she was sick might change something when the time came, but it seemed like it hurt just the same.

I parked and got out to open Grace's door, but she'd already let herself out. Probably thought I was too tired. Eva always said that if you were too tired to be a gentleman, you were too tired to have a woman in your company—

Grace didn't wait for me to shut the door behind her. She was out of the car and walking at first, then faster, then running. I slid behind her, catching up just as she crumpled to the cement in front of a broken picture frame. It had been a beautiful print, I could see that. A black-and-white of an African woman, whose peaceful face was now sliced in half. I reached for Grace and pulled her close with one hand. I called the police with the other.

She buried her face in my hair. "Not again."

I stroked her face. There'd be no more peace. Not tonight.

They left the door open.

"Like last time, they wanted to make sure she knew they were here. That's what the picture was about. A message," the officer said, his words aimed at me this time.

I squeezed Grace's hand.

"The team will assess the evidence and catch this person. They were foolish enough to return to the scene. We'll get them this time."

"If it was the same person," Grace mumbled. I knew she was thinking about the phone calls I'd gotten earlier. So was I. I hadn't thought that Lottie would go this far.

I tried to stay calm. "It's the same nut."

The officer narrowed his gaze. "Do you have something to add, Dr. Mayfield?"

"He doesn't, Officer. We've been at the hospital all night with our principal, Joyce Rogers." Grace interjected before I could respond.

"I'm sorry. About all this. Where are you going to stay tonight?" the officer asked.

Grace pointed toward Zeely's, even though there was no car in the driveway. "I'll stay with a friend, Zeely Wilkins."

The officer nodded and flipped through the case file, noting Zeely's phone number and address. "Do you need an escort?"

I shook the man's hand. "I'll handle it. Thanks again."

As Grace and I walked away, a wiry woman in a uniform whispered something in the detective's ear.

He stopped us. "One more thing, Ms. Okoye. We found a gum wrapper in the kitchen. Do you chew gum?"

Grace shook her head but she stumbled back as though she knew someone who did. It took me a minute, but it came to me too. Sean McKnight. The math gum. I tried to call the officers back but Grace begged me not to, said I didn't know for sure. It could be anybody.

Yeah. Right.

No matter how hard I tried, nothing could slow down the anger flooding my veins. If the officer hadn't already left, he might have arrested me next. I banged my fist on the hood of my car.

Grace cringed, watching me pace back and forth. I hurled my keys to the ground. "I knew it! I told Joyce to get him out." I spun toward Grace. "And I told you to watch out for him. I—"

STOP. YOU'RE SCARING HER.

As quickly as the storm began, it ceased. I picked up my keys, took a deep breath. "It doesn't matter. I'll take care of it. Let's get you safe."

Grace looked like she wanted to ask how I'd take care of it, but was scared to find out. And with good cause. If Sean was capable of doing something like this after all Imani and I had done to help him, the boy deserved whatever he got.

We walked to Zeely's in silence and stood in the cold moonlight ringing the doorbell.

Ding. Dong.

Okay, so Zeely's car wasn't at the shop. Despite the crazy hour, she really wasn't home.

My head started to throb. "Okay, look. You can't go home and I can't leave you here, so come with me. I'll take you somewhere. Thelma's maybe—"

"No. Zeely will come home. She always does. Probably out shopping somewhere."

She was back across the yard and into her place almost before I knew it. I caught up quickly. And followed her inside. The officer had ordered us out and here she was back at the scene of the crime, hitting redial.

This makes no sense.

My body hit the couch. It was all I could do to keep from losing it, just stop and drop. Something stuck me, cut into my jacket. Glass. No wonder the cops had ordered us out. The closer I looked, I could see little bits of glass on the couch and on the floor. I got up and took the phone from Grace's hand. "You can't stay here. Do you understand that?"

She grabbed it back. "I'm not staying here. I'm just waiting until Zeely gets back. She must have run to the superstore for something to go with her outfit tomorrow."

"You'll be waiting awhile then. That's twenty miles away." I fought off a wave of nausea from lack of sleep. "Look, come home with me. I'll sleep on the couch. I'll sleep in the car if you want. Just don't stay here."

It was her turn to pace. If I'd seen this coming, I would have taken a longer nap at the hospital.

She slammed the phone into its charger. "I can't spend the night at your house. This is messy enough. If someone saw me leaving there, it'd be on the front page."

Better than an obituary. "Be reasonable, Princess . . ."

One look at her eyes told me I'd crossed the line.

And so had she.

Grace took my hand and tugged, moving toward the door. "If I were reasonable, I wouldn't have moved back here."

I stepped between her and the door, ready to restrain her if necessary. Instead, I fell backwards from an unexpected shove. I got up, but on the wrong side of the door. Maple wood almost smacked my lips as the door slammed shut. The lock clicked with finality.

Eva was wrong.

Sometimes being a gentleman was just too tiring.

78

Grace

I don't think I'll talk anymore. It makes me tired.
People are only thinking of what they're going to
say better, faster—instead of hearing the words. No
one listens except God, and I can no longer hear his
answers. I can only hear the drums.

Diana Dixon

I dragged myself toward my bedroom then, not wanting to hear him start his car and drive away. I'd forgotten that they'd come through the back window this time and gone out the front. A chill whistled through the sliced screen that sent me running back to the front for the phone. Redial. No answer. No car. And now Brian was gone too.

I walked to the front door, trying to remember Brian's cell number. Was it in my purse? I couldn't think. There were just windows going through my mind, windows with a blank face pressed against them. And here I was trying to pull Zeely into it.

I should have listened to Brian. About Sean. About everything. It had only been a few minutes since I'd shoved him outside, but it seemed like forever. I opened the door anyway.

My foot hit something soft. And something not so soft. Muscles.

"Watch it. I'm trying to sleep, you know." It was Brian, stretched out across my porch.

I dropped the phone. Brian got up and raised one hand. "Don't hit me, okay? You know I couldn't leave you here—"

"Thank you," I said, folding into him. "I'm sorry. I'm just so, so sorry." I pressed against his cold, wet body, felt his tangle of hair, freezing lips . . . Snow soaked through my tights as we held each other. The coconut oil from his hair smelled better than ever.

Almost as good as he tasted. Delicious, just like I knew he would.

Brian spent a few seconds trying to figure out what was going on. I couldn't figure it out myself. So far I was only sure of one thing—I needed this. I needed him.

Maybe if we'd been more rested, less hungry and afraid, I might not have started it, running my hand under his sweater, up his back . . .

But I was all of those things and as it was, when I kissed him, I forgot about Joyce in that hospital, the picture on the front lawn, the gum wrapper the police found . . . For a minute, I think I forgot my name.

We were lost in each other but Brian tried to stop, tried to pull away while he still could. Well, I was past that. Way past it. This was why I didn't date much. I was as scared of myself as I was of men.

Brian almost got away, but I wasn't having it. I grabbed a handful of his hair and kissed him thoroughly.

Completely.

He started talking about praying and saying hold up a minute and how I didn't mean it, when I took my fingernails and raked them through his beard.

He stopped talking.

We started moving back toward the door, in the house with the glass and the hurt. And at the moment, I didn't care. At least not until my foot slipped out from under me.

We went down hard, both of us. Hard like how we'd fallen for each other that first night in the cafeteria. We held on tight, tumbling as the porch seemed to slide away.

Finally we came to a stop in a bank of fresh snow so wet and cold that I started to sneeze. Brian wiped his mouth and helped me to my feet.

"I'm going to call the police back. They can keep you at the station until Zeely comes back. You're right. You can't come to my place—"

I just stood there, horrified. "I—we—"

Brian shook his head. "Just call 9-1-1 before we kill ourselves out here."

Before I could reply, we heard someone behind us.

"Umph umph umph."

Zeely stood behind us in a leather trench coat and bunny slippers.

"Y'all won't have to worry about the boogeyman. If that didn't scare him, nothing will."

Though she hadn't wanted to listen to me lately, Zeely hung on to my every word.

"I am so sorry. I should have come to dinner with you." Zeely waited with a towel in the doorway while I splashed my face with cold water. "First Joyce, now this? What a rough night."

Rough? Tonight was downright crazy.

"Sorry I wasn't home when it happened. I stopped by Dad's for a while. Left my phone in the car. When I left there, I saw your messages."

I followed Zeely upstairs, trying both to remember and forget what had happened with Brian. Zeely had been right all along. Staying away from men was the best policy. I hoped Zeely would be smart enough to take her own advice. She looked like she'd had a hard night too. Whatever she'd talked about with Reverend Wilkins must have been some heavy stuff.

We got into bed. Zeely pulled up her perfumed sheets. I sneezed.

Zeely fell on her knees at the edge of the bed. I turned to the wall, hoping she wouldn't pray out loud. After the way I'd dived on Brian, I could hardly face myself, let alone God. I just wanted to get to sleep. Fast.

Zee scooted closer to me, her elbows touching mine as she prayed. "Lord, thank you for keeping my girl safe, for bringing Doc Rogers through the night . . ."

I sighed. Joyce. Once I'd explained what had happened at the hospital, Zeely had called for a report. Joyce was stable and resting. Zeely praised God for that news as she concluded her prayer. Then she slipped her hands under the covers, clasping my fingers. "We thank you for Jesus, who is able to keep us from falling . . ."

Too bad that didn't apply to rolling off porches with men attached to your face. I sneezed again as the cold wetness of the night soaked into my bones. As my father used to say when he felt a cold coming on, I had an ache in my pocket. It had been near midnight when we left the hospital. It had to be after 1:00 by now.

Zeely squeezed my hand one last time. "In Jesus' name, amen."

"Amen."

Satin rippled as Zeely slipped in beside me. "The snow's falling fast now. We might be off school Monday."

I watched the clumps of white fall past the window. It seemed hard to believe that I'd been outside not long before. I wanted to pray that school would be closed Monday, but praying didn't seem right, especially with Brian's kiss still sweet on my mouth. I'd brushed my teeth with the new toothbrush in Zeely's bathroom that I didn't want to ask about, but Brian's kiss was still there.

What was missing now was the kiss of Christ.

I thought I'd had things under control, but in the end, I'd caved.

They didn't call it warfare for nothing. Regardless of what had happened tonight—delicious dinner, hospital prayers, juicy kisses—Brian wasn't safe for me. It didn't seem like I was much good for him either. I'd been so concerned about me playing with fire and getting burned that I hadn't realized I'd set his life aflame too.

We could never work. And I'd gone and dug the hole deeper.

And I had holes enough. The holes in my window, in my heart . . . After what had happened tonight, I couldn't fool myself about having the gift of singleness. I was the marrying kind.

How Brian could seem so right and be so wrong I didn't know, but I was tired of trying to protect myself, to control myself. Sure Brian had prayed a few times during emergencies, but I'd been down that looks-like-a-Christian-so-maybe-it-is road with my first husband.

And I'd been wrong.

Dead wrong.

What I did know was that for every temptation there was a way of escape. A trap door. God promised that. Somehow though, I was missing it.

I couldn't think anymore. Instead, I tucked my hand under Zeely's pillow instead of my own. There was something under the pillow. Something sharp and cold.

A knife.

That made me laugh through my fog of sleep.

That Zeely. Always prepared.

When the doorbell rang, I rolled from my side to my back, trying to figure out when it was, where I was. The clock helped me out as well as the scented, slippery sheets. Two a.m. Zeely's place. Nobody came to Zee's at that time of the morning. Maybe I'd imagined it.

I hadn't.

My eyes barely open, I sat up and grabbed for Zeely's curtain and peeked outside. With a sigh, I sat back on the edge of the bed.

"Grace, who is that?" Zee whispered.

"Mal."

"Do you want me to tell him to go away?"

"No. I'll go down. They probably called him about Joyce and he saw my place—"

"Grace—"

"It's okay. I'll get rid of him."

I couldn't have been more wrong.

My feet downed the stairs two at a time while my mind searched for the right words. Mal didn't sleep well when he was worried, so all I had to do was set his mind at ease, let him know that Joyce was okay and I was too. I bunched the robe Zeely had tossed at me in one hand and clicked the deadbolt open with the other.

Malachi pushed past me, his eyes darting around the dim room. "Are you all right?"

"I'm fine."

One step brought him to the foot of the stairs. "Who's here with you? Mayfield isn't up there, is he?"

I caught him on the second step and pushed him off it. "Nobody's up there but Zeely. Now be quiet before you wake her . . . again. And the police have been out here once tonight. We don't want the neighbors calling them again."

At the mention of the authorities, Mal's expression sobered. "Sorry," he said quietly.

"You should be," I whispered, wondering if Mal had lost his mind.

He took a seat on the couch, his eyes locked on me. "I saw the mess outside your place. Why didn't you call me? You know I want to protect you. You should have stayed with me."

"I'm where I need to be right now."

Zeely appeared at the top of the staircase. A silk scarf meant to be tied on her head was looped around her neck.

I cut my eyes at Mal for making so much noise. "Sorry for waking you."

Zeely pivoted back toward her room half-asleep. "Um-hum."

Mal waited for Zeely to disappear before he moved closer. "You see how this goes, being with him? It always puts you in danger."

"Come again?"

"You and Mayfield—Brian. I saw you out there rolling around in the snow."

This just got better and better.

I squinted at him. That was hours ago. "What were you doing, spying on me?"

His expression softened. "No. I wasn't spying. Just worried. I came by to check on you. Then I saw you two on the porch like that . . . Not that you would have noticed."

He had me there. "I'm sorry you saw that, but in truth, it was a private moment after a long, hard night."

"You were outside—"

There was a neediness I'd never heard in Mal's voice. For once, I truly had nothing to give him. "I appreciate you being concerned, but it's over with us. You got your ring back. As for Brian, that kiss, well, I don't know. That's basically the end of it."

Malachi chuckled softly. "It won't be for him. Trust me." He reached over and picked up Zeely's phone.

I teetered on the edge of the couch, staring at this man who I'd almost married. A man who had always been so reserved with me. Who would have thought that Brian would drive him over the edge? Jealousy was a green-eyed monster indeed.

He held out the receiver to me. "Call Mayfield and tell him there can't be anything between you. That'll squash it."

It was way too late for this conversation. I placed the phone on the charger. "I know this is hard, but it's late and I don't feel well.

This isn't even my house. It's time for you to leave." I stood up and started for the door.

Malachi reached for my arm. He pulled me toward him by the belt of Zeely's robe. "Kiss me. Kiss me like you kissed him." He took a deep and desperate breath. "Please."

A stab of fear went through me. Was he on something? Everything about him tonight seemed . . . odd. Or maybe it was just the night. I'd been acting rather odd myself. Maybe it was nothing.

"Mal—"

His mouth clamped over mine, now demanding the kiss it had just requested. A reflex from too many self-defense classes, I stomped his foot and tried to pull away. My bare feet had no effect on his boots. He held me fast and pressed something sharp and cold against my neck.

A knife.

"You'll never know how much I loved you. Don't call your friend. I don't want to hurt her. Let's just keep this where it belongs. Between us," he whispered in my ear.

Somehow, I managed a nod, despite my shock. How had I gotten everything so wrong?

"Don't look at me like that. It didn't have to be this way." He yanked me to my feet, his hand on my mouth. Snow blew in as he pushed the door open.

Zeely's sleepy voice floated over the stairs. "Grace? You still down there? Come to bed or you'll never wake up tomorrow."

I hoped that wasn't prophetic. I paused for a second, considering the knife under Zeely's pillow. Maybe she could, we could . . . No, I couldn't risk it. The blade pressed against my throat as Mal lifted two fingers from my mouth.

"Go back to sleep, Zee. I'm fine—"

He pulled me tighter. "Tell her you're going out for a minute."

Outside? Panic started to set in as I tried to figure out a way to stay in the house. Outside, I'd be totally at his disposal. The knife pressed harder against my throat, cutting a little. "We're going to get some food, Zee. You know how I get sometimes. I'll be back in a minute."

"In your nightclothes?"

I pointed to the hall closet. He led me there. I took out my coat and stabbed my feet into my boots. "I've got my coat. We're just riding through the drive-thru."

"Well, be careful," Zeely said from the throes of sleep. "We've had enough trouble for one night."

She had no idea.

79

Brian

The driver behind me blared his horn and called me a few choice names before I came to myself and pulled over into the 7-Eleven in the middle of town.

When I looked in the mirror, Grace's lipstick was still on my mouth.

And in my mind.

One more kiss like that and I'd be done for.

With a napkin from my glove compartment, I got the top layers of color, leaving me with a stain. It made sense that it didn't wipe away easily. This whole night was like that, something that would stick around for a while.

Tired and cold, I headed into the store to get something to keep me awake the rest of the way home. I'd slept in my car in Grace's neighborhood for a while just because I couldn't go any farther. But the snow woke me soon enough.

Somebody pulled my hair. I swung around and smiled as Ron gave a hug.

Man, I was glad to see him. "What are you doing out this late?"

He shrugged as we entered the store. "I could ask you the same. You're usually getting up about now, aren't you?"

Pretty much. "Not quite. A few more hours yet." The heat felt good, but now I was getting sleepy again.

"Right. Well, I went out to the hospital. I was out of town and missed the initial call. They told me you were there. How'd your dinner go? That was last night, right? Did the hospital call before or after?"

"During. We both went to the hospital and spent the night. I dropped her off not long ago." I picked up a candy bar and put it down.

He squeezed my shoulder and shook his head. "Just like old times, huh? Crazy times. All we need now is some food and a place to sleep off our blues. I could go for some chitlins right now. . . ."

Some things never changed. "No thanks. I think I'm going for a Slurpee."

Ron laughed. "You're funny. Drinking a Slurpee in a snowstorm. You and Mal are the only people I know who'd drink frozen drinks in winter. I came through here for gas on the way to the hospital and he was getting one."

The cup I'd just grabbed started to collapse in my hands. Mal and I had always liked the same things. Especially lately.

"Mal was in Testimony? Tonight?" My heart beat in my temples. "Did you see which way he went when he left?"

Without hesitation, Ron pointed in the direction I had come from. Grace's direction. "That way. I only remember because he peeled out of the lot. He always was a jerk."

The cup hit the trash where I aimed it. I motioned for Ron to come with me. He followed, no questions asked. At least not until we were in my car.

"What gives, man?"

"Remember how I always knew when your mom was coming? Even before I saw her?"

Ron nodded. "Yeah, I remember. That last time . . . she would have killed me."

"I feel like that now. Only worse. It might be nothing, but I just want to go by. She's at Zeely's tonight."

Ron stiffened at the mention of Zeely's name. "Let's check. Just in case."

80

Grace

*I crocheted a blanket. It's crooked because I keep
forgetting to turn it over. I don't really know what
I'm doing, but I want the baby to know that I tried. I
really, really tried.*

Diana Dixon

I tried not to fly away as Mal dragged me to a patch of trees behind one of the model condos. Something in me wanted to let go and look down on the whole scene, but something else wanted to be free.

Wanted to live.

That was the part of me that bit him until he bled. That was the part of me that ran. Only now with my feet freezing and sinking in the snow like quicksand, that same part of me seemed to be fading away.

Mal tackled me and stroked my hair. "Will you stop? I don't want to hurt you. Don't make me."

That did it, flipped my switch back on. The first time I'd been held against my will, I hadn't known what would happen. Now I knew what came next. This time I wanted a different ending and I'd have to use my head to get it. I went limp in his hands.

"Give up? Good. I don't know why you had to make this so

difficult. This could have been our honeymoon." Mal's breath curled away from my ear like smoke.

I took a deep breath, strengthening myself for what would come.

The righteous are as bold as a lion.

I looked to a star overhead. God would tell me when.

He was going to kiss me again. I closed my eyes, let myself disconnect. The dreaded kiss never came.

"One last chance. Will you marry me?"

I tried to say something that he'd want to hear, something that would save my life, but my disgusted look must have betrayed me.

He shook his head. "I thought as much."

In the white of the snow, I could see his shadow moving, his body coming down on me. This was it.

Now.

I shoved my knee into his groin. Mal crumpled to his knees, still grasping my robe. He swung the knife as I pulled away. The blade sliced my palm, but I kept going, crawling backward, lobster-style toward the street, toward the lights. Mal was still down, but not for long.

Scream.

I screamed, hoping, praying that someone would hear. He was up now and coming at me. Before I could scream again, Mal's hand clapped over my mouth. He jerked my face toward him and pulled something out of his pocket.

A ski mask.

As he pulled it down over his face, I gasped. Only once before had I seen someone's eyes look like that. Like then, those eyes were the last thing I saw before my soul broke away and everything went black.

81

Brian

There were no lights at Zeely's. They were probably asleep. I couldn't look at Ron. "You probably think I'm nuts for sure."

Ron was still looking up at Zeely's windows. "You did the right thing."

Embarrassed, I lifted my foot off the brake, ready to ease down the street in silence.

"Wait." A light appeared in Zeely's upstairs window. I put the car back into park. Another light, downstairs. Ron and I looked at each other. He was almost out of the car when I heard the scream.

Grace's scream.

We took off in two directions.

Ron's words came over my shoulder as I cut behind the building. "I'm going in for Zeely. I'll call the cops. I'll find you . . ."

Lights clicked on in other condos as I stumbled past them, willing my sleep-starved body to keep going. Thinking, praying one thing:

Faster.

A light flicked on across the street, three condos down. I propelled myself forward, pushing a clump of bushes and trees. He had on a ski mask, but when I saw his back, I knew. It was Mal, with a knife in his hand and Grace at his feet. She wasn't moving.

A scream of my own came somewhere from the depth of me as I charged him. The knife came at me, but I ducked and chopped at his wrist with a martial arts move I'd thought I'd forgotten. The knife flew away.

He tumbled back, but came up ready, both fists raised. "I knew you'd come."

I head butted him. He kicked me. And all the time I was looking at Grace, hoping that her chest was really moving and that it wasn't just the wind.

He was watching her too. "I did love her, you know. Always. Even the first time. I just didn't know it yet."

That dropped me quicker than any blow he could have landed. Grace had never told me what happened to her, but Testimony was a small town.

It'd been Mal all the time.

I tried to get up, but fell down on one knee.

He laughed as he ran away. I was up now, running after him. I saw Ron, up ahead of me, pulling at Zeely's arm. I slid to a stop when I saw what she had in her hand.

A gun.

"Zeely, no!" Ron shouted before something exploded in front of me.

Mal was down, grabbing his shoulder. Zeely was shaking. The gun dangled from her fingers. It looked like it weighed more than she did. Ron pried it from her fingers.

With her hands free, she pointed at Mal, screaming at him. "You come into my house and do this? You never loved her, but I did. She was finally going to be okay. We all were." Tears washed over her chin.

Sirens echoed as what sounded like our entire police force approached. Zeely ran toward Grace. Ron and I stayed put, watching as Mal managed to stand.

A few strides brought me to him. It was a good thing Ron had the gun and not me. "Why did you do it, huh?"

Mal spat in my direction as the police approached. "The first time? Gang initiation. This time, I was going to make it right—"

I punched him then, right where he'd been shot. Put him in a headlock, squeezing off his air.

Ron came to me, but he held the gun out of my reach and unloaded the bullets, threw them in the snow. "Thou shall not kill, bruh. Don't."

I let him go. He curled into a ball on the ground. Laughing. "You're pathetic, Mayfield. A punk. You always were."

I snatched the empty gun from Ron and raised it over Mal's head.

Someone grabbed me from behind. Slapped handcuffs on me.

"This is the police. Put down the weapon."

The gun fell onto a sea of fresh snow. Virgin white. I tried to breathe as the police pulled me past Grace, just laying there as the medics loaded her onto a stretcher.

Once they got the whole story from Ron and confirmed there'd been no bullets in the gun, someone uncuffed me. I didn't relax until I saw Mal in custody, heard them say the words.

"You have the right to remain silent . . ."

Mal kept going until the end, looking like a pitiful boy now instead of a man who'd done so many horrible things. And still he wouldn't shut up. "I had to make her understand. Don't you see? God sent her back to me," Mal said as they dragged him past me.

I turned from his lies toward Zeely's sobs, wondering how I could have ever thought of him as a friend. Ron flanked my side as I headed for Grace.

"Can you hear me?" the medic asked once Ron pried Zeely away from Grace's stretcher.

A weak voice answered. "I—I can."

"Thank you, Jesus," Zeely said, quiet now, almost whispering. She spoke soft enough for me to hear my own voice.

I was saying it too.

82

Ron

I stayed with Zeely. The police had questioned her, but I'd done a lot of the talking. She was out of it. All the neighbors gathered around, letting the officers know that she had done what any of them would have, defended herself against an intruder. There was some discussion, but she was let go pending further investigation. Let go, but then she didn't really go anywhere but into my arms.

"Are you okay?"

She shook her head. Started crying. "I never should have bought that gun."

"I know."

When one of the officers bagged the gun for evidence, Zeely covered her eyes. "I really shot him, didn't I?"

I smoothed her hair. "You did. I couldn't believe it. Where did you get that gun anyway? You're scared to death of guns."

She wilted against me, squeezing as she hugged my waist. "Yes, I am afraid of them." A sob shook her body. "I shot somebody. Did I kill him?"

"Unfortunately not."

"Ron . . ."

"I know. I don't mean it. He'll be fine. Probably better than any of us. Come on. I'll drive you to the hospital."

She shook her head. "No, I'm going in the ambulance. They're not going to hurt her anymore."

I sighed. We'd all been hurt tonight, and not just by bullets. I helped her to the ambulance. "Okay. I'll meet you there."

"You sure?"

"Unless—"

"What?"

"Do you want me to call Jerry instead?"

She stiffened, then climbed up into the ambulance. "No. I want you. I'll see you there."

The ambulance doors slammed in my face. I knew that Mal was in the other one. When they'd taken him past me, he'd avoided my eyes. I could hardly believe that this was a guy I'd driven over an hour to hear preach. And tonight, I could have killed the guy. Easy. Brian could have too. But thank God, we hadn't. As horrible as all of this was, vengeance belongs to God. It had to. I joined Brian sitting on the curb, giving a statement. I'd had to drag the guy out of the snow not long ago, but he seemed to be okay.

Another officer tapped my shoulder. "And your name?"

This again. "Jenkins. Ron Jenkins."

"You were with, uh, Wilkins, correct?"

"Correct."

"What's your relationship? Why were you here tonight?"

I shrugged and looked at Brian. "Friends? We're good friends. All of us."

Brian nodded, then looked back at the ground. He pounded his fist against mine as the officer took his statement. We'd been through a war tonight. A battle fit for the two musketeers. We'd called ourselves brothers back in the day, then spent so long struggling to be friends. Something in this ugly night with its screams and guns had made us remember how to be brothers again. It seemed to have made Zeely remember too. I sure hoped so.

83

Grace

Jenny is going to teach me to make booties and a hat too. Pink ones, because I still think it's a girl. I picked a name. Melony. Corny, but I like it. I rewrote my letter. I told her that I was just a kid and Mom says I have to give her to someone grown who wants to have a baby. I told her I didn't know if that was right, but everyone says it's best. I told her I'll go to college and get a good job so she'll be proud if she ever comes to find me. I hope she does.

Diana Dixon

I looked like a monster, but there was a beauty in the cuts and bruises obscuring my features, the lump that had been my eye. I couldn't see much, but I knew when the nurse came at me with that little box in her hand what she wanted to do. I tried to scream, to yell, but all I could get was a weak, tired voice.

"Please don't." Going through a post-rape exam once was enough for a lifetime.

Standing nose-to-chest with a nurse holding a pair of tweezers, Zeely tapped the nurse's shoulder. "She wasn't raped."

"I know that's what she says, but we need to do a rape kit just in case." The nurse reached beneath the drape.

I cried out, clutching Zeely's hand. Zeely pushed the nurse's hand away. "I think you're the rapist tonight. She's traumatized enough."

"Ma'am, you don't understand—"

Zeely squeezed between the stirrups and pulled out the rest of the bed. Put my feet gently down on the bed. "The man is already in jail."

"But there is some question of a previous case—"

Zeely rubbed her nose in circles, snorting—the warning for complete meltdown. I rolled toward the window, bracing myself for the next wave of pain, sure to come after they carted Zeely away: a speculum, a needle, or some other instrument. I waited so long that I fell asleep. When I woke up, I smelled something wonderful, something scary. Cucumbers rolled in pine needles. Gingerly, I rolled over, lifting the pillow from over my face to look at him.

Brian.

I covered my face again. As much as I was glad he'd come, I didn't want him to be here now, to see me like this. He took one step at a time, finally reaching me. He put his hands on the pillow and held it, waiting until I moved it out of the way. Someone shut the door behind us and the room went dark. Was it night? I'd lost all track of time.

I wasn't sure what time it was, but for once I was thankful for the darkness between us. He moved slowly, putting his arms around me, and bringing his lips to my swollen eye, my bruised cheek . . . He kept on, finishing with my bandaged hand. It was as though he'd memorized my wounds in the few seconds that I'd let him look at me. A fragmented thought came to me from somewhere far away.

Jesus with skin on.

He lifted me off the bed just a little, held me in his arms. I was crying now, both from the pain and from the pleasure. As he lowered me back to the bed and eased the pillow behind my head, something wet hit my face. He was crying too.

He pulled the blanket up to my neck. I knew he was moving easy to keep from hurting me, but I could see that he'd been hurt too. His breathing was shallow and ragged. Desperate. It was more than I could take.

I turned away from him.

He gently turned my head and leaned over me, close enough to kiss. But he didn't. Instead he kissed me with his words.

"I've been waiting for you all my life. I can wait. However long it takes."

The tears kept coming as I listened to him drag himself across the room. I wanted to stay silent, to just take everything in. He wouldn't have blamed me if I did. But I couldn't.

"I love you," I said in a voice I didn't recognize. A voice that brought him running right back to my side.

He kissed my fingertips. "I know. I love you too. Now get better so I can show you."

Even though it hurt, I laughed.

Maybe we were going to be okay.

All of us.

Acknowledgments

Jennifer Leep, thanks for always believing in this story. It means so much.

Jessica Ferguson, thank you for "getting it" when nobody else did. You made me brave.

Claudia Mair Burney, thanks for loving this book and for loving me.

Isaiah, thanks for waiting to be born so I could finish this. You're a big boy now, but you'll always be my first book baby.

Fill, you didn't let me give up, even when I tried. There are no words for how much I love you.

Michelle and Ashlie, thanks for all the days you helped with the kids so I could write this book and all the others. You are the best.

Shonie Bacon, Maurice Gray, Aisha Ford, Tanya Marie Lewis, Suzette Harrison, LaShaunda Hoffman, Yolanda Callegari Brooks, Amy Wallace, Jennifer Keithley, Staci Wilder, Nan Toback, Beth Ziarnek, Susan Downs, Susan May Warren, Tracy Bateman, Colleen Coble, Members of the Black Writers Alliance, thank you for reading this in its various forms over the years.

Wendy Lawton, thank you for being you.

Dr. Joseph Smith of Central State University, Olokikijulo! This bantu finally made it back to you.

Cat Hoort, thanks for all your support and marketing efforts (and for reading the book so fast!).

Nathan Henrion, thanks for all the laughs and insight into the sales side of publishing.

Cheryl Van Andel and the art department, thanks for another great cover.

Special thanks to Barb Barnes for her many reads of this book. Thanks for your hard work.

Jesus, my everything, who taught me so much during the writing of this book and all that came after. Thank You. You were right. About everything.

Reader Note

Dear Reader,

Thank you for reading *Rhythms of Grace*. I hope you enjoyed it. This book is very special to me because it is my true first novel, the first book I ever wrote. If you've read my other titles and enjoyed them, then you'd already enjoyed this story in a way, because it was during the writing of this book that I became the writer that I am. During the revisions of this book, I became the writer I hope to be.

Please visit RevellBooks.com for book club questions and other information about this book and the others to follow it. Visit my website at http://www.MarilynnGriffith.com as well, or drop me an email at MarilynnGriffith@gmail.com.

Until next time, keep dancing to God's glorious rhythms of grace.

Blessings,
Marilynn

Marilynn Griffith is a freelance writer who lives in Florida with her husband and seven children. When she's not helping with homework or tackling Mount Fold-Me, her ongoing laundry pile, she writes novels and speaks to youth, women, and writers.

Watch for the sequel

COMING FALL 2009